HEART OF THE RAVEN

Karl, transfixed in the doorway, was deaf to the banshee howl of the wind. His enraptured gaze raced over Anne's face. "There is no one here," he said at random, desperately struggling with the forbidden heat that snatched at his resolve like the wild, wicked wind outside.

"M-my clothes were wet," she whispered. "This was all I could find."

The rosy firelight gleamed through the translucent fabric of her gown, outlining her hips, her . . .

"Anne, I give you my word, I will not take advantage of this . . . this situation."

"And if I want you to . . . to take advantage . . ."

"You don't know what you're saying."

"I love you," she whispered.

Banishing sanity to a far corner of his mind, he swept his arms around her and yielded to desire.

HEART OF THE RAVEN

DIANE WICKER DAVIS

AVON BOOKS ◆ NEW YORK

HEART OF THE RAVEN is an original publication of Avon Books. This work has never before appeared in book form. This work is a novel. Any similarity to actual persons or events is purely coincidental.

AVON BOOKS
A division of
The Hearst Corporation
105 Madison Avenue
New York, New York 10016

First Avon Books Printing: October 1989

AVON TRADEMARK REG. U.S. PAT. OFF. AND IN OTHER COUNTRIES, MARCA REGISTRADA, HECHO EN U.S.A.

Printed in the U.S.A.

K-R 10 9 8 7 6 5 4 3 2 1

To the members of RAH
With special thanks to
Marnie Ellingson,
who shared her interest
in the Regency period with me

Chapter 1

May 1813
Bragg House
Lake Windermere, Cumberland

"Is any woman worth the loss of a prince-dom?" Franz Grillparzer's burly frame shook with ill-suppressed anger.

"Is any princedom worth the loss of this woman?" Karl Auguste Wilhelm II, a prince without a prince-dom, a man without a country, asked, more of himself than of his man.

"Raise your right wrist and bare it, *Majestät!*" ordered Franz, like the officer he had been before his willing exile. "See the crown there, the birthmark inherited only by the Master of the Ravens. The crown worn by your father and his father and his father before him. You are not free to choose as you may. You are not free to shirk your duty."

Already it had begun, Karl thought, that tearing of himself between duty and desire. Duty! God, he hated the word! Yet its meaning—obligation, sacri-fice, service, loyalty—had been bred in him bone-deep from the cradle. Just as he could not escape it, neither could he escape the need to see *her* once more.

Lady Anne Ransome. Sweet Anne, who had, for a few short weeks, made him forget who he was, what he was, what he had to do. Like the Lorelei

1

luring a sailor to his death on the rocks of the Rhine, she had lured him to the abandonment of onerous duty for a chase as old as man and woman. A chase cheated of its full fruition by the duty he could not, in the end, abandon.

His vivid blue eyes stared through the ivy-draped peel tower window, across the broad yew garden to the classic Palladian mansion. The purpling twilight bathed its sparkling white facade in a watercolor wash of rich lavender and turned its thick window glazings to a deep plum hue. The lustrous, unwinking eyes of Bragg House revealed nothing. Not the secrets held close for thirty years. Not the hopes and dreams that had died there. Certainly not the woman newly arrived, who waited in the immense and gloomy Blue Room.

Whether Anne's presence was a blessing or a curse, Karl did not know. He only knew this chance would not come again.

"I will see her," he said, his normally deep and melodic voice flattened by resolve.

"This is beyond all reason," thundered Franz, his beefy hands curling into fists.

"Yes, but . . ." A reminiscent smile softened the austere line of Karl's mouth. "There are times, my old friend, when a man grows weary of being wise."

"Do you grow weary of life, too? For that is what you risk!"

Karl's smile vanished. A frown knit his tawny brows. His life had been at risk since he slid squalling into the world. What did another danger matter if it came couched in the guise of heart's ease? That was what Anne had once given him, and he would have it again, if only for a night.

His frown darkened, and his gaze shifted to the glossy black raven, alert on her perch. Always she was nearby. Watching him, watching over him, she never allowed him to forget he was the Master of the Ravens, and so, not his own man. She would not free him, nor would Franz, nor would those others lying in their restless graves, nor would the man who had put them there.

"Anne's father would not have sent her here, using her, if he had a choice," he said.

Franz's breath whistled in his throat. "Do you think he has told her—"

"No, her innocence is her safety." Innocence. It had been her utter lack of guile that had first attracted, then seduced, Karl. His dusky gold lashes fanned down to shield his pain.

He moved abruptly, as if he could shake her hold on his thoughts. His tasseled Hessians trod on the glorious hues of a Kashan carpet. His fawn pantaloons, molded to his muscular horseman's thighs, brushed the gilded arm of a brocade settee. All around him was elegance, shimmering with light and color: the glitter of crystal, the sheen of silver, the soft patina of fine polished woods. All wasted in this secret chamber at the top of the crumbling peel tower. This secret chamber furnished for a secret man.

He paused beside the piano, his strong warrior's body angling against it, while his supple musician's hand stroked the lacquered top. "Petworth," he said to Bragg House's burly butler, standing sentinel beside the door, "you will send word to Lady Anne that a visitor has arrived."

"And what name shall I give?" asked Petworth, his broad, flat face as impassive as stone.

Cantor. Across the span of four years Karl heard the gentle cadence of Anne's voice whispering the name by which she knew him. Sweet as it was, it would have been sweeter had it been his own. The corners of his mouth crimping in distaste, he responded quickly, "Cantor Cartwright. You know the tale to tell."

"*Majestät,*" began Franz.

"Enough!" Karl rounded on him, his cornflower-blue eyes smoldering. "If the earl risks his daughter in order to communicate with me through Lady

Bragg, we dare not await Lady Bragg's return from Bath. While I dine with Lady Anne, you must search her chamber. If there is a copy of *Sense and Sensibility*, remove the message from the spine and bring it to me."

"But *you* need not see her! Petworth can—"

"Do not press me too far, Franz! I left her once. I can do it again."

"And what did it cost you to leave her then?" Franz burst out impatiently. "What will it cost you to leave her now?"

Their eyes locked, Franz's dark with pity, Karl's bright with shock. He should not have been surprised that Franz had guessed his deepest, most private feelings. Stolid and faithful Franz, who had stood guard by his orphan's cradle, guided his first steps, and followed him into a life of subterfuge and deceit, of desperation and danger. Minion, companion, and mentor, Franz had always known his thoughts, his heart, before he himself knew either.

"Leave me," he commanded in a thready whisper.

With Franz and Petworth gone, he was alone, as he had always been alone. He sank into a wing chair. His butter-yellow curls nestled against ruby-red velvet, and his graceful hands squeezed into fists on the broad velvet arms. It had been four years since he had kissed Anne and departed from her, leaving her with the best part of himself. He had nothing more to lose—and nothing but pain to gain. Yet he would count that pain as nothing for the pleasure of one evening with her. Another memory to carry him through the darkness ahead of him.

In the immense and gloomy Blue Room surmounted by a lofty coffered ceiling, Lady Anne Ransome dismissed her abigail, Bess, and watched that worthy chatterer trundle away. Scant weeks ago she would have smiled at the way Bess rubbed her generous buttocks, which had been unmercifully abused by the jolting journey. Scant weeks ago she would have welcomed any excuse to escape the sooty, stifling atmosphere of London and the stultifying whirl of the Season's entertainments. Now, no smile touched her pale lips. No excitement rose at the prospect of solitary ramblings in the fresh country air. She wanted—needed!—to return to London at the earliest opportunity, but she could not discharge her father's commission until Lady Bragg returned from Bath.

Bess vanished through the door, her sigh of relief heaving through the closing crack. Anne relaxed her stern guard. Alone, there was no need to square her shoulders, to tilt her chin at pride's rigid angle, to press the betraying tremor from her lips. Alone, she could yield to her ever-present companion, despair.

She moved slowly, stiffly, drawn to the roaring hearth fire. The fire that would not warm her, for the chills that racked her slight and slender frame did not rise from the cool of the waning day. It had been a se'nnight since her father had pressed a copy of *Sense and Sensibility* into her hands and said, his voice dropping low in the intimate murmur of conspiracy, "You will put the book in no hands but those of Lady Bragg. I will have your word on it, Anne."

Until that moment she had hoped she was wrong. She had hoped her father was not a spy. She had hoped that she and her mother and her brother Robbie were more important to him than king and country.

The disappointment that knifed through her was a childish one. Only a child insisted on being the center of her father's world, first in his affection, first to be protected. Life, a sinuous tangle of loyalties, was never so simple as that. Who knew that better than she, the last person—did he but know it—that her father should trust.

Her gaze drifted to the massive bed. An eagle rampant glared from atop the scrolled headboard into the blue shadows cast by the satin draperies, as if he contemplated tearing away the India scarf wrapped around the copy of *Sense and Sensibility* lying on the silken coverlet. No simple gift need travel by stealth and secrecy in the guise of innocence. No simple gift need be protected by four outriders prickling with arms enough to guard the crown jewels. This book, then, was something more. What that something was, she dared not discover, lest she be forced to betray her father . . . and her country yet again.

Treason. It was an ugly word, an uglier deed. One that could send her, the daughter of a peer of the realm, to the gallows as quickly as any scullery maid sluicing out chamber pots below stairs. One that could make her family's old and honored name anathema the length and breadth of the kingdom. But a deed she had and must continue to commit if she hoped to save Robbie's life. Robbie, the brother only she could raise, like Lazarus, from the dead.

The fire failed to melt the ice riming her heart. The light failed to banish the horrors lurking at every turn of her thoughts. Seeking the window in the forlorn hope that the spring greenery might give birth to a more cheerful mood, she thrust aside a silken panel with a pale and trembling hand. Below, encroaching night cast long shadows. In the distance, beyond rippling blue Lake Windermere, above the sharp fell peaks, the brassy-yellow sun sank in a blood-red sky.

Anne shuddered from head to toe. She must return to London! She would give Lady Bragg three days, then she would leave the book with the butler. Her father could not fault her. She was not supposed to know that he was the director of the Raven's Nest, a network of spies burrowed deep into the heart of Napoleon's Empire. She was not supposed to suspect the book was more than his gift to an ailing kinswoman. She could plead innocence to her father—she, who was tarred by the taint of treason. The hypocrisy of it threatened to choke her.

She swallowed hard and turned from the window, her weary gaze searching the darkening corners of her chamber. No one waited to leap out on her. No one observed her every move. For that she could be grateful. For these few days, she would not be forced to help her country's enemies or to betray her father. Here, at least, she would be free of fear and pain and—

A sharp rap on the door jerked Anne's head up. Her ebony curls trembled, and her heart pounded. "Who is it?" she called out, her light voice cracking with strain.

"Petworth, milady. May I enter?" asked the butler.

"One moment." She moved to a massive wing chair and placed one hand across the tawny velvet back for support. Her chin climbed precipitously, her shoulders squared rigidly, and her spine assumed the cast of iron. "Enter," she called as imperiously as a dowager duchess of imposing years.

Petworth stepped through the door, his white wig askew and his chest heaving, as if he had come on the run. "Milady," said he, "I pray your indulgence. A visitor solicits the favor of your company at dinner."

Anne's hard-won dignity threatened to crumble. Von Fersen? she wondered wildly. The oily German, the man who held her in his clutches as surely as a trap held a rabbit. He would not dare follow her! But he would! He would dare anything.

"If I may say so, milady, he is a man of excellent repute. A man well-known to us. Almost like a . . . a son to Lady Bragg."

A rush of relief steadied Anne's jangled nerves. Her dove-gray gaze focused on the butler's homely face. "You say he is known to you?"

"Yes, milady. He is Cantor Cartwright, Esquire . . ."

Color drained from Anne's face, leaving it an alabaster white untinged by any hint of life. Her quivering knees bled of strength, she sagged onto the tawny velvet cushion of the wing chair.

Petworth leaped forward on his thick legs clad in white silk stockings and black knee breeches. "Shall I summon your woman?" he asked, his dithering over her even worse than Bess's over a choice between sweetmeats and bonbons.

"No," whispered Anne, fixing her haunted gray gaze on him. "It was only the . . . the shock . . ."

What a mild word for the rush of pain that shattered the armor of indifference she had girded on four years ago. Why did he come now, when it was too late? Much too late.

She drew an unsteady breath. "I pray you, be good enough to tell . . . your visitor that I cannot dine with him tonight. I am . . . indisposed."

"But, milady, he particularly wished to—"

"His wishes are not mine!" she cried with a cutting knife's-edge of panic.

"Very well, milady." Petworth escaped with the haste of a man expecting a deluge of feminine tears.

But no tears came when he was gone and Anne was alone—a new and grievous sensation for one who had, until recently, sheltered in the lee of a loving family. She burrowed into the depths of the wing chair. Her ebony curls nestled against the tawny velvet, and her fragile hands squeezed into fists on the broad velvet arms. Though she struggled against it, the memory came, as it always came, swiftly, ruthlessly. Grief and pain, hopes and fears, all fled before the deep, melodic voice that filled her mind, peeling away four years of questions. . . .

"The Lakeland is like a woman, Lady Anne," Cantor had said, while the candlelight turned his yellow hair to Midas gold. "Now fiery-tempered, now soft and gentle, now quiet and . . . dangerous. Its nights can be as black as your hair, its mornings as silvery-bright as your eyes, and its twilit evenings as rosy and . . . inviting . . . as your lips."

With every word his voice grew deeper, huskier, as if the musicians playing on the dais, the dancers swirling around the floor, the people pressed five-deep against the walls, did not exist. With every word her pulse lurched and sprinted, and her heart lowered its firm guard and left her, in the end, defenseless.

"Anne," he whispered, "you should not walk with me in the garden."

"No, I should not," she answered, and moved with him to the broad terrace doors and into the cool of a night drenched in starlight and promises.

While she strolled the cockleshell paths at his side, she forgot everything: that she was the daughter of the wealthy Earl of Darenth and a great matrimonial prize; that he was a penniless younger son, addicted to gambling, fast horses, and, so the tattle-mongers said, faster women; that even her brother, Robbie, who had his share of those vices, had said, "Puss, Cantor Cartwright is not the man for you."

In a far corner of the garden, lit by a wedge of moonlight that wielded an artist's brush of mysterious light and shadow, he turned to her in unaccustomed silence. She longed to see the smile whose every nuance she had learned in their few short weeks of acquaintance. She longed to hear the masculine ripple of his laugh, to hear the liquid song of his voice. She longed to have her sudden doubts and rising fears laved with the assurances that only he could give. But he neither smiled nor laughed nor spoke, and the tense sigh she heard might have been the breeze murmuring through the old oak tree.

His strong, supple hands cupped her shoulders, heedlessly crushing the pouf of muslin in a gentle grip that communicated the heat of his body, the power of his need. A need that she, even in the innocence of her first Season, recognized and felt as strongly as he.

He caressed the length of her arms, leaving desire tingling in the wake of his touch. His hands captured hers, pulling them to the moist heat of his lips. His breath steamed through the palm of one gloved hand, then the other.

"Anne," he said gently, sadly.

"My father wants nothing for me but my happiness," she whispered, answering the questions she feared he asked of himself.

"Your father wants your safety," he said, his eyes glittering enigmas in the dark shadow of his face.

"You would never hurt me."

"But I would, Anne. I would, and if your father was aware of . . . us, he would know it, too."

The protest parting her lips was dammed by his mouth. The hot, sweet mouth that had never before touched hers. Rising on tiptoe, she was caught in a muscular, enveloping embrace. His broad shoulders blocked the moonlight, leaving them alone in a black night scented of damask rose.

His kiss was all her dreams had imagined it would be. A petal-soft exploration of her mouth, defining every contour as exquisitely as a melody defined a song. A deepening of passion, avid, desirous. A reluctant parting that left her like a starveling unassuaged by a crust of bread.

He released her. The iridescent moon climbed into view over his shoulder. The world intruded with distant lights knifing between the black silhouettes of the trees. She stood alone, unsupported, untouched, forever changed.

"Anne," he whispered, a tormented whisper that tore from his throat, as if he meant never to say her name again.

His adoring hands cupped her cheeks. She covered them with her palms, her gaze searching his face. A terrible premonition flew as swiftly as an arrow from a twanging bow, piercing her peace and stabbing deep into her defenseless heart.

"I hope you will someday understand," he said,

and spun away, melting into the night like a man long-practiced at stealthy retreat.

Cantor Cartwright vanished from her life as effectively as he disappeared from the London scene. Pain silenced her during the next few weeks, pride through the months and years that followed. Garrulous gossips had him wedding a Cit's daughter for her fortune, bedding a duke's daughter for her beauty, retiring to the country in disgrace. He was even seen in Borodino during the bitter Russian winter of Napoleon's defeat. The bitter winter, just months past, that had seen her brother Robbie, an attaché to the British Embassy in St. Petersburg, reported dead.

That new grief of her brother's loss, unendurable and overpowering, had banished the old pain. But she had not forgotten Cantor Cartwright, or those few shining weeks that had changed her forever. Those weeks that had made her more of a woman, and less of one. . . .

. . . and less of one. Anne shifted uneasily. Where once she had greeted each day with excitement and had looked to the future with anticipation, she had now learned to walk softly through life.

Her gray gaze lowered to the crackling hearth flames. Flames that faithfully replicated the spectrum of yellow, from the golden glow of Cantor's face to the tawny gold of his sharply arched brows to the butter-yellow of his waywardly curling hair— tormenting reminders of the man who had loved her, but not enough.

If he had left her cruelly, callously, he might have become a dim, unhappy memory that made her ache only when she was beset by a melancholy mood. But he had left her with regret, with reluctance, with a soul-shattering kiss, and with words that were burned into her mind: *I hope you will someday understand.* Words that implied a promise that he would someday return to explain.

Her speculative gaze sought the tapestry bellpull, richly colored and daintily stitched. If she did not see him, she might never find responses to the questions he had left unanswered, the hopes he had left unfulfilled, the dreams he had left lying in ashes.

Chapter 2

In the hurry and scurry of summoning Bess and completing her toilette, Anne had no time for thought. Now, with the time drawing nigh, questions sprang up like dragon's teeth in the fertile soil of doubt. What if the man she remembered had never existed except in her dreams? What if the answers she craved crushed her dormant hope?

As if that doubt was not enough to try her soul, she had to find a safe place to hide the book. She dared not let it fall into any hands by those of Lady Bragg. The solution was the very simplest—if only she could break the freshet of Bess's endless chatter.

"Not eatin'! Not sleepin'! Ye're wearin' down to a string!" Bess leaned over the awesome jut of her bosom to tug at the Brabant lace collarette ringing Anne's throat. "And don't tell me ye're pinin' over our darlin' Robbie! God rest his soul! He'd be the first to tell ye to plump up on jam tarts and learn to smile again. Ain't nobody knew how to live like our Robbie did."

The reminder of her brother's passionate love of life pierced Anne with guilt. Always she must remain silent while those who loved him suffered in their grief. She bit back the cry of *He's alive! Robbie is alive!*

"Ye got bottom, as his lordship 'ud say—"

"Bess—"

"—and rightly so! Not like them flirty, flighty,

13

flitty misses with their die-away airs—and thank the Lord for that!"

"Bess!" she said sharply, drawing the woman's wounded gaze.

"Yes, *milady*." Bess used the stiff tone she used only when in a dudgeon.

Anne stared at Bess's pinched mouth and stifled a sigh. "I need your help," she said softly. "I must descend to dine now, and I want you to leave with me. Take the servants' stair and make your way to the library, unseen. *No one* must see you! Put this book"—she lifted the light volume from her dressing table—"on a shelf with others like it. Then retire for the evening."

"Retire?" Bess questioned, as if parroting a heathen language. "Who'll help ye disrobe?"

"I won't need help this once."

"Of course ye will!" declared that addict of order and regimen.

Anne's guilty gaze dropped. "I don't know how late I will be, and I won't have you sitting wakeful through the evening."

Bess folded her hands beneath her daunting bosom and settled a jaundiced gaze on Anne. "I don't like it." She sniffed, incurably top-lofty on behalf of her mistress. "I don't like it at all! Who is this . . . this person? This *Mister* Cartwright."

Much as Anne loved her abigail, there were times when the woman drove her to the last ditch of exasperation. She thrust the book into Bess's hands and towed her, resisting, to the door. "Hurry! Let no one see you!"

Bess sailed off on tiptoe, her broad hips heaving like a ship in high seas. Anne traversed the opulent corridor, pausing at the triumphal arch of the doorway. She pressed her hands to her hot cheeks, fighting the desire to seek the safety of her chamber.

She could not turn back now. She had to see the man who had stolen her heart and left her without a backward look. She had to know why Cantor had deserted her.

Did he remember . . .

. . . everything, Karl thought. He remembered everything.

Awaiting Anne in the cozy Red Salon, he stood before the terrace doors, staring out into the ink-black night. Behind him, red silk walls were wed to the lofty ceiling with an elaborately carved and gilded cornice. Vibrant Italian velvets upholstered mahogany chairs in the ponderous style of William Kent. Pier glasses topped by gilded eagles reflected the celestial gold light of girandoles and chandeliers. The setting was designed for a prince, but his thoughts were far from princely.

He was cursed with the undying memories of every look, every touch, every brief moment they had shared. Anne's skirt, the yellow of Grasmere daffodils, flying around her trim ankles as she danced a rigadoon. Her eyes sparkling in the summer sunlight. The feel of her fragile hand nestled in his palm. Her lustrous curls, black and soft-spun, bouncing gently with every step. Her alluring lips, rich with the tantalizing promise of unawakened passion.

Those memories taunted him with stronger impressions of how she had made him feel. As if he would never again need to be alone, never again need to know the darkness of defeat. As if he had reached a haven of peace, a sanctuary that admitted neither pain nor sorrow. Yet both of those emotions had penetrated that sanctuary. His time with Anne had been nothing more than a fleeting dream, a last illusion. And, in the end, the fury of vengeance had proved a stronger lure than love's promise of contentment.

Vengeance, years in the making and unrealized as yet, had called him away from Anne, but he had really left her because he feared the gentle nature that insidiously nibbled at his hard resolve and the growing love that made him question every belief he held dear.

Franz was right. He was a fool to chance seeing her now. A fool to—

The whisper of a light step sent a thrill of anticipation through him. He turned slowly.

Anne stood in the gilded frame of the doorway, a wisp of woman with the bearing of a queen. Anne, the fulfillment of one dream, the threat to another.

He was a fool, and he was glad of it.

But the smile he remembered did not touch her lips. The sparkle he recalled did not brighten her solemn gaze. Sweat beaded Karl's brow. Had her love become hatred or, worse, indifference?

Indifference. Anne strove for it, but found it as elusive as her efforts to forget him. How could she be indifferent when he stood before her, a regal figure of heroic proportions? How could she be indifferent when she was besieged by the memories of every look, every touch, every brief moment they had shared?

"It's been a long time," she said softly, her gaze racing over his face. He looked harder somehow. The years had stolen the last boyish fullness from his face, leaving his jaw resolutely square and his cheeks taut and lean.

"Too long," Karl said, his gaze taking in every detail. She had been more child than woman when last he'd seen her; she was all woman now. Her small heart-shaped face was thinner, its exquisite bone structure more pronounced. Her eyes seemed larger, pools of silvery-gray hedged with a thicket of ebony lashes. Once, those eyes had been the guileless mirrors of her loving heart. Now, cautiously shuttered against him, they revealed nothing of her thoughts. Karl swallowed a lump of pain.

"I own to being an unrepentant Philistine, my lady, but I cannot tolerate dining in that elegant barn Lady Bragg terms the 'Great Dining Chamber.' I have taken the liberty of having a table set here before the fire, where we will not have to scream the length of the table.''

A sharp edge of strain dulled the mellow music of his voice. A strain that Anne felt, too. Her gaze strayed to the small table, backlit by the fire dancing in the hearth. ''Dining *tête-à-tête?* It sounds''—she chanced a glance and found his graceful hands balled into fists at his sides—''delightful.''

He nodded stiffly, gesturing to the table thickset with steaming bowls and platters and presided over by Petworth. ''I have taken another liberty, as you can see. I hoped that you, like I, would choose to dine without retainers. It is more . . .''

''Intimate?'' Anne finished for him, in a tone as soft as swansdown. It wasn't done, an unmarried woman and a man dining alone. Should the gossip-mongers learn of it, she would be ruined.

He neither spoke nor nodded, though his eyes darkened to a smoldering blue. Anne's pulse stutter-stepped. The tip of her tongue peeped out to slick across her dry lips.

This was the man who had loved her and left her, she reminded herself to no avail. Unwise it might be, but he was the man she still loved.

If she was to trust herself at all, she must believe what she had sensed and seen in him four years ago: a strength that would make him follow his chosen course to the bitter end; a pride that might break him, but would never bow his head; a capacity for love unequalled in her experience, and that love given to her alone. And yet he had left her. Why?

''Petworth, you have our leave to seek your leisure,'' she said softly.

The impeccably correct butler slipped silently away, and Karl found the short distance to Anne looming like an unbridgeable chasm. Her delicate scent of damask rose permeated the air. Tension pulled his bold features taut as his gaze embraced the gentle face, the memory of which had been a talisman against the harsh realities of his life.

That talisman drew Karl across the unexplainable chasm of four years' separation. "Anne," he whispered, in a suspiration of repentance and regret.

"Cantor," she sighed.

Karl's gaze dimmed for the briefest of moments. He ached to hear his real name on her lips. He ached to know that she saw through "Cantor" to the man hidden behind him.

She reached out. His breath caught in his throat. The tips of her fingers seared his. The hot mulled wine of forbidden desire flowed through nerve and vein and sinew, leaving his loins heavy, his face flushed, and his mind spinning . . . far away from the knowledge that he would never be free to wed her.

His hand closed around hers. "I have missed you, Anne," he said, the bitter admission harsh with longing.

A fleeting look of pleasure, then pain crossed her face. Her lashes fanned down, fragile ebony crescents that trembled against the cool ivory of her cheeks. "How, Cantor? How did you know I was here?"

A tremor raced through his hand, giving Anne a warning that was emphasized by the ruddy flush that darkened his face. "I didn't. I came to dine with Lady Bragg, and Petworth told me you were here."

"I—I see." What a fool she was to hope he had come simply to see her. She attempted to slip her hands from his, but he held them tightly.

"Don't," he pleaded.

She went still, desperately seeking to regain her poise. Her gaze found a spot just over his shoulder, a gargoyle grinning from the carved mounting of a pier glass mirror. "You . . . you must live nearby. I—I don't remember your mentioning exactly where," she said at random, in the disinterested tone reserved for polite conversation.

"Don't expect a dandy's petty prattle from me, Anne," he warned harshly.

Her gaze, a bleak pewter-gray, clashed with his. "If not, then what are we to have? Will you tell me how you have spent the last four years? Will you tell me why you left me?"

The questions Karl dreaded. The ones he could not answer. His secrets were too old; the danger was too great.

"Is it enough," he began in a voice devoid of all emotion, "to say that I would not have left you, if I did not have to?"

Anne's breast ached with the pressure of anger and grief. "No, it is not."

"I can tell you nothing else," he said stiffly.

Her disappointment scoured deep, scrubbing away at the last remnants of hope and abrading her pride. The pride that sucked her tears back to their source and set a stern finger beneath her chin, tilting it up. Her hand slipped away from his, abandoning its heated strength. "Why did you request that I dine with you tonight?" She cleared the betraying tremor from her voice. "Why, Cantor?"

He reached out, his fingers gently coasting from the crest of her cheekbone to the trembling corner of her mouth. "Do you have to ask why?"

Though she saw it all in his eyes, the loneliness, the longing, and the love, she said fiercely, punishingly, "Yes! I have to ask!"

His thumb glided over her lips. "Because I left my heart with you, Anne."

The wisp of a wounded breath whispered through her parted lips. She plunged deeper into her hopeless, helpless love.

"And you took my heart with you," she said, so softly he leaned down closer to hear. So close she could see the golden roots of his tawny lashes and feel the warm wash of his breath stirring the tendrils spilling across her brow.

"Then let us, for this one night, feel whole again, Anne."

"Must it be for only one night?"

He broke the tender tether of her gaze with a visible effort. "I would make it a lifetime, if I could."

Why couldn't he? Anne leaped from the impossible to the improbable to the outlandish. If he had married another, the gossip-mongers would have spread it through the *ton*. If he thought a marriage between them would be a mésalliance—as the *ton* surely would—he must know how little his lack of rank meant to her. If he, like she, was trapped in some clandestine—impossible! Her imagination ran away with her!

Yet it was a haunting reminder that she should be relieved that he sought no future with her, for she dared not seek a future with him. She dared not drag him into the web of treachery that surrounded her. Not while Robbie's life rested in her hands. Not while she, a traitoress, might be exposed at any moment. She could not protect her family from her scandal and shame, but she could protect Cantor.

She blinked away tears and reached out. His hand folded around hers, warm and strong and sure. "Then let us make the best of the time we have," she said softly.

It was a bittersweet victory for Karl. There would be no more questions. He would have minutes, when he wanted a lifetime. The quicksand of need tugged at his heels, but he could not yield to it. He could not seek to engage Anne deeper in love, then leave her. He must make of this evening lightness and laughter and sweet, sorrowful parting.

Only his tightening grip spoke of the turbulence buried beneath the smile forcing up the corners of his mouth. "I see," he began, his melodic voice plumbing breathless basso depths, "that you never grew as tall as you hoped you would."

That light observation told Anne what he wanted to make of the evening—a memory as bright as a newly minted coin. No hopes were to be born anew. No dreams were to arise, throbbing with life. They would share nothing more than frivolous chatter and laughter, shields for the pain of loving where they should not love.

"And now it is too late," she said, as breathless as he, her smile as tentative as his. "I have one foot on the shelf, with youth and growth behind me."

"And have your fears been realized?" There was so much about her that he didn't know, so much he would never know.

"To a wretchedly tiresome degree," she responded. "No man will take a woman of my diminished size seriously. Carroty-pated youths in their first Season persist in ignoring my consequence and patting me on the head."

His smile died. Despite a valiant effort, it could not be summoned back. Was the surety of a throne worth the loss of Anne? Would the satisfaction of vengeance ever equal her promise of peace? Duty! Always duty! He was claimed by a sudden desperate need to escape his duty and to seek his desire.

"Anne, I—"

"Don't!" Her fingers drifted over his lips. "Don't say something both of us will regret. Don't make a promise you cannot keep."

His heart burned with rage and rebellion. Even as hot promises formed in his mind, Karl knew he would not make them. He could not draw Anne into the web of danger that surrounded him. He could only accept, as he had always accepted, that the wishes of a prince meant little.

He bowed his head, fighting the rage, fighting the rebellion. He gathered his strength, offered Anne his arm, and began leading her to the table.

"You have had long acquaintance with Lady Bragg?" Anne asked, surely a neutral topic. But he hesitated, reminding her of the many times he had turned her questions about his family and himself into paeans of praise for the Lakelands. Accus-

tomed to the *haut ton*'s worship of family history
and consequence, she had found this a mystifying
quirk of character. One that, apparently, had not
changed.

"Our acquaintance is an old one," he said at
length. "She was a close . . . friend of my mother's."

Anne, cursing herself, could not resist probing
that crack in his guard. "Was?"

"My mother is dead," he clipped out, effectively
quelling her questions.

Cantor held her chair. Anne settled with a rustle
of black crêpe, glancing at the clock ticking on the
mantel. Time, that sullen despoiler of dreams.

Her gaze fled, restlessly roaming the salon, skimming over the red silk walls, the lush appointments,
and settling on a marble Aphrodite, naked and demure atop a mahogany pedestal.

Cantor sank into the chair opposite, his exquisitely tailored coat of Bath Superfine molding the
muscular swell of his shoulders with lazy elegance.
The hint of a smile played along his beautiful mouth.
"What do you find so amusing, my lady?"

"Myself, I fear." Anne's sparkling gaze flitted to
the demure Aphrodite. "I feel deliciously wicked.
Like a barque of frailty being wined and dined in a
lusty boudoir."

His smile became a boyish grin. "I own to a pro-
found shock, my lady, and no small amount of curiosity. What do you know about barques of frailty
and lusty boudoirs?"

"No girl raised with a brother like mine could fail
to lose her delicacy of thought and expression."

"Do you mean he told you—"

"Certainly not! He assumed that odiously superior masculine attitude that sprouts with a boy's
beard and refused to discuss his more . . . singular
pursuits with me. So, I . . ."

She paused, and he leaned forward, bracing one

muscular forearm along the edge of the table. ''So, you?'' he prompted.

''I became quite attached to a limb of the oak tree outside his window at Darenth Hall. Whenever his friends visited—aspiring Pinks of the *ton*, who spent hours perfecting the folds of their cravats—I would hie myself away to my favorite spot and listen to all they said. It was positively''—she gifted him with a radiant smile—''edifying.''

''No doubt.'' The corners of his mouth quivered with a laugh that came forth with a deep, throaty resonance.

It shattered the last of Anne's restraint, leaving her feeling as reckless as he. He exuded the vigor and zest of old, an irresistible combination. A trill of merriment spilled from her, flutelike and clear. How long it had been since she had laughed, since she had felt . . . alive, as if every moment was a challenge to be met and every minute a gift to be cherished.

''And here I thought your Robbie was the only devil in the Darenth brood of two,'' Karl said. No sooner did the words leave his mouth than he wanted to drag them back. His gaze raced over her black crêpe gown, pausing to linger on the fluted collarette at her throat. Mourning's black and white. The remnant of his smile faded.

He wanted to tell her he had suffered with her, that he had been in Russia eight months ago, that he had heard her brother was missing after the Battle of Borodino and presumed dead. He wanted to tell her that he had abandoned a mission dear to him to search for her Robbie, but that his efforts had yielded no trace.

But ''Cantor Cartwright,'' penniless younger son of a penniless knight of the realm, could tell her nothing. A rakehell with a touch of the scoundrel, a gamester and a wastrel, Cantor would not have been riding with the Tsar's fierce Cossacks.

The mantel clock ticked the seconds away. Time

fled, now and always beyond his grasp. Would he always exist in the shadows, watching life but never living it?

All he could offer Anne were the insipid condolences of any acquaintance, and none of the sympathy of a man who loved and, in that loving, shared her grief. His hands curling into fists, he studied her face. With that closer attention, he saw the slight hollows beneath her cheekbones and the lavender shadows beneath her eyes. He saw the marks of sleeplessness, the faint etchings of grief, a new and terrifying fragility.

"I was sorry to hear about your brother's . . . death," he said, offering useless words when he wanted to give so much more. "I know how close you were."

Anne looked away, staring blindly into the fire. If only she could tell him Robbie was alive, held hostage to her every act. If only she could share her fears for her brother.

Her leaden gaze lifted to Cantor's face, turned now to the seductive heat of the fire. She longed to throw herself at him, to shift the burden for saving Robbie's life to his broad shoulders.

"Cantor," she whispered, "let us bar sorrow from this room. Let us pretend there was no yesterday, there will be no tomorrow. There is only now."

"I wish—"

"No wishes," she said quickly. "Only the reality of tonight."

"Reality, sweet Anne," he said, bitterly dreading the loneliness of the morrow, "is cold comfort."

"But better than none. Come." She forced a smile. "Will you let that champagne age yet longer?"

"So commanding, my lady," he said, his smile a ghost without depth or humor. "I cherish the gloomiest expectations for you."

"And what are they?"

"I predict you will someday be a poker-faced dowager with a shocking want of delicacy."

"Wretch," she said softly.

Her caressing tone stole the sting from the word and washed gently over Karl, a healing balm for a man bathed in the muck and mire of dark deeds. His eyes locked with hers, hot blue to misty gray. *I love you, Anne*, the forbidden avowal lingered unspoken on his lips. He wrenched his gaze from hers and raised his champagne glass in a toast. "To Lady Anne Ransome, the most beautiful woman born of England's peerage."

Anne's raised glass dipped low. She had no illusions that she had more than a passably pretty face, lacking any singularity. Her features were too fine for arrogance, too small for resolution, too ingenuous for strength. "Cantor," she chided, "you are coming it too strong, surely."

Coming it too strong. The cant expression, never used by ladies in polite society, pricked Karl's tawny brow into an inquiring arch.

"Robbie, again," Anne confessed with a laugh. "I fear he has left me with a . . . a 'shocking want of delicacy.' "

Karl smiled, relaxing as he had not done in years. He brought to Anne a blemished soul and a dark, unhappy heart. She gave him peace, pleasure, and laughter, and more important than all, the hope that there were others like Anne in his rapacious world. Others who lived their belief in loyalty, truth, and love.

She had shown him the emptiness of his life through the richness of hers. For him *family* was only a word. For her it was a way of life, the reason for life. Her family was the source of her serenity and happiness. She loved her parents, but she had adored her brother Robbie. Seeing his flaws and foibles clearly, she loved him all the more. And that had been a lesson, too. Love did not require that a man always be strong or right or good. Only that he be himself—and that was the one thing he could not be.

Even that thought could not blight Karl's mood. Time was too short to waste on regrets.

The meal cooled and congealed, for Anne dared not waste a moment of the time that tramped past as inexorably as Napoleon's *Grande Armée*. She talked and listened and laughed—and wept inside, for Cantor watched her as if every look might be his last, as if he must drink in her very essence to carry with him into a lonely night.

She followed his lead, discussing everything from the latest peccadilloes of the *ton* to the wars in Europe and America. But beneath the conversation she waged a bitter battle. The lightly etched streak of cynicism she had seen in him four years before had become a deep, ineradicable vein—why, she would never know, as she would never know so much about him.

The candles guttered one by one. The black of night yielded to gray. Dawn came, thief of the night. A chorus of linnets sang a hymn to the rising sun, while Anne, standing at the terrace doors, mourned its coming.

Karl stood behind her. Close, so close, but not touching, not daring to touch. He had to leave her, melting into the darkness, becoming the shadow he had always been.

Another moment, he promised himself. Another moment, and he would leave.

The moment came. The moment passed. Then another, and his hand raised, hovering over Anne's shoulder, so close he could feel her warmth—

"You must go," she whispered, as much question as statement.

A tremor raced through his fingers. His hand moved back, away from Anne. His long sun-browned fingers curled into a fist.

"Will you once more tell me that you hope I will someday understand?" she asked.

It was a plea for an explanation Karl could not give. He studied the soft tendrils curling across her tender nape and yearned to press a kiss to her fragrant flesh. Even that he must deny himself.

Anne closed her eyes against the rising day, against the knowledge she would shun. ''Cantor,'' she whispered helplessly.

Only the ticking clock answered her.

And on the terrace, gray with night's stubborn shadows, there landed a raven, cawing.

Chapter 3

Karl's one night of pleasure cost him more than he expected. His unholy Grail—the need to take his revenge on the man who had stolen his heritage—had taken him from "lusty boudoirs" to filthridden slums to jeweled palaces, all in the shadows of intrigue where a knife in the ribs awaited him around every corner. Never before had he doubted the worth of his quest as he did now.

He raced up the stone stairs spiraling through the heart of the peel tower. Outside, the borning day was bathed in the light of the rising sun. Inside, all was dark and drear, as dismal as his mood. He must read Darenth's message. He must flee Anne, and her dangerous promise of peace. He must liberate himself and leave her free to seek another love, to make a life without him.

Yet the thought of another man making Anne his own was a pain beyond bearing. Karl wanted to bask in the loving light of her gaze. He wanted the right to touch, to take, to give. He wanted that right to be his into the twilight of their years. He wanted . . . everything he could not have, everything he dared not reach out to take. Even if he could give up his quest, he could not draw Anne into the web of danger surrounding him.

He reached the top of the stair and burst through the door, sending it slamming against the wall. Franz, dozing before the fire, woke with a start, his beefy hand slapping against the knife sheathed at his waist.

"Where is it?" Karl bit out in a cold, implacable voice Anne would not have recognized. Nothing of the lover remained, except the fathoms-deep pain buried beneath his hard blue eyes.

Franz levered his thick body from the chair, an arrested expression in his penetrating gaze. He searched Karl's face, as if he would rip all away to see if the core remained staunch and true.

"I won't be quitting on you after all of these years," Karl said, every word sharp with the futile anger roiling inside him. "Where is it?"

"I could not find it." Franz's grizzled brows frowned a lowering ridge across his forehead.

"The message wasn't in the book?" Karl paused beside the piano.

"There was no book," Franz responded flatly.

"There has to be! Darenth knows that French and German agents watch his every move. He would never allow Anne to lead them here for a simple visit to Lady Bragg."

"I searched every nook and cranny of her chamber, every bandbox and portmanteau. I even had Petworth call her abigail away on a pretext. Then I scoured her chamber. I tell you, there is no book. There is no message!"

"Damn!" Karl strode to the window. The garden glistened in the sunlight, diamonds of dew sparkling against the green velvet background of turf and yew. Seeking Anne's window, Karl was blind to the morning's beauty.

If Franz could not find the book, there could only be one of two reasons: there was no book or Anne had hidden it. If she had, she knew its significance, and she could only know that if her father had told her. Was this message so important that the earl had trusted her with a secret he had kept for twelve years?

Karl dared not confront her, thereby revealing

more than her father had—if Darenth had revealed anything at all. He dared not stay where her presence threatened a goal toward which he'd strived all his life, a goal he must reach, not only for himself but for others. That victory hovered now, just beyond his reach, but so close he could taste it, smell it, feel it.

Step by slow step, he, with the earl's aid, had moved ever nearer to that victory. This message might thrust him across the threshold, leaving him free of danger, free to live. He could not leave. He must stay near Anne, the fount of his every doubt, the center of his every hopeless desire.

In the Blue Room, Anne, too, thought of hopelessness and desire. Needing solitude and silence, she had slipped into her chamber like a thief in the night, careful not to rouse her abigail in the small maid's closet. Bess, who otherwise slept like the dead, had an irritating habit of waking at the drop of a pin when she was least wanted.

Hurriedly shedding her black mourning crêpe for a voluminous dimity gown awash in Buckinghamshire lace, Anne wrapped a shawl around her shoulders and went to the warm marble hearth. Her chin cradled on the crest of her updrawn knees, she folded her arms around her legs. The fragrant oak log burned red before her blind gaze, which saw nothing but the man painted with infinite care on her mind's eye.

Though sadness tugged at the depths of her soul, like dark earth at a rose's roots, she did not yield to a storm of tears, healing though they might be. Tears would not bring Cantor back. Tears would not change those things that kept them apart.

She told herself they shared something rare and unique, a love that could not be dimmed by the passage of years or cooled by separation. Tonight it had grown stronger than ever, bonding them as one in heart, soul, and mind. It was there in Cantor's vivid blue eyes, those eyes that spoke so eloquently the words he did not say. It was there, a perfume wafting on the air, a taste of honeyed sweetness on her lips. It was real. It was hopeless.

"Cantor," she whispered. But in her grief, there was relief. However painful, it was best that he had left her. If he had not, would she have found the strength to deny him?

Not a thought to dwell upon. Anne burrowed into the vast blue cavern of the bed. She promised herself she would not look back, only ahead, but she fell asleep on thoughts of Cantor and dreamed sweet dreams of all that might have been.

Sleeping through the sunny day and peaceful dusk, she awoke with a jarring jerk from deepest slumber, alert and watchful in the Stygian night.

She heard . . . music? Surely not.

But there it was again. The furious, glorious music of a virtuoso surged through the window. Though the pianist was a mystery to Anne, the music he played was not. The sonata was a musical form marked by emotional restraint—until composer Karl von Dannecker had imbued it with passion and fire, with anger and audacity. That music had carried her through the early weeks of her grief over Robbie's reported death. That music had been both solace and release as she eased her sorrow and guilt at the keyboard. Though she was a talented pianist, she had never achieved such an effect as this. Every exquisite note throbbed with emotion.

She eased from the bed, drawn inexorably to the window, enraptured by the music spilling into the night. Music that came from the ancient peel tower, where a single tiny window glowed.

Anne sank to her knees, her hands clasped in reverent prayer. The pianist in her marveled at the awesome talent of the unknown musician. The music lover worshipped at the shrine of every note. The woman responded to the emotions created, as if she were the instrument and her heart its vibrating strings.

The music stopped abruptly.

Disappointed, Anne shifted restlessly. Who was it that played? Who . . .

A crashing chord splintered into a dynamic allegretto movement that raged against bitter fate. Anne sighed blissfully. Von Dannecker's *Sunset* sonata. She knew it well. Swept into his angry vision, she forgot herself, Cantor, her fear for her brother. She was one with the music and the musician. Soon the rage wore itself out in a despairing *fortissimo* that thundered through the darkness. The pianist's fingers flew through the modulation to a plaintive minor key. *Pianissimo, pianissimo*, softly, softly came the lyrical passage, a plea, a prayer, a demand for acceptance. A demand that grew stronger, rejecting pleas, rejecting prayers, rejecting acceptance. *Presto, prestissimo*, passion and pride returned in a flurry of notes that rushed toward the *glissando* of defiance— the stunning end that always took Anne by surprise and left her, heart pounding, to wonder where that defiance led.

Crickets chirped wanly in the silence that fell.

A shadow darkened the tiny square of light that hung against the sky. A masculine shadow, broad-shouldered and slim-waisted—and hauntingly familiar. Cantor, Anne grieved, knowing her mind was playing tricks on her. By now, he must be far away from here.

Who played von Dannecker's music, as if he were both player and composer? That angry, mystic music whose publication four years before had presaged the excitement roused by Byron's poem *Childe Harold*. Where the sullen, sultry Lord Byron gloried in his lionization by the *haut ton*, the mysterious German musician had royally snubbed his would-be worshippers. Invitations to fêtes and routs, balls and soirées poured into his hapless publisher's office, leaving the inundated man with no recourse but to make an announcement through the *Times* that Herr von Dannecker regretfully declined. Rumors spread and grew, as rumors do, but never a fact saw the light of day. Except the one fact that the "Mystery Composer," as he was dubbed, did not care a cinder's worth for the adoration of society—which, of course, made him all the more desirable.

Had Anne just been privy to a private concert given by the Mystery Composer himself? It was possible. Lady Bragg was a German, whom Cousin Richard Bragg had met and married during a visit to Venice. Perhaps Lady Bragg had maintained her ties to her—

"Praise be, I heard ye stir!" said Bess, all atwitter, her mobcap askew and her white gown billowing like a sail in full wind. She carried a single candle, its flame streaming flat, and the little light it emitted shone in her round blue eyes. "There ye were sleepin' the sleep of the innocent this morn, and me not knowin' what to do. How shall I contrive to tell . . ." Her plump hand trembled against her breast. "Indeed, it is not to be believed! Here! In Lady Bragg's . . . really it is quite, quite extraordinary!"

Accustomed to her woman's extravagances of expression, Anne climbed to her feet without haste or alarm. Bess described even the sighting of a mouse in words of drama and imminent doom. "Surely, there is no need to enact me a Cheltenham tragedy," Anne said, the hint of a smile playing about her mouth.

"No, *milady*?" said Bess, stiffening like a Grenadier on review, an image quite at odds with the drunken drape of her mobcap. "I scruple to tell ye what has happened," she said loftily. "Shabby, shabby, it is! And in Lady Bragg's own—"

"And what has happened?" interrupted Anne.

The question induced an immediate melting of Bess's cool mien and brought her tiptoeing across the chamber. At Anne's side, she ducked and brought her lips near to her mistress's ear. "Milady," she whispered, as if ears pressed at the walls could hear, "yer chamber was searched last night and so was mine!"

The alarm that had previously escaped Anne came now in an icy deluge. "Are you certain?"

"Certain? Of course, I am certain! I always—always—leave your silver-backed mirror—the one your father gave you on your Christmas of two-and-ten. Such a lovely gift with the comb and brush to match. So thoughtful his lordship is!" she apostrophized, while Anne waited impatiently. "I always—always!—leave it one finger's length from the edge of the dressing table and, milady!" Bess gasped, as if she were just discovering it now. "It was moved!"

Had the news come from someone else, less well-known to her, Anne would have hesitated to accept such paltry proof. But Bess performed every duty with clockwork precision. No doubt she could reel off—and would in breathtaking detail, if asked—an arm's-length list of the disorder she had discovered.

"The book, Bess! Did you hide it on the library shelves? Did anyone see you?"

"It's hidden, as ye asked. None saw me," said Bess. "Do ye think—"

"I don't know." Anne turned away, staring through the panes at the lonely shadow of a man in the peel tower window. "Seek your chamber and rest, Bess. I must be alone to think. And, Bess, you will speak of this to no one, ever."

For once, her woman left promptly and without argument. Anne listened to the snick of her closing door and allowed the trembling that began deep within to have its way. If she needed proof of her suspicions, she had it now. The book was more than a simple gift. Her mission was more than a simple visit. Come what may, she must remain until Lady Bragg returned.

In the cool peel tower chamber minutes passed like hours and hours like days. His hearty nuncheon

lying untouched on a small piecrust table, Karl sat
in a broad, upholstered, thronelike chair—Lady
Bragg's most pretentious purchase. Though he normally eyed it with amusement and avoided its ex-
ceedingly comfortable depths, today he sat in the
shadows of its deep side wings with the carved mahogany crown soaring above his head and the living
raven perched on his knee. Both were reminders of
hopes and dreams, of sacrifices made and steps
taken. Both were meant to banish thoughts of Anne.
Both failed.

Franz came in slapping a broad-brimmed yeoman's hat against his thick knee and frowning
mightily. He threw his hat on a cluttered side table,
sending a dainty gold snuffbox sliding to the edge.
He sank into a chair and leaned forward, propping
his elbows on his knees and tapping his knuckles
against his hard mouth. "A stranger in the village
is asking questions."

"About Bragg House?"

Franz leaned forward, his fingers curling into fists.
"About you . . . and Lady Anne."

"Anne!" Karl burst out.

The raven flapped her wings and took flight with
a grumbling *Pruk, pruk.*

Karl's hands, with their hunter's strength and
musician's grace, gripped the armrests with white-
knuckled power. "Is she in danger?"

"*Nein,*" said Franz. "The villagers know Lady
Bragg has been ailing, and that a kinswoman has
come. Nothing more. His interest was in the 'mysterious man of Bragg House.' "

"How did he—"

"The new footman prattled. Petworth is sending
him to the seat in Surrey, none the wiser. The old
staff has been given a new warning."

Karl sank into the chair under the gleaming mahogany crown. So many tongues to wag. So many

secrets to keep. God! He was tired of it all! "If the stranger comes too close—"

"He won't," Franz vowed grimly.

Anne's shock of the night yielded to a morning laden with questions. Did the book hold a message for Lady Bragg to pass to another? Had that agent searched her chamber?

She spent her morning in those idle pursuits expected of a country manor guest. She ate a late breakfast served by a ham-handed footman with a face like a Newgate inmate—and wondered about Lady Bragg's choice of servants. She plied her needle in the Yellow Salon, ablaze with the sunlight that pierced the row of tall windows—and noted with a chill of foreboding that a burly footman stood guard on the portal. She laid her needlework aside with a shaking hand and left the palatial confines of the house to stroll along Lake Windermere's rippling blue rim—and found that a husky, hard-faced gardener followed her progress, ostensibly clipping balding yews and flowering lilacs.

She was being watched, closely. Her heart misgave her. She had been so sure she had left watchers and danger behind her. She had been so sure she would find peace in the Lakelands. She should have known that peace had vanished when von Fersen first came to her, telling her that Robbie was alive and what she must do to save him. He trapped her between her loyalty to her brother and her father, her brother and her country. Now she was trapped at Bragg House with obvious watchers and unseen searchers and a message she must deliver for the good of the realm.

Should she trust Petworth, the impeccable butler? Her father said to put the book in no hands but those of Lady Bragg. But she must trust someone! If only Cantor was here! If only—

She could not drag him into danger! But Cantor could tell her who among these people were Lady

Bragg's oldest and most faithful servants. Surely Petworth could send a message to him.

She lifted her skirts and raced toward the house. A reed-slim figure in unrelieved black, she flew through the lemon-bright day as fleetly as the rusty-red roe deer frolicking in the sprawling gardens. Looking and sounding like the hoyden she had been in the innocence of her youth at stately Darenth Hall, she burst through the door and snagged the startled Petworth by the arm as he crossed the cool checkered marble of the entry hall.

"Petworth, I must send a message to Mr. Cartwright. Have a groom prepare—"

"Milady!" Discomfort lighting his pale gaze, he pulled away and craned his thick neck, confined by a snowy stock. "I regret to inform you that Mr. Cartwright has—ah—been called away from the Lakelands."

The soft, searching "ah" betrayed him. Anne realized he knew where Cantor was. Yet he refused to tell her. Why?

"How . . . how very provoking," she said, the comment at odds with her spinning thoughts.

"May I be of service, milady?" he asked with strained decorum.

He was refusing to tell her where Cantor was. It was clearly an attempt to keep her isolated here, but to what purpose? Was he, like Lady Bragg, in league with her father? Or did he work against him?

"No," she said softly, her gaze searching his.

"Very well, milady." He turned to leave.

"Petworth!" she said quickly, then could think of nothing more to say. She wanted to hold him for a moment, to hear him speak again, to learn what she could.

"Yes, milady." He turned back to her, stiffly correct.

"I . . ." She sought wildly for something to say. "I—I heard music in the night."

He started violently, his heavy lids rising to reveal a wary blue stare. "Music, milady?"

Such an innocuous comment to rouse such a reaction. Unease snaked down Anne's spine. "Yes." She winced at the breathy hiss of the word. "Someone played the piano."

His eyes did not meet hers. "I fear you are mistaken."

"I think not." She studied his broad, flat face intently. "It came from the peel tower."

"Impossible, milady," he said dismissively. "The tower has been abandoned for years."

He crossed the hall, every tread regally measured, leaving Anne with another mystery. Why would he deny the existence of the man in the peel tower? Unless . . . that man was the searcher, the one who wanted the message she carried. Still, she did not know if he worked with her father or against him.

No sooner did Petworth vanish than a beefy footman came to stand in the hall. Huge feet set apart and thick gloved hands clasped behind his back, he stared straight ahead, obviously on guard. Anne hurried to the Yellow Salon and settled down with her needlework, while her heart pummeled against her ribs. Surely, there could be no danger for her here at Bragg House. No danger where her father had directed her, for he would not be party to murder and mayhem.

Yet he was the director of the Raven's Nest, the leader of men who lived by their wits in the shadow of danger. Men driven by their allegiance to king and country, by their love of the chase, by the thrill of danger. Men who would do anything to protect themselves and their mission. Would she, her father's daughter, be safe if they thought her a threat?

The salon, snugly cluttered and warmed by streamers of sunlight, assumed a malevolent, stifling air. She needed to escape it and her wardens. She needed freedom to think alone.

Plying her needle with shaking fingers, Anne watched the footman, standing sentinel outside the door. She waited until she thought she must scream with the tension building inside her. She waited until she thought tedium had dulled his wits. Then she tiptoed through the golden sunbeams and slipped through the terrace doors and left her watcher guarding the empty parlor.

She fled around sculpted yews, seeking the far reaches of the garden. The acute sensation of imminent peril followed her into the wilderness beyond the formal plantings. She paused in the shade of the crab-apple tree blazoned with pink blossoms and crimson buds. The geometric trellis of a spider's web anchored a drooping limb to the bright green turf. At its heart was the spider, its long legs entrapping the writhing body of a butterfly.

Anne shuddered and hurried on, rubbing her arms against the cold that rose from within her. When would Lady Bragg return? she wondered frantically. Two days, and she felt she had been here for years. Cantor, Cantor, she thought. Could he help her, if only she could see him now?

Delicate white umbels of wild parsley quivering with her passing, she stumbled on with no destination, only a need to escape the questions that snapped at her heels like snarling hounds. Her gaze climbed to the Troutbeck Hundreds, craggy peaks ascending to the clouds. Peaks of slate-gray boulders and screes of rock, luxuriant emerald-green turf, mist and cloud and, in the distance, rain, all lit by the golden sun. A scene as exquisite as a Turner landscape, beautiful, fearsome, and in her uncertain mood, frightening.

In that wilderness of jewel-toned wildflowers and bronze-foliaged oaks, she found a three-sided rectangle of neatly clipped yews and scythed green turf. Within, a marble angel gazed benignly on two sunken graves. Etched into the pedestal beneath her was the vengeful statement, *An eye for an eye*, and below, Sir Richard Bragg, 1763–1793, and Wilhelm von Cramm, 1783–1793.

Lady Bragg's second husband and the son of her

first marriage, both lost in a fire when the stable
burned. Anne remembered her parents discussing it
when she was a child, her mother grieving and her
father strangely angry. It was a tranquil resting place
with the wooded hill climbing above it and the lake
spread blue at the distant foot of the slope. She
stared down at the fringe of wet meadows painted
with the brassy yellow of marsh marigolds and the
silver-white of lady's-smocks. The tranquillity seeped
deep, blunting the edge of agitation and fear.

"Hssst!" came a whisper to shatter her hard-won
peace.

Anne spun quickly, her black skirt swirling on the
breeze.

A gangly scarecrow of a man enwrapped the corner of a yew, his clothes hanging from his spindly
body like rags from a hook. His blade-thin face was
deep creased with grime behind a long, sharp needle of a nose. A nose that lifted to stab the air.
"Alone, yer ladyship?" he rasped, like a saw
through wood.

Her every panting breath sucking in sweet spring
air corrupted by the stench of old sweat and gin,
Anne fell back a step. "Who are you?"

"Von Fersen's man." A gaping grin split his face,
revealing a ghastly row of rotting teeth. "Ye might
say we're mates."

The bile of revulsion bubbled at the back of her
throat. "What are you doing here?"

"Watchin' ye, yer ladyship. The Dutchman ain't
a trustin' sort, if ye get me meanin'."

She should have known. She should have expected
a watcher to follow. Hadn't von Fersen warned her
that she could do nothing without his knowledge? Yet
here, where all was such a tangled coil!

"What do you want with me?" she asked, her
voice sharp and shrill.

"There's somethin' I'm needin' to know." He
leaned forward with a leer, a rattlebones in the
breeze. "Ain't none as can tell it but ye. Who's the

mysterious man of Bragg House? Him what the footman says comes and goes in the night with none to see his face.''

The musician. It could be no other. Anne's hand crawled to her throat, where her pulse throbbed furiously. ''M-mysterious man?'' She played for time. ''I—I cannot think what you mean.''

''Ye haven't seen him then? Out back in the old peel tower. That's where he lives, so the footman says.''

The musician. The lonely man standing in the lit window. The man whose presence Petworth denied. Her father's man or another's? Anne's tongue slicked over her dry lips. ''Why does . . . this man . . . interest you, if you were sent to watch me?''

''Ain't me, yer ladyship. 'Tis the Dutchman. I'm to report anything what ain't on the up-and-up. Has a devilish interest in Bragg House, he does.''

''I—I see.'' But, of course, she didn't. She didn't *see* anything anymore. She didn't act on her own. She only jumped to act, when von Fersen twitched the string of his threat to Robbie. But she would give him nothing she was not forced to give. She would betray no one she was not forced to betray. ''Whatever his interest,'' she dared to say, ''you are mistaken about a mysterious man. I have seen nothing''—her heart hammered, trembling the lace at her breast—''and heard nothing of any mysterious man.''

''That's as may be, but he's there all the same.'' He twitched back the ragged skirt of his coat, fingering the knife at his waist. ''Ye'll meet me here at dusk on the morrow an' tell me who he is—or the Dutchman'll be hearin' of it.''

Chapter 4

$\sim\!\sim\!\infty$ O O $\infty\!\sim\!\sim$

Anne spent a sleepless night. Karl knew, because he spent one, too. While the moon nudged the stars across the sky, he watched her window. She returned to it again and again, a Raphaelite angel framed in light.

A somber fog ushered in the day. Hour by sullen, inexorable hour passed with Karl pacing his elegant chamber. He paused, his gripping hand turning white against the royal-blue window frame.

"Majestät."

His blood ran as cold as an ice-flecked beck tumbling down a fell peak. *Majestät.* The reminder that he lived by his wits and survived by whatever means it took. He was darkness, where Anne was light. Despair, where she was hope. Death, where she was life. No matter the dream that haunted his weakest hours, he could never take her for himself. Even if he were free, marriage to him would kill the best part of her. His life had been too hard. His scars ran too deep. Her innocence could not survive his devil's own knowledge of what the world really was.

Survival demanded that he bury unruly emotions. He sucked in a bracing breath and turned to Franz, a deadly gleam in his hard gaze. "You learned who sent him?"

"The Weasel, von Fersen," came the sour answer.

The old rage welled up, hot and strong. A furnace

blast that shriveled tenderness and love. Karl looked forward to the day when no ties would bind him, no woman would hold him, and he could yield himself up to the black night of vengeance. "Friedrich's mad dog," he said, his voice guttural with loathing.

"Do you think he suspects?" asked Franz.

"How could he?" Every word came drenched in the bile of bitterness. "He thinks I am long dead."

"There is more." Franz paused, shifting his big feet and removing his floppy yeoman's hat to run his fingers through his grizzled brown hair. "Before von Fersen's man . . . died, he said that Lady Anne . . ."

Karl stiffened, rigid, waiting. The split second of silence lasted a lifetime. "Out with it, man! What about Lady Anne?"

Franz straightened, his dark eyes seeking a spot high overhead. "He said that Lady Anne is spying for von Fersen."

Had Franz run mad? He must have, if he could believe this of Anne! Karl's darkening gaze took searing survey of his man: the steady hands, the prideful jaw, and most damning of all, the lucid gaze. A black frown sprang to Karl's brow.

"Impossible!" he said flatly. Anne? All that was innocent and good? It was too ridiculous for credence! No man who knew her would believe it!

"So I thought, *Majestät*, but . . ." Franz's leathery face remained impassive, but his eyes spoke eloquently of the pity his tongue would never betray.

Karl felt cold of a sudden, as if the warmth of life was bleeding away, as if gelid fingers were wrapping around his heart, squeezing breath and strength from him. His lips and tongue formed the soundless word, "But?"

"But a coward with a knife at his throat does not lie! Lady Anne spies on her father for von Fersen, and through him, for—"

"Enough!" Karl hissed, and wheeled away. Franz did not know her, Karl told himself. He did not know Anne's fierce loyalty to her family or her capacity for love. She would never betray her father! Yet Karl stood with his back to his man, his body rigid with roiling fear, for he knew Franz as well as he knew Anne. Franz would never accuse her without proof.

One balled fist slammed into the back of a chair, pressing deep into the horsehair stuffing. His eyes, dark with anger and dread, stared at the raven, hopping on her perch with her shiny black head bobbing a yes-yes-it's-true. "A coward with a knife at his throat will say anything. What proof do you have?"

"She arranged to meet him at your . . . grave, *Majestät*. Fitting, don't you think?" added Franz bitterly. "Go now, and you will find her there. You will learn what she does—and know to protect yourself from her."

As if he could. Where had his instinct for survival gone? If Anne, sweet innocent beloved Anne, could not be trusted, what was the point in sacrificing and striving? What was the point to life?

He would never believe it! *Never!* came a violent cry from his heart, while the coldly calculating core of his mind ticked off points with the precision of a Borgia measuring drops of poison. Franz had no reason to lie. Franz would not accuse her unless he believed it. And Anne? Every man, woman, and child had a price. Even Anne.

It sounded so simple. Find her and learn what she had become. There was only one problem. He did not want to know. He had, he realized with ominous foreboding, lost his nerve; and a man without nerve was easy prey in the game he played. But if he did not go, he would never know whether she was accused falsely, whether the flame of hope should burn brightly. And he needed that hope, if he was to go on sacrificing and striving.

He moved quickly, lest his sudden resolve desert him. Sweeping his cloak from its hook, he lunged down the spiral stair and plunged into the thick, swirling fog. He cursed the quaking of his belly and the gorge rising acid in his throat and the fear that he would find her, waiting fruitlessly for a man who could not come.

He knew every inch of the sprawling grounds. Sight was unnecessary for movement. With a lifetime of practice at stalking his prey, he fell easily into the sleek, stealthy strides of a hunter. Not a twig snapped, not a blade of grass broke to betray his passing. But while his body conformed to those old habits, his mind spun wildly out of control.

The blossoming crab-apple tree loomed out of the mist, a ghostly presence grasping the curtain of fog with yearning arms. He angled down the slope, his black cloak rippling. His long legs ate the distance, while his mind screamed, *Stop! Stop now! Before it's too late!*

But it was already too late. Directly below the gravesite, he dropped to his knees and crawled beneath the dripping branches of a fragrant bog myrtle. The rich, fecund odor of the wet soil filling his nostrils with the earth's promise of renewal, he dared to look.

Through the shredding mist he saw her. His Anne, pacing beneath the marble angel.

She arranged to meet him at your . . . grave, Majestät.

If she had not planned to meet him, how had von Fersen's henchman known she would be here? If she had not, then why was she waiting and watching in the thick, chilly fog?

Anne threw back the hood of her cloak. Opalescent pearls of mist glistening in the black curls piled atop her head, she stepped around the yew hedge and stared anxiously up the slope—looking, Karl admitted, for a man who would not arrive.

He closed his eyes. Was Franz right? A pain too deep for rage claimed him. Did Anne spy for von Fersen and through him, for Friedrich, prince by murder and deceit, the uncle Karl had never seen, his father's twin, his father's murderer? The man responsible for the deaths of his mother and Sir Richard Bragg, that kind and gentle man who was the only father Karl had ever known.

Those three lost lives cried for vengeance, and its black night yawned before Karl, an abyss from which, once entered, there would be no return. He stared into that abyss, seeing a man beyond redemption, wandering through a wilderness, lost and alone. He shrank from that vision, clinging tightly to the hope that Anne had given him.

In the distance the raven cawed a forsaken warning that echoed through the billowing fog.

Looking at Anne, a slight figure swathed in black with the moist air caressing her pale cheeks, Karl could not see an enemy. Yet he would be a fool to believe in her. He knew too well the frailty of the human spirit and the strength of its vices. She was a woman, not a saint. But he knew—in that tender retreat where love dwelled—that she could not have changed so much. He would have seen those changes.

Like the changes he was seeing now? Karl frowned, watching her intently. Her rigid posture spoke of tension and fear. Her hands, the smooth white hands that gave him ease with a touch, were nervously clasping, unclasping, and stroking her cloak, as if her palms were sweating. Most damning of all, she stared up the slope, watching . . . watching for who, if not von Fersen's henchman?

Was it possible for the Anne he knew to betray her father and her country? Karl was no longer sure. He only knew he had to find out.

Impulse urged him to demand the answer of her, but impulse was a deadly weakness in the game he played. He had left such weakness far behind, in the youth ended abruptly in his tenth year.

Unseen, he waited with Anne while the moon climbed high in the foggy sky. He watched her pace back and forth, rubbing her arms beneath her cloak and casting worried looks up the slope. At last, she relinquished her vigil, and so did he. Following her, he wondered whether he was the lover seeing her safe from harm or the enemy stalking her.

Anne hurried through the oddly luminous night with the fog purling around her and the trees dripping their sodden weight of mist. She wanted nothing more than a fire to warm her from without and a steaming cup of tea to warm her from within.

So seldom of late had she been blessed by good fortune, she hated to question it. But why had von Fersen's gaunt man not come? It was possible he had learned the identity of the "mysterious man of Bragg House" from another source. She would like to believe it, but could not. Petworth was too secretive. His underlings would not be less so. She could only believe von Fersen's man had been discovered and . . .

Beyond that she trembled to think. If the gaunt man had been discovered, had she been betrayed?

The windows were ablaze with welcome as she approached the terrace and eased into the Yellow Salon. Lady Bragg, a tall reed-slim blonde trailing sheer draperies, stood before the fire, warming her hands. Nearby was a thickset man dressed in the russet browns of a laborer. Anne froze, her cloak dripping audibly on the carpet and fingers of fog curling around her, as if reaching for the light.

"Pray, forgive me," she began haltingly.

"Anne." The woman moved toward her with a cool, distracted smile.

The man assumed a militant stance, feet spread, hands clasped behind his back, thick shoulders squared, and smooth-shaven chin lifted. Above that chin was a severe face burnished by the sun and marked by pride and purpose. That in itself was remarkable, but it was his suspicious nut-brown eyes that captured Anne's attention.

"How lovely that you have come to visit," said

Lady Bragg, the guttural syllables of the Germanic tongue lightly evident in her precise English.

Anne clasped her cousin's hands and found them colder than her own. Tearing her gaze from the man, who was frowning so heavily that his grizzled brows shadowed his searching stare, she summoned a smile she feared was as weak as her watery knees. In Lady Bragg's face she saw the remnants of a stunning beauty ravaged by time and grief, a sweetness of disposition, a melancholia of the soul.

"You have made a handsome woman, *leibling*," said Lady Bragg. "The very image of your mother, and she, you know, was once a diamond of the first water."

Tears sprang to Anne's eyes. Her mother was no longer a beauty. Grief had stolen the blush from her cheeks and carved them with deep lines of sorrow. A sorrow Anne could eradicate with the few words— *Robbie is alive.* Though she tried to tell herself that the good to be achieved in the end was worth the pain of the present, she could not banish her deep-seated guilt.

Lady Bragg's grasp tightened painfully. "Your mother—"

"Is well." Anne blinked back the tears. "I fear her grief for my . . . my brother—"

"Yes, *leibling*," Lady Bragg murmured, a corpse-cold finger stroking Anne's cheek. "A mother's grief is a fearsome thing."

"Yes, you know . . ." Anne stopped abruptly, biting her quivering lip, appalled that she had wakened that old grief for her sad and sorrowing cousin-by-marriage.

Lady Bragg's gaze dropped to the hands she withdrew from Anne. "Yes, I do," she said in a voice as colorless as her pale gaze.

Colorless as the words were, there was a false note in them. Anne promptly dismissed the thought. Tangled deep in her father's and von Fersen's cunning webs, she saw deceit, she told herself, where it did not exist.

"You are cold and wet, *leibling*," said Lady Bragg gently. "Go above and change. I will order a tea tray for us here."

However gently said, it was a dismissal. Anne, making her way to the door, nodded briefly to the man and received as brief a nod in return. She could feel his eyes on her back, boring deep with suspicion, and wondered who he was, what he did here. Though he moved with catlike quiet, she heard the whisper of his steps and the firm snick of the door at her back.

In the vaulted hall she hesitated, staring at the library entry, adjacent to the Yellow Salon. No one was nearby. Petworth did not linger in the hall. No footman stood guard. She moved swiftly to the library and passed into its gloomy precincts. It was the work of a moment to find the book and slip it from its shelf, then breathe a sigh of relief that her father's task would soon be done. As she turned to go she heard voices through the crack in the door that led to the Yellow Salon:

"Franz, I am so frightened! In the village I was asked to identify a man who had been killed in a fall from the fells. He was a stranger to me, scrawny and needle-nosed, but he had been asking questions about Bragg House and its 'mysterious man.'"

Scrawny and needle-nosed. Von Fersen's man. Anne's heart surged into her throat, pounding a frantic rhythm. Dead in a fall from the fells, but . . . but he had no reason to be scaling those dangerous heights! Though the blood drained from her head in a giddy rush, the crack in the door pulled her toward the sliver of light, the whisper of voices.

"Do not fret, Elisabeth," said the man, his voice a low rumble. "He became known to us as von Fersen's man. You have nothing to fear now. Dead men carry no tales."

Dead men carry no tales. Nor dead women either!

Terror claimed Anne. A suffocating, choking terror that sucked the strength from her knees. Weakly she slid to the floor, the book clasped to her breast, as if it could shield her from her rising panic. She wanted to run, but there was nowhere to go. If they were against von Fersen, then they worked for her father. She wanted to hide, but if she did, what would happen to Robbie?

That thought steadied her. Her back straightened. Her chin climbed. She must go on, for there was always the chance she had not been betrayed. Tonight she would deliver the book into Lady Bragg's own hands. On the morrow, she would leave at first light—if she was allowed to leave.

In the gloom of morning Karl read again the message he'd taken from the spine of *Sense and Sensibility*. It was characteristically crisp. The Earl of Darenth neither minced, nor wasted, words. No salutation, no closing, no name to betray the sender or intended recipient; yet the spare and decisive style was one Karl would recognize anywhere:

> *A spy has invaded my household. I suspect the Weasel and need a Raven to pluck his eyes.*
> *Send M.C.*

The message fluttered to the surface of Karl's walnut kneehole desk, a scrap of white littering its stark surface. Unlike the surrounding peel tower chamber, which betrayed Lady Bragg's love of ornament and her belief that Karl should live amidst the finery that fit his station, his desk was as his mind had been before Anne—uncluttered by the unnecessary. Now, though he struggled for reason, all he found was confusion.

A spy has invaded my household.

Was Anne that spy?

Traitors were born of many natures: avaricious, ambitious, and weak. None of those natures be-

longed to Anne. Yet there had to be something! A
secret she wished kept. A deed she wished done or
undone. What was so important that she would betray her country for it?

Her father? Karl thought of the elegant Earl of
Darenth, whipcord-lean and tough, with a mane of
steel-gray hair and arctic-blue eyes that could cut a
man to the bone. Forged of equal parts of rigid rectitude and unflinching loyalty, Darenth would die
before turning traitor to the country he loved.

Still Karl wondered if this was a trap to lure him
to London and into von Fersen's clutches. But the
German did not know he was alive. He believed his
assassination attempt those many years ago had suc-
ceeded.

Karl tunneled long fingers through his golden
curls and settled his forehead on the heels of his
palms. Dare he refuse this summons, breaking faith
with the man who had been his father's friend and
his own?

Send M.C. The last resort he and Darenth had
agreed upon long ago. Though Karl would be in disguise, he would move into Polite Society, meeting
the same people who knew him as Cantor. There
was the danger, the earl had said, that someone
would recognize him. Neither had suspected then
that Anne might be that one.

Anne. Ah, God! Anne!

If she did work for von Fersen, Karl could not believe she did it willingly. If she did not, he dared
not abandon her to that lonely and dangerous struggle. If he did, he would abandon himself, too. He
would forfeit his right to leave his world of shadows
for the light of a real life.

Climbing to his feet, his powerful legs sheathed
in buckskin and the muscular vee of his upper torso
clad in a loose shirt and a coat of creamy soft chamois, he moved to the piano. His speculative gaze
roamed along the keyboard. His supple fingers
spread, striking a minor-key chord. The plaintive,

unfinished chord echoing to silence, he quit the peel tower chamber.

If Anne was willing, if she spied out of avarice, ambition, or weakness, then . . .

He would treat her as the traitoress she was.

While Karl's fleet-footed Welsh bay flew down the rutted track circling Lake Windermere, Anne bade nervous farewell to Lady Bragg. She had delivered the book. Her task was done. Now she wanted only to escape. To escape the secrets held close by Bragg House. To escape the memories of Cantor.

She climbed into her fashionable post chaise and sank onto the azure-blue squabs, her heart pounding a rackety rhythm and her mouth as dry as dust.

"Hie, me beauties! Hie!" bellowed the coachman, and the chaise lurched and began to roll.

Anne sighed, a soft sound replete with relief, rested her head on the smooth velvet, and laced her ice-cold fingers together. She was safe now, but— she trembled—for how long?

Chapter 5

June 1813
London

In the sooty dusk of the London evening Lady Anne Ransome's post chaise wheeled into St. James's Square, only to be caught in the crush of barouches and landaulets delivering the cream of the *haut ton* to Lord Robert Stewart Castlereagh's door. Reckless excitement permeated the crowd that jostled for precedence like Billingsgate fishwives hawking their wares. Anne had seen the same reckless excitement the previous summer, when the literary lion of that Season, Lord Byron, had appeared.

Too exhausted to wonder who had received the *ton*'s cachet, and its consequent adoration, she stared instead at the lamplighter threading amidst the throng of carriages and liveried footmen, like Diogenes in search of an honest man. Were there any of those left? Her lashes drooping over her disillusioned gray gaze, she laid her head back on the azure squabs. At every turn she met insidious lies and terrifying venality, even from her father. Did he know what his minions did? Did he approve of cold and calculated murder?

At least she would be spared a meeting with him tonight. He and Lord Castlereagh were as thick as Seven Dials thieves. An unfortunate choice of words. She sighed softly. Castlereagh was the Foreign Secretary; her father was a patriot. No doubt they shared a common interest in the plots and plans of the Raven's Nest. They were men who, scheming for the good of the realm, would consider one man's life a small price to pay, whether that man was in the pay of foreign spies, as the gaunt man had been, or held hostage by them, as Robbie was.

"Puss!"

Her father's face appeared in the narrow rectangle of her window. Anne's startled gaze leaped guiltily away, as if he might read the questions springing into her mind. If he knew Robbie was alive, would he defy king and country to save him? Or, as she feared, would he forfeit his son's life to save the many?

"Father," she whispered, the word as frayed as a beggar's rags. Struggling against weary muscles and aching bones, she put steel to her bowing spine and sat as straight as his blackthorn cane. She could order her body to her will, but she could not scrub from her mind's eye the imagined sight of von Fersen's henchman lying broken and dead at the foot of the soaring fells. She could not scrub away the memory of her father's elegant hand ruthlessly shifting a lapis lazuli queen as he said "Checkmate!" with the arrant satisfaction of a man who played to win.

He would ask about the book. Fighting back a shudder, she prepared to give innocent answer to that inquiry fraught with the danger of exposure.

He opened the coach door and held out his hand, helping her to alight. "You must have been on the run in good earnest to have returned so quickly," he said in the low, mellow voice that had once lulled her to sleep with cradle songs. "Any . . . trouble?"

"N-no." The lie stumbled from her lips. No trouble for him, but for her there had been a shattering of faith as absolute as the breaking of a Wedgwood plate. Her father had become a stranger to her, a man capable of the cruelest deeds.

Her gaze shied away from his face, carrying an indelible impression. Nothing was changed. Not the long high-bridged nose. Not the thin mouth that often hinted of a smile. Not the finely arched brows or the mane of steel-gray hair. The youthful glint in his arctic-blue eyes still belied his two score and fifteen years. He was the same man he had always been. The man who had sniffed her childish gifts of wilted ragwort, though they sent him into fits of sneezing. The man who had tossed her into the air, skirts flying and laughter pealing, always catching her and holding her close and making her feel safe and secure. Would she ever feel that way again?

Her icy fingers linked at her waist, seeking comfort where there was none. Waiting for him to ask of the book, she mentally formed a light response.

"You look pale, Puss. I trust you are well," he said, sending her calmly reasoned response scattering on a rush of confusion. A confusion that deepened when he stroked her cheek with a gentle black-gloved finger.

The lustrous ebony crescent of her lashes fanned down, shielding the yearning that welled up to sting her eyes. Unwillingly, she leaned into that touch and the affection that prompted it. He was her father, and she loved him. He was her father, and she feared him. But whatever her doubts, she could never question whether he loved both her and her brother. It was only that he loved his country more.

"It was the journey," she murmured. "I—I fear I am quite overset by it."

"Then you must rest, Puss. I shall tender your regrets to Lady Castlereagh," he said with an air of finality.

Anne watched his lean, impeccably tailored form angle away, as if he meant to leave. A frown crept across her brow. A question formed in her mind. It was not possible that he would not ask, when the answer must be important to him. Little as she wanted to speak of it, she found herself calling out. "Father?"

"Yes, my dear?" He turned back to her, his expression of polite interest tinged with the impatience of a man of affairs eager to be about his business. Yet all he meant to do was attend the Castlereaghs' soirée, another in the endless round of soirées, levées, and balls that made up the London Season.

"Lady Bragg asked that I convey her best good wishes, and her thanks for your"—Anne's gaze narrowed, alert for any flicker of response—"gift."

No widening of his coal-black irises heralded an inner relief, no twitch of a muscle betrayed a secret tension. Anne saw nothing more than a softening of his features, the growth of a fond smile.

"A woman of excellent sensibilities is our Lady Bragg, eh, Puss?" he said carelessly.

He had already known! He had already known the message had been delivered! But how? Who had ridden from Bragg House to London, carrying that answer before her?

"Darenth! You sly devil!" The swarthy Earl of Audley approached, prinked up like a bandbox dandy. Bess would have sniffed had she not been snoring in a corner of the chaise.

" 'Evening, Lady Anne." He tapped his deep beaver brim and flashed a white-toothed smile. "What do you think of your father's stealing a march on the whole of the *ton*?"

Anne blinked once, twice, struggling to make sense of what he said. "I—I fear I am at a loss, my lord."

"By gad, my lady!" He canted over his ebony cane, the cluster of seals dangling from his fob chiming musically with his every move. "Your father has pulled off the coup of the Season! Imagine! The Mystery Composer himself as your houseguest!"

Karl von Dannecker! Anne's hand smothered her gasp. It was too neat by half: that she should think von Dannecker was at Bragg House; that someone should precede her to London with news that her father's message had been delivered; that von Dannecker should *happen* to be her father's houseguest.

Was he the mysterious man of Bragg House? The man capable of cold and calculated murder? Had the gaunt man betrayed her before he died? A chill raced up her spine, prickling across her scalp with spidery feet. Did her father know, even now, that she was a traitor?

"I say, Darenth!" Audley was saying. "I'm dashed if I can see why you would yield the honor of von Dannecker's first musical evening to Castlereagh."

Her father flicked a speck of lint from his French cuff. It was a languid, apparently thoughtless gesture, but he never wasted effort or action. Dread dulling the sheen of her heavy gaze, Anne watched a slow, unamused smile curl along his mouth.

"You always were a glutton for glory, Audley."

Clearly unruffled, the swarthy Audley bared his startlingly white teeth in a grin. "Let's hope our Mystery Composer is worthy of the humdugeon he's created. If he's ham-handed at the keys, Castlereagh won't thank you for giving him the honors and the . . . glory." He winked an onyx eye, dipped a scant bow to Anne, and strutted off, twirling his ebony cane.

Her mouth arid and gritty, Anne waited for her father to turn to her. She had seen no knowledge of her guilt in his eyes nor heard condemnation in his voice. Yet he had concealed his thoughts and his actions before, keeping the secret of the Raven's Nest from her . . . and from her mother? Did he dissemble so easily that even her mother did not know?

His cool blue gaze touched her. The frown lingering in its depths sent chills scrambling across her nape. Anne, waiting for an accusation, heard instead: "I begin to believe, Puss, that Audley is, after all, the frippery fellow he appears to be."

"A-Audley?" she stuttered.

His frown deepening, her father stepped closer. "You are as white as wax. Are you ill?"

Anne searched his face, whose every nuance of expression she knew so well. Worry darkened his eyes and concern tugged his brows into a frown, but there was not a hint of aversion, of disappointment, of anger.

"Puss!" he said urgently, his voice thick with concern.

"I—I am quite well, Father." It was a lie. She was sick with fear. "It is only that . . . that I am weary."

"Then you must rest."

But she could not. There could be no rest for her until she knew whether the Mystery Composer was also the mysterious man of Bragg House.

The Castlereaghs' musical evening was what Robbie would have called a "fashionable squeeze." Guests squeezed into corners. Footmen, carrying silver salvers laden with glasses of ratafia and claret, squeezed through clustered groups. Anne, her every muscle quaking with tremors of tension and fatigue, squeezed into the drawing room.

Her skin dewy from a hurried bath and her ebony ringlets warm from the curling iron, she paused to catch her breath and search the crowd. Lady Castlereagh, a patroness of Almack's, the seventh heaven of the *ton*nish world, had invited everyone who was anyone. The Duke of Cumberland, that gimlet-eyed lecher, held court in one corner, a fat finger tickling the blushing cheek of a miss scarcely out of the schoolroom. The Prince Regent, that less than jolly gourmand, held court in the opposite corner, his fat fingers delving into a bowl of sweetmeats. Morose Lord Liverpool, stately Lord Castlereagh, and her father huddled in converse too serious for this frivolous gathering. Nowhere did

Anne see anyone who might be the broad-shouldered, slim-waisted shadow sighted in the peel tower window.

A rill of awareness moved across the surface of her tension and fear. A rill of pleasure as fragile as the ruffles of soft black lace rimming the hem of her tiffany gown. She sensed a presence, familiar and loved. The presence of Cantor Cartwright.

Impossible! She thrust the thought away. He would have told her if he planned to come to London. Yet the feeling persisted, honey-sweet and warm.

It was nothing more than a whiff of sandalwood riding the air thickened with perfumes and scented powders, she assured herself. Perhaps a glimpse of a bold, masculine face with a sturdy jaw, or a deep, liquid laugh buried beneath the rumble of voices. Despite those assurances, the search for the peel tower shadow became, instead, the search for her tall, strong Cantor.

Her gaze roamed restlessly, eagerly. Scanning the men's faces, she discarded one after the other. Dark and fair, they laughed, smiled, and frowned, flirted, and dipped snuff, while she made a visual circuit of the room. The circle closed on the Earl of Audley, stifling a yawn at her side. Disappointment sluiced through Anne. Cantor was not here, but she had not expected him to be. She had only wanted him so desperately that she imagined he was near, as she sometimes imagined that Robbie was home. That she could hear her brother's step on the stair and his rich laugh flowing from chamber to chamber. Delusions that could lead only to madness, when she needed her wits crisp and clear.

She must know if the Mystery Composer was the musician of Bragg House. She must separate fact from fancy, reality from fear. A stir came from her right, the rustle of skirts, the shifting of feet. Hissing whispers surged toward her.

"Von Dannecker," murmured the Earl of Audley.

"Have you seen him?" whispered a woman at his side.

"Dash it, I have!" he choked out, stifling a laugh. "I've not seen such a sight since Sheffield appeared at the Raeburns' *bal masque* dressed as a Saracen dancer."

Anne darted a quick look his way, seeing the dancing black eyes, the broad cynical smile. His portrayal of von Dannecker was hardly the stuff of nightmares, of villains and murderers.

The stir quickened. A pair of dandies decked out in their Bond Street best bowed elaborately toward the door of the Ladies' Salon, then stepped back with the deference due to royalty. Anne's brows arched over eyes shining with equal measures of curiosity and dread. What would she do if he was the musician of Bragg House?

A trio of ladies, decked out *à la militaire* in plumed Prussian helmets, epaulets and gold braid, swayed into graceful curtsies, like primroses making their *devoir* to the sun. Anne steeled herself, her mind's eye filled with the broad-shouldered, slim-waisted shadow seen in the peel tower window.

A path opened with Anne at its foot and at its head stood her mother on the arm of a . . . masked man! A tall, broad-shouldered, barrel-waisted man dressed in the gaudy, garish style of a Macaroni— the dandy of her father's youth.

The mask alone was startling, a confection of pink satin studded with rose-cut brilliants and rimmed with lace. Anne's gaze, unable to find a safe place to light, danced from the outlandish to the outrageous. Pink-tinted powder sifted like snow from a moth-eaten pigeon's-wing wig with every regal nod of his head. Silver-thread embroidery and tarnished spangles, worked over the bilious green-satin ground of his square-cut coat, glittered with every movement of his great frame. A pink brocaded waistcoat rippled over the whalebone struts of a corset. Heart-stoppingly tight, gaudily striped breeches undulated down muscular thighs, punctuated at each knee with a bouquet of multicolored ribbons trailing streamers to the ankles clad in bilious green stockings.

Von Dannecker flourished a lace handkerchief, making what was called in her father's day "an elegant 'leg." With that corsetted paunch and fluttery manner he could not possibly be the musician of Bragg House. That man had exuded vigor and power. Anne doubted this one could summon the mettle to swat a bothersome fly, much less engage in the dangerous game of spying. Relief came on a sigh of pent-up breath, an easing of the apprehension knotted in the pit of her stomach.

The Countess of Darenth captive at his side, he struck a theatrical pose in the doorway, obviously waiting for the murmurs to die away, for every eye to focus upon him. Though how any eye could fail to do so, Anne was at a loss to understand.

The woman at Audley's side gasped back a giggle. The earl cleared his throat raucously. Anne chewed on her lip so hard that tears of pain shimmered in her eyes. The Mystery Composer was, to put the kindest face on it, a ridiculous figure perched midway between mummer and mountebank, with nothing of the musical maestro about him.

"*Meine Damen, meine Herren!*" he sang out in a shallow, flutelike tenor. "It joys me dat you vill haf de pleasure of *meine Musik.*"

The drawing room exploded into clapping and cheers. Von Dannecker fluttered his handkerchief, accepting the adulation he obviously considered his due. Nodding to first one, then another, he moved into the drawing room, limping heavily. Anne thought he would go to the piano. Instead, her mother at his side, he began a halting but purposeful progress down the opened pathway that led to her.

She was his host's daughter. It was courtesy,

nothing more. Yet every halting step sent alarm skittering along her nerves.

She searched the mask, whose rose-cut brilliants captured the candlelight, sparkling and twinkling like stars in a pink satin sky. Sparkles and twinkles that lured the gaze away from the dark, seemingly empty, eye slits. To keep any from probing that seeming emptiness? From seeing his eyes and the thoughts dwelling in them?

It seemed to Anne that those hidden eyes were riveted upon her. Even when he paused to accept a nosegay of violets pressed upon him by a stuttering, blushing miss in virginal white. Even when he paused to brandish the handkerchief like a scepter and kiss Lady Jersey's hand. It was fancy, not fact, fear, not reality, that made her feel she was the focus of his every thought, that his halting steps were not so much halting as stalking, that she somehow was the prey he sought.

He stopped before her, frills of lace spilling over his hands and concealing all but the sun-browned tips of his fingers. Her gaze climbed to the mask and dropped to the firm, square jaw, cording with tension. She saw the ripple of muscle beneath taut, sunkissed skin. The youthful skin of a man in his prime. Not, as she had thought, a man of her father's years. A wave of familiarity washed over her. The lean jaw, the chin with its hint of a cleft, the thinly compressed lips, all were—

"Herr von Dannecker," her mother said in that newly soft and sad voice, bleached of life since Robbie's reported death, "I would make you known to my daughter, Lady Anne Ransome."

Anne's impression of familiarity fled, routed by the burning sensation of torment flowing from Karl von Dannecker like heat from the sun.

"Vat a pleasure dis is for you, *Fraulein!*" he simpered down from his great height, wafting the handkerchief by two daintily crooked fingers, delicately tapping the nose concealed by the lace bordering his mask.

The strange sensation of torment linking Anne to him snapped like a weak thread, leaving her with no recourse but to believe it had been imagination—or madness. This vain peacock could never suffer such depth of feeling.

He bowed deeply, posturing before her. A ridiculous, puffed-up, self-important man, he preened in the garish feathers of the Macaroni, strutting for the crowd like a Covent Garden player. "Someday, you vill haf de honor to tell your children dat you haf heard dat great genius, Karl von Dannecker."

He inclined his huge body on a whisper of satin and a creak of a corset, while gracefully poising his hand in midair.

Though Anne shrank from his touch, courtesy impelled her to offer her hand. His fingers, sunbrowned and warm and hard as a sporting blood's, closed around hers in a shockingly strong, almost painful, grip that shattered her illusion of softness.

He gently tugged her resisting hand up to his mouth. The moist heat of his breath washed over her knuckles. His lips touched the back of her hand, and something powerful, unnameable, arced from flesh to flesh. Sensations of emptiness and loneliness echoed through Anne, finding their twins in the secret places of her heart. The same emptiness and loneliness that emanated from her Cantor.

Anne's tender gaze hardened, pewter-gray and resentful. How could this pastry-puff of a man remind her of Cantor? Her Cantor, who was all strength and masculinity, tenderness and joy!

His lips lingered on her hand, not kissing but caressing. Warmth tingled through her fingers and shimmied up her arm. Anne snatched her hand from his, pressing it to her waist and surreptitiously scrubbing the feel of him away.

Her wide gaze climbed to the mask, searching the dark eye slits that protected his every secret. She could feel those hidden eyes watching her, measuring, questioning. She could feel his sudden burst of confusion and anger, as though those feelings were her own.

His head tilted up. Tension tugged at the corners of his mouth, but her gaze lingered on the cleft in his chin. So familiar, so like Cantor's. She was going mad. There was no other explanation for it.

"Lady Anne," he whispered for her ears alone, his voice thrumming deep and low, as if her name had been forced from him by some emotion beyond his control.

The mellow music of his voice touched Anne with a tortured caress. Her beating heart seemed to stop, pausing, poising for the answer lurking in the shadows of her mind.

Rills of tension chased through his lean jaw, while his mouth pinched together in a relentless line. With a curt nod, he turned to her mother. *"Gnädige Frau—"* Candlelight glinted from the rose-cut brilliants into the flat pink of his powdered wig. "I should to *das Klavier* go, *ja?*"

Her mother's lips moved, but Anne heard nothing but the questions, the fears, the possible explanations swooping through her mind like swallows through the sky. She found no answers, no comfort, no possible explanations.

An electric air of excitement raced through the crowd, now melting around the rim of the drawing room. Footmen scurried about with shield-back chairs. Anne, her mind spinning with wild confusion, sank into one, gripping her hands in her lap. Who was von Dannecker? More importantly, what was he?

He posed in the golden light of a brace of candles, and Anne watched his hands with attentive desperation. Those strong, hard hands that did not belong to a mummer, a mountebank, a musical maestro, but to a man of action. Yet the man of action was belied by the paunch, the affected airs, the eccentric costume.

Solemnly, he bowed to the Prince Regent, who acknowledged him with a regal inclination of his head. Another punctilious Germanic bow graced the Duke of Cumberland, whose lecherous gaze lingered on the schoolroom miss. A third bow paid gracious obeisance to the room at large. Could he hear her heart throbbing in the silence, wondering who he was, what he was?

More solemnly still, he turned to the piano bench, flicked up his bilious green coattails, and sat. Tucking his handkerchief into a cuff, he fastidiously pulled on the lace frills at his wrists and poised his hands over the keyboard.

Anne's heart seemed to stop, waiting for the first notes, waiting to hear, to know. And she would know when he played. A practiced and talented pianist herself, she would recognize the phrasing, the fire, the fury of the musician of Bragg House. Or would she? she worried. Her senses were unreliable. They had teased and tormented her with untruths and impossibilities. Watching von Dannecker, the candlelight gleaming over his moth-eaten wig and sparkling off the gaudy mask, she saw nothing but the self-important eccentric and sensed nothing beyond her own hopeless confusion.

A crashing chord splintered into a dynamic allegretto movement that raged against bitter fate, and Anne went cold as winter sleet. Von Dannecker's *Sunset* sonata. She knew it well. She had played it herself. She had heard it at Bragg House.

She sat forward, stiff and alert. The passage raged through notes thundering with fiery audacity. Was the phrasing the same? One moment, she knew it was. Another moment, she knew it wasn't. Soon the rage wore itself out in a despairing *fortissimo* that danced through the cut-glass lustres and brought a sigh of satisfaction from the woman sitting behind Anne.

The sonata played to its inevitable end, despair yielding to demand, demand yielding to the abrupt *glissando* of defiance. Silence fell, acute, penetrating. The guests surged to their feet in a thundering ovation. All but Anne. Anne, who was blind to the sight of Karl von Dannecker rising to take a bow. Anne, who was deaf to the cheers echoing from the medallioned ceiling and papered walls.

There was so much at stake! Robbie's life, and her own. Alert as she had been, she still did not know whether Karl von Dannecker was the mysterious musician of Bragg House. Von Dannecker, who was now her father's houseguest—perfectly placed to watch her every move, to ferret out her every intention.

"The hour is three," sang the nightwatchman patrolling St. James's Square. "God's in His heaven, the devil's in his hell, and all's well."

The deep baritone rolled around the corner of Darenth House, climbing to the window where Karl stood, a cruciform image with his hands braced high on the window frame, his head bowed, one knee bent. Silvery moonlight flowed across his pale, shimmering hair and danced across the tarnished spangles of his square-cut coat. A pearly shaft slipped beyond his broad shoulders to reach deep into his chamber, alighting on the wig and mask abandoned on the bed.

All's well, he thought bitterly. With Anne sleeping in the chamber beneath him? With her father waiting in the library for their first private meeting? With his own decision still to be made?

Betray her or save her. Which would he do?

Rising from the patch of a garden below came the sweet scent of lily of the valley and the musty smell of martagnon lilies, and stronger than both, the heavenly perfume of damask rose. The perfume that never failed to summon memories of Anne and the kiss that had rocked him to the depths of his soul.

He felt again that tearing of himself between duty and desire, but the sensation was stronger, more painful than it had been. He yearned for the once-simple choice between his happiness and his quest. Painful as it was, it had been easy to sacrifice himself. But if he sacrificed Anne for the good of her country and the hope of his own future, there would be more than her happiness at stake. If she was a traitoress, she would be ruined at best and hung at worst—and he could live with neither.

Closing his eyes, he saw Anne as she had been in the Castlereaghs' drawing room. Small and pale and tense, with her hands knotted at her waist and her eyes huge in her fragile face. There was a haunting quality to the pallor of her cheeks, to the lavender smudges beneath her eyes, to the proud set of her shoulders. The free and easy movements of the girl he had known were lost in this woman whose every gesture seemed to be consciously ordered. He had thought the changes were wrought by her grief for her brother. He suspected now that they were not.

"Anne!" He sighed her name into the indifferent night, and turned his back on the moonlight.

One supple sun-browned finger touched the mask, trailing gently over the cool rose-cut brilliants. He had feared she would recognize him. Insanely, a part of him had wanted her to. A part of him wanted the tie between them to be so strong she would know him and love him no matter what disguise he wore. For a moment he thought she had. He had seen the widening of her eyes, the stunned awareness leap into her face, suffusing it with vibrant life. The moment had passed quickly, dying like a snuffed candle. Even now, the taste of ashes lingered in his mouth.

Her love for him had not been strong enough to part the veil of his disguise, just as his love for her was not strong enough to kill his doubts. Every man, woman, and child had a price. Some secret they wished kept. Some deed they wished done or undone. If those prices were met, they would do anything. Even Anne. Even . . . her father.

Karl would know soon if the earl plotted a trap. He placed the mask over his face, hiding an expression as grim as death, while he tied the ribbons at the back of his head. He would know soon whether he would betray Anne or save her.

He swept up the wig and settled it over his soft golden curls. The queue hanging over his rolled collar and the fat pink powered rolls over his ears, he picked up a gold-knobbed cane and quit his chamber with the sleek, silent steps of the hunter.

Minutes later, the lace handkerchief trailing from his fingers, Karl von Dannecker limped into the drawing room. He paused, searching the corners, probing the shadows. He listened for the susurration of a breath that was not his, for the whisper of a nervous movement. Satisfied that he was not being followed, he limped to Darenth's library door, lit by dim candlelight.

"*Ach*, I disturb you, my lord! I could not sleep," he said in a light tenor.

"Nor I." Darenth set his pen aside and leaned back in his chair. "I would be honored to have you join me, sir."

"*Natürlich!*" said Karl with von Dannecker's pomp and pride, while his gaze scoured the library. A long, open rectangle with bookcases lining the walls, the room contained only one place a watcher could be hiding—behind the red velvet curtains.

A smile toyed with the corners of Darenth's thin mouth. "I have here a fine brandy, if you would care to join me."

A long-suffering sigh fluttered the lace rimming the mask. "I vill never survive dis barbarous country! Surely, you haf *schnapps*, my lord?"

"Forgive me," said Darenth, his eyes alight with laughter at the charade they played.

Karl closed the door and moved into the room. Silent, padding steps carrying him toward the win-

dows, he twisted the gold knob of the cane he carried and pulled forth a hidden sword. That sword
at the ready, he tore one curtain back, found nothing but the cool night breeze, and moved to the next.

"Was that necessary?" asked Darenth with an acid
edge of anger.

Karl, turning, shot the sword into its hidden
sheath and studied the man he had served faithfully
since he was eighteen years old. "A . . . precaution,
my lord," he said, dropping the accent and sliding
into his own mellow baritone. "The kind of precaution that has kept me alive these last twelve years."

"And you think it is necessary in my house, in
my library, in my presence."

Karl stripped away the wig and mask, striding
easily to the chair before the desk. He used those
precious seconds to covertly inspect the vein ticking
in Darenth's temple, the icy expression in his eyes,
and the anger betrayed by his tight-lipped mouth.
The righteous anger of a man honestly insulted, not
the manufactured anger of a guilty man. They had
worked together too long for Karl to mistake one for
the other.

"I pray your pardon, my lord. My company, as
you know, has not been of the best." He sank into
the chair, dropping the wig and mask on the floor
beside him and propping the cane against the bouquet of ribbons at his knee.

Darenth leaned back, steepling his fingers and
narrowing his eyes. "Do you trust even yourself,
Karl?"

A bitter smile curled across his mouth. "No, my
lord."

The brooding silence was broken by the sharp,
shrill caw of the raven landing on the windowsill.
Darenth's gaze shifted to the fluttering curtains.
"Most men," he said with the hint of a wry smile,
"have a watchdog. I own you are the first in my
acquaintance to be guarded by a raven."

"I am not most men, my lord."

"No, you are not." Darenth's gaze dropped, his lashes fanning down to hide his eyes.

It was a technique he used to great effect. The lowering of the eyes, a long silence, the sudden up-sweep of the lashes, a piercing look, and a staccato question to knock his quarry off guard. Karl had seen its effectiveness too often not to react now. He stiffened, waiting, telling himself to pause and think before he answered.

It came in a rush. The sudden piercing look that seemed to stab into every secret Karl wished to hold close. "What is my daughter to you?"

Wary though he was, Karl was not prepared for this. "Anne?" Her name spilled from his lips, quickly, thoughtlessly.

Darenth's brows, a startling black against the steel-gray of his hair, scaled his forehead. "Anne?" he asked softly, ominously. "You are so . . . intimate you don't use her honorific?"

A damning flush heated Karl's cheeks. "We met briefly four years ago, my lord, and we dined together at Bragg House," he said stiffly. "She knows me as Cantor Cartwright."

"Why did you make a point of approaching her today?"

Karl quelled the unendurable restlessness roused by the earl's cold, cutting stare. "She is your daughter. It was courtesy to my host—"

"You have never lied to me. Don't begin now," ordered Darenth, every inch the earl. "You have a . . . *tendre* for Anne?"

Karl's chin climbed, his gaze frigid. "You and I, my lord, know that whatever . . . *tendre* I have can come to nothing."

"And my daughter? Does she have a *tendre* for . . . Cantor?"

His gaze locked with Darenth's, with those arctic-blue eyes that seemed capable of dissecting his every thought, hope, and dream. His own eyes hot and prickling, he wrenched his gaze away. "Yes, my lord."

Darenth leaned forward, bracing his forearms on the desk and lacing his fingers together. "My daughter is a woman of excellent understanding. I am neither surprised by, nor disappointed in, her attachment for . . . Cantor. However, it will not suit. You will someday assume your throne, and there will be no place for her at your side. I will not have her hurt."

"Nor will I, my lord," said Karl, knowing that he could never hurt her, never betray her. There had to be a way to save her, guilty or not, threat to him or not.

Darenth frowned, tapping his fingers against his chin. "Under other circumstances, you would suit each other very well," he said softly. "It's a pity . . ."

A pity. Karl gritted his teeth. Impatient of a sudden, he sat forward. "Let us discuss why I am here, my lord."

"My secret papers," began the earl quickly, as if he were as eager as Karl to put discussion of Anne behind them, "papers concerning the agents of the Raven's Nest and reports of their work, have been disarranged several times."

"You are sure?" Closely watching Darenth's expression, Karl saw no heaviness of spirit to suggest the earl suspected Anne, no guilty twitch of a muscle to suggest this was a trap.

"I should have mentioned it straightaway," said Darenth. "After my first suspicion, I began to secrete the most important reports and to particularly arrange the rest. I know when each foray took place; I don't know who. That is why I summoned you."

Karl frowned, alarm bells ringing inside his head. "You don't need me to set a trap for a spy in your own house."

"No, that I could do easily myself. However, I am certain the man behind the culprit is von Fersen, and he is the man I want. Meanwhile, he has given us the perfect opportunity to use our enemies."

This was more like the wily earl, who let no opportunity pass. Karl's alarm shrank to the subliminal vibration that kept him ever alert, ever cautious. "Use them, my lord. How?"

"You know the situation on the Continent. Napoleon emerged victorious at Lutzen, Bautzen, and Hamburg, but without a *decisive* victory. The Russo-Prussian Alliance is holding him. They need only be joined by the Austrians, and France will be beaten."

"I thought the British were staking all on success in Spain," said Karl.

"We do not stake *all* on success anywhere. Word of an armistice signed between Napoleon and the Alliance will reach London in a few days. Officially, that is." The earl's black brows climbed over an amused gaze. "Austria is the key. She cannot be allowed to sustain her *nominal* alliance with France."

"What does this have to do with your opportunity to use our enemies? How will you use the spy in this house?"

"How, indeed!" The earl folded his hands over his lean middle and smiled with saintly innocence. "With distortions, deceptions, and outright lies, all embedded in truth enough to make them believable. I will lard my papers with false reports to be stolen by our traitor. You will tie him to von Fersen. Franz must infiltrate his ring, learning who his agents are and where they are placed—and I believe we will find them everywhere from the servants' quarters of our leaders to the very precincts of Whitehall. When we are ready to strike, we can destroy them. Meanwhile, we can help ourselves."

It was hardly a trap baited for Karl. While he found that a small relief, he suffered a greater fear for Anne. If von Fersen discovered the information she fed him was false, what would he do to her? Yet what choice did Karl have? This plan would give him time to learn what hold the German had over

Anne. It would give him time to wrest her from von Fersen's clutches.

It was a Machiavellian plan, worthy of the wily earl. One that would put Anne at risk, but without it, she could not be saved in the end. "I would suggest, my lord," said Karl, "that you leave only papers of the least importance for our . . . spy to find until you have the false papers drawn up. How long will it take?"

"A week at the most," said Darenth. "I must be sure to do the most damage in the time we will have."

"Excellent," said Karl. "We will want our . . . man hungry for the information . . . he will find. And, my lord, I would suggest that, once we learn who he is, I alone keep the secret of your spy's identity, since you—"

"Would find it intolerable to deal with the knave day-to-day if I knew who he was?" said Darenth. "Excellent suggestion."

Not a flicker of relief showed on Karl's face. Anne would be safe now. Safe from her own father, but not safe from von Fersen . . . or from himself.

Chapter 6

Chumley's was a prosaic name for a milliner's shop that had the London ladies as aghast at the proprietor's top-lofty arrogance as they were dazzled by his exquisite creations. Millinery, as Anne had learned, was not Chumley's only occupation. For the shady, the seedy, the thrill-seeker, the dishonest, there were rooms above for private transactions of an illicit or amatory nature. In one of those tastelessly opulent rooms Heinrich von Fersen awaited her.

Since her return to London, she had slipped into her father's library during the wee hours of each night. She had planned to continue as she had begun, by sifting missives, letters, and reports, copying only what was common knowledge or patent conjecture, with a sprinkling of facts that would not threaten her country or her countrymen. Once, there had been sheaves of papers from Lisbon, Trieste, Paris, and Madrid. Papers that listed troop movements, casualty figures, rumors, and predictions. Now, there were few, and those devoted to rumors.

With Wellington on the march and the Peninsula in turmoil, reports might be delayed from Lisbon and Madrid, but Anne was suspicious of this sudden dearth of information.

She feared her father had learned what she was doing, but he treated her as always, with loving affection untainted by guilty knowledge. Even he could not dissemble as easily as that.

At first she had feared that Karl von Dannecker and the mysterious man of Bragg House were, after all, the same one—a spy in her father's pay—but that made no sense either.

Her father had confided that von Dannecker's mask hid a deformity, but Anne was convinced it was an affectation that garnered him the attention he craved. After a week's association, her pity for his ridiculous vanities had become disgust for his overweening conceit. A gusty trencherman, he spent every meal complaining of his delicate digestion. He sought his bed as early as a country squire, rose as late as the finest sprig of fashion, and napped the afternoons away—all due, he complained, to his delicate constitution. He was as delicate, Anne was certain, as the oxen plowing the hop gardens at Darenth Hall.

If she pitied anyone, it was his valet, Josef Hummel. A dun-colored cricket of a man, hollow-cheeked and hollow-chested, Josef was forever hopping between the chambers above and the kitchen below, stirring up nostrums and potions and broths to build his master's strength.

Anne did not dispute Herr von Dannecker's personal claim to genius, but he was so impressed with himself, he left no room for her to be impressed by him. She was thoroughly out of patience with his pretensions. She was also thoroughly convinced that he was nothing more or less than he appeared to be.

That left her with no explanation for the dearth of information. What von Fersen would say about it, she shuddered to think. What he would ask about the gaunt man, his man, murdered at Bragg House, terrified her—for she planned to lie.

She had considered it carefully. She would say the gaunt man had never contacted her. Von Fersen might suspect, but he could not prove, that she knew what had happened to him.

* * *

"General Junot, governor of the Illyrian Provinces, is rumored to be going mad. Fascinating," Heinrich von Fersen said drily, his buffed nail flicking the creamy sheet of vellum.

Anne quivered, as if that flicking finger was a lash laid to her back. Not a sound climbed from Chumley's shop below. Not a sound passed from room to room or pierced the heavy oak door leading to the carpeted hall. She was isolated in the tawdry splendor of this "lusty boudoir."

Her gaze roamed restlessly, avoiding von Fersen. The crimson curtains flowed like blood from ceiling to floor. The massive four-poster bed was draped in crimson and gold. *Bijouterie* vulgarly crowded gleaming mahogany surfaces and were hideously multiplied in the pier glass mirrors.

She drew an unsteady breath, suffocating in the stale chamber, in the presence of von Fersen—the man who had taught her to hate.

"The French poet, de Béranger, has written a song, 'Le Roi d'Yvetot,' which is being sung in Paris. It is an affectionate mockery of a king who makes pleasure his code of law. I am overwhelmed, my dear," he said gently, but he had nothing of gentleness or kindness in his relentless face.

Anne's resisting gaze met the steely, implacable blue of his eyes. She saw a flicker of amusement, the deadly humor of a cat toying with a helpless mouse. He enjoyed her grief, her pain, her fear. He even enjoyed the hate that washed over her in a choking tide.

"Let me forbear to warn you, my dear," he said in the precise English of the foreign-born, retaining the merest hint of his origins, "my master expects more than . . . this." He flung the papers onto the bed, where they scattered on the crimson coverlet.

My master. Always *my master.* Never his name. Never the name of the man who held her brother prisoner and herself hostage to his fate.

Von Fersen planted his bloodless hands atop the gold filigreed knob of his ivory cane and bent one knee, as if he posed in White's bow window with an array of blasé dandies. He was a small man with narrow shoulders and a sunken waist and tiny feet, exquisitely shod. Though he affected the dandy's costume and tortured his thinning, mouse-brown hair into Byronesque curls, he was as sharp, hard, and pitiless as the blade of an ax.

"I have told you before, my dear, my master is a powerful man and utterly ruthless. The choice is yours: to save your brother or to condemn him."

With his eyes upon her, as cold as death and as ruthless as he claimed his master to be, Anne showed not a tremor of fear. It was there, buried deep, a silent scream, a dark despair. But she dared not reveal a glimmer of it, for he fed on fear, like fire fed on the wind's breath. Her shoulders squared, her chin lifted, and her eyes grew as cold as his. "I own it is little, but it is all I found."

"Then I suggest, for your brother's sake . . . and your own"—he paused, his small hawk's nose twitching like a beak preparing to rend its prey—"that you find a way to get what I want."

"I will try," Anne said stiffly.

"Try?" The word hissed between his teeth. "You will succeed, Lady Anne, or suffer the consequences."

But those consequences would not be hers. They would be her brother's. Robbie, with the laughing violet eyes and the ever-ready smile. Robbie, who reveled in life, wringing from every moment its last drop of pleasure. Robbie, who might, even now, be dead and beyond saving. A thought not to be borne.

With delicate steps, Von Fersen moved to the japanned writing cabinet. Fingering a goose-quill plume, he exuded an air of nonchalance that failed to set Anne at ease.

"How did you find Bragg House?" he asked idly.

Anne's heart lodged in her throat. "Lovely."

"And your visit?"

"Pleasant," she lied. Waiting for the question she dreaded, she ached to moisten her dry lips but dared not.

His bony fingers shredded the plume, while his eyes cut toward her with an expression of speculation and suspicion. "I sent a man to watch you in the Lakelands. Did you see him?"

"No." The lie whistled through her arid throat.

"You do not seem surprised," he said, his small eyes watching her narrowly.

"You told me I could do nothing without your knowledge," she responded, with what she hoped was cool disdain.

"The man has not returned. Do you know anything about him?"

"No." Swallowing the acid bile of fear, she assured herself he could not know. Whatever he suspected, he could not *know!*

He studied her for long moments, while she struggled to suppress her guilty knowledge, to keep her features bland and cool.

"I will see you here one week from today. I trust you will have something for me, or . . ." A ghastly smile pulled at his mouth. "We have no need to repeat that, do we?"

While Anne hurried down Pall Mall, her abigail chattering at her side, Heinrich von Fersen's fingers, now gloved in canary-yellow, eased between the crimson curtain panels. Her abigail bobbed like a buoyant cork at sea, while Lady Anne glided along the path cleared by her footman's sturdy arm—as all paths were cleared for the aristocracy.

English or German, it was the same, he thought, sneering, coveting. *Der Adel's* paths were smoothed by a title, while the common herd of men—better, wealthier—lurched and skidded as if on ice. Soon, he promised himself, his path would be smoothed as theirs were. He would be *Graf*

Heinrich von Fersen, equal to the Earl of Darenth not by an accident of birth, but by hard service well done. The title he used in England would be his in truth. Only this one small task to finish, and he would return to the country of Schattenburg, as rich in honor and glory as a complacent *Bürger* was rich in gold and gelder.

Only this one small task . . .

He turned from the window, a frown wrinkling his brows, his nose twitching as at the odor of rotting fish. And there was something rotten about this. Why had the wily earl sent his daughter to Bragg House? Lady Bragg was a kinswoman to the Countess of Darenth, but was she something more? Something more, as she had been long ago, when she protected a boy who could have toppled Prince Friedrich from the throne of Schattenburg? A boy whom he, Heinrich von Fersen—soon to be *Graf* at his prince's pleasure—had destroyed. But not without paying a price.

His finger climbed to the deep puckered pockmark on the crest of his cheekbone. Memory assailed him on a bone-racking chill of superstitious fear. His nostrils flared, catching a forgotten whiff of heat and wild thyme, of hay and horse. He heard the hum of bees pillaging a sprawling sweet-briar and a chorus of thrushes warbling hymns of praise to the translucent blue sky and, in the distance, the caw of a raven, so innocent in the summer day. In a yeoman's scratchy, dirt-crusted wool, he had slipped by stealth into Bragg House's vast and vaulting stable. There, hidden, he had awaited his prey. . . .

Distant sounds of revelry had floated on the summer breeze, while he smiled, self-satisfied. He'd chosen his moment well. Sir Richard Bragg considered the occasion of his marriage so fortunate that he shared each anniversary celebration with his neighbors and all in service to him. With the revels in full swing none would enter the stables. None but the child, who would seek out his new pony, whatever occurred elsewhere. So von Fersen had been told by a local whose gullet had been sufficiently oiled by ale to overcome his scruples about talking to an off-comer.

Minutes later the boy came whistling out of the brilliant light into the dim, cool shadows. "Blueberry," he called out, and was answered by an eager whicker from a distant stall.

The boy, von Fersen's prey, laughed the light, rippling soprano of childhood, while von Fersen stole from his hiding place with stalking steps, raised his cudgel, began a deadly downward arc—

"Wilhelm?" a masculine voice called out.

"Papa!" The boy's head turned toward the door, and the cudgel crashed along the back of his head, tearing at his scalp, ripping at fluffy butter-yellow curls.

As the boy crumpled to the straw-covered floor, von Fersen nimbly leaped into the deepest shadow by the door and heard the fierce scream of a raven, closer now. A single set of footsteps approached. He waited.

"Wilhelm, your mother—"

Von Fersen swept the cudgel in a long horizontal arc with all of his strength behind it, catching the man at the base of the neck and bending his head at an impossible angle.

He leaped for the lantern and tossed it into the mound of hay. The voracious flames licked out and spread, while he spun for the door. But through that door came a feathered fury of beating wings and tearing claws and sharp beak. And von Fersen, raised on the ancient legend of Schattenburg, suffered a mindless, screaming terror. . . .

Even now, in the dim room over Chumley's Millinery Shoppe, von Fersen could feel that terror: the quaking of every nerve; the trembling of every muscle; the bruising power of the raven's wings; and the needle-sharp gouging of its beak. He wondered now, as he had often wondered since, why the raven broke off its attack. Whatever the reason, it left him free to report the boy dead and Prince Friedrich safe, free to begin his own journey up the ladder of his prince's esteem toward his dream of a title.

Trouble rising from that quarter was highly suspicious. The boy was dead. They had nothing else to hide—or did they? He would wait two weeks for his man to return. If he did not, he would send another to Bragg House to see what could be found.

While Heinrich von Fersen tapped his ivory cane along the promenade of Pall Mall, three men discussed his fate in Lord Robert Stewart Castlereagh's gracefully appointed library.

"You know the latest, of course." A frown furrowed Castlereagh's brow. "Von Fersen, insinuating himself into the *ton* as a violently anti-Bonaparte German count, has received Lady Jersey's ultimate cachet, a voucher to Almack's."

The Earl of Darenth's gaze settled on his friend's austerely handsome face. A fey smile tilted the corners of his mouth, cleaving creases in his spare, sun-browned cheeks. "The disobliging creature! What I wouldn't give to see her face when she learns that she, the highest of sticklers, has vouched a foreign spy into the holy of holies."

"An edifying prospect," said Castlereagh, a smile flickering across his mouth. Then he shifted restlessly, a frown banishing the mild humor. "I have a plan that will put the German in the palm of our hands. It will mean"—his grave gaze shifted to Karl—"raising Cantor Cartwright from the dead."

Behind the mask of sapphire-blue, lavishly embroidered in silver gilt thread, Karl's face remained as impassive as stone, revealing not a flicker of his dismay. He could not, would not, fling Cantor in Anne's face. He would not hurt her more than he already had. He would not subject himself to that pain. Being near her now was torture enough. It would be even worse playing the role of Cantor Cartwright, returned lover.

"Franz will infiltrate von Fersen's ring, my lord," Karl said. "He will learn who his agents are, where they are placed, who they have bought or blackmailed. Franz will be able to directly tie von Fersen to them all." Karl leaned over the stuffing of his belly. The corset creaked, and he silently cursed the earl's long-ago inspiration—demonically inspired, he was sure—of the Macaroni disguise. "Surely that is enough."

"I beg leave to agree," said the earl, with a sharp glance at Karl, which said he well-remembered his daughter's *tendre* and would protect her if he could. "Resurrection of Cantor Cartwright at this moment would be disastrous."

"Disastrous?" Castlereagh questioned. "How?"

The Earl of Darenth, usually articulate, sputtered.

Karl swept up the fallen gauntlet. "For . . . personal reasons, my lord."

Castlereagh's perceptive gaze shifted from the earl's reddening face to Karl's shimmering mask. "I am loathe to insist, gentlemen, but we are approaching a time of critical importance. Napoleon has retaken Hamburg. Our exports into Germany are choked off once more and our economy with them. We must act now to crush the spies in our midst. We must act at any cost! *Any* cost," he reiterated.

"There must be another way." Darenth shifted uneasily.

"None, I am afraid."

"Damn!" The earl's gaze sought the ceiling medallion, as if he would find an answer written in the sworling honeysuckle pattern.

Karl watched his tug-of-war between daughter and duty, family and country. Regardless of the earl's decision, he himself planned to refuse. But he wanted to know what that decision would be.

"Damn!" The earl heaved a sigh, his chin dropping, his eyes lowering. "We will bring Cantor Cartwright back."

In the shadows of the mask, Karl's eyes narrowed. So, now he knew. If Anne was to be saved, he would have to do it alone. He would have to protect her, not only from von Fersen, but from her father. "No," he said flatly. "We will not."

"It is imperative," said Castlereagh.

"We will find another way."

"Will you hear me out?"

"It will change nothing," said Karl.

"Perhaps not, but . . ." Castlereagh leaned forward. "If we take the body without the head, we accomplish nothing. We must have undeniable proof of von Fersen's personal involvement. If I hire our gambling-addicted Cantor as assistant to my secretary in the Foreign Office, he will be a target von Fersen cannot resist. Then, gentlemen, we will have him."

And they would. Von Fersen would leap at the opportunity to subvert a man with access to the secrets and plans of the Foreign Office. Especially Cantor Cartwright, ever in need of the ready to wager at the gaming tables. As Castlereagh said, Cantor would be a target von Fersen could not resist. A target that might lessen Anne's importance to him. Anything that would accomplish that, Karl could not refuse. No matter how much it hurt her . . . or him.

"When should Cantor . . . arrive?" he asked, seeing the glimmer of relief in Castlereagh's steady gaze, hearing the earl's tense, noncommittal sigh.

"As soon as possible. I want him working in the Foreign Office within the week."

"And von Dannecker?" Karl asked.

Castlereagh frowned. "We may yet need him."

"Very easy, dear boy," said the earl, with a humorless bark of laughter. "My wife has mentioned what a fine attention our composer pays to his health. Indeed, she fears he suffers from hypochondria. An exaggeration of that, continued use of the secret stairway leading from my chambers, and you will be free to come and go as you please."

"When does Franz begin infiltrating the German ring?" asked Castlereagh.

"Tonight," said Karl. "We begin tonight."

The stench of Spitalfields hung like a vapor in the air. Karl leaned against a crumbling brick wall in the black shadows of Blue Ruin Alley with a sliver of clean, star-studded sky overhead and the filthy refuse of gin-sodden poverty underfoot. A battle-scarred tom eagerly sniffed an odorous midden-heap, scouted out a rat, and gave chase. A child's thin wail wafted through a rag-stuffed window above. A woman's spine-chilling scream pierced another.

The sounds, the smells, and the dull, penetrating taste of hopelessness were not new to Karl. Whether in London, Paris, Madrid, or St. Petersburg, a slum was the same. Children cried. Women screamed. Cats chased rats. Men, sodden with drink, stumbled through slimy, offal-strewn streets, like the man shambling through the door of the Cock and Roost opposite the alley.

Timid light, creeping through the door, shrank from the man's mammoth frame. His hand, the size of a Yorkshire ham, raised in greeting, and his voice, a boom of thunder, rolled into Blue Ruin Alley: "Meg, a blackjack o' blood an' step lively. Got a thirst could drain the Thames dry."

The man shouldered his way into the inn. In the crack of the closing door, Karl saw the stiff shock of black hair. Milling-Jemmy Shadwell, the wolf that led von Fersen's snarling pack. Karl could only hope the man wouldn't kill him before the night was done.

The plan was risky at best: Karl baiting Shadwell into a fight; Franz leaping to the man's rescue and beginning the work of befriending him. If it didn't work, there would be no second chance. Another way would have to be found.

Not an eyelash flickering, not a muscle rippling, Karl leaned against the cool wall, arms folded over his broad chest. If anyone probed the dark shadow, he would see a denizen of Spitalfields. Karl's russet coat was tattered, his shirt stained, and his trousers, hitched up beneath a broad leather belt, were crusted with dirt. A scrubbing of grime filled the lines at the corners of his eyes and darkened his hair to muddy brown. He stank of gin and sweat, and dreamed of clean, sweet Anne, until danger threatened with a furtive step.

Only his eyes moved, sliding to the corners, studying the pale-gray light edging the building. His senses hummed at fever pitch, drawing in the fishy smell of the Thames, the cool of the night, the sigh of a breath around the corner. Soundlessly, he reached into his boot, felt the chill of the bone handle—

"C'or, gov, ain't a Redbreast on the prowl tonight."

Franz. Karl eased the knife into its sheath. "And who'd want a Bow Street Runner," he whispered.

Franz eased around the corner, meshing with the shadows.

"You followed her?" Karl asked.

"To . . . Chumley's."

Karl's throat ached with tension. Chumley's. Von Fersen's favorite spot for trysts that were anything but amorous.

"Von Fersen came out a few minutes after she left," Franz added.

Neither doubt nor hope was left. Von Fersen's man had not lied. Anne spied on her father for her country's enemy—and his. Loving her, he must save her. But if he could not, would he be forced to expose her before she did more harm?

"Ready?" Franz asked, his eyes gleaming in the dark.

"Treat me gently, old friend." Karl attempted a smile.

"Gently as a swaddled babe," Franz responded with a low, rough laugh.

Moments later, Karl swaggered through the door of the Cock and Roost, a malodorous gin mill that no Bow Street Runner dared enter. He posed with his thumbs hooked into his leather belt and his eyes glittering a challenge beneath the drooping brim of his black felt hat—a man looking for trouble and sure to find it.

A jack-tar snored in one corner, oblivious to the drab turning out his pockets and rifling his purse. A hostler, emitting the sickly-sweet smell of manure, was draped across the bar nursing a tankard of ale. Laughter bellowed from a scurvy quartet gathered round a trestle table, while a maudlin Irish ballad lilted from an adjacent trio.

Karl's cold gaze slid over Milling-Jemmy Shadwell, guzzling his blackjack o' blood—a heinous way to treat a claret, even the swill no doubt served here—while a carroty-pated doxy perched on his trunklike thigh.

Carroty-pated youths in their first season, came the whisper of Anne's voice, with a vision of her smooth ivory skin, her silvery-gray eyes, her lips and laughter and loving warmth. A warmth that could bathe and bind a man to his last breath. Nothing to be thinking of now, when he needed his wits about him.

Karl swaggered into the room, his lean hips rolling and his broad, thick shoulders squared in a primal dare. The pall of smoke, partly tobacco, partly greasy tallow candles, purled away from his body. The toe of his boot sent a pig's knuckle skidding over the foul floor. Shadwell's glittering black eyes, the soulless eyes of a hunting hawk, stared over the tarred leather rim of his blackjack, and a prickle tickled the vulnerable center of Karl's back. The plan would work. Shadwell would be easily stirred to offense and anger. But would it work too well?

The doxy bounced off of Shadwell's thigh, wriggled her lush body, and jutted her plump white breasts, revealed to the rim of pink nipples. She ogled Karl up and down. "Wot'll ye have, dearie?"

A slow, lascivious grin stretched Karl's mouth wide, wolfishly revealing his straight, white teeth. "Blood n' Thunder, wench." He paused, leering at her jiggling breasts. "Fer a start."

"Oy, now! Get on w' ye!" she simpered, and squirmed, setting her breasts to rolling like two round melons. "I ain't that kind o' laidy."

He shouldered past a stumbling drunk. Abreast of his quarry, Karl joggled Shadwell's raised elbow with a careless arm. Watery red claret, liberally diluted with Adam's Ale, spilled down the corners of the man's pink mouth, pooled at the end of his round chin, and dripped onto the yellowing cravat tied with the care of a dandy.

The lilting Irish ballad choked off. The laughter died. The doxy scuttled around the end of the bar. Silence descended, so thick Karl felt he could cut it with his knife. The prickling between his shoulder blades became a sharp stab of warning. As if unaware of what he had done and oblivious to the horrified silence, he stepped past Milling-Jemmy Shadwell.

A sledgehammer blow to the center of Karl's back propelled the breath from his lungs on a long *Oooof!*—telling him he should have waited for Franz's arrival. A sure-handed scrabbling of fingers hooked the collar of his shirt, yanking him upright and spinning him around. A smile curled along Shadwell's full pink lips below his empty, soulless eyes—telling Karl he had started something that might be finished for him.

Milling-Jemmy aimed a ham-sized fist at the cleft in Karl's chin. He dodged and threw his strongest punch, aiming just above the belt, just below the joining of the ribs. His fist connected squarely with muscled flesh as hard and unyielding as the woody trunk of an oak. Pain shot from arm to elbow, from elbow to shoulder. Two great arms wrapped around him, crushing the breath from him, threatening to snap his back. He slammed the flats of his hands against Shadwell's ears. The man bellowed like a wounded bull, his grip loosened, and Karl wrenched away, dancing on the balls of his feet, landing one blow, two, to no effect. Where was Franz?

He chanced a glance and saw the door fly open and Franz charge in. Quick-witted Franz, who immediately saw that he would need to rescue not Shadwell, but Karl.

"By God! I've snabbled ye now!" Franz roared, giving pause even to Milling-Jemmy. "Slumguzzled me out o' me woman he did, and a game pullet she were. Swore I'd carve out his liver and lights!" he said furiously, yanking a knife from his boot and brandishing it like a sword. "If ye'll step aside, sir"—he motioned to Shadwell—"I'll rid us o' this Queer Nab and stand ye to a pottle o' whatsomever yer tongue craves when I've readied him for the Carrion Hunter."

"It'll have to be more than a pottle," said Milling-Jemmy, his voice a rough whisper.

"Ah!" Franz grinned. "A man after me own heart! A tun it'll be, if ye let me at him."

Shadwell moved aside. Karl snaked the knife from his boot, and wondered how Franz would solve the little problem of killing him. Chairs and tables were tumbled aside, making room for the fight, while Franz closed on Karl, his nut-brown eyes wary.

Franz feinted to the left, leaped back, and jabbed

for Karl's belly, hissing under his breath, "Hesterman."

Karl, a faint smile touching his mouth, arced back, and danced away. Hesterman. The German agent who had neatly escaped the trap he and Franz had laid in a filthy alleyway of Madrid. It wouldn't be easy to duplicate his and his partner's feat, and it would be painful. Leave it to Franz to remember it! The man never took the easy way out of anything!

His breath whistling through his dry throat, Karl feinted and stumbled and struggled not to shrink from Franz's knife, stabbing at his belly. The move had to be judged to the finest hair. The appearance of a wild thrust, pausing at the last moment, slicing deep enough to draw blood, and turning aside while the blunt edge slammed into him, as if the blade had pierced him fully.

Pain flamed on the bony curve of Karl's rib cage, burning across the ridge of muscle beneath his heart. He grunted and felt the warm wash of blood and saw in Franz's eyes the shocking awareness that he had misjudged the depth of the cut. Karl groaned and fell forward, flinging his arms around Franz. His mouth at his man's ear, he whispered, "Gently as a swaddled babe? You need lessons, old friend."

He relaxed every muscle and slid down Franz's body, crumpling to a heap on the filthy floor with the blood pooling beside him.

"Ye'll not slumguzzle another man o' his woman!" crowed Franz, wiping the bloody blade of his knife on Karl's dingy shirt. "Give me friend whatsomever he wants," Franz growled to the doxy, while he jerked his head at Shadwell. "I'll dump the cove in the alley and be back to sluice me gob."

He hefted Karl's limp body, tossing it over his shoulder. Karl gritted his teeth against the pain, sweat sheening his face while he fought to keep from crying out. Jarring steps carried them into the cool June night, steps that hastened into the blackest shadows of Blue Ruin Alley.

Gently Franz lowered Karl's feet and propped him against the crumbling brick wall. *"Gott im Himmel,"* said Franz, unconsciously slipping into German, "I've spitted you!"

Chapter 7

❧❧

It was not Karl's first brush with death. That had
come when he was ten and Friedrich's assassin
had murdered Sir Richard and nearly murdered him.
Even now, in odorous Blue Ruin Alley with Franz
fumbling at his belt, raising it to the sliced flesh spitting gouts of blood and yanking it so tight Karl could
not breathe, he remembered the terror and confusion of the child he had been. His innocence and
youth had died with the knowledge that evil respected neither, nor the goodness of a man like Sir
Richard Bragg. It was then that he had looked on
the face of evil, and that face, featureless and un-
formed, was his uncle's, Friedrich, prince by murder
and deceit. It was then that he had coldly, calculat-
edly determined he would have his revenge. It was
then that he had embarked on the road that had led
him to . . . Anne.

"I've got to get you back to Darenth House," said
Franz.

"No!" Karl whispered as fiercely as choked-off
breath and fiery pain allowed. "We haven't come
this far to fail! You will return to Shadwell, now!"

"You'll never make it alone!"

"That's an order, Franz!"

It wasn't easy convincing him, and that sapped
more of Karl's waning strength. He shrugged into
the cloak he'd hung over a rickety barrel and left

91

Franz standing in the inky dark of the alley, staring after him.

Merging with the shadows, Karl crept onto the street, heading for the Strand. Blood, warm and thick, seeped into his trousers, clotting and turning cold. Every beat of his heart throbbed in the wound; every misstep on the rutted cobbles sent shards of pain stabbing through him.

Yet it seemed he had never smelled air so sweet as the stench of Spitalfields, nor seen a moon as silvery bright as the one peeping over the eaves above. Never had life and the promise of the future beckoned him more urgently. The future that now crooked a gentle finger, promising not vengeance but the hope of love and happiness. And he, who believed in so little, discovered that he believed in that future. For the first time since a boy of ten lost his illusions, the man, who should have known better, believed.

The fishy smell of the Thames pulled him into the Strand, thick with the mist crawling up from the river bank. He hailed a passing hackney coach and fell onto its welcoming seat with a breathy order for the jarvey, "St. James's Square. A quid if you're quick about it."

While the hackney flew across the City, Karl's mind flew over the times he'd felt the cold breath of death. Once with a fever in Madrid. Once when stabbed in the back in a putrid Parisian alley. Other times, all melding into one long memory of pain, but never of fear.

His forearm, sticky with blood, pressed to the flesh beneath the belt, and he experienced for the first time the fear that he would die and life would be lost. Anne had given him the fear, as she had given him the hope. He reveled in both, for they meant he was alive now as he had not been before.

That feeling of life spun through his veins, lending him strength. He directed the jarvey to the alley behind the Square, flipped him a quid, and descended from the coach. It rattled off behind him, and he hugged the concealing fences.

The blood seeped beneath the belt. The wound throbbed with a dull ache. His head spun with dreams and fears as he stumbled through the latch-gate into the tiny patch of a garden ripely scented of damask rose.

On the crest of the roof the raven, watcher and watchman, hopped from foot to foot and pierced the night with her raucous cries. Karl paused by the privet hedge. His face tilted up, shiny with sweat and white as the moon overhead. His gaze rose, seeking the herald that summoned him back to duty, back to existence without life.

Accept it or deny it?

He found he could do neither. The duty was too deeply ingrained, too imperative to free him now. Just as the wrenchingly painful sense of life and hope and future, though newly come, were too strong to let him go.

He slipped through a break in the hedge and found the cunningly hidden door. He stumbled and sprawled and finally crawled up the secret stair to the earl's bachelor chamber.

"It has begun, my lord," he muttered to the earl, who bolted from his bed with an oath.

Karl's milk-white cheek sank to his bloody hand, and he rushed toward oblivion.

"I own you have more mettle than sense!" the earl whispered urgently, his back to Darenth House's graceful salon, stuffed to bursting with the *crème de la crème* of the *ton*. "This could have waited until you were stronger."

"I am strong enough," said Karl in a low undertone.

It had been a week since he had crawled into the earl's richly appointed chambers. He still had a low-grade fever, but it was not as bad as the incessant, infuriating itch of the stitches buried beneath the

stuffing, the corset, the disguise of von Dannecker.
Tonight, he wore livid purple and saffron-yellow
thickly crusted with gold embroidery.

It was not physical weakness that worried Karl,
but another weakness that reached into the root of
his being, blurring his beliefs and his perceptions of
himself. He had always known who he was, what
he was, what he had to do. Now that knowledge
seemed a mirage. The only substance was Anne and
his desire for a future with her.

Reality was Anne, a traitor to her country and not
to be trusted. Yet he did trust her. He knew, as
firmly as he had ever known anything, that there
was a reason for what she did. And he would understand, if not approve, when he learned what it
was.

Reality was the throne that awaited him. A throne
he would gladly abandon for the woman who meant
more to him than the power of a crown. The thought
shocked him, for the throne had been the Grail directing his every step—until now. Now he knew
there was another power afoot in the world: love.

Yet he dared not yield himself up to love.

He felt sapped of strength, unequal to the task he
must begin, for Anne's ultimate protection and for
his own. "The papers—" he began.

"Are in the case in my desk for our spy to find,"
the earl said crisply. "You know who he is, don't
you?"

A wary stillness descended on Karl. "Yes, my
lord."

The earl's frosty gaze shifted away, narrowing on
a footman dodging Princess Esterhazy's gesticulat-
ing hand. "Dreadful that a man is not safe in his
own house. I agree it is best that you haven't told
me who he is. Having neither your patience, nor
your detachment, I fear I should act with a haste
that would destroy our plans. It has become my
greatest pleasure to imagine our spy kicking at the
end of a rope."

The earl turned away, melting into the crowd, and Karl's pent-up breath eased on a sigh. Darenth had, unwittingly, drawn a vivid picture of Karl's worst nightmare, of Anne . . .

He couldn't think it. He wouldn't let it happen!

Nausea churning in his belly, Karl scanned the drawing room, his gaze drawn to Anne. She stood near the fireplace, as graceful as the pair of Grecian-draped caryatids supporting the mantel. The nausea lessened. She was safe, for now. And so beautiful he would never tire of looking at her, of seeing more than the outer adornments of face and form, of seeing the beauty, born of a loving heart, that would last beyond the ravages of age.

She wore a silk tulle gown with mameluke sleeves—puffs slashed in white and separated by ribbons that marched down her slender arms. The black of mourning became her, lending the luminous glow of moonlight to her smooth white skin. Hugging the fragile stem of her neck was a rope of diamonds, and there Karl's gaze lingered while the nightmare returned.

If von Fersen discovered the papers were false, he would believe Anne had tried to dupe him. He might slit her throat in a rage. Cold sweat sprang from Karl's every pore, oozing beneath the mask, soaking into the padding beneath the corset. If that happened, his would in a sense be the hand directing the knife, his would be the responsibility for her death.

But no matter what course he took, she would be at risk. He could only hope von Fersen would believe the lies. He could only hope that Cantor's appearance would lessen Anne's importance to von Fersen.

Tonight. Tonight Cantor would reenter Anne's life.

Across the width of the room, he saw her eyes shift to him. He felt more than saw the infinitesimal pinching of her lips, the darkening of her eyes. She disliked von Dannecker, and that had helped him maintain the necessary distance between them. But there would be no dislike to distance her from Cantor . . .

"Herr von Dannecker," said the earl, approaching with a bow, "our guests await your pleasure."

Across the room Anne watched von Dannecker's limping progress to the rosewood piano, set in a bower of candlelight before the bank of windows curtained in summery white lace. She would have wept with relief had she not been so intent on edging away from the formidable Duchess of Wrexham. Her Grace, one hand pressed to her nonexistent bosom, the other wafting a hartshorn vinaigrette, had spent the better part of an hour bewailing the follies of her inattentive son, the swarthy Earl of Audley. That gentleman, no one's fool, had stationed himself on the opposite perimeter of the drawing room near the library, where Anne had, earlier in the day, surprised her father in the act of stacking a sheaf of papers in his red morocco case.

She edged beyond the grasp of the duchess's fingers and trod on Lady Melbourne's toe. "I pray your pardon, my lady," she said breathlessly, slipping out of range of her Grace's nasal whine.

If only she could reach the library door, she could slip inside during the concert. Tomorrow she must meet von Fersen. She had to know if those papers were more than gossip and rumor. If they were not— her hands clenched into fists—she must, before the evening was over, seek out young Sir George Darcy. Sir George had sadly failed pretensions to Corinthianism. He, also, had a tongue—seemingly unattached to his brain—that clacked at both ends. It was a dangerous failing in a War Office clerk. One Anne would be forced to make use of, if the papers were worthless.

Easing around the front of the drawing room, she was stopped near the entry by the crowd greeting a

trio of latecomers. Welcoming that respite to gather
her strength and courage, she closed her eyes for a
moment. Her heart throbbed against her ribs, as if
it would break those bonds and burst. She almost
wished it would. Spying on her father was horrible
enough. Knowing she would, if she must, use sim-
pleminded and kindhearted Sir George made her
something so despicable she felt faint with revulsion.

Thank God, Cantor was not here to learn what
she had become. While she yearned fiercely for the
cleansing power of his love, she knew that nothing
could make her feel clean again. Not even Robbie's
safe return home, so desperately needed by her es-
tranged parents. She longed for her life as it had
been, but she could never go back. Innocence lost
could never be reclaimed. That thought above all be-
deviled her sleepless nights.

"Anne!" cried an eager voice that held vestiges
of fuzzy-bearded youth.

A voice she recognized instantly. "Brat!"

She watched the crowd at the door part, watched
him stride toward her with a gangly gait that had
not yet found the firm footing of manhood. Her eyes
locked on the empty, pinned-up sleeve flapping at
his side, the blood-red sleeve of a heavy dragoon
officer.

She wrenched her gaze from it. A black leather
helmet, piped in shiny brass and sporting a horsehair plume, was wedged between the long arm and
the body that was too thin. Epaulets flanked his wide
shoulders. A blue collar piped in yellow framed the
angular face that had, at last, shed its baby fat. His
melting brown eyes had lost their innocence, but not
a whit of that something-wonderful-is-about-to-
happen expression that had made him Anne's favorite of her brother's friends.

Brat Raeburn—spinner of dreams of martial glory
in the long, sweet summers of their childhood—had
followed Wellington to Salamanca and left an arm

there. Never again would he tie an intricate cravat or race her up the hardy ivy scaling Darenth Hall to tumble, breathless and laughing, through her bedroom window.

But he, at least, had come back. How many other young men would not? How many would die because she gave aid to the enemy?

"Hey, Cork! Catch!" He tossed the helmet to the young man following at his heels, swept out a long arm, and in careless defiance of convention, pulled Anne to him for a boisterous hug.

She scraped her nose on a brass button, welcoming the pain she knew she deserved, while her arms wrapped around his thin waist. "Brat," she whispered. "I'm so glad, so glad, you're back safe."

"It'd take more than a Frenchy to stick my spoon in the wall." He buried his nose in her crown of ebony curls and sniffed suspiciously. "Hey, Anne? When did you stop smelling like horse manure?"

She swallowed a sob compounded of equal parts of happiness and guilt, thumped his ribs, and pulled back. "You're as rag-mannered as ever."

"Shameless," he agreed.

Her eyes swimming with tears, she stared up at his funny, lopsided grin, sandwiched between dimples. Was it enough that she winnowed her father's missives and reports, seeking not the kernels, but the chaff? Was it enough that she never gave von Fersen anything she thought truly dangerous? Did it make it right that she did it to save her brother's life?

Brat's grin died abruptly, his brown eyes losing their sparkle. "Anne, I . . . I heard about . . . about Robbie."

Her gaze dropped, carrying with it the pain of Brat's grief. *He's alive! Don't grieve for him! Not yet! I'll bring him home, Brat! Whatever it takes! I'll bring him home!* The thoughts screamed for a voice she dared not find.

"Ladies and gentlemen!" her father shouted over

the babble. Tall as he was, he was dwarfed by Karl von Dannecker, who posed beside him, a monarch deigning to give audience to his subjects. "I pray you, take your seats."

Brat touched Anne's hand. "It's good to see you again," he said, summoning his crooked grin, "even if you don't smell like the stables anymore."

She watched him stride away, her heart aching with guilt and grief and regret. When Robbie returned to them, would he, like Brat, smile his old devastating smile and look out through eyes that had seen hell?

The choice is yours: to save your brother or to condemn him, von Fersen had said. Anne's gaze slid away, finding the library door. It wasn't right. She knew it. She knew, too, that she had no choice.

The room stirred to life, groups breaking up and seeking the rows of chairs. Anne sought the fringes of the crowd, quickly and surely, despite the hesitation in her heart.

Karl's eyes, glittering behind the mask, followed Anne's progress. He knew where she was going. He knew why. It did not surprise him to see her station herself near the library door. He did not need to hear that she planned to slip inside the moment everyone was enthralled by von Dannecker's music.

The musician's simper clung to his mouth, like paint on the lips of a porcelain doll. He was too well-practiced at playing his role for what he saw to affect the facade of von Dannecker.

He had set the bait. The earl had filled his official morocco case with reports that were a mix of truths and lies. Anne, all unwitting, would become the funnel through which they misinformed the French, while waiting to spring the trap laid for von Fersen's agents. And if she was caught . . .

Karl frowned. He could not go through with it. He could not let her take the step that would begin her destruction.

The earl spoke beside him, words Karl did not hear. His audience burst into clamorous applause while he sought a solution. He preened and posed and bowed, his lace-trimmed handkerchief dancing through the air. The solution came with the last clap of lagging hands.

"*Meine Damen, meine Herren,*" his flutelike tenor rang out. "I vill begin tonight vit a love song. De story of a prince and de lady he loved, but could not haf. I dedicate dis song to"—he paused dramatically, his gold-crusted, purple-clad arm sweeping out to encompass the room—"Lady Anne Ransome."

Anne started, as if the burst of applause had physically thrust her back against the wall. Only Karl knew it was shock and chagrin that froze her there with a wan smile.

"*Fraulein*, you vill sit here!" He stabbed an imperious finger at the empty chair nearest the piano. He saw the widening of her eyes and the incipient shake of her head. "Ah, *das madchen*, so shy," he said. "But you vill. I do you great honor."

He saw the moment he won and waited while she made her graceful way forward. Her cheeks flaming, she dipped him a scant curtsy, murmured, "You do me too much honor, Herr von Dannecker," and sank into the chair.

With a flourish of his coattails, he plumped onto the piano bench and rippled an *arpeggio.* "Imagine if you vill, *Fraulein,* a pine forest whose tops caress de clouds"—his supple fingers picked out the sigh of a breeze—"a summer day"—he trilled the liquid notes of birdsong, the scamper of a small animal's feet—"a prince at his ease"—his fingers languidly flowed into a deep basso song—"a maiden filling her basket vit buttercups"—the song surged into the upper ranges, light and airy with flutters of sound like soft, loving laughter—"a meeting"—his long agile fingers lifted from the keys, leaving a waiting silence, thick with suspense—"and love striking like lightning from a cloudless sky. A love dat vas not meant to be.''

He launched into the song in a languorous waltz time, poignant and sad. While he played he told the tale of the prince and his lady, the mythical story of his earliest ancestor, the first Master of the Ravens.

The prince was pledged to another, not for love but to end a longstanding and deadly feud. But his love for the lady of the forest grew through stolen meetings in the woodland glade. They suffered desperation and pain and a hope that would not die. But in the end, his lady had more courage than he. She denied her prince to save his people from the vengeance that would be inflicted upon them by the rejected bride's family. Alone, she sought the deepest reaches of the forest where the sun was seldom seen. There she grieved unto death and after death, as a shade, a shadow, a curl of mist clinging to the woodland where first they met. It was then that the ancient gods took pity on her and gave her a single wish. And her wish was to return as a raven, watcher and watchman, to guard her prince and the rightful princes of his line unto eternity.

His heart heavy, Karl's fingers stilled on the keys. The last note trembled into silence. Staring through the prison of his mask, he saw the tears that slipped unheeded down Anne's cheeks. He longed to take her in his arms, to kiss away the tremulous quiver of her mouth.

The clapping began on a faltering note, growing louder and louder, until the chandeliers chimed with it. He hauled himself up, struggling for the character of von Dannecker, hating himself, hating the world for the loss he must endure.

When the concert ended, Anne was desperate to escape von Dannecker and the memories he engendered with the voice that had grown mellow and deep and melodic during the telling of his tale. He sounded so much like Cantor she wanted to scream him into silence. He brought Cantor so close she felt that if only she looked hard enough, she would see him.

And the thought that she might terrified her, for the reflection in his eyes would be that of the girl she had been. That girl brimful of faith and trust and hope—and blissful ignorance of the evil afoot in the world.

She was neither the girl she had been, nor the woman she should have become, but something else. Something less innocent, less trusting. A woman she never wanted Cantor to know. For the first time, she was glad he was gone from her life.

While shouts of "Encore! Encore!" raged above the applause, Anne began edging toward the library door.

Karl, damning his imposture, helplessly watched her go.

Chapter 8

A single lamp burned on the massive mahogany desk. Repelled by the light, by the desk, and by the hidden morocco case, Anne stood with her back to the door and felt the vibration of the thunderous clapping beyond. Clapping that died away, leaving an acute silence broken only by the sound of her pounding heart.

She had so many happy memories of this room: of Robbie dragging her away from Shakespeare's sonnets to see the first snowbells dangling on their stems; of Robbie sauntering in after a night of gaming at Watier's, a wicked smile teasing his mouth as he dropped his hazard winnings in her lap and said, "For the Forlorn Females' Fund of Mercy, Puss. Your favorite charity . . . and mine."

But there were unhappy memories, too. They flooded back on a wave of resentment.

Robbie had always been devil-may-care, leaping from one hair-raising scrape to the next, while she trailed behind, setting all to rights. As the years of their youth sped by with her brother lunging from daring to danger, she became the island of calm in the stormy sea of the Ransome family. Her parents, though passionately attached to each other, were sorely divided by their wayward son. Her mother claimed he was a high-spirited boy; her father, driven to the last ditch of exasperation, declared him a harum-scarum hotspur and too old for such games.

103

It was Anne who soothed the outraged earl with reminders that Robbie had never committed a cruel or dishonorable act. It was Anne who reminded her mother that Robbie, as a young man of the first rank, needed a firm hand. It was Anne who, seeing the peril of leaving Robbie to his own devices, conceived the idea that sent him to the British Embassy at St. Petersburg as a military attaché.

It had seemed the perfect solution. The Czar's court was far from the deadly Peninsular War. Robbie, beneath the vein of recklessness, had a serious core that needed the discipline such a post could provide. They were all convinced he would return a changed man, settled and prepared for his duties as Viscount Langley.

But he hadn't returned. His thirst for adventure led him astray once more. Moving to the Russian front as an observer, he was lost and reported dead. Her mother blamed her father. Her father blamed Napoleon. Anne blamed herself.

Wracked by grief and guilt, she had wept that she would do anything to bring him back. Then von Fersen had told her what *anything* was—and she had agreed.

Pulling Robbie's irons out of the fire was an old habit, but she was tired now and too much had been asked of her.

Still, her footsteps carried her toward the desk where the papers lay concealed—one step closer to the hope of bringing her brother home.

While Anne's shaking hands clasped the red morocco case, Karl burst into his chamber above, ripped off the mask, and flung an order at Josef: "Make haste, Hummel! I don't have a minute to waste!"

He was too late to stop her. She would have seen the papers by now, but a sliver of hope urged him on. Though a voice of sanity said that confronting Anne and stopping her would warn von Fersen and

ruin the earl's plans, Karl cared for nothing but protecting her.

Hectic minutes later, the hated corset lay belly-up
on the floor, the despised padding beside it. Karl
emerged from his chamber, a fashionably garbed
Corinthian. White pantaloons rippled over his muscular legs. A claret-colored tailcoat spanned his
broad shoulders and hugged his narrow waist. The
time-consuming cravat had been abandoned for the
lace frills of a jabot, pristine white beneath the face
flushed with fever and furious rush.

"*Majestät!* Your hair!" wailed Josef, hopping after
him with a silver-backed brush.

"I don't have time, Hummel!" Karl tunneled long
fingers through the curls flattened by the wig and
raced down the stairs.

Neat rows of scripted figures marched down the
page: casualty lists from the spring campaigns
waged along the Russo-Prussian front; lists that
showed the slaughter of the French and the lesser
losses of the Allies.

Anne's heart ached for the bereaved. She knew
the pain of losing a loved one, of seeing a family
broken. Her mother cherished her grief in solitude,
while her father refused to yield to his. Neither
turned to the other for the solace they both needed.

She thrust that sorrow away, sliding the casualty
list aside. Beneath was a report headed *El Señor, Old
Castile, June 4, 1813.* She scanned it quickly. *Wellington planted King Joseph a facer*, it began in colorful
boxing cant. Joseph Bonaparte's line had been taken
in flank, and the French had evacuated Toro and
Valladolid and were expected to evacuate Palencia
within days. Wellington's army, eighty-one thousand strong, was concentrated north of the Douro,
preparing to march across the great plain of Tierra
de Campos. Supplies were plentiful and the men,
in good heart, were eager to meet the French.

A sigh of relief whispered through Anne's lips.

This she would gladly pass along to von Fersen. It was real information, but already three weeks old. By the time he sent it back to the French—as she was sure he would—it would be of no use to them. Wellington would have done whatever he set out to do.

She swept the papers together, aligning the edges and preparing to slip them into the case topped by a gilt etching of the family crest. Tonight, she would return to copy them. Tomorrow, she would meet von Fersen.

The caw of a raven pierced the night. Anne's startled gaze swung to the curtains, billowing gently in the balmy breeze. Between the undulating edges of the red velvet panels, she saw a raven perched on the windowsill. Shiny black against the sapphire night, it watched her with a beady stare that seemed as old and as wise as time.

A chill prickled the fine hairs on the back of her neck. The chill was roused by nothing more than von Dannecker's mythic tale of the prince and his lady and the raven she became, Anne assured herself. This was simply a bird, out of place in the City and more curious than most.

The raven's strong beak parted. *Pruk, pruk,* it called with a deep croaking, almost like a warning, then launched itself into the night with a noisy flapping of its wings.

The sound was muted by the babble of chatter and laughter pouring into the library through the slowly opening door. A spear of light arced across the red Turkey carpet. A shaft of terror tore through Anne. Her father! It could be no one else! And her with the evidence of her treason guiltily searing her hands!

Her head whipped around. Her wide gaze sought her father's lean and elegant frame, but another, taller, thicker, broader, darkened the wedge of light. She blinked, as if the sight could be washed away like a speck of dust in the eye, but the sight was unchanged. The gay and golden light haloed Cantor Cartwright's majestic frame.

Anne's heart trembled, like a sparrow ensnared by an alien hand. The papers slid from her nerveless fingers, fanning across the desk with a whisper as soft as her fearful cry. "Cantor!"

Karl stood in the door, staring at the damning proof of Anne's treachery shining in the lamplight. He was too late. She had found the papers larded with, as the earl had said, "distortions, deceptions, and outright lies, all embedded in truth enough to make them believable." Which would be safer for her? To confront her now? Or to wait until he had von Fersen in hand?

Karl shrank from the answer. She would never be safe until von Fersen was caught. He must leave her to suffer fear and danger now, so that he might save her in the end. It was the best he could do for her, he told himself, but a prodding voice wondered if he remained silent because he could not betray all he was, all he was meant to be.

The persona of Cantor Cartwright slid over him like an ill-fitting suit. Karl had never felt more like a scoundrel or less like a rakehell.

Firmly closing the door behind him, shutting out light and laughter, he strode toward Anne. "Do I intrude?" he asked, casting a disinterested glance at the papers.

"No," she said quickly, hurrying around the desk. "I—I had not expected to see you after . . . after . . ."

"Bragg House? Nor had I expected to come to London."

"Then why have you come?" she asked, with an edge of panic. It would be the cruelest trick of fate if he was free of that which had kept him from her. Free, while she was snared ever deeper.

"Not for the reason I—" Karl frowned. That wasn't what he meant to say. "Castlereagh has offered me a position in the Foreign Office. I am now assistant to his secretary.''

''How . . . how fortunate for you,'' Anne said softly. He was so close she could feel the heat of his body and the sturdy strength that could be her bulwark, if she was willing to drag him into treachery and treason with her. Weakness urged her to tell him what she had been doing and why, to lean on him like a frail reed.

''Perhaps,'' he said with a slight smile, ''my way in Society is made.''

''You haven't come to tell me this.''

''No, I came because''—Karl's every purpose scattered before an onrush of desire—''because I could not stay away from you.''

Her small face tilted up to his, like a flower seeking the sun. He could see, think, feel nothing but the need to taste and touch. His hands closed around her waist, fingertips meeting in the graceful hollow of her spine, thumbs touching in front.

''No,'' Anne whispered hopelessly. ''No, Cantor, don't.''

But Cantor wasn't there. Only Karl and a desire he would not deny himself. Gently, he pulled her toward him, his head lowering, his lips hovering over hers.

''Nothing has changed, has it?'' she questioned desperately. ''We still cannot—''

''Don't deny me, Anne,'' he pleaded in a tortured whisper, and his lips touched hers. Touched them with reverence and prayer and gratitude for the love that filled the empty night of his soul.

Her feeble resistance melted away, and his mouth slanted across hers, moist, hot, desirous. Her tentative caress tickled through the silk of waistcoat and shirt to the gilded thatch of hair on his chest. His heart pounded the pagan rhythms of his ancient Saxon forebears. Her finger feathered across a sunbrowned tendon above his high collar. Innocently erotic, it found no answering innocence in Karl.

He pulled her to him tightly, wrapping her in his arms. Her slender body quaked against his, and a shaft of pain dulled the exquisite joy of having her near. He could take no pleasure if he roused in her nothing but fear.

He pulled his lips from hers with a soft and sighing "Anne," and was answered with a mewing of regret. Her mouth, seeking his lips, landed on his chin. Her lashes fluttered up, revealing an unfocused gaze of misty gray wonder amid the glowing embers of newfound passion. The trembling, he realized with a fierce thrill, was her need soaring to meet his.

He caught her in a crushing grip that said he would never let her go, one arm molding her slight frame to his, one hand cradling the back of her head. His fingers delved into her ebony tresses, while his lips plied hers with passion's rising hunger. Her hands slipped around his nape, deliciously cool and soft. Her heart beat against his, matching its wild rhythm. Her fingers threaded his hair, pulling him closer and filling his heart with love and his soul with dread.

His mouth eased from hers, gliding across the flushed warmth of her cheek, seeking the tender hollow beneath the lobe of her ear. That tender hollow that might never be his to touch again. Breathing the heavenly scent of damask rose and Anne, he found unwelcome thought treading where feeling had reigned. He nuzzled the silk of her skin.

Over the crown of ringlets that teased his chin, he stared at the papers shining in the lamplight.

Why, Anne? Why do you do it?

"Cantor." She whispered the most beloved name in her world, unaware that it was becoming the most hated name in his.

Anne absorbed his heat and strength, like a cooling rain on sun-baked skin. She drank in his nearness and his need, wondering at the answering need roused in her. His lips had treasured and plundered hers with a sweet savagery that left her weak and wanting and aching for more. His hard body had sought the curves and hollows of hers. Yet close as he was, she wanted him closer still.

Before, her love for Cantor had been as chaste as a girl's. Now, his demanding lips and hard, seeking body had lured her over the threshold of innocence into a woman's world of desire, where a kiss was heaven, and heaven was not enough. She wanted him as a woman wants a man, her man.

She dredged up the courage and strength to deny him. Still, she could not let him go. Her head tilted back, her heavy gaze seeking his. "You must go away," she whispered past the pain crowding her throat.

A rill of tension flowed along his clenching jaw. Only his eyes spoke to her. The heady blue of cornflowers warmed by the summer sun, they expressed a soul-deep sadness and painful acceptance.

Her hands cupped the powerful tendons of his neck, her fingers stroking the silky curls at his nape. There was no need for her to say more, but the words spilled out, more to assure herself than him. "You must see that we have nothing lasting," she said, the lie a hesitant whisper as broken as her heart. "A *tendre* of youth that will lead to bitterness with age. We don't really know each other at all, Cantor. We have nothing more than this . . . this . . ."

Karl's lips touched hers in an achingly gentle caress that offered solace without hope. She was sending him away, and he suspected why. To protect him, to protect herself. Knowing that, it still hurt.

Reaching up, he tenderly shackled her wrists with his hands and pulled them down. Her smooth white fingers curled around his thumbs. He pressed a kiss to the knuckles of one hand, the other, released her and stepped back.

"I won't seek you out again, Anne," he said, knowing that he would, that the next time it would be in this very room, when she stepped into the trap he laid for her.

He strode away, pausing at the door to look back. The light played a game of advance and retreat, finding the soft black ringlet quivering over the white fire of a diamond clip, finding the curve of Anne's cheek and the tilt of her chin, finding the grief-stricken gaze that shied away from his.

Cantor's last look, dark, enigmatic, and loving, lingered with Anne during her return to the library to copy the papers in the wee hours of the night, during her meeting with von Fersen the next morning, during the lonely afternoon. Though beams of sunlight streamed through the parlor windows to frolic amidst the cut-glass chandeliers and playfully dart away from the beeswax shine of the rosewood piano, Anne, caught in her own morbid musings, was blind to the golden glory of the day.

She sat in a dainty Adam chair with legs as straight as her spine and a lyre-shaped back that gently angled away from her rigid shoulders. Thomas Gray's melancholy meditation, "Elegy Written in a Country Churchyard," lay forgotten in her lap. Over the printed pages hovered her hands, fingers threaded and clutching, as if they held her last vestige of control. It was not enough that she committed treason against her country and betrayed her father's trust. She must also watch her mother suffer, knowing that three simple words—*Robbie is alive!*—could end her suffering.

On the satin-striped sofa in the small sitting area arranged for conversation *tête-à-tête*, her mother sat as stiffly as she. So recently acclaimed for her youthful beauty, Agatha Bragg Ransome, Countess of Darenth, looked neither younger than her years, nor beautiful, any longer. Since Robbie's reported death her willowy elegance had withered to gaunt simplicity. The silvery depths of her eyes, once aglitter with her son's bright gaiety, were now haunted by grief.

The thick and luminous black hair that had once won admiring looks was now dull and streaked with white. The skin, so recently as fresh as a girl's, was now frighteningly pale.

For months she had languished in the solitude of a grief that permitted no one to intrude. Now, for the first time, she noticed something outside her own pain—the last thing Anne wished her to see.

"My dear, you have not been yourself of late," she said, her voice a wan parody of its former throaty richness. "Something is wrong. Won't you tell me what it is?"

Her loving gaze moved across Anne's face, searching the eyes Anne dared not turn away, touching the cheeks that blushed too easily. Her nape crawled with the fear that her mother would see her guilt, her shame, her treachery.

"It is . . . summer, Mother," Anne said quickly, her voice thin and high. "I've been remembering . . ."

Knowing that her mother, too, remembered Robbie in this, his favorite season of the year, she left the hideous lie unspoken. She told herself that her brother's life was worth any humiliation, any disgrace she must endure, but her very soul cringed from the pain she must inflict on others, pain reflected in her mother's somber gaze.

"I fear, my child," she said gravely, "that you are troubled by more than your—"

"Please!" Anne burst out, surprising both of them.

Lady Darenth's mournful gaze flickered away uncomfortably. "I have neglected you abominably in these . . ." She paused, her lips pinching together, as if to hold back a sob.

"No, Mother," Anne protested quickly, faintly. It would be unbearable if her mother added guilt to her grief.

"No, my dear?" she questioned sadly. "We both know it is quite true. You must think I've forgotten I have a daughter."

Anne's gaze dropped to her hands, clenched so tightly her knuckles were bled of color. She had always realized that, though her mother loved her, Robbie was the axis around which her world revolved. A fact Anne accepted without regret, for she, too, loved him.

"I have never understood how you and I could look so much alike yet be so very different," her mother whispered, as if to herself.

Anne's stricken gaze lifted, intense, seeking. "Are you sorry that I am not like you in—"

"No! No, I am not!" her mother exclaimed with the first animation she had shown in months.

For a moment Anne thought her mother would abandon her grieving loneliness and reach out to her. The moment slipped quickly into the oblivion of lost opportunities.

"You have a strength that I have always lacked, my child." She sighed wistfully, drawing Anne's skeptical gaze. "Oh, yes. It's true. Even as a babe you were quiet and steady. Now, as a woman, you are strong and sure."

"Is that really how I seem to you?"

"All of us face dilemmas and doubts, my child," her mother said with a sad smile. "Some of us sink beneath them. Others, like you, rise above them."

"I wish I could believe—"

"You can. But even the strong sometimes need help. I would help you now, if you would let me. Won't you tell me what is troubling you?"

A desperate, selfish desire seized Anne—to confess all, to share the burden that pillaged the strength her mother claimed she had. It seemed she had used it all up in sending Cantor away.

Her gaze lifted to her mother's delicately refined face, etched deep with lines of sorrow. Weak as she felt, Anne could not force her mother to choose between love and loyalty: her son or her husband; her son or her country. She could not force her mother to live with the fear she suffered, that her sacrifice would be for nothing, that Robbie would never come home and bring the light back into their lives.

"It's of no consequence, Mother. Truly, it isn't," she said with as much assurance as she could summon.

A shadow of bitterness flowed across her mother's face. "Perhaps you would prefer to discuss it with . . . your father."

Your father. Said as frostily as if he were a despised stranger, when once she would have spoken his name with a loving lilt. "It is nothing for either of you to fret over," Anne said softly.

Of all that Robbie's reported demise had wrought, the slow strangling of her parents' love for each other was the hardest for Anne to bear. As desperately as she wanted to heal the breach between them, only Robbie could do it. Only he, alive and well, laughing and loving, could make her family whole again—and set her world aright.

Hoping that she had eased her mother's worry, Anne entered the drawing room in the twilight of that evening. Ripe summer scents wafted in from the garden. Tension emanated from her father's tall, spare frame. Noting the ticking muscle in his cheek, she darted an anxious glance at her mother. Each had stiff, set shoulders. Each avoided the other's glance. Each looked as if he held his own gloomy expectations for this rare dinner *en famille.*

A shaking hand smoothing her gauzy silk tulle skirt, Anne pasted on a bright smile and stormed the barricade of tension with lissome grace. "Evening, Father," she said, her voice sweetly melodious, despite the jarring hammer of her heart. "You look as fine as fivepence."

He turned slowly, dipping a restrained but polished bow. "And you, Puss, look lovely as always," he responded with the light air of a courtier, while his eyes narrowed intently on her.

In those arctic-blue depths she caught a glimmer

of worry and something . . . determined, almost ruthless. A daunting expression that the director of the Raven's Nest might easily wear, but one she had never, before now, surprised on her father's loving countenance. He looked like a man with a mission, and that mission was Anne herself. Fear prickled through the fine tendrils artfully escaping the satin ribbon banding her crown of tumbled curls.

Though dread hounded her every light step, she continued to the Wedgwood blue-and-cream-striped sofa on which her mother reclined. Anne sank down beside her in a gossamer whisper of tulle and placed a fleet kiss on her cool cheek.

"How are you feeling?" she inquired, embracing her mother's cold hand in her warm one, and avoiding, carefully avoiding, her father's searching, searing stare.

"Quite well, my dear," Lady Darenth responded, with a sharp edge in her voice and a challenging glance at her husband that brought a frown to his brow.

Anne's low spirits plumbed new depths.

"Your mother and I have noted—" He stopped to shoot his wife a glance as dagger-sharp as the aside he cast. "Yes, Agatha. In spite of my *eminent affairs*, I, too, have apprehended that our daughter is vexed by an affliction of the spirit."

Anne's hand went as cold as her mother's, now flexing tensely against her palm. Her startled gaze flew from her mother's ashen face to her father's sternly unyielding and equally pale countenance. The air reeked of icily civil rage, of the argument that must have occurred moments before Anne had arrived.

"Father—"

"John," her mother interrupted faintly.

"Damn!" Swiveling on a heel, he strode to the wall niche where justice-loving Cicero's marble bust sat silent and condemning in the evening's gathering shadows. He turned slowly to face them as ruddy color sprang to his cheeks. "I beg your indulgence of my . . . curst temper," he said, as if he could not bear to address his wife directly.

"It doesn't signify," her mother said to the flames dancing in the wall sconce above his unbowed head. "It is of more import that—"

"Of course." His gaze shifted to Anne's face with an expression as inexorable as the sun's daily rise and fall. "Puss, you are all that is left to us. Though you have been well-loved by your mother and I, you are even more dear to us now. You must tell us what trouble afflicts you."

Though he spoke gently, it was more order than request. Anne's heart lodged in her throat, beating, beating, while her mind frantically raced. Her mother watched her with a patient gaze. Her father waited with equal patience but stronger will. He would accept nothing less than the truth.

"Puss," he said softly, the harshness bled from his voice and gaze, "let us help you."

Puss. He sounded so much like Robbie. Anne's eyes burned. She shifted awkwardly, releasing her mother's hand. Rising awkwardly, she moved across the narrow circle to a dainty Adam chair and gripped its curving lyre-shaped back for support. Her gaze moved from the bright Aubusson carpet to the dining room, where a spindle-shanked footman stood narrow and straight. Passionately, she longed for the peace of Darenth Hall in the countryside of Kent, for the comfort of the bright blue ribbon of the River Darent winding through the greening hills. But both peace and comfort were denied her.

Her father waited, the candlelight glistening across his mane of steel-gray hair. Her mother sat in the shadows. Anne must tell them something. She stared at the nimble footman, neatly squaring first one dining room chair, then another, under the eagle eye of the elfin butler, Rumford.

"I . . ." she began, and promptly felt the giddying rush of breath from her lungs. "Robbie," she began again, her voice so faint her mother came to the edge of the sofa and her father leaned forward. "Robbie would not have been lost to us, save for me. It was I who conceived the idea that—"

"No!" Her mother swept forward in a rustle of bombazine skirt. Her outstretched hands caught Anne's and drew them to her breast to nestle against the cameo brooch that held locks of hair from the three people dearest to her. "You cannot labor under a guilt that is not yours! John"—her eyes, silvered with welling tears, turned to her husband, now at her side—"I pray you will convince our daughter that no guilt attaches to her. She is blameless, innocent—"

"Quite true, my dear."

The painful grip of his hand on her shoulder pulled Anne's shamed and sorrowing gaze to his sternly handsome face.

"You would take the worry of the world on your shoulders, if we'd let you, Puss," he said, holding her hand like a precious chalice. "You cannot do it, you know. If any should suffer the guilt of Robbie's passing, it should be . . ." He paused to clear the roughness from his throat, his darkening gaze sliding to her mother's bowed head. "It should be I, who could not accept him as he was, but must forever be attempting to remake and remold him."

Her mother's head tilted up slowly. A tremor of emotion, poignant and sad, stirred her pale, parting lips. In the melting depths of her eyes was the power of a love that would not die, the pain of a grief that would not be assuaged, the sorrow of a breach that would not heal.

Uniting them hand to reluctant hand, Anne stepped away, not daring to hope, not daring to think.

"Aggie," her father's low voice threaded the silence, "can you forgive me?"

"John," her mother said brokenly, and needed to

say no more. She had not forgiven him. She could not. She might never.

Anne stood aside, knowing that three small words—*Robbie is alive!*—could change them all. Three small words could allay her father's guilt, return her mother's love, and bring the joy back to all of their lives. Three small words that, if spoken aloud, might in the end destroy Robbie, destroy them all.

The stricken silence was broken by Rumford's measured tread. ''Dinner is served, milord,'' he intoned, like a church bell ringing in the darkest hour.

Chapter 9

~~~~∽◯◯∾~~~~

For all of the pretensions of its Lady Patronesses,
Almack's was hardly the temple of the *beau
monde*. Not if they could, Anne thought icily, vouch
Heinrich von Fersen into the *sanctum sanctorum*.
Could they really believe he was a German *Graf*, a
title he had obviously bestowed upon himself?

Sitting in a rout chair with the unadorned wall at
her back, she watched von Fersen converse with her
father in the lee of a gilded column on the far side
of the ballroom. Both were garbed in the knee
breeches and white cravats that were *de rigueur* for
Almack's, but where her father wore his with the
thoughtless elegance of a man born to the best, von
Fersen seemed ever conscious of his appearance and
his pride in it.

Her father was deliberately cultivating the German, and tonight was not the first time, Anne realized with a new fear. Astonishingly, von Fersen, in
this last hectic week of the Season, had attended
a rout at the Liverpools', a dinner at the Castlereaghs', and an assembly at the Melbournes'. How
he contrived to worm his way into the highest ranks
of Society was a fascinating puzzle for Anne. One
she quickly forgot for a riddle more fearfully intrigu-
ing.

Von Fersen snapped a stiff Germanic bow at her
father and turned away. The sharp blade of his face
was not softened by his stingy smile, both trium-

phant and contemptuous. The triumph frightened
Anne. The contempt did not surprise her. She had
seen it often in this past week, when the German
seemed to be everywhere the *ton* gathered for entertainment. The first time she had wondered—as von
Fersen must have—how the director of the Raven's
Nest could be ignorant of the foreign agent under
his nose.

Now she suspected her father was not ignorant at
all, that he was using von Fersen for some purpose
of his own. Her gaze shifted back to her father. He
had been accosted—her only method of approach—by
Cousin Knox, whom he was fond of calling the requisite eccentric on the Ransome family tree. Befeath-
ered, bejeweled, squat and square as a box, she
gestured with her lorgnette, while he nodded ab-
sently and his eyes searched among the dancers flying through the steps of an energetic Scotch reel. On
his face lingered an expression akin to von Fersen's.
The merest touch of triumph. The merest curl of
contempt. His wandering gaze stopped on Castlereagh, who returned a questioning look. Her father
dipped the scantest of nods, as if to say, *It is done,*
then turned his full attention to Cousin Knox, who
was peremptorily rapping his arm with a fan.

Castlereagh, in turn, searched along the wall till
he found the broad door of a small anteroom. The
dance spun him away, but when he returned, he
caught Lord Liverpool's eye, shot a glance at her
father, and nodded.

So they all knew who and what von Fersen was,
Anne thought with frigid foreboding. How long
would it be before they snapped the jaws of their
trap—and found her snared in it with the German?

"Well, gel, you're looking pale as a frog's belly,"
bellowed Cousin Knox, bearing down on Anne like
a runaway coach.

She dutifully climbed to her feet, wishing she was
anywhere but here. At the best of times her father's
cousin was a trial. At the worst of times she was

unbearable. Lady Jersey—another of whom it might have been said—had stated that Arabella Knox wanted both manner and sense.

"Cousin Knox," Anne said, "how delightful to see you here."

"Delightful, indeed!" She snorted, having no patience for the amenities, despite being a social arbiter of the rules of good *ton* and bad *ton*. Rules which she felt compelled neither to abide by nor respect. "If you weren't just wishing yourself on the Hebrides or some other godforsaken spot, I will eat my fan!"

The hint of a shamed smile tugged at Anne's mouth. "Not precisely the Hebrides."

Cousin Knox shot her a keen glance atwinkle with humor, then gestured to the rout chairs with the dainty lace fan. "Sit! Sit! If you had to carry around my *embonpoint*, you would waste no opportunity to rest your feet!" she shouted gracelessly, bringing heads swinging around to stare.

Anne sat. Cousin Knox plumped into the chair beside her, heaved a blissful sigh, and stuck her feet out in front of her, wriggling the broad toes in her satin slippers.

"Have you danced?" she asked abruptly.

"Of course not!" Anne replied, aghast at the idea of contravening that convention of mourning.

"Good gel!" Cousin Knox nodded briskly, and her aigrette of ostrich feathers abandoned the stalwart effort to stand upright and reclined among her pomaded curls with the brushy tips swaying beyond her ear.

Anne choked back a horrifying urge to giggle. "Ah, your aigrette—"

"Fell again, did it?" Cousin Knox probed her dusty brown curls and detached it from her hair. "I always envied your mother, you know. A day on a country picnic, and she looked like she had just stepped from her abigail's hands. While I can step from my abigail's hands and look like I've spent a day on a country picnic!''

"You refine too much upon nothing, Cousin Knox," Anne said earnestly. "Why, you look quite . . . quite—''

"Don't pitch me any gammon, gel! I look like a yeoman's fat wife. Always have! Always will!''

If Robbie had been here, he would have chucked her under the chin, dropped a kiss to her cheek, and said, "What a shabby thing to say, you delicious creature. I would far rather a sturdy wench of the yeomanry than these swooning misses on the Marriage Mart.'' But he wasn't here, and Anne had not developed what her father ironically called "Robbie's fine art of discriminating praise.''

Her gaze slid away to the bustle and noise at the door. Cantor had arrived in a trio of bucks of the first blood. They made a splendid picture, all young and handsome men in the prime of life and in very merry pin. There was a duke, called Old Nick by the town beaux for the devilish arch of his brows and the wicked slant of his smile. The Earl of Audley, clapping Cantor's back and laughing, was called the Spaniard for his swarthy skin. Each had a sobriquet. Anne wondered what Cantor's had become.

They didn't appear to be foxed, but they were in high gig, eyeing the ladies through their quizzing glasses and hailing cronies on the dance floor. All but Cantor, who had found her.

Anne had seen him often during this last week, but never to speak to, to touch as she had in her father's library. It seemed an eternity ago.

His eyes, bright and burning, met hers across the room and asked the age-old, unspoken questions of parted lovers: *Have you missed me as I have missed you? Do you remember? Have you changed?* Her own eyes, hot and dry, answered: *Yes! Yes, I have missed you! Never could I forget! Never could I change!*

He would come no closer, for he had kept his word and not sought her out. It was relief, and it was pain. The pain was never stronger than when he reluctantly turned away from that initial meeting of eyes and hearts, as he did now.

"Handsome rapscallion, ain't he?" Cousin Knox studied Cantor through her lorgnette, as if she were a cat and he, a bowl of fresh cream. "Have you heard the latest *on-dit*? He's come into a healthy fortune. Uncle died. Baron Cartwright of Mersey. The man pared his cheese so thin you could read the *Times* through it. Let's hope our young buck enjoys the results of his uncle's parsimony."

"How . . . how wonderful for him," Anne said softly, wondering if this would have changed everything and brought him to her. If only . . . if only . . .

"You'll not fool me, gel! That young buck has turned your head! About time, I say!" blared the bane of the Ransome family. "You're looking pasty-faced and blue-deviled! It don't do to repine! Won't bring that brother of yours back! Ramshackle, care-for-nobody hellhound he was!"

Embarrassment fled on a rush of rage. "Cousin Knox, Robbie is . . . was the kindest, most loving brother a girl could—"

"Put you out of temper, did I? Always wondered if there was a spark of fire in you." A mischievous smile played about the small mouth pinched between chubby, sun-blushed cheeks. "No need to fly up in the boughs! I'm partial to ramshackle hellhounds!" she boomed. "He put me in mind of the men of my day. Now, those were *men*! Not like these flummery, frippery sprigs of fashion! Not a dram of mettle in them! Although"—the lorgnette climbed to her twinkling brown eyes—"your beau's got a way about him to set a gel's heart to thumping."

"Cousin Knox!" Anne whispered faintly, under the titters of laughter rising around them.

"Climb out of the dismals, gel, and take a tipple o' that!" She stabbed her lorgnette Cantor's way, gave Anne a significant look, and sailed off, flinging back over her shoulder, "That'll put the color in your cheeks!"

With a crimson blush, Anne rose from her chair with as much grace as she could muster and fled to the Assembly Room for a cooling cup of orgeat.

Her parents were there, standing together for once. Her mother was thin and pale and her father spare and dark. Each, when they chanced to exchange a glance, looked tender yet strained. They had not shared their grief, but there was a new rapprochement between them, as if they wanted to reach out now but still could not. That, Anne thought, was better than before, with her mother bitter and her father cold and hurting.

"Ah, Cartwright! I had not expected to see you here."

The voice came from behind Anne, rooting her to the spot.

"*Graf* von Fersen."

Cantor's voice was warm enough for an acquaintance to mistake it, but underlying the deep bass melody was a thread of tension and distaste and, deeper still, a current of triumph.

"I have the most extraordinary feeling we've met before," said von Fersen in a speculative tone, as if he mentally searched for a face, a gesture, a voice to match Cantor's.

There was the slightest pause, which seemed to Anne pregnant with an ominous threat. Though she told herself she was pouring all of her own fears into that moment of waiting, the feeling persisted that this one was, somehow, significant.

"You'll put me quite out of temper if you suggest that mine is a face that could be forgotten."

That air of arrogance was not like Cantor at all. Though he had a matchlessly handsome face, he seemed oblivious to it. She had always thought him like Robbie, who paid inordinate attention to detail while dressing and ignored his appearance thereafter.

"Quite," responded von Fersen, obviously at a stand and none too pleased. "I should have thought you would be celebrating your uncle's legacy."

"And I shall be, later tonight at Osprey's."

Osprey's. Anne's breath fluttered in her throat, caught there like a butterfly struggling from its chrysalis. She had—and now wished she hadn't—heard Robbie and his friends whisper about the notorious gambling hall that offered more than games of chance for its members. She trembled like blancmange.

She had never thought of Cantor in that light, as a man who had known other women. Women who offered him more than she had: who yielded up not only their lips, but their bodies; who touched him physically and emotionally, and were, in turn, touched by him. She wanted to spin around and see him in this new light, but fear kept her still and silent and hurting.

"Osprey's," repeated von Fersen, with a licking-his-lips tone. "It should be a . . . fascinating evening."

"Quite," said Cantor.

Anne could hear a smile in his voice, but suspected that none graced his lips.

"I would be honored to have you join me at gaming, *Graf* von Fersen," he continued, with the merest stress on the title that made Anne wonder if he, too, suspected its authenticity. "I'll be throwing the bones. I hope that is your pleasure."

"The limit?"

"None."

"Then the bones it will be, Cartwright."

Now the smile that Anne heard was in von Fersen's voice, with the accompanying suspicion that there was none touching his thin slash of a mouth. She heard the tapping of his cane as he moved away and knew a terrible fear for Cantor. All the murmurs of the gossip-mongers came rushing back. Cantor's addiction to gaming. His refusal to stop when Lady

Luck turned her back. Now he had a healthy fortune and was heading to Osprey's with von Fersen. She must warn him.

She turned slowly and found his brooding gaze upon her. Lagging steps carried her to him, and she saw a flicker of surprise cross his features and tension pull at his mouth. The beautiful mouth that had kissed—only a fool would think it had not!—lips other than hers. She suppressed that pain, knowing it would come back to haunt her in the empty, lonely night.

"Lady Anne," he said formally, as if he were as aware as she of the scandal-hungry *beau monde* that could take the least lint of impropriety and weave a tapestry from it.

"Mr. Cartwright," she said with equal formality, "may I offer my condolences on the loss of your uncle." She moved closer still, tilting her head up and studying the face turned down to hers. There was strength in the bold bone structure and a powerful force of will in his eyes. Whatever the gossipmongers said, she could not believe that he would ever yield to the capricious impulses of a gamester. Yet he had never denied what he was.

"I am honored, my lady," he said, with the hint of a frown.

"Cantor," she whispered, "I overheard you talking with *Graf* von Fersen."

The light fled his eyes, leaving them flat and blank. "A man of excellent sensibilities," he said, with a penetrating look and a wary tone.

"I pray you, do not meet with him. He is . . . dangerous." She wanted to say so much more, but dared not.

"A German count, Anne," he whispered, his gaze scouring her face as if he might read her thoughts. "What danger could he pose for me?"

"More than you know!" she whispered fiercely, blinking back angry tears. "He is a . . . a *despicable* man! I pray you, heed me and have nothing to do with him!''

Afraid she would burst into angry tears, Anne spun away—and left Karl nursing a disastrous desire to drag her back. She had confirmed his belief that she was no willing ally to von Fersen. A belief strengthened during the last week, when he had seen her repeatedly watching Friedrich's man with a look of unmistakable loathing.

Whatever Karl wanted to do, he could not. The plans had been laid and von Fersen had leaped for the bait as eagerly as Napoleon following the retreating Russians. Karl could only hope his ploy would be so successful. Tonight, he would lose his ''inheritance'' to Friedrich's man. Then he would wait.

Osprey was a retired pugilist reknowned for having the ferocity of a wolf in the ring and the manner of a lamb outside it. He had a body like a wine tun, a cauliflower ear scarcely hidden by the woolly white fleece of his hair, and a nose whose oft-broken bridge wandered at will toward jutting brow and thick lips. When a night of hazard play turned into a day, he sent the weary groom-porter off to bed and acted in his place.

The hazard-room was stuffed to bursting. Even the midday sun tried to sneak between the curtain panels, its bright spears of light as gold as the guineas piled at Heinrich von Fersen's elbow. Despite the crowd, the sounds were few. The Earl of Audley, sprawled over a chair in an exhausted stupor, snored softly. An onlooker sniffed a pinch of snuff. Another shifted his weight, scuffing a shoe across the carpet.

''Will you cover, or do you refuse the bet?'' Karl repeated with the slurred tongue of a heavy tippler. He was a trifle foxed, having been forced to consume an inordinate amount of port during the night—not to maintain his masquerade as a reckless chuck-farthing but to quell an irritation that mounted to outright fury. He had been beset by a wholly unwelcome run of luck, while opposing an utter flat at the hazard table. No matter how hard he tried to lose, he won.

Fortunately, the sinking moon had taken his luck with it. Unfortunately, luck was not required to best an opponent who was unaware that hazard was a game of not only odds but also skill. Karl thought longingly of an escape he'd once made over the baking plains of Spain with pursuers hot on his trail. That had been easier than the effort to dump his lately acquired "fortune" in von Fersen's lap.

The green baize table-cover was, at last, littered with his golden guineas and vowels promising payment, all gathered around his opponent. The time had come, at last, to chance all on one game. But here von Fersen sat with his pomaded Byronic curls straggling over his sweating brow, timid as a mouse. The man had a merchant's dread of losing his gold.

"Do I understand correctly?" Von Fersen looked up, and Karl struggled for the proper blend of the inveterate gamester's eagerness and the town buck's ennui. "You are betting the entirety of the fortune left you, and I am to match it."

"On one game." Karl swept up his glass, allowing the port to slosh over the rim and onto his hand, and saw a look of cunning replace the former timidity.

"Done!"

As one, the onlookers expelled their breaths. "Ten pounds on Cartwright," murmured one.

"Fifteen pounds on von Fersen," said another.

Karl took up the dice-box, rattling it with a nice indifference.

"Main of seven," said Osprey as groom-porter, in a voice like pulverized gravel.

"Twenty pounds he nicks it," drawled Old Nick, cocking a devilish brow over a dark, bored gaze.

"Done," cried Audley, having awakened from his snooze and struggling up from his chair.

The dice rattled onto the table, pulling the onlookers forward.

"Chance of nine," intoned Osprey.

Karl held the dice-box steady, relishing the moment, while beads of sweat gathered on von Fersen's brow like drops of blood. Karl must continue to throw until he matched the main to win or the chance to lose. Though he wouldn't mind winning a small fortune direct from Friedrich's coffers, he must put himself at a disadvantage—penniless once more and prey to the offer von Fersen would surely make.

The box rattled. The dice rolled. "Four," called out Osprey.

Von Fersen's eyes glittered, and his tongue raced across his lips. Karl called for another tumbler of port and bets flew around the table. While Osprey poured, Karl adjusted his cuffs and stifled a yawn. He took a leisurely swallow, and threw once more.

"Six," called out Osprey.

Von Fersen arched over the table like a vulture over its prey. Karl casually chided Audley over the sorry state of his cravat and suggested to Old Nick that they meet at Cribb's that night, while the box rattled in his hand.

His friend's dark gaze lit with a rare sparkle of humor. "Take care. Another late morning and Castlereagh will be giving you your *congé* like a dismissed lover."

Karl grinned. "Haven't you heard? The Foreign Office couldn't run without me."

"Nine!" intoned Osprey. "The chance is matched! The game is lost!"

Von Fersen stared blankly, as if he had not heard. Karl calmly wrote out a voucher and slipped it across the table. It was fortunate that the hallmark of the true Corinthian was his disregard for the ready, for he could not have looked properly chastened if his life depended on it. He had just taken the first step toward destroying von Fersen and saving Anne. The night's exhaustion faded beneath an upswell of eagerness and energy.

"A glass of port, sir?" he asked, seeing the stunned awareness of his win flush von Fersen's face. "I would like to toast your good fortune."

"I would be delighted." His spidery hand crawled across the green baize and leaped upon the vowel. Minutes later, the toasts quaffed and Karl preparing to leave, von Fersen smiled and requested him to step aside for a moment.

"This is a trifle awkward, Cartwright," he began, "but if you find yourself purse-pinched, I may be able to offer some assistance."

"For what in return?" Karl asked bluntly, eager to have this done.

Von Fersen's cold gaze scanned the room, the look of ruthlessness returning now that his gold was not threatened. "This is not the time. Later, perhaps we can discuss it."

Though they met often in the waning rounds of the Season's entertainments, von Fersen said nothing beyond the commonplace and suggested nothing out of the ordinary. Losing his "fortune"—direct from the coffers of the King's treasury—was not enough, Karl suspected. He needed the real desperation of the deeply indebted.

With companions who were ever ready to drop the blunt, Old Nick and the Spaniard, Karl launched into a spending spree that could rival the Prince Regent at his best. He bought a high-perch phaeton and a curricle, whose thin wheels were picked out in yellow. He haunted Tattersall's, buying a team of matched bays and a team of matched grays and a riding hack, a glossy black sweet-goer. He foraged through the shops of Bond Street, acquiring a wardrobe that was all the crack. He gambled at Watier's and Osprey's, sinking deeper and deeper into debt.

By mid-July impatience plucked at the taut strings of Karl's nerves. Anne seemed to be as restless as he, with dark circles rimming eyes that mirrored an unquenchable fear. He, as von Dannecker, could do nothing but flutter around her and act the fool. Even that was better than the role of Cantor, who must look but not touch, see but not speak, and writhe under the lash of a gentle gaze that condoled the loss of his fortune even as it expressed a deep, perhaps unconscious, disappointment in the Out-and-Outer he had become.

The tag end of the Season saw the *ton* fleeing to Bath and Brighton and Tunbridge Wells, carrying a delectable *on-dit*. At a ball hosted by Beau Brummell and three friends, the Prince Regent had given his foremost dandy the cut direct. As he walked away, Brummell cried out in a clear, carrying tone, "Alvanley, who's your fat friend?"

It was a calculated and unforgivable insult to the vain and sensitive regent. It was an unending source of titters and whispers to the *haut ton*, who had little respect and no love for their prince.

As July began ebbing away, a grand public fête was held at Vauxhall to honor Wellington's victory at Vitoria. Detaching himself from his friends, Karl strolled down the Grand Walk beneath the vaulted colonnade supported by slender iron pillars and hung with lamps in golden globes. It wasn't difficult to look haggard. Though most might assume the taut expression in his eyes and the suggestion of circles beneath them were caused by the duns of importunate tradesmen and the vowels strewing his wake, he knew it was the waiting that was wearing him down. It wouldn't be long now. He had learned just today that someone had paid his bills and made good his vowels. That someone could be none other than—

"Cartwright, I hoped I would see you here tonight."

Karl's heart leaped in his chest, sending his blood strumming through his veins. Too long-practiced at deceit to show that relief, he turned an indifferent gaze on the man striding up beside him. "*Graf* von Fersen."

"I would like to speak to you privately, if I may."

Karl cast him a jaundiced glance. "So long as you do not intend to repeat Brummell's jibe. I've had enough of it."

Von Fersen shot him a startled glance. "Hardly, Cartwright. Only a fool bites the hand that spreads his butter."

They strolled beneath the stars with the music of the concert swelling through the night and the fireworks bursting overhead. On Lovers' Walk, with nightingales trilling in the verdant canopy above, Karl paused in the dark and turned to the man who had tried to assassinate him when he was ten. It would be so easy to break that scrawny neck. His hands balled into fists.

"I can contrive, should I desire it, to return your fortune to you, Cartwright."

Karl listened to the ring of triumph and smiled to himself. "I should be forever in your debt. However, I cannot imagine why you should wish to do so."

"Ah, debt." Von Fersen's spiderlike hands folded over the gold filigree knob of his cane. "I can, also, return your every vowel and tradesman's bill."

Karl dredged up the requisite anger. "I knew someone had bought them up," he said icily. "Not quite the thing, von Fersen. Bad *ton*, you know."

"Let me forbear to warn you, Cartwright. You are in a dangerous state. I can, should I choose to, demand payment of your debts, which we both know you cannot meet. You could be sent to Newgate, possibly transported."

"Dire consequences, indeed," he said with the nonchalant air of the town buck, who would not under any circumstances show a quiver of discomfort or fear. It had the desired effect.

Von Fersen's anger boiled up. "*Der Adel!*" he spat

with loathing. "I shall enjoy destroying you, if you do not choose to help me."

"Ah," Karl said softly, wondering how far he dared go. "Now we come to it. I presume my debts will be forgiven should I render you some service. Surely you must realize there is little I would not do to escape debtor's prison or transportation. Simply tell me what it is, and do me the honor to forgo the threats."

"I need information—"

"The devil, you say! Pray continue! I have the ear of every frippery fellow and, among them, the worst scandalmongers in the *ton*."

"Do not overestimate my good temper!" von Fersen burst out.

"No need to lather up, old boy. You have me on tenterhooks."

"The information I need comes from the Foreign Office."

"You must be quizzing me!" Karl started back, as if stunned and outraged.

"Hardly. I need to know what the Austrians will do when the Armistice is over. Will they stay loyal to France or join the Allies?"

"You are asking me to commit treason, with far worse possible consequences than prison or transportation. You must be mad. I've a mind to report you to the—"

"And I shall be delighted to have my good name vouched by the highest worthies in the *ton*. The authorities will surely be impressed by such men as the Earl of Darenth, Lord Liverpool, and Lord Castlereagh, all explaining that I have lost my homeland through my opposition to Napoleon. Those men have been carefully cultivated for that very purpose, while you, sir, are a chuck-farthing ne'er-do-well without rank or prospects. Who do you suppose they will believe?"

"I may have more debts than expectations, sir,"

Karl blustered, not daring to give in too easily, "but—"

"But you will report me to the authorities? Don't talk fustian to me, you shatter-brained fool!" von Fersen said malevolently. "If you do, I will see they are presented with evidence that you have been selling the secrets of the Foreign Office to French agents."

"False evidence!"

"Real enough to send you to the gallows, if you do not meet me in Hyde Park one week from today with the information I have requested."

"And will that be the end of it?"

"No," von Fersen said coldly, and walked away.

Behind him, Karl permitted himself a single, swift, and deadly smile. It was begun. Now, for Anne.

Chapter 10

~~~ೲ~~~

The whisper of Anne's footsteps slithered into the reaches of the library, as if shunning the bright nimbus of the solitary candle trembling in her hand. Flanked by the pilastered Corinthian columns framing the doorway, she hesitated, not daring to turn back, fearing to move forward. The room, as familiar as her father's ascetically handsome face, was obscured by shadows.

As always, her inner arguments and doubts raged. Even now Englishmen were dying, beardless boys, on the barren shores of the Peninsula. What was the weight of one life—Robbie's life—in the balance of untold numbers of lives and the future of nations?

She stared through the darkness, finding the black hulk of the desk where her father sought to spin a web to snare Napoleon, but had, instead, snared his son and daughter.

Her lashes feathered down to caress her icy cheeks. She saw Robbie, his black hair thick and careless, his violet eyes bright and loving, his mouth curved in a reckless smile. He, too, was a youth with a life to live and none but she to save him.

Before further doubt could creep in, she hurried forward. Luminous bars of starlight striped the flowing folds of her cambric night-robe with light and dark. At the corner of the desk, she stopped. Her wide and frightened gaze guiltily probed one inky shadow, then another.

She sensed a presence in the room, but that was nothing new. She had accustomed herself to the feeling, knowing it was a product of imagination prodded by fear. Yet the presence seemed stronger tonight, as if it lingered in the corners, awaiting its moment to spring out. A shudder shook her from the tips of her black satin slippers to her crown of modishly disheveled curls *à la Titus*.

Her fleeting glance scanned the red velvet curtains, hanging dusky-dark and still. She set the candle on the edge of the desk and pulled open the drawer. The creak, subdued by heavily waxed runners, seemed as loud as a pistol shot. Anne sucked in a deep breath and listened with quivering apprehension. No sound intruded on the silence. No watcher leaped into the flickering light. Her pent breath eased out, its soft susurration lost in the thunder of her heartbeat.

She wedged the red morocco case beneath her arm, lifted the candle in a trembling hand, and slipped around the desk, eager to quit the library for the safety of her chamber.

An alien sound intruded on the silence. Anne froze, her wide, wild gaze searching the room. In the folds of velvety darkness fanning away from the windows, she saw the glimmer of a hand hooking back the curtain. A scream gathered in her throat and died from lack of breath. A man stepped out, his face a smudge of white beneath pale, gleaming curls.

Slow, inexorable steps brought him to her. The smudge of white resolved into individual features: tawny brows, strong nose, and grim mouth. Cantor! Why had he come to her in this stealthy manner?

His pale, drawn face forcibly reminded Anne of the rumors spread by scandalmongers: that he had lost his fortune to von Fersen; that he had launched into a spree of gaming that left him hopelessly indebted. Only one thing could have brought him here.

"You are in trouble," she murmured, drawing a step closer and feeling anew those emanations of heat and strength and tightly leashed power. "Do you need help?"

A rush of emotion darkened his eyes. A look of anguish and anger and something almost like shame. "Not I, Anne"—his gaze dropped to the red morocco case—"but you."

The flame of her candle quivered on its wick. He still stared at the case. Surely, it was curiosity, nothing more. He could not know! "I—I cannot conceive what you could—"

"Don't!" The word tore from Karl's throat, strangled by warring emotions. Anger, betrayal, and bitterness vied for supremacy over sadness and regret. "I know, Anne," he said flatly. "I know . . . everything."

His meaning was unmistakable. Shock leached the color from her face, leaving it a ghastly white. Yet she would not believe it!

"What . . . what do you *think* you know?" The question leaked past her lips in breathless horror.

Karl's heavy gaze raced over her alarmingly pallid features. It would do neither of them any good to prolong this encounter. Though he ached to soften the blow, he dared not succumb to that weakness. She threatened every sacrifice he had made. She risked herself, and that he would not tolerate. But which of those reasons was more important to him, even he was not sure.

"I know," he began harshly, "that you copy your father's secret papers and take them to von Fersen."

Her endless nightmares should have prepared her for the shock of discovery, but they had held not a tithe of the horror of this moment. Her hand trembled so violently the flame quivered on its wick, threatening to extinguish itself. She struggled to calm the tremors racing through her hand, but they were beyond her control. Turning jerkily, she took a faltering step to the desk. The silver chamber-stick clattered dully against the gleaming mahogany surface. Chaotic light stabbed at the red morocco case she dropped on the desk.

"How . . ." Breath failed her. "How did you learn?"

The flame of the candle silvered the black fringe of her curls and shone through the sheer draping sleeves of her robe. That light betrayed her failed efforts to control her trembling, and Karl discovered he had not courage enough to watch her. His gaze dropped to the case, to the fragile hand caressing its gilded crest, as if she sought comfort and strength.

"I learned at Bragg House."

"Bragg House?" Anne whispered.

"The book you delivered there had a message meant for me."

"You are an . . . an agent for my father," she said bleakly.

"Yes."

Her stricken gaze raced over his closed, cold face. Only his eyes were alive and watching her with soul-searing intensity.

"For how long?" she asked.

"Twelve years."

Cantor's strange comings and goings, his inability to tell her why, his arrival in London—all of it made sense now. Assailed by the memory of the moonlit garden, Anne remembered his deep voice murmuring, *I hope you will someday understand.* She had not understood then. She did now. Oh, God! She did now! Her lashes drooped over her eyes, squeezing out hot tears.

"Von Fersen's man at Bragg House." The jolting beat of her heart shuddered through her. "He was murdered . . . by you."

The line of his jaw went rigid. "By my order."

He didn't try to justify himself. Even she could see that the gaunt man had posed an untenable threat to him. But now . . . so did she. Though her every muscle was aquiver, she faced him boldly. "What will you do with me?"

His cold, forbidding expression grew hot and hard. A daunting anger flashed in his eyes. "Do you believe I could harm you?" he asked in a stark tone. "Do you know me so little?"

"I—I don't know you at all." She looked away and swallowed hard. "I only thought I did."

It was the perfect opening to tell her who he was, what he was, what he had to do. It was the perfect time to tell her everything, but she no longer trusted him and Karl no longer trusted her.

"And I, Anne? Have I ever known you? Why?" He moved toward her, his hands leaping out and clamping around her arms. The light cast satanic shadows across his angry face. "Why would you betray all you hold dear?"

His voice and his darkening eyes held too much torment for her to fear harm at his hands. But he was still an agent for her father. She could not trust him with the secret of Robbie's life. Even as she thought it, her palms climbed to his broad chest and her fingers curled around his lapels to hold him fast.

"I cannot tell you!" she whispered urgently. "I dare not trust you with—"

"Not trust me! If you could not trust me, I would not be here alone! Do you know what I have done for you?" He glared down at her. "I have kept this from your father! He sleeps peacefully in his bed, unaware of what his daughter is."

Anne sighed, weak with relief. "Thank you for that. I could not bear it if—"

"Don't thank me yet!" he said fiercely. "If you don't tell me, I'll go to him now. One way or the other, I will stop you!"

His eyes held the cold glitter of diamonds, promising a will stronger than hers and a resolve that would neither be softened, nor swayed. Panic leapt in the pulse at the base of Anne's throat.

"Cantor, I pray you! Don't stop me! If you have any feeling for me, let me—"

"Go on risking your life and all I have—" He halted abruptly, his grip on her arms painful and a scowl clouding his face. "For what? For what, Anne?"

His ruthless will preyed on her every weakness: on the panic that vanquished coherent thought; on the fear that she would fail, see her brother killed, and her family shamed; on the terror that her father, in learning, would stop her. Her eyes, spangled with tears, mutely beseeched him to ask no more.

"For what, Anne?" he demanded mercilessly.

None of Cantor's love and tenderness softened his face. He was a stranger without pity or compassion. An agent for her father. What drove him? she wondered. Feeling his will sucking the strength from her, she hoped that somewhere, buried in the heart she thought she knew, was the man who loved her and would help her. Feeble it might be, but it was her only hope.

"For my brother," she whispered. "For Robbie."

His scowl vanished, leaving blank surprise. "Your brother is dead."

"He is alive and held hostage!" Her strength returned and, with it, her will. "Cantor! Cantor, I pray you, help me! Help me to save him!"

God help them both! Karl thought. Grief had unhinged her mind! Seeing the blaze of hope in her eyes and feeling the vibrant tremor of her body against his, he suffered a black despair. "Anne, Anne," he said gently, "I was in Borodino when Robbie was reported lost. I searched for—"

"But you didn't find him, did you? Cantor, he is alive! Von Fersen told me things that only Robbie and I knew! Things—"

"Von Fersen!"

"His master holds Robbie! I don't know who or where he is!"

But Karl did. Friedrich! As *Prinz-General* of the

Lancers of Schattenburg—a cavalry troop of Napoleon's German Legion—Friedrich had fought under Ney at Borodino. Ney had flung his men again and again at the heights of La Flèche. On those heights the Russians had broken and fled in disorder, leaving behind—so he had been told—the valiant young Englishman, wounded. Friedrich could have found him. Robbie, expecting honorable treatment, would have told him who he was—and set the seal to his fate. There was an old and deep-rooted enmity between Friedrich and the Earl of Darenth. And Friedrich missed no opportunity to wreak his revenge on an enemy. The Earl, despite Anne's fears, would have to be told.

"Anne"—Karl's hands climbed to her face, cupping it tenderly between his palms—"he may have been alive when he was taken, but you cannot know he is now."

Fear flared in her eyes. Her lashes swept down to hide it. The small hands grasping his lapels knotted into fists, and Karl saw that this was not a new thought for her. It was a fear that plagued her daily. Yet she continued to risk herself to save her brother.

"I won't believe it! I can't believe it!" Her gaze swept up to meet his, luminous and sure. "Don't you see? I can't take that chance! If there is any possibility that Robbie is alive, I will do anything— anything!—to save him!"

She had not abandoned all she believed in after all. She had only been forced to choose between her loyalties and her loves, and she had chosen her brother. Karl should have welcomed this revelation, but somehow he could not. Anger grew within him, honed by a fear he could neither name nor understand.

"Do you know what could happen to you?" he asked sharply. "The daughter of a peer can hang as readily as any other!"

"He's my brother! A part of me, as I am a part of

him! If there is any chance that I can save him, I will take it!"

"Would Robbie expect this of you? Would he want you to risk your life for him?"

"You must know he would not!" Anne cried. "You must know, too, that I have no choice!"

"Just as I have no choice but to summon your father."

Anne wrenched away from him, backing to the desk. Her hands clamping around the cool rim, she struggled for control. She couldn't fail Robbie. Not now! She ignored pain, disillusion, and fear for the terrible need to make Cantor understand.

"My father, if he is forced to choose, will leave my brother to die before he will give aid to England's enemies. It will hurt him. It may destroy him, but he will do it. If he learns that I . . ." Her voice trembled out of control, but she dared not stop. "I beg you, don't force him to make that choice!"

She saw a fleeting pain mark Cantor's face before he turned away. His strong profile etched the darkness beyond. Slowly, the pain vanished. In its place came stern resolution.

"Your father has long known that von Fersen placed an agent in this house," he said, without turning to face her. "He used that agent to plant false information, and I, knowing it was you," he emphasized, as if to punish himself, "allowed him to do it."

Anne stared at Cantor's hard profile, unable to believe what she had heard. She stumbled weakly to the wing chair and sank onto its cool leather seat. Oh, God! She struggled for every breath. What would happen to Robbie now?

Karl, waiting for her to cry out, to accuse him, to deny him, heard only the pounding of his own heart and the shallow, wounded pant of Anne's breath. He wanted to kneel at her feet and plead for understanding. He had done it for her! he wanted to say. He had to stop her, and this, though fraught with danger, had been the safest way. But how could he tell her that when he doubted it now? Had his need to thwart Friedrich through von Fersen been so great that he was willing to use Anne—to endanger her!—to do it?

He had existed too long in the shadows. He had struggled too long, forced to make use of anyone and anything that would move him a step closer to Friedrich. Even now he could see a way to use the situation to the earl's good and his own. But Anne's? The threat to her and her brother must continue if he hoped to destroy von Fersen.

He shifted restlessly. There was more at stake here than one man! Anne must be made to see that! Neither her brother, nor his own crown, were more important than a Europe free of Napoleon's tyranny. The lives of millions might rest on a cog as small as von Fersen.

Reason succumbed to doubt. Anne had everything to lose, while he had a crown to gain and vengeance to be won. Did he care more for that than for her? Though he searched his heart, he didn't know. He only knew he had come too far and fought too hard. He could not give up now.

Karl turned slowly. She sat wilted over the arm of the chair, her face as white as the buttercups that bloomed in the summer heat of the Schattenwald. Desire tugged at him. He yearned for the peace and pleasure and laughter, the hope Anne had once given him. He was tired of being a rootless wanderer. For a moment he allowed himself to dream of a happy hearth, of sons tumbling on the carpet, of Anne smiling the secret smile that promised, *When we are alone, my love* . . .

His dream was as hopeless as her belief that her brother was alive.

He could not keep this from the earl. Robbie was his son; Anne, his daughter. Only he could decide what should be done.

Anne's head tilted up. Her eyes, dark and tor-

mented, searched his face. Karl waited, his every
nerve taut.

"Have I ever known you?" she asked softly, more
of herself than him.

Karl flinched and turned away. "Wait here," he
said brusquely. "I will bring your father to you."

Utterly defeated, Anne sagged over the arm of the
chair, her cheek pillowed on her arms. She was too
frightened for anger, too desolate for tears. She
closed her eyes, remembering the long-ago night
when Robbie had risked his life to save hers. She
had failed her brother, who, for all his rash and feckless ways, had never failed her.

The door burst open. Her father strode in, the tail
of his brocade dressing gown flapping around his
ankles. His flushed face was carved by the grim line
of his mouth and scored by deep grooves of anger.

Behind him, Cantor paused to close the door before stationing himself beside it. Anne's hostile
glance found him as grim as her father, his lips
pinched bands in a face as cold and still as marble.
His gaze met hers briefly, enigmatic and foreboding.

A chill prickling up her spine, she stood slowly to
face her father.

"What you have done is unforgivable!" His arms
folded across his chest and one brow arched high
over a relentless stare, while his slippered toe tapped
an irritated rhythm.

He had used this dominating pose often on his
wayward son, but never on Anne. Had Robbie with-
stood those silent clashes of will because some things
were more important than personal fears or misgiv-
ings? For Robbie it had been his independence, his
determination to live his life in his own way. For her
it was the need to patch the torn fabric of her family
and move into the future together, loving and
happy.

Her chin climbing, she met her father's hard stare
without flinching. "I did it to save Robbie, Father,
and I would do it again if need be."

"You should have come to me!"

Beyond the anger burning in his eyes, Anne saw the deep and bitter disappointment she dreaded more than anger. Disappointment meant a loss of trust, and that was a corrosive that even a father's love could not withstand.

"I could not ask you to make this choice—"

"You dared not ask me, you mean!"

Just so had it always gone with Robbie. Her father used his anger and his words like bludgeons, but beneath them was his love and his adamant determination to see that *right* was done. For him there was right and there was wrong, and there was nothing in between. And that was what made him so dangerous to her brother and to her.

"No, Father, I dared not." She paused, her chest squeezed by a vise of pain. "Not when Robbie's life was at stake."

He didn't move. Not a muscle rippled in his face. Not a flicker of an eyelash betrayed any inner emotion, but it seemed to Anne he flinched.

"Your brother is dead," he said hoarsely, the grief he had never been able to express seeping through his anger.

"No! I—"

"Your brother is dead!" he repeated furiously, but Anne sensed in him a need, a wish to believe his son alive. A wish so strong he could only deny it. "Friedrich," he continued, "would never allow a son of mine to live!"

"F-Friedrich," she faltered. "Y-you know who has—"

"I know who von Fersen's"—his lips curled back over his teeth in a snarl—"*master* is."

"Then you must rescue Robbie!" she cried. "You must—"

"Anne!" He caught her arms, his fingers biting deep and his face bending low to hers. "You must listen to me carefully."

"But Father—"

"In our youth Sir Richard Bragg and I," he began, as if she had not spoken, "took our Grand Tour together. In Paris we met Friedrich von Schattenburg and . . . his brother. We invited them to England. Your mother and I were affianced, with plans to marry the following year. Friedrich . . . attempted her. I called him out and injured him quite seriously. He swore then that he would have his revenge, no matter how long it took or what he had to do. Anne, if Robbie has fallen into his hands, there is no hope. Do you understand? No hope!"

She pulled away from him, horrified by what she had heard, unwilling to believe, as he so obviously did, that there was no hope for Robbie. "But Father, we cannot—"

"Anne, you too are a part of this. If von Fersen betrays you, Friedrich will have taken my last child from me. I cannot allow that!"

"Will you accept Robbie's death so easily?" She swallowed hard, struggling not to scream. "Won't you try to find proof before you condemn him to it?"

"Friedrich," he began with cold loathing, "is the man behind von Fersen and a ring of, up until now, very efficient agents gathering intelligence here in London. That intelligence goes straight to Napoleon. It draws out these damnable wars. It weakens England. It must be stopped! And you, my dear, are going to help us do it!"

"I—I don't understand."

"Ka—" He stopped abruptly and turned to Cantor. Their eyes met in wordless communication. "He," her father said at length, "has a plan. He will tell you about it."

Cantor moved forward into the flickering light. Though his face was pale and drawn, his eyes held a ruthless determination akin to her father's. Anne backed to the chair on legs too unsteady to hold her. Sinking to the leather cushion, she laced her fingers and stared up at him, awaiting what she feared would be a final blow.

"Though we have been aware of von Fersen's activities for some time," he said in a cool, emotionless tone, "we have not been able to trap him in the act. Something we are not yet ready to do, in any case. You have provided us with an opportunity to continue feeding him false information, thus confusing and confounding our—"

"No! No!" Anne leapt to her feet. "You can't do this! If Robbie is alive—"

"Anne!" her father shouted. "Sit and listen!"

Her heart burning with rage and rebellion, she perched on the edge of the cushion. Her eyes, hot and hard, met Cantor's, promising that she would never forgive him for this betrayal.

"Von Fersen now believes he has me at his mercy," Cantor continued, a hint of strain in his voice. "He has demanded that I bring him information from the Foreign Office. If you and I take him similar information, he will accept it as legitimate, however erroneous it later proves to be."

"Anne, we must do this to protect you," her father said. "Von Fersen will not allow you to stop, nor can I allow you to take him anything that—"

"To protect me," she said bitterly, her heated gaze locking with her father's. "And if Robbie is alive and von Fersen learns of—"

"Robbie . . . Robbie is alive?" came a soft voice quavering with joy.

Three pairs of eyes filled with varying degrees of dismay turned to the Countess of Darenth, standing by the door.

Chapter 11

Dust swirled above the flagstones, driven by the sweltering wind funneling down Pall Mall. August had arrived with a vengeance, drying air and earth and leaving London a seared and dirty brown. Anne noticed neither dust nor wind nor discomfort.

What she had wanted to do was so simple: to bring her brother home and unite her family in happiness once more. What she had actually done was disastrous. Her brother was in more danger than ever. Her parents were at daggers' drawn, her father refusing to entertain any hope that Robbie was alive and her mother refusing to believe he was not.

The simmering blue sky lacked a wisp of a cloud, while a nascent storm gathered strength inside Darenth House. Black disillusion, anger, and accusation boiled beneath a tension that threatened to snap, bringing lightning strokes of destruction and devastation. Anne feared she would be the catalyst whipping that storm to life.

Her father had told her precisely what to do. She was to give von Fersen the information he requested about the Austrians and, with it, the papers he had drawn up—misrepresentations, misconceptions, and outright lies, all threats to Robbie's life. She had meekly said, "Yes, Father," and "No, Father," knowing she had no intention of following his instructions.

She had a plan of her own, one that would answer

her father's doubts and—could she admit it?—her own, but one he would see as her last and most grievous betrayal. She would prove that Robbie was alive. Then her father and . . . Cantor—though the thought of him clutched at her heart, her eyes burned as hot and dry as the simmering sky—would have to help her.

Yet the closer she came to Chumley's Millinery Shoppe the slower her steps dragged and the faster her heart raced.

She was late. Heinrich von Fersen, in a foul mood, paced through the red gloom. His eyes, gleaming like a cat's in the darkness, probed the crimson curtains, as if he might pierce the draped velvet to see her hurrying along Pall Mall in the dusty heat of the day. He pulled his heavy gold watch from his waistcoat pocket and frowned at the time. He had an hour yet before his meeting with Lord Castlereagh. A meeting he would have avoided but for Friedrich's strict orders.

Those orders. His nostrils flared away from the sharp blade of his nose, while a frown beetled his brow. He could hardly believe what he was to do. Less could he believe what he was to say. Had the hand not been Friedrich's unmistakably sharp, tight script, he would have thought the billet had been sent by another. But only Friedrich could have written it, only he could have demanded that they seek to work for the English, while continuing to work for the French. Whether it was a masterstroke worthy of the Byzantine workings of Friedrich's mind or a lethal error, von Fersen did not know. He only knew it was a change undirected by himself, and he did not like it.

Resist it he might, but change was coming. He could smell it, like the acrid taste of a brewing storm. If he needed proof, it came in the message Friedrich wanted relayed to Castlereagh: an illness had left Napoleon bloated and pallid, lethargic and hesitant;

he had become more and more indecisive, weakening his grip on the Empire; he could not be stirred to action even by the discontent rumbling through the Confederation of the Rhine; Friedrich's spies had learned that Duke Frederick II of Württemberg was negotiating secretly with Prince Metternich in order to ally himself with Austria, and if he switched allegiance, the Confederation would crumble.

His frown deepening, von Fersen pulled out his watch. Where was she? He had the meeting to follow and the dispatch to send on its furtive way. And in that dispatch he wanted confirmation of Cantor Cartwright's whispered confidence that the Austrians would be deserting Napoleon for the Allies when the Armistice was over. Another nail in the coffin of the Empire. And if they took Württemberg with them, it would be the beginning of the end.

Tap . . . tap, tap came a knock. The door swung noiselessly, and Lady Anne stepped through. Small and neat in mourning black relieved by a ruching of white at her throat and wrists, she settled a gray gaze dark with turmoil and fear upon him. Von Fersen's narrow chest expanded with his thin-lipped smile, like the slash of a wound, cleaned but seeping blood at the edges.

"You have what I want?" he said, his voice full-bodied with the power of having her helpless and at his whim.

"Yes."

"Give it to me," he commanded, extending a soft white hand.

"No."

His triumphant smile lingered for a moment, then vanished behind a pinched line of rage. "Do you forget—"

"I forget nothing!"

His nostrils flared. Her pulse hammered in her throat and fright dilated her eyes, but still she thwarted him. He itched for a club to beat her into submission.

"I want proof that my brother is alive," she said.

"You will have proof that he is dead, should you—"

"And you will be without the information your *master* craves."

He paused at that, his own pulse hammering in his temple with a dizzying heat and speed. Something was different. Something was wrong. She had never been timid, but with the sword of her brother's life hanging over her head, she had been malleable. "How am I to prove it? He is far, far from here," he said tightly.

"He is to be asked this question: What happened to Anne on her eleventh birthday? I will give you what you demanded from me today, and nothing else—nothing!—until I have my answer."

"That will take weeks! I need—"

"Nothing!" Her chin climbed.

Tremors of rage spread throughout his body, leaving his hands trembling and his mouth working convulsively. "I have but to whisper one word in the right ear and you will be charged with treason. Are you willing, *Lady Anne*," he sneered, "to risk that?"

"If you do, you will have nothing more from me. Are *you* willing to risk that?"

Though he had other sources in London, none had proved as fruitful as she. "Give me what you have," he snarled. "You will have your answer, and then, *my lady*, you will do as I say."

Moments later, she was gone on a whisper of swirling dimity skirts. He shuddered in the overheated room, glaring with narrowed eyes at the door. Too many straws in the wind promised disaster. Napoleon's weakness. The Austrians' defection. Lady Anne's dismaying determination. Two of his best-placed men in the City had vanished without a word, without a trace. And, worst of all, the second man he had sent to sniff around Bragg House had neither returned nor sent word.

He shifted restlessly, his frown turning into a

scowl. Two men now swallowed up by Bragg House.
A chill of superstitious fear shuddering through him,
he fingered the deep, puckered pockmark beneath
his right eye. Though he shrank from the thought,
he knew he had to do the deed himself. If he must
he would dig up the grave to make sure the boy was
in it, and if he was not . . .

Von Fersen trembled with frustrated rage and fear.
The howling storm of change . . .

. . . was breaking. Anne felt it the moment the hot
wind whipped her into Darenth House.

Rumford, his pixie face carefully expressionless,
stood guard in the salon, keeping footmen and
housemaids away from the raised voices spilling
through the closed library door.

"Yes! I tell you, yes! Even Friedrich von Schattenburg could not be such a monster!" Her mother's
voice, so lately low and drugged with grief, pierced
the door with ringing authority.

"Agatha"—her father's voice vibrated with tension—"you more than anyone know what Friedrich
is capable of doing."

"How long?" Anne asked softly, shedding her
black straw hat with its crown of white roses, her
gloves and reticule and shawl.

"Too long, milady," said Rumford, pity darkening the round, brown buttons of his eyes.

Too long. Once, a moment of screaming dissen-
sion between the earl and his wife would have been
too long. Could love die so easily? Anne wondered,
pausing with her hand on the etched silver knob
and fearing, with a painful thought of Cantor, that
love could die when faith and trust were gone. She
must stop her parents, halt this argument, before
they said the unforgivable.

"Agatha, the man committed fratricide! He murdered his own brother on the very altar of the
church! Do you think he would hesitate to murder
my son?"

Fratricide. The word vibrated through Anne, weakening both her grip and her belief that she was right and her father wrong. A man who would murder his own brother would not hesitate to murder the son of his enemy. Rather than saving her brother, was she merely making her father's task harder?

"But what if he hasn't, John? I beg you! Robbie must be rescued!"

Before her father could refuse, Anne pushed open the door. Squared off like opponents at Jackson's Boxing Saloon, her parents stood in the flood of sunlight pouring through the windows. Her mother's cheeks were stained a hectic red, and her father's were blanched a dead-white. Both wore the black of mourning, her mother's unrelieved by any touch of white, her father's softened only by his stiff-starched shirtfront.

Her mother stretched out her hand. "Come, my dear, and help me. I have just been telling your father he should—"

"Don't encourage her, Anne! Hope now will only make her disappointment more bitter!" he ordered.

A look akin to hate flashed in her mother's gray eyes, and Anne hurried forward. "I must tell you what I have done, Father."

He turned from her mother, tension pulling his lips thin. "You saw him?"

"Yes."

"You gave him the false papers?"

"No."

A frown tugged his black brows together over the bridge of his nose, flattening the arch. "No?"

The very mildness of his tone was more threatening than a shout would have been. Even her mother sucked in a sharp breath and held it, waiting for the storm to strike.

It was what she wanted. Their argument was forgotten. Their attention was focused on her. Even as Anne breathed a sigh of relief, she suffered a terrifying urge to run.

"No?" her father repeated, quietly, emotionlessly.

"I—I gave him the information about the Austrians," she said, her voice a thready whisper. "I—I refused to give him anything more until . . . until he brings me proof that Robbie is alive."

The tenderness and concern of husband and father yielded to the implacable resolve of spy and king's man. "You will meet with him again and—"

"No, Father, I will not." She struggled to meet his icy stare.

Anger blazed in his eyes and rippled along his clenching jaw. His effort to subdue it brought a sheen of sweat to his brow. "You don't understand what you are doing, Anne," he said in a ruthlessly controlled tone. "We have begun to close in on von Fersen, picking off his men one by one. The Prime Minister's coachman, fuddled with ale, has *signed on* with the Army. A servant at White's has been impressed into the Navy. This is a beginning, but we need you to complete it. You, and the information you give him, will allay von Fersen's suspicions while we move in for the kill."

He watched her carefully, as if, Anne thought, she were an enemy to be thwarted if necessary and manipulated if possible. In the heat of the day she felt cold.

"I can't," she cried, sensing with him, as she had with Cantor, his ruthless determination to have his own way. "I can't condemn Robbie to death. Father!" She moved closer, reaching out to touch his hand. "What if you are wrong? What if Robbie is alive? Could you ever forgive yourself—"

"Anne"—he lifted her hand, holding it between his—"I tried to teach both you and Robbie that you must always do what you believe to be right. You must trust me now—"

"Trust you, John," her mother interrupted bitterly. "When you have never trusted us. Had I not learned that Robbie was alive, I would never have learned the secret of the Raven's Nest—"

"Kept to protect you," he said.

Anne saw the hurt in her mother's face and the guilt in her father's, and knew that the schism between them ran deeper than their division over Robbie.

"No, John," her mother said, "you have never shared your life, your secrets. How can you ask for trust, when you have never given it?"

It seemed to Anne she could hear the air whispering around her. The threads of love binding them one to the other were slowly unraveling, whispering in the silence.

Her father turned to her, a mute question overlaying the pain shining deep in his eyes.

"I can't," she answered, and feared that nothing would ever be the same again.

Karl noticed it at dinner: the brooding aftermath of an emotional storm that had left everyone in its path dazed. A clamoring silence greeted every scarcely touched course. A silence that even he, in the garrulous persona of von Dannecker, dared not break. Over cigars and brandy in the waning light of the evening Darenth told him what Anne had done.

"You cannot be surprised, my lord," he said.

"No." With an expression mirroring both pain and pride, the earl stared at his daughter's empty chair. "I taught her to do right without regard as to who it hurt."

It was a sentiment Karl understood only too well. He, too, had tried to do right, for himself, for Anne, for the country that had sheltered him from his birth. Yet the memory of her hostile gaze, promising that she would never forgive him, sucked his confidence from him.

At noon of the following day he stared through von Dannecker's cerise mask trimmed with satin forget-me-nots and watched Anne from the shadows of the stairwell. Framed in a square of hot, bright light and caressed by the curtains billowing gently on the sultry breeze, she gazed at the brown garden below.

I don't know you at all, she had said. *I only thought I did.*

An ache beat in Karl's heart. His name was false and his life was not his own, but he was the man she had met and loved. He was the same! he wanted to say. The same man who had found in her all he desired in a woman. Loyalty, truth, and love: what more could he want?

Yet there *was* something more he wanted: an unnameable, unknowable something that only Anne could give him. But what it was, he did not know. It remained frustratingly intangible, a tantalizing thought that lurked in the dark corridors of his mind.

The search for that elusive thought was vanquished by a new awareness. Anne was frightfully thin. Her once gently molded features were sharp and pinched. Her skin was a translucent white. Her eyes, shaded by a luxuriant sweep of glossy black lashes, were ringed by the delicate mauve of sleeplessness.

The tremor racing across the sweet curve of her mouth and the ragged sigh fluttering the lace at her breast pulled him out of the stairwell. Limping across the salon on the mute murmurs of cerise and lemon satin, his violet hair powder sifting onto his shoulders and his cane tapping lightly, he approached with the courage given him only by his disguise. Von Dannecker would not turn Anne's eyes a hard pewter-gray. He would not be greeted by anger. Thus, he could go to her, wanting . . . wanting what?

The sadness emanating from her clogged his aching throat. "*Fraulein, bitte,*" he said gruffly.

Her gaze lifted to his mask, slowly focusing, as if she had been miles or years away. With her brother, he thought with that strange feeling of fear and anger. His eyes met hers and both feelings died. She looked—he groped for the word—shattered, as if her spirit had been fragmented beyond redemption.

"Herr von Dannecker," she said, her normally light voice low and uncertain.

Blindly, he reached for her hand, gently rubbing her icy fingers with the pad of his thumb. "Nothing, *Fraulein*, not even pain, lasts forever."

A flicker of surprise lightened the gaze that raced over his masked face. Quickly the surprise and the curiosity were gone. Sorrow tugged at her mouth and a suggestion of tears glistened in her eyes. "Nothing, Herr von Dannecker," she agreed. "Not even love."

She turned away to stare through the window once more, leaving Karl feeling as though he had been dealt an unexpected blow. Had he done this to her? Had he destroyed her vibrant sense of life, her limitless capacity for hope, and her belief that love could endure?

He could not leave her like this! Not if it cost him everything! His hand climbed to the mask, fingers hooking over the border of forget-me-nots. "Anne—"

"Herr von Dannecker!" called the earl, one arm elegantly draped across the mantel, as if he had been watching for some time. "I pray a moment with you."

Karl turned slowly. "I would have a word with—"

"A moment," said Darenth with a frown. "It is of the utmost importance."

Karl wanted to tell her and be done with it. He wanted to assure her that love could endure. He wanted everything that duty said he could not have. Duty and desire. Would the first never stop throttling him with what must be done? Would the latter never stop tormenting him with what might have been?

He followed the earl into the library. "Anne—"

"Shut the door." Darenth sank into the leather chair behind the desk and steepled his fingers, staring warily over them.

The door clicked shut, and Karl abandoned the limp, striding angrily to the wing chair. "This cannot continue with Anne, my lord. She is—"

"Grieving for her mother and for me. We are . . . sorely divided by . . ." One hand fanned out, as if to say, *There is no need to repeat that.* "Anne cannot accept that her family may not always be what it once was. We have seen that in her refusal to accept Robbie's . . ." One finger tensely tapped the enameled lid of the pouncet-box. "There is nothing either you or I can do for her."

Karl sank into the chair, still gripping the knob of his cane. That unnameable, unknowable something was slowly coming into focus. The strange, unwanted fear was finding expression. She needed her family's love, not his. She needed her parents and her brother, not him. She was tied to them in ways she would never be tied to a man. Her family would always be first with her. And that was his fear. Even if he could claim her for his own, she would never be wholly his. And he, having lived a secondhand life, needed a woman who would give him her all.

"We have a more immediate problem now," said Darenth flatly. "Von Fersen has approached Castlereagh with an offer to work for him."

Karl slipped off the mask and wig and let them tumble to the floor. His head sank back against the leather upholstery. "You know what he is doing," he said tiredly.

"Of course, and so does Castlereagh, dear boy," said the earl, his steepled fingers tapping against his grim mouth.

So much had been begun. The nibbling away at von Fersen's agents, preparatory to taking the man himself. And here, another delay. Karl should be angry, but he felt drained. "He isn't to be trusted," he said, raising his hands to his face, fingertips kneading his arching brow.

"Castlereagh knows von Fersen is playing both sides, hoping to win, whoever triumphs. But the information he has given and will give is of exceptional value."

"Is it possible he does this on his own?"

"Without Friedrich's knowledge?" The earl frowned. "No. Friedrich's fine finger stirs this broth. In a way, it is a good sign. The German states must be strongly uniting against France, or he would not chance it."

Karl should have been glad to hear that, and a part of him was. But that part was buried deep beneath a numbing sense of loss. "What would Castlereagh have us do now?"

"Nothing, dear boy," said Darenth. "Von Fersen is not to be touched. We must wait."

"Wait, my lord? I may not have time for waiting." His head lowered, his gaze meeting the earl's. "I have just come from Franz. Lady Bragg sends word that another of von Fersen's men came sniffing around Bragg House. He will sniff no more, but . . ."

August continued hot and dry. Fashionable London was dead, the *ton* having fled the heat for Brighton or Bath or their country seats. Normally, the Darenth household would have removed to Darenth Hall, and Anne would have been rejuvenated by the peace of the Elizabethan estate and the lush Kent countryside. But nothing was normal in this summer of 1813. Her world had shattered into ever smaller pieces. Everything and everyone she relied on had proven to be faithless. Her parents' love had died, leaving them icily polite strangers. Her mother, once trapped in lonely grief, was now caught in solitary bitterness. Her father, once loving and thoughtful, was now distant and preoccupied. Cantor . . . spy for her father . . . stranger to her.

She longed for the willow-draped banks of the

River Darent, for the neat rows of hop fields, and the fragrant meadows of blooming lavender. Those places she had inhabited as a child now seemed to be her only safe sanctuary. And she needed a sanctuary. She should try to effect a reconciliation between her parents. She should try to understand why Cantor had never told her he was a spy. But she could summon neither the strength nor the will for either.

She could only wait. It would be weeks before von Fersen brought her an answer. So she fed the pelicans in Regent's Park and watched the milkmaids in Green Park and strolled the meandering paths of Hyde Park. In self-imposed solitude, she waited to hear whether her brother was alive or dead.

Behind his own self-imposed prison of von Dannecker's mask, Karl discovered that the patience of a lifetime had deserted him. He wanted to see color in Anne's cheeks once more, to hear her laugh. He wanted her to be at peace with herself . . . and with him.

He shed the mask and ribbons and wig, and dressed in Cantor's exquisite style. He sought her out at Hookham's Lending Library; she ran away. He followed her to Regent's Park; she hurried elsewhere. He tried to see her no more.

August progressed. The stifling weather broke with a turbulent storm that left the promise of autumn in the cool air.

Every day Karl watched Anne trudge through the dawn light, heading for the stables. Every day he waited for her to return. One finger stroking the raven's sleek head, he leaned against the windowsill while she passed below, her riding crop drooping from one hand, the demi-train of her skirt falling from the other.

In the dusky evenings von Dannecker dined *en famille*, and Karl stared out of the mask. Tension ringed the table with an undercurrent of anger. Anne watched her parents, while they watched each other. In every eye he saw disappointment and disillusion, but in none was it stronger than in Anne's. She looked, he thought, like a snuffed candle. The light was gone from her eyes.

She did not need him, but she did need her family. There must be something he could do, something he could say. He told himself to give her time, but day by day she grew thinner and quieter. Unable to wait longer, he laid his plans . . .

Astride one of Cantor's extravagant purchases—a dainty-limbed riding hack he called Blueberry after his childhood horse—he secreted himself in the shrubbery and waited for her to come trotting around Hyde Park's Ring. The grass was greening and the birds were singing and the trees were showing the first signs of rusty-yellow. High in the branches of a mulberry tree the raven fluttered from limb to limb, like a restless playgoer in search of the best seat.

Anne appeared in the distance, a slight figure with her black skirt flowing in the breeze and a snip of a hat perched at a jaunty angle atop her ebony curls. As she drew nearer, he saw that the hat was the only jaunty thing about her. Her expression was melancholy, her eyes brooding. She wouldn't welcome him.

He dismounted and stepped into the middle of the Ring, his Hessians crunching the gravel and the breeze wafting a lock of his hair. Anne's widening eyes held recognition and fear. Her mouth became a thin, angry line. She yanked on the reins to wheel her snow-white mare around, and Karl leaped forward to catch the bridle.

The mare danced, rolling her liquid brown eyes and showing her teeth. "Whoa, girl. Steady now. Steady," Karl soothed, stroking her sleek neck.

She settled slowly, her hide quivering beneath his hand while she huffed her pleasure. Karl's gaze found Anne's, and a slow smile tugged at his mouth. "I could wish you were so easily tamed, my lady."

The admittedly feeble attempt to win a smile failed. "You have been avoiding me," he said softly.

She struggled for composure. The lines of tension softened. Her rigid posture relaxed.

"You flatter yourself, sir," she said icily. "I do not give you the thought necessary to *avoid* you."

"Don't you, Anne? I own that I have done little but think of you." His gaze wandered to the color staining her cheeks. He stepped closer, tilting his head back, revealing his powerful throat. "You are unhappy."

Her hand clenched around her riding crop, wrinkling her supple glove. "My brother is hostage and my parents are at daggers' drawn. Am I to dance in the streets?"

He listened to the new and brittle tone in her voice, remembering her softness, her sweetness, her ineffable belief that right and good would prevail. There had to be some way he could convince her that von Fersen would never tell her what she wanted to hear. He had to soften that blow. "Your father—"

"Should trust," she said, turning an embittered gaze on him. "You do know what that means: belief, faith, hope."

"Trust is for those who can afford it, Anne."

"Trust is for those who love!" she shot back, then looked away and bit her lower lip, as if she would recall those hasty words.

Nothing could have better said that she had thought of him as often as he had thought of her, that her recollections were as painful as his. He knew suddenly why he had come. To help her understand, if he could, but more, to heal the wound he had dealt her. "Four years ago was no lie, Anne," he said urgently. "Nor was Bragg House."

"And now, spy for my father?" She leveled a hard gaze on him. "What is now?"

What was now? Nothing had changed. Love her he did and protect her he would, but his life was still not his own. There was his vengeance to seek and his throne to gain. And when that was done, he must take to himself a woman of his people to heal and bind the wounds of war. He could not wed a hated and feared Englishwoman—*die Engländerin*—who would keep those wounds fresh.

"Anne, I pray you will believe that I have meant only the best for you," he said softly.

"God save me from your worst!" she said, wrenching at the reins and galloping away.

Chapter 12

God save me from your worst! Karl heard the echo of Anne's parting shot in the twittering of the birds flitting through the garden, in the rumbling of dray wheels and the clatter of carriages. He heard it in the skittering of alley rats in Spitalfields when he should have been listening to Franz; and in the chink and clink of silver plate when von Dannecker should have been attending to the winsome miss on his right and the Friday-faced dowager on his left. It soured his food and his mood, and left him aching to right the wrongs he had done Anne.

There was only one thing to do. He, who unflinchingly met every danger and threat, now planned to turn his back and run.

He limped into the library with a curt greeting for the earl. Grateful this once for the mask that hid his face, he slammed the door behind him and strode to the windows. In the garden below the damask rose was studded with red hips and a wan scattering of ragged blossoms. Soon they would be gone, too, and nothing would be left but the memory of a long-ago night, of a kiss, of a love that never had a chance.

"I am leaving," he said flatly.

"With so much undone," replied the earl mildly.

"Yes."

"And you think that will help Anne."

He should have suspected that Darenth would know. "No one can help her now."

"You are wrong about that."

He turned from the window to study the earl, who relaxed in his wing chair, leaner than he had been but harder somehow, like a rapier that had been tempered in the fires of hell. "She will never forgive me for telling you."

"So you will leave her to grieve alone once von Fersen fails to provide the answer she wants. I had thought better of you than that."

A cynical smile pinched Karl's mouth. "So, my lord, had I." He moved to a chair and sank down with a sigh. "I cannot face her."

"Or yourself?"

Karl's hand curled into a powerful fist. "I never realized I was a coward."

"A woman can do that to a man." The earl leaned over the desk, restlessly tapping it with neatly pared nails. "I may yet need von Dannecker, Karl. You cannot leave."

"You ask much of me, my lord."

"And will, no doubt, ask more."

There was nothing to do but wait in the encroaching prison made of others' decisions. Where once Karl had waited with assurance and ease, he did so now with a new and dreadful impatience, and with a fierce yearning for action—any action!

It came in the dead of night, an urgent summons from Franz. Eagerly, Karl hastened into a rustic drayman's garb, pulled a knitted cap over the betraying gold of his hair, and rushed down the earl's secret stair. The September moon, peeping through a swirling mass of clouds, found him entering the King's Arms, better known as Cribb's.

Scents of smoke and sawdust, ale and roasting beef greeted him at the taproom door. A seething mass of odd-sorted humanity, from dukes to boot-catchers, bulged against the wainscoted walls. While his narrow gaze searched for Franz, snippets of conversation climbed above the babble.

"The Austrians are in the war," said a fastidious dandy, idly thumbing the lid of a Sèvres snuffbox at the table adjacent to the door.

"For all the good it'll do," said his companion, a hollow-eyed Corinthian with a fluffy mop of chestnut curls. "First campaign after the Armistice, and the Prussian Blücher loses six thousand men to Napoleon. Damn if we'll ever see this end."

But one campaign, as Karl had learned, did not win or lose a war. He was proof of that. He had waged battle after battle, winning some and losing others, and now found himself closer to final victory than ever. It took nothing more than the will to win and the determination to see it through without regard to the cost . . .

He thrust that thought away and spied Franz, huddled over a tankard in a far corner. Moments later, he eased into a sturdy Windsor chair and eyed his man's grim expression. "What has happened?"

"Milling-Jemmy is in charge here now." Franz drained the tankard to its dregs and swiped the back of his thick hand across his mouth. A frown knitted his grizzled brows, and a grimace twisted his lips. "Von Fersen left for Bragg House at dawn this morning. No doubt he wonders why two of his men have vanished in its environs. He can suspect only one thing—that you are alive."

"Then he will dig up the grave to make sure I am in it"—Karl's eyes turned as hard as flint—"and we will have him at last."

Franz cocked his chair back on two legs and hooked his thumbs beneath his broad leather belt. "Castlereagh won't like this. He wants von Fersen free and his agents unaware that suspicion has fallen on them until we are ready to take them all in one sweep."

"So does the earl, but even he would agree that we dare not leave von Fersen free with the news that I am alive. He would report it to Friedrich, and Friedrich would use Robbie once again—this time to get me. Darenth will agree that we should take whatever measures are necessary," Karl said on an exultant note. No longer did he consider himself bound by any purpose but his own. No longer need he chafe under restrictions imposed by others. Von Fersen would, at last, pay for Sir Richard's death. "How does he travel?"

"Hard and fast," said Franz. "He takes but one man, and he is armed to the teeth like a Spanish *guerrillero*."

"Damn!" said Karl, frowning. "There will be no time for von Dannecker to take a leisured leave of Darenth House. It must be in haste. He'll leave at dawn. I'll meet you at Tyburn Hill soon after. Be ready to travel like the wind."

Franz heaved himself up and slapped a hand to Karl's back. "We have waited long for this," he said, his wolfish smile revealing the even row of his white teeth.

Karl watched him go, then signaled for ale. A long pull of the yeasty brew sent the lingering remnants of tension fleeing. His hands had been tied so often, bound by old loyalties and new. At every turn his purpose had been thwarted, but no longer. A smile as wolfish as Franz's pulled at his lips and lingered, a rough promise of a deed to be done.

A short time later, he rousted the earl from his bed.

Darenth, the tassel of his nightcap dangling at his ear and the hem of his crumpled bed-gown of India cotton swaying around his bare ankles, folded his rigid arms over his chest and scowled into the embers of the hearth fire. "You cannot kill him!"

Karl, lounging against the bedpost, his ankles crossed and one fist riding low on his slim hips, arched up, stiff and straight. A frown wiped the satisfied smile from his mouth. "What?"

"You cannot kill him. We need him alive." Dar-

enth swiveled around, his gaze hard and cold. "He
must be returned to London under close arrest. Who
knows what we shall have from him with the threat
of hanging to loosen his tongue."

"You ask too much!" protested Karl, trembling
with a slow-building rage. "For twelve years I have
done all you asked—"

"For a price, Karl! Don't forget."

"Yes, for a price! A price that will cost you nothing and gain me much. Now I demand this one—"

"No!"

"He killed Sir Richard. Your cousin, your friend.
He has used Anne. Terrified her. Held out the hope
that Robbie is alive. You cannot think he deserves
to live!"

"Deserves to live!" Darenth's thin face twisted
with hate. "If it were left to me, I would kill him
myself! But there is too much at stake here, Karl.
We cannot be ruled by our passions. You *will* bring
him back alive. And when this war is done and your
throne regained, you can return here to see him
hang. We will have justice, if not vengeance."

But it was vengeance Karl wanted. An eye for an
eye, a death for a death, von Fersen's life for Sir
Richard's . . . and his own. God! His own.

Von Fersen's assassination attempt had abruptly
ended Karl's childhood. He had learned he was not
simple Wilhelm von Cramm, but Karl Auguste Wilhelm II, Prince of Schattenburg—whose uncle
wanted him dead. He had lost his identity, his security, and the only parents he had ever known.
Lady Elisabeth Bragg née von Cramm had, she told
him, been a lady-in-waiting to his real mother, Princess Magda. With Franz and Josef, they had fled
Schattenburg after the murder of Karl's father. Sir
Richard had come to them in Venice, planning to
bring Princess Magda, the wife of his old friend, to
England, but she had died at Karl's birth. Meanwhile, Richard and Elisabeth had fallen in love. They
decided to marry and raise Karl as her child by a

first marriage. He would have been told all of this,
Lady Bragg had said tearfully, when he was old
enough to understand—but von Fersen had made it
imperative that he learn to be ever watchful and cautious.

So Wilhelm von Cramm had been buried, and
Karl, with yet another name, had been sent to a cottage in the Lakeland's bleak vale of the Wastwater.
Raised by Franz and Josef and a bevy of closemouthed tutors, he had taken a child's rage and
molded it into a man's cold purpose. A purpose that
had been thwarted again and again by events and
men beyond his control. And now . . .

"Karl?" asked the earl in a warning tone.

"You ask too much," he responded bitterly.

"You will do what is right," said Darenth.

What was right? The question tormented Karl
through the dark and hectic night. Impatience chafed
him, for every moment saw von Fersen drawing
closer to Bragg House, closer to the secret that could
destroy them all. The raven fluttered on the windowsill, as if she were as impatient as Karl. Josef
hopped around the chamber like a cricket on a griddle, folding and packing and giving vent to dire
warnings.

While the blue of night yielded to the gray of
promised day, Karl struggled into the padding and
corset, the ribbons and frills of his disguise. At least
he need not do this again; he could abandon von
Dannecker forever. At least he need not see Anne
again; he could leave her in peace.

A parade of sleepy-eyed footmen carried port-
manteaux and bandboxes and a carved ivory chest
of music to the chaise-and-four creaking and stamp-
ing in the foggy predawn light. Karl descended the
stair with the musician's halting step, making von
Dannecker's fluttery farewell to the earl for the sake
of the eyes and ears of the footmen and the gossip
they would spread.

"My lord, I—"

"What . . . what is . . . Herr von Dannecker!"

Karl spun around at the first breathless whisper of Anne's voice. She stood in the entryway, her cambric night-robe adrift on swathes of lace. Touseled ebony curls strayed in wanton disarray from a dainty lace cap. Sleep still misting her gray gaze, her bare toes curled away from the cool marble floor. Karl felt a tightening in his loins, a constriction of his chest, a need to sweep her up and carry her away.

"I—I heard a commotion and feared something was wrong," Anne said softly, her hand climbing to the pulse beating visibly at her throat. It was a lie. It hadn't been fear that pulled her from her bed to fly heedlessly down the stairs. It had been a strange, surreal awareness that Cantor was nearby. Forgetting that he had betrayed her, forgetting that she had hurt him, she had fled her lonely bed, only to find, not her Cantor . . .

"Herr von Dannecker is leaving us," said her father.

Anne's curious gaze never left the blood-red mask. She could still feel Cantor's presence . . . emanating from von Dannecker! She studied the beautiful mouth, slightly parted and exquisitely formed beneath the mask, the lean square jaw, and the hint of a cleft in his bold chin. The image of Cantor's! She couldn't be wrong! A cold chill washed over her.

Karl saw the startled awareness in her eyes, the knowledge that blossomed there. "Lady Anne," he began, forgetting the musician's light and lilting tone, speaking instead in his own low, mellow voice.

A sharp breath escaped her throat.

He closed his eyes and silently cursed himself. Would he ruin it all now? "Ah, *Fraulein . . .* "

Too deep, too low. He wafted the lacy handkerchief beneath his nose, sending a lemony scent spiraling through the air. "*Fraulein*, I must leave you desolate, but it cannot be helped. Vat a pleasure dis has been, but . . ."

A halting step brought him to her. His supple, graceful hand captured the small fist at her throat and pulled it, unresisting, to his lips. It trembled against his light and lingering kiss. Attuned, he wondered, to the trembling of his heart?

Cantor! Anne thought, her hand growing rigid in his. But why? Why would he not tell her who he was?

His hand relaxed, as if he would release hers. She caught it and held it fast, her fingers gripping the graceful hand that was too hard, too strongly muscled for a simple musician's. As she had once before, she felt the force of something powerful and unnameable arcing from his flesh to hers. "Herr von Dannecker," she asked, "do you return now to Bragg House?"

Shock struck Karl immobile. He struggled for a breath, smothering in the confines of the padding and corset. "Bragg House, *Fraulein?*" he echoed on a guttural note.

His shock communicated itself to Anne through his stiff hand with its residual quiver of surprise. "Yes, I heard you play there when I visited," she said, wondering if it had indeed been him, if it had been . . . Cantor.

"You haf the good ear, *Fraulein,*" Karl said cautiously, remembering that Petworth had warned him she had heard music in the night. How could he have forgotten? His mind spun wildly, searching for some solution that would allay the suspicion darkening her gaze. "Of course, I vas dere. Vat do de Spanish say . . . ah, *incógnito. Der Vetter* . . . ah, de cousin . . . but *natürlich!* You know him!" he said, with a spurious feathering of joy in his voice. "Cantor Cartwright!"

Ah, God! Had it worked?

"C-Cantor?" Anne faltered. Was that why she felt Cantor's presence in him? The family resemblance in the mouth and the chin. And beyond that a grotesque travesty of her Cantor's unrelenting masculinity. It had to be true. He had no reason to keep from her a masquerade as the musician.

"*Ja!* He arrange vit de *Gnädige Frau* for my use of de peel tower. A place for me to be alone, to commune vit myself, vit my art, to compose, *Fraulein*, as I must. It is"—he swept his handkerchief in an elaborate arc—"de curse of genuis, *madchen*. Say *Danke* to de good God dat you are not cursed vit it."

She couldn't let it go. The feeling was so strong it would not be denied. "But you have not seen your cousin while you were here, Herr von Dannecker."

"*Ach! Nein!*" His hand clapped against his chest, as if he had suffered a blow. "My cousin and I share nothing, *Fraulein*. He is"—he shuddered delicately—"a sporting blood vit none of de finer feelings. A barbarian! He offends me!"

"No doubt," murmured Anne, now utterly convinced that this pastry puff of a man could not possibly be Cantor. "Forgive me, Herr von Dannecker. I keep you from your . . . communings."

The tiny bite of sarcasm in her voice and the shadow of contempt in her eyes told Karl that he had allayed her suspicions. Whether he was glad or sad, he did not know. He only knew he had to leave before he aroused them anew. Whatever happened, he dared not confront Anne as von Dannecker again.

An hour later, having effected a hasty change of attire at a wayside inn, Karl pounded up to Franz on the crest of Tyburn Hill. Buckskins tucked into his Hessians and a soft chamois coat clinging to his shoulders, he easily controlled his restive steed with the pressure of his powerful thighs and a gentle touch with the bit. He said nothing, nor did Franz, as they set out at a mile-eating gallop, merging like wraiths with the mist.

And overhead, winging through the first stream-

ers of dawn's golden light, flew the raven, heading
north.

The silvery disk of the moon perched atop the
Troutbeck Hundreds when Heinrich von Fersen and
his heavily armed man came slipping and sliding
over the crest of the hill. The bracing air had been
washed clean by a daylong rain that had left the thick
turf wet and treacherous. Below, Lake Windermere,
agleam in the night, slapped gently at the shore.
From the craggy peaks above there echoed and re-
echoed the harsh warning caws of ravens.

Von Fersen paused, shovel in one hand and
shielded lantern in the other. The puckered pockmark on the crest of his cheekbone stinging as if the
flesh had been newly gouged, he searched the dark,
looming fells. Fear raised the fine mouse-brown hairs
on the back of his neck as he remembered the legend of the House of Schattenburg, the tale of the
raven who watched over its prince. The ravens had
vanished with the death of Friedrich's brother, an
event foretold in the ancient myths. They would
dwell on the heights of the Reisenberg, bringing
peace and prosperity only when the rightful prince
sat on the throne.

Von Fersen assured himself he was a modern and
practical man, not given to flights of superstition,
but the fear prickled now through the rising hairs
on his arms. Shuddering, he turned his back on the
sharp fell peaks and the sharper caws of the ravens.

"Co'r, guv," said his man, rolling his eyes fearfully. "Ain't never heard a raven cawing i' the
night."

His nose wrinkling against the odor of sour sweat,
von Fersen cast his man a quelling look. "Come
along," he growled, stepping out sturdily.

His foot skidded over a patch of mud. His legs
flew out from under him. The shovel sailed in one
direction, the lantern in the other, and his fleshless
rump hit the ground with a breath-stealing whack.

He careened down the hill, his backside gathering mud, and fetched up against the neatly clipped yews in a tangle of arms and legs.

Loping after him, the shovel and lantern hastily grabbed, came his man in a clatter.

"Quiet, you cork-brained fool!" said von Fersen, his spidery hands crawling across his buttocks, gathering mud as they went. He flung the viscous earth away, yearning for the day he would travel in state, gathering nothing more than the dust of the road. Someday, he vowed, he would have it all. A mansion like Bragg House rising in elegant black silhouette against the blue of the night. The respect of the lower orders, of which he had tried to forget he was one. A title of his own and a titled wife to give him added consequence. He would have it all!

"This is it," he said, moving down the long leg of the rectangle of yews and finding the open end.

Moonlight bathed the marble angel gazing benignly on the two sunken graves. Moonlight bathed the lustrous raven, perched atop the angel's halo.

Von Fersen stopped in the full glare of a beady eye. His man stumbled and fell against his back, sending him sprawling over the small child's grave of Wilhelm von Cramm. A menacing *Pruk, pruk* issued from the raven, followed by a fierce *Caw! Caw!* and the whipping of wings.

Von Fersen, rolling onto his back, saw the bird fly from the halo led by its fierce pointed beak, aiming straight for his eyes. He flung a crooked arm over his face, and the powerful wings beat against it while the strong beak tore a gobbet of flesh from his brow. A wild cry of pain and terror wrenched from his throat.

The raven was gone so quickly he thought he had summoned it from the deep hell of nightmares, until he sat up with the blood streaming down his face.

"God! God!" he breathed, staunching the flow with a handkerchief and wallowing in the muddy, sunken grave. "Fool! Fool! Where are you?" he hissed for his man, and heard the unmistakable slither and slide of boots scaling the hill. He scrambled to his feet, rounded the end of the hedge, and saw his man fleeing, chivied on by the diving, screaming raven.

Von Fersen backed into the gravesite, the chill chattering his teeth roused by more than superstition now. His wary eye settled on the shovel slanting against the yews. Overhead, a cloud crept across the moon.

He wanted to run as his man had, fleeing this fearsome place, never to return. But the thought of failing Friedrich was more fearsome than the scream of the raven vanishing in the distance and the agitated caws echoing through the fells. Friedrich forgave no failure, accepted no defeat. If the boy had not died . . . if he was still alive . . .

Von Fersen's trembling hands knotted the handkerchief around his bleeding brow and reached for the shovel . . .

Four days of hard riding on relays of hired hacks brought Karl and Franz to Bragg House in the dark of night. Avoiding the drive, they galloped across the park, hugging the tree line. A stop at Kendal to bait the horses had seen them hiring new hacks in order to press on. Von Fersen, they had learned, was but hours ahead of them.

It had been a long four days of catching naps beneath hedgerows and eating in the saddle. Dust, wind, and exhaustion rimmed Karl's eyes red, but the end was in sight and the bone-deep weariness fled. Soon, soon, he thought, he would have Sir Richard's murderer. But what he would do with him he still did not know.

He dismounted in a grove of limes and wrapped the reins around a low limb. There was only one place von Fersen could seek his answer. Karl beckoned Franz and set off.

As once before, he fell easily into the sleek,

stealthy strides of the hunter. Not a twig snapped, not a blade of grass broke to betray his passing. Behind him, Franz moved with the same ease, the same silent menace.

The crab-apple tree, its limbs sagging with fruit, loomed out of the darkness. Karl angled down the slope, heading for the rectangle of yews.

From high overhead came the caw of the raven. He watched her swoop in ever tighter, ever faster, ever lower circles. Watcher and watchman. She knew. His blood began to strum. The raven screamed and dived, and a wolfish smile pulled Karl's lips from his teeth. She vanished behind the tall carved yews, and a scream, human and shrill, pierced the air. Karl broke into a run. There was no need for silence now.

Franz at his heels, Karl pounded up to the edge of the desecrated grave. Heinrich von Fersen huddled atop the exposed coffin in its muddy depths, his bleeding hands fending off the feathered fury while mud scudded down the ragged walls around him.

"Der Rabe!" Karl said firmly, and the raven broke away, circling the trees before settling gently on his shoulder and nuzzling his cheek with her beak.

Von Fersen, muddied and bloodied, struggled to his feet with a terrified sob. The thick cloud obscuring the moon slid away. A shaft of pearlescent light poured over Karl, revealing the lustrous raven and his grim expression.

Von Fersen cocked his head back, gaping up. "Cartwright!"

"Nein, mein Herr!" He dipped a scant bow. "Karl Auguste Wilhelm the Second, Prinz von Schattenburg."

A choked gurgle issuing from the gaping maw of von Fersen's mouth, he stepped back on the coffin and sagged against the mud. "You are dead! I . . . I—"

"Tried and failed. I am, as you see, very much

alive—as Sir Richard is not." The old rage welled up, hot and strong. His hands ached to wrap around von Fersen's scrawny neck, to choke the life from him.

"Shall I kill him here, *Majestät*?" said Franz, stepping into the light. "We could bury him where he is and none the wiser."

Von Fersen, his irises ringed in white, scrambled against the back wall of the grave, pressing into the mud. "No! No! It was not my fault! Friedrich! Friedrich is the one you want!"

Karl's lip curled with disgust.

Franz drew the knife from his belt, running his thick thumb along the honed edge. "A single thrust would end him," he said with a caress. "A slice across the throat would be better yet. How, *Majestät*, do you want it done?"

Von Fersen threw himself the length of the grave, his long fingers crawling over Karl's boots. "Don't let him touch me!" he screamed. "I can tell you much that you don't know! The agents I have! Where they are placed! Anything! Anything!"

"Anything, *mein Herr*?" Karl asked cruelly, stepping back from the edge. "And can you tell me why I, who have long awaited this moment, should care what you have to say?"

Even as he said it, Karl knew he did care. If von Fersen's confessions could save Anne one moment of worry, he would be well served by sparing the man's life. But he still felt the painful tug-of-war between old loyalties and new.

"So you didn't kill him?" asked Darenth, days later.

Shortly after Karl's return to London the earl had sent a billet to Cantor Cartwright's bachelor lodgings in Ryder Street. It requested attendance in a private game of macao at the fashionable hour of midnight. Karl had not been surprised when he was directed not to the macao-room, but to a private antechamber.

Garbed in the elegant Corinthian guise of Cantor Cartwright, he settled in a *bergère* chair and eyed the earl with disfavor. "He wasn't worth it."

"Come, come, dear boy. It does you no dishonor to admit you have no stomach for murder."

"I've done my share, as you well know."

"In the line of duty, dear boy. It doesn't signify."

"Perhaps not to you, my lord, but to my victims . . ."

The earl laughed. "Point well-taken."

Darenth studied the glowing tip of his Havana cigar, as if nothing were more important to him. Another little trick of the earl's, Karl knew from long experience. This time he would not be caught unawares. He would let Darenth broach the subject of this carefully arranged meeting in his own good time.

"Main of seven, chance of four, odds, two to one," the groom-porter's monotone droned from the hazard-room.

"Old Nick at it again?" asked the earl.

"He's mad for the bones," said Karl, lifting his claret and sniffing its bouquet.

"Castlereagh tells me that von Fersen, once the laudanum wore off—by the by, a prime piece of work that. Your idea?"

A genuine smile touched Karl's lips. "You may tender your encomiums to Lady Bragg, my lord. Franz and I would simply have trussed him up like a fair-day goose and tumbled him into the chaise."

"Ah, leave it to a woman to find the more devious route."

"I doubt, my lord," Karl said pointedly, "that any woman would find you amiss on that head."

"Patience, dear boy. Patience," said the earl, settling back with a sigh. "I'm given to understand that our *friend* suffered from a splitting head and a foul mood, but that he sang quite admirably in spite of it." He paused and frowned. "I can't agree with

Castlereagh's refusal to put him in Newgate. It seems to me that the assurance of secrecy is outweighed by the threat of escape."

"His windows are barred, and the house is guarded inside and out by handpicked men. Not much more can be done."

"Humph! You're right. Still . . ." The earl rolled the cigar between his fingers. "I believe it was Franz who put the fear in von Fersen?"

"He can be a bloodthirsty brute," Karl said equably, though his nerves were aquiver. He'd never seen the earl prose on to no point. The fact that he did so now could only mean he had something to say he expected to be taken in the worst way.

"How have you solved the problem of von Fersen vanishing? Won't this Milling-Jemmy Shadwell wonder what has happened to him?"

"Franz has told him that he met with von Fersen, and that he sends word he doesn't know when he will return. An emergency has arisen, and Shadwell is to carry on."

"And the man who did go with him?"

"Dead, my lord. An . . . accident in the fells." A shudder racked Karl. Being chivied over the edge of a cliff by a flock of ravens was hardly an . . . accident. Even he had not known to what length his black-feathered watcher would go.

"Excellent. No loose ends. Excellent," said the earl, sitting forward with a purposeful frown.

Karl stiffened in his chair, carefully setting the claret aside. "So, my lord, I am now to learn why I was summoned here."

"Dear boy, you know me too well." A faint flush crept into the earl's cheeks. "Our musician's disappearance leaves us with a small problem. We must have a socially acceptable reason for Cantor Cartwright to visit Darenth House, and I own I have found the solution. He must begin courting Anne."

Chapter 13

Anne gaped at her father. "You are roasting me, surely!"

"I own it must seem so," he responded, with the grace to look uncomfortable, "but I assure you I am not."

"He is to . . . to *court* me!" Her fulminating gaze shifted to Cantor, standing rigidly silent before Cicero's bust. He was dressed in the first style of elegance, yet in spite of his carefully expressionless face, he managed to seem as savage and untamed as the tigers pacing in their cages at the Tower of London. "And what do *you* have to say to this?" she asked bitterly.

One tawny brow rose into an arch of displeasure. "As little as possible," he said flatly.

So, she thought, she was to be used by them both with no regard to her feelings. She was a fool to let it hurt her, but hurt it did. "If you had a grain of proper feeling, you would tell my father to whistle down the wind!"

"Make no mistake, my lady," he said in a neutral tone with an underlying bite of sarcasm, "I like this no better than you do."

"And do you, my lord father, expect the *ton* to accept this? You, the highest of sticklers, giving the nod to a gazetted fortune hunter?"

"Perhaps I should have mentioned straightaway that I have engaged Cousin Knox to give this courtship the air of propriety," her father hastened to say.

"Cousin Knox!" Anne whispered, convinced by this news as by nothing else that her father was in deadly earnest.

"She will spend the Little Season with us."

"A sacrifice indeed!"

The suggestion of a smile curled the earl's mouth. "My atonement for insisting—and I do insist, Puss—that you convince Polite Society that you find him both an eligible and an acceptable *parti*."

"There must be another way!" she cried, flinging a harried glance at Cantor.

"He must have *entrée* to Darenth House—therefore to me—in such a way that will not be remarked," her father said.

"You could engage him as your secretary."

"And put Smythe in a snuff? I dare not, dear girl. Besides, it would not suit. He must continue in the Foreign Office."

At her wit's end, she cast a pleading look at Cantor and found him singularly indifferent to it. That indifference struck to her very soul.

"Let us end this brangling. I had enough to do in convincing Ka . . . Cantor to do this," said her father sharply. "I must have access to him at will. Have you not considered why, Anne?"

She had thought of nothing but of having Cantor near and unwillingly so. She had not considered her father's reason, nor did she want to now.

"I will have my revenge on Friedrich for Robbie's death," he said viciously, "and no man better than Cantor can aid me."

But revenge was what had gotten them here. A glance at her father's unyielding expression said he would not care to hear that. "And if Robbie is alive?" she asked.

"Then Cantor is the only man who can rescue him for us."

"Rescue!" Her wide gaze streaked to Cantor. "Is it possible?"

"Yes."

"W-won't that be . . . dangerous?"

He eyed her coolly. "Every care will be taken of your brother."

But her first thought had been for Cantor, whose level gaze now pressed hers down to the hands knotted fearfully at her waist. "Of course," she murmured breathlessly, shame staining her cheeks.

"I take it I may expect your compliance in this matter," said her father, pulling his watch from his waistcoat pocket. "Damn! I must be on my way! I want you two to spend the next hour—"

A clatter and chatter burst from the entry-chamber, flowing through the stairwell and into the drawing room. Hard upon it came the bellow of an unmistakable voice: "Announce me? Announce me indeed, nodcock! Step aside!"

The earl groaned. Anne turned to the doorway, her gaze wide and wondering. A moment later, the Duchess of Worth, more familiarly known as Cousin Knox, erupted through the portal, her bonnet askew and a fur tippet sailing behind her.

"What disaster has befallen?" she trumpeted, her pink pagoda parasol assuming the *en garde* position of a fencer. "Has that wretched gel absconded to Gretna Green with her . . . no, I see she's here. Aha! There you are, you delicious creature. So! You haven't made away with her. More fool you!" she enfiladed Cantor before turning on the earl. "It can only be Agatha. Well, tell me what it is. I shall forbear saying that I warned her—"

"Good God!" interrupted the earl. "What are *you* doing here?"

"Good God, indeed! You provoking ninnyhammer!" Cousin Knox rounded on him with a flame in her fine brown eyes. "You summoned me here."

"For the Little Season. Which happens," the earl added at a roar, "to be a fortnight away!"

"Am I to understand there is no disaster? No one ill, maimed, or dead?" The point of her parasol punctuated the list.

"I said in my billet—"

"Fustian!" crowed Cousin Knox, her squat, square body aquiver with indignation. "A piece of fiddle-faddling nonsense! What need have you of me to give countenance to Anne and her *parti*? There is more to this, Coz," she said ominously, "and I shan't oblige you until I know what it is!"

Despite the fury engorging his face, the earl flung Anne a desperate look. In no better humor than Cousin Knox, she was equally unwilling to oblige him. His gaze darted to Cantor, still standing before Cicero's bust.

He bowed deeply, a lock of golden hair falling across his brow. "This battle, my lord, is yours," he said, with a you'll-get-your-own-back-at-last smile.

"Well, Coz!" said Cousin Knox, her plump shoulders squared and her head reared back.

The earl heaved a disgruntled sigh. "Arabella, you could try the patience of a saint."

"And you, Coz, are no saint," she huffed on swelling notes. "I well remember the time you filled my bed with toads."

"Good God, Arabella! I was only nine—"

"And a wretched boy you were!"

The earl's rigid arm rose to point. "We will speak in the library."

She turned, pink ruffles adrift on the air, and aimed her parasol at Cantor. "You, my fine Corinthian, shan't leave till I've had a word with you."

"My pleasure, your Grace," he said equably.

They were alone: Anne and Cantor; Karl and Anne. Each conscious of that separateness, of each other, of the disappointment that scoured deep.

He had known she would object, but had not suspected how strongly. He had not known how much that would hurt. Damn Darenth! The earl had overborne his every protest, until he had conceded that

a courtship would serve their purpose as nothing
else could. Somehow now—his frowning gaze followed Anne to the bellpull—the prospect of Darenth's rage was less daunting than the disconsolate
curve of Anne's lower lip. They would have to find
another way!

His gaze skimmed her simple morning gown of
unadorned velvet, lingering on the square neckline
that revealed the vulnerable hollow of her throat and
the generous swell of her breasts. A thick, honeyed
heat sent his thoughts skipping along forbidden
paths. He reined them back with a vicious yank.

"Shall I arrange for tea, sir?" she asked, as if he
were a stranger.

A stranger, when they had shared . . . not enough
. . . never enough. "Brandy would be more in order," he found himself saying.

Her soft gaze touched him, set his heart to thumping, and skittered away. "I own there are times I
envy a gentleman his resort to strong spirits."

While he ached with a sense of coming loss, she
looked as if she could not be rid of him soon enough.
Resentment scalded him like lye. "Then join me,
Lady Anne," he said frostily. "I daresay the prospect of being courted by me has earned you that . . .
resort."

She looked up. Dwelling in the quicksilver depths
of her eyes was a shadow, like the bruise he felt
throbbing on his soul.

"No doubt, sir," she said softly, "it has."

A moment later the elfin butler entered, silent as
a cat. "Brandy for the gentleman, Rumford," said
Anne, adding, "and for myself."

His round eyes stretched to their limits. "F-for
you, milady?" he faltered.

"She has need of it," said Karl.

Rumford eyed Anne warily. "If you are sure, milady?"

"Quite sure."

The butler was gone. The log burning in the fireplace hissed and snapped. Outside, the wind sang an intimate song. An angry voice issued through the library door.

"Cousin Knox and Father . . ." She hesitated.

"Rub together like pumice stones," Karl finished for her, winning an all-too-brief, all-too-wan smile.

Looking more child than woman, she sat on the Wedgwood blue-and-cream-striped sofa, her small feet neatly aligned and her hands folded in her lap. But there was nothing childish in the gaze that lifted to search his, as if she sought the answer to a painful puzzle.

Now was the time to tell her he would not force her to this lick-penny courtship. Now was the time to say that this had been none of his doing. But his throat was so tight it was strangling him. Stretching his chin to ease it, he parted his lips to speak—and Rumford entered with a high-rumped expression, a silver tray in his hands.

"Sir," he said to Karl, his tone as flat as a griddle. "Milady?" he questioned Anne.

"Thank you, Rumford. That will be all."

With the butler vanished into the hinterlands of the house, Karl raised his fluted stemware in a toast. "To courtship," he said challengingly.

Anne paused, her glass at her lips. "To courtship," she echoed. The brandy pooled on her tongue and slid down her throat in a molten stream of bracing fire. Its thick aroma stung her nose and brought the sparkle of tears to her eyes, even as a spreading warmth aroused a heady glow of well-being.

She blinked rapidly, clearing away the tears and bringing Cantor into sharp focus. He had angled an elbow into the wall niche and leaned now upon it, his Hessians crossed at the ankles, his coat folded back and his thumb hooked into the pocket of his waistcoat. He had tossed off his brandy and set the glass aside and regarded her now with the beginnings of a smile.

"And do you still envy gentlemen their resort to strong spirits?" he asked.

"More than ever," she said, with a deplorable tendency to return his smile. To cover that failing she downed the healthy dollop that remained. The delicious heat came again. She blinked the sting of tears from her eyes and drew a breath that whooshed like the wind down her burning throat. "So much better than a hartshorn vinaigrette," she whispered, with the suggestion of a wheeze.

The smile hovering about his mouth was more a promise than a fact, but its warmth joined with the brandy's to induce in her a liquid languor. Though she yearned to yield to it fully, she couldn't forget her shock at her father's plan and her overwhelming disappointment that Cantor had obviously and bitterly opposed it. For that, it seemed, there could be only one answer. She had so disgusted him, he could not bear to be near her. She, who was traitor to her country, her father and herself, should have expected it sooner. She, who had refused to grant him the trust she demanded for herself, should have known that justice—cruel, blind justice—would be hers in the end.

She tilted her chin, searching for her battered pride. "I—I shall contrive to make this *courtship* as painless for you as possible."

His face grew as hard and cold as the marble bust at his elbow. "I doubt, my lady, that would be possible," he clipped out, as if he begrudged the breath that gave the words life. "Nor will your *sacrifice* be necessary. I shall inform your father that I will not be a party to this . . . travesty."

"T-travesty," Anne whispered, drawing a sharp look. Her lustrous lashes drooped over her eyes, shielding her despair. "Of course, it"—she swallowed the lump blocking her throat—"it could be nothing else."

Tears burned her eyes. Standing unsteadily, she moved to the window and turned her back on him.

"If you would care to leave now, I will tell my father."

"I won't leave you to bear the brunt of his anger."

But her father's anger meant nothing at all to her, while Cantor's throbbed in her heart, like an ache in old bones. And that ache pushed at the tears, forcing one through her lowered lashes to track slowly down her cheek. Surreptitiously she wiped it away and gathered her strength.

She turned briskly, her lips parting on an excuse—and surprised on Cantor's face an expression of anger and torment and longing. He looked away, his frown smoothing out and his mouth thinning. So quickly did he resume the cold, expressionless mask, she thought she had imagined it all. But loneliness and longing palpated through the chamber.

He stiffened and straightened, his broad shoulders squaring and his hands balling into fists. "It would seem that his lordship will be longer than we expected," he said harshly, as he turned to leave. "I will return—"

"Don't go!" cried Anne.

He wheeled around, caution in the gaze that sought hers. "What good will it do?" he began bitterly, breaking off with a visible struggle.

"There . . . there is something I must tell you before you go." She moved across the lush carpet, approaching so near she could have touched him had she dared. This might be her last opportunity, hard as it was. Her gaze climbed to search his face, moving lightly from the bold square of his chin to the firm set of his mouth, to the acquiline bridge of his nose, to his eyes. The cornflower-blue eyes that could sparkle with laughter and glow with passion were now blank and flat. An inauspicious beginning for the apology her pride demanded she give.

"I am so desperately sorry for what I said to you in Hyde Park. It was c-cruel and unfair. I should not have blamed you for doing what you believed to be

right. I cannot now blame you for never wishing to
see me again, but—''

''Anne, do you mean that?'' His strong hands
clamped around her arms, pulling her so close she
could feel his heart pounding in unison with hers.
''You can forgive me for telling your father—''

''Yes,'' she said breathlessly. ''Yes, I—''

''But you objected to his plan,'' he said, his gaze
probing hers with an intense question.

''As you did! You were so angry—''

''Because I wanted it too much and I knew—''
He leaned down, his voice low and husky, his lips
a breath away from hers. ''There are so many
things you don't know, so many ways I can hurt
you, and this, Anne''—his voice throbbed—''not
the least . . .''

His mouth claimed hers with a fierce desperation,
and Anne melted against him, welcoming the painful prison of his arms, the painful pressure of his
lips. Lips that tasted of brandy and desire's sweet
promises. Languor stole through her once more . . .

''I should say,'' shouted Cousin Knox, ''that we
needn't take pains convincing the *ton* which quarter
the wind lies in here!''

Anne and Karl parted, flushed, to see the earl
trudging into the drawing room, dragging a damp
and crumpled handkerchief over his sweating face.

His gaze met Karl's with a glower. ''The wretched
woman has had everything from me!'' His eyes narrowed meaningfully. ''Everything!''

Cousin Knox marched up to Anne and sniffed
suspiciously. ''Good God!'' She raised an accusing
glare to Karl. ''The gel is foxed!''

Cousin Knox became, Karl came to think, not so
much a chaperon as a bloodhound ever sniffing at
his heels. ''Persons of your order don't marry to
please themselves, so I shan't permit you to attach
the gel's attention, Cartwright,'' she warned. ''Not

at all the thing, and you—you provoking man!—are not, I trust, such an Out-and-Outer as to do it."

He was not. Nothing had changed—except the desire that grew minute by minute. Though he spent the days in Anne's company in a blaze of painful pleasure, he spent the nights in his bachelor lodgings in Ryder Street trying to find a way—any way—that he could marry his Anne.

He longed to forget everything and revel in her gentle smile, in the fleeting touch of her hand, and the healing properties of her loving gaze. But his duty did not vanish simply because he wanted to be happy. There were furtive exchanges of information and orders with Franz in the dark of night. There were meetings with Milling-Jemmy Shadwell, von Fersen's second-in-command, who demanded of Cantor the news from the Foreign Office. And that news was good. Napoleon had experienced his last great victory at Dresden in late August. Since then, his lieutenants had been thoroughly trounced by the Russo-Prussian–Austrian Coalition. Though the Confederation of the Rhine still maintained its allegiance to France, for the first time there was real hope of seeing Napoleon's end, and with him, the fall of Friedrich, Prince of Schattenburg. Karl could not abandon his quest now.

Though Cousin Knox was an incessant irritant, she was also a reminder . . .

At a card party at the Liverpools', Anne was partnered by a gawky youth and Karl by . . . Cousin Knox. When his attention wandered to the adjacent table, to Anne and the youth caught in the gawking throes of puppy love, Cousin Knox's peremptory fan rapped his knuckles and returned his attention to the cards.

Refreshments were served at midnight. While Cousin Knox gave the Prime Minister an unbridled critique of his domestic policies, Anne joined Karl at the sideboard laden with sweet biscuits, fruits, and clotted cream.

"I see that you've found another admirer, Lady Anne."

"Another?" Her inquiring gaze sparkled with ill-suppressed laughter.

"That sprig of fashion, who aspires to be a town buck of the first cut," Karl responded caustically, while reaching for a peach.

"Dashwood is quite charming, but"—deliberately reaching for the same peach, Anne caressed the knuckles that had been rapped earlier—"he has taken no wounds on my behalf."

Karl's grin spread slowly. "Perhaps, my lady, an apple would be more appropriate."

"And if I tempted you with it?" she asked softly.

"I should—"

"Good God, gel! Of all the Bath-miss manners!" cried Cousin Knox.

At a dinner at the Melbournes', Anne sat at one end of the table and Karl at the other—partnered by Cousin Knox. Said the wretched woman in an undertone that managed to travel the length and breadth of the table, "I trust you will devote the removes to Miss Fasham"—she indicated the singularly lackluster miss on Karl's right, whose only conversational ploy seemed to be nodding in agreement—"for it don't do to follow your own inclination to study Anne, as if she were a blooded mare at Tattersall's."

While the young ladies of the dinner party showed off their musical talents, Cousin Knox cornered the uninspiring Miss Fasham, giving her a lengthy list of topics for Polite conversation should her future dinner partners prove to be so unforthcoming as that coxcomb, Cartwright. Anne joined Karl on the settee. Under the cover of a vocal rendition marked by more enthusiasm than talent, she asked, with a quiver of laughter, "And did you devote the removes to—"

"As if you were not watching," Karl growled softly.

Anne covered her smile with her fan. "I pray you will forgive me, but you looked so . . . so exquisitely pained. It was quite a lesson for me."

"A lesson?"

Her eyes danced. "I had never realized how disagreeable being agreeable could be."

"A problem, sweet Anne, that you will never—"

"Fuss and botheration! I cannot turn my back for a moment," said Cousin Knox. "The *Oracle* had it right. We've nothing these days but 'Bucks without blood, Beaux without taste, and Gentlemen without manners.' "

In the crush of the Darenths' first at-home of the Little Season, Karl escaped Cousin Knox's eagle eye and found Anne at his side.

"She is, I believe, informing Prinny that his renovations of the Pavilion at Brighton are an insult to the delicate sensibilities of all of those with a sense of style."

Karl stared at Anne. "A trifle encroaching, even for Cousin Knox, isn't it?"

"A duchess of her standing could never be encroaching," Anne informed him with a laugh. "However, she can be aggravating—"

"Infuriating—" he added.

"And maddening," Anne finished.

Though they were ringed about, they formed a private circle of two. She settled a small hand on his arm, a hand that seemed to burn through the fabric of his coat and shirt to his flesh. Her gaze lifted to his, a lustrous silvery-gray that stroked away his irritation. A smile curled her mouth, simple and sweet and loving, and he thought his heart would burst with joy—until Cousin Knox's stubby finger prodded his shoulder.

Despite a frustration that had been pushed to explosive limits, Karl had no intention of further seeking out Anne—until Franz warned him that Shadwell had received Friedrich's answer to Anne's question.

Karl conceived an idea. It was borne of desperation and he executed it with military precision. In
the cool of the autumn noon, the Darenth barouche
bowled along country lanes with the top-hatted
coachman perched on the high seat and a liveried
postillion bouncing on the rumble. The tray of the
elegant black-lacquered body held Karl and Anne
and the ubiquitous Cousin Knox, and with them,
the earl and his countess. Darenth, fretted raw by
his nettling cousin, could be persuaded, Karl was
convinced, to give him a moment alone with Anne.

They dined in a private parlor of the Star and Gar-
ter atop Richmond Hill. When the last of the apple
tarts and cheese had been cleared away and the earl
had savored his brandy, Karl asked lightly, as if he
had not planned it all night, "Would anyone care to
enjoy the view?"

The earl, a dab hand at thwarting his cousin, sat
up in his chair, but it was the countess who settled
a restraining hand on Cousin Knox's thick arm. "I
confess to an astonishing lack of interest in a view
of the Thames." Her warm gray eyes flicked over
Karl with the sheen of a cognizant smile. "I pray
you, Cousin Knox, remain with me here."

The earl sprang from his chair with alacrity. Karl,
stunned by the ease with which he had obtained his
wish, was a second behind him. Anne rose as
quickly, gathering her pelisse and parasol with a
soft-voiced "The view is so exquisite here." All the
while her gaze lingered, not on the autumn scene
sprawling beyond the broad window, but on Cantor.

"Coz," blared Cousin Knox, jerking the earl up
short, "I am not persuaded that you know your
duty!"

"My duty, Arabella," he said frigidly, "is whatever I deem it to be!"

On the furzy broken ground outside the inn, the
earl stuck his cigar—that abominable contrivance of
the devil, Cousin Knox called it—between his teeth,

rammed his hands in his pockets, and ambled along. "I know now what it must mean to escape Newgate," he said with a sigh, then cast Karl a vexed glance. "I quite understand that I am *de trop*. Get along with you while you can. That wretched woman will come cackling quick as thought."

Karl needed no further inducement, nor did Anne. Though he would like to have taken her hand in his to flee, laughing like carefree children, he set out at a sedate pace and kept a proper distance. He had to tell her she would have her answer soon. He had to warn her she would not have that answer from von Fersen, but from Shadwell, a man more dangerous than the German.

From the brow of Richmond Hill spread the tranquil prospect of the broad valley of the Thames. The trees, burnished in autumn colors, spread down to the winding blue river speckled with skiffs the size of toys. Far off, in the purple haze, the hills of Buckinghamshire undulated beneath russet-red beeches, the downs of Surrey rolled beneath a golden carpet of gorse and heather, and the Berkshire heights rose humpbacked against the setting sun. Farther still, and dimly seen, was the majestic crown of Windsor, where the poor mad king strolled the North Terrace in his plain blue coat.

The air was perfumed by the scent of the sea rising from the Thames and of wood-smoke spinning up from the hamlet of Petersham, cradled in a loop of the river. The cool breeze lifted a lock of Anne's hair and sent it drifting out to lightly caress the smooth wool of Karl's coat. A caress that he felt as if it had been on his bare flesh instead. He swallowed hard and wrenched his gaze away from her delicate profile, only to find it returning, lingering, yearning.

"Lovely," she said, gazing into the distance.

"Lovely," he echoed, on a husky note of intimacy.

Her head turned, and the ebony lock clung to him,

the curl stretching straight until it ripped reluctantly away. Her small chin climbed slowly. Her silvery gaze meshed with his.

He was acutely aware of the nearby couples strolling on the brow of the hill. He was more acutely aware of the pounding of his heart and the weakening of his will. "Friedrich has sent an answer to your question," he said softly. "You will be summoned to a meeting on the morrow."

The inner light of hope illumined her face. "The answer?" she asked eagerly.

"I don't know what it is, only that it has come." He stared out over the broad valley below. "You will not be meeting von Fersen, Anne."

"But he—"

"Is being held under close arrest by Castlereagh's order."

"Why? He is the man who—"

"Learned too much about . . . me." He should tell her who he was, what he was, what he had to do! Still, he could not. Why? Why was it so hard to trust her in this matter?

"He . . . he learned that you are an agent for my father?" Anne, studying his face, saw the taut rigidity of emotions ruthlessly controlled.

"Yes," he said shortly, with an unfinished sound, as if there was something more he wished to add.

When he did not, she touched his arm and felt the muscles wrench tight and hard. "Then who will I see?"

"Milling-Jemmy Shadwell." His gaze lowered to hers with a frown. "Take care with him, Anne. He is more dangerous than von Fersen ever thought to be."

"Cantor," she said softly, "if Robbie is alive—"

"Don't hope for that!" His hand covered hers, pressing gently. "You will be bitterly disappointed."

"But I know he is alive. Even before von Fersen came to me, I could not *feel* that he was dead. Can't you see?'' she pleaded. ''If anything had happened to Robbie, I would know it. Just as I would know if anything happened to you. Some ties of the heart are so strong that—''

''Don't say it, Anne! For God's sake, don't say it!''

Chapter 14

Milling-Jemmy Shadwell's mammoth frame overflowed a scratched and battered Chippendale chair whose joints creaked with his every move. He had flung the crimson curtains wide, permitting the mid-October light to pour over the dusty surfaces of Chumley's irregular room. Caught in the sun's full glare while Shadwell claimed the shadows, Anne longed for the concealment of gloom.

Shocks of black hair, untamed by the bone comb tapping his thick knee, lurched around his head in a satanic halo. With von Fersen Anne had sensed pleasure in her misery. With this man she sensed nothing. The soulless black eyes glittering from the pale round moon of his face told the tale. He was utterly without humanity, lacking even the avarice and ambition she had sensed in von Fersen. Cantor was right. He was more dangerous than the German ever thought of being. Her hands trembled in her swansdown muff.

A powerful man, all muscle and bone, he stood slowly on the massive trunks of his legs, like an ancient oak reaching for the sky.

Anne's heart pounded against the fall of goffered muslin spilling across her breast.

He curled the great hams of his hands into fists and jammed them against the thick swell of his hips, setting his meaty arms akimbo. His huge head tilted back, and his black eyes rolled down to stare across the leathery planes of his cheeks.

Anne retreated a step. She wanted to demand the answer to her question, but her lips were frozen stiff.

"The murder hole," said Milling-Jemmy, each word rolling like thunder.

Anne blinked.

His full pink lips puckered beneath a ghastly frown. "The murder hole," he repeated, louder, as if he doubted her hearing.

A memory came to her, resonating with the thunder of Shadwell's answer. *Don't be afraid, Puss!* Robbie's voice, shrill with youth and fright, shouted across the years. *I'll save you! I'll save you!* Only he knew of their dangerous moonlit exploration of the crumbling ruins of Darenth Castle. Only he knew that she had fallen into the dark, seeping depths of the murder hole.

Robbie was alive!

Tension, fright, and grief draining from her in a rush, Anne stumbled to the massive four-poster bed and sagged against a dusty column. Her head drooping and the swansdown muff pressed to the runaway beat of her heart, she whispered a silent prayer of thanksgiving while tears of relief streamed down her cheeks.

He was alive! Someday he would come home again with his violet eyes atwinkle and his smile wide and loving. Pray God, it would be soon!

"Ye'll come again on the morrow, milady," rumbled Milling Jemmy matter-of-factly, "and ye'll bring me what I'm wantin'."

Her gaze climbed to his empty eyes. Her ordeal wasn't over, but she hadn't expected it to be. Now, at least, there was hope.

In the cool elegance of the drawing room at Darenth House blue velvet draperies barred the sunlight and a fire burned in the hearth. Lady Darenth, parchment-pale and trembling, had resorted to sip-

ping brandy. The earl, with a fine inattention to the
liquor's heady bouquet or fruity flavor, gulped his,
bellowed for more, and began to pace once again.
Cousin Knox reigned over a corner of the settee, her
bronze gown crumpled around her, her plump fingers drumming on her empty glass, her eyes following Darenth as if she longed to trumpet a command
to sit and be still. Karl, his elbow angled into the
wall niche and his Hessians crossed at the ankles,
had discovered that his clenched throat admitted
nothing more than a trickle of air. His brimming glass
remained untouched at the foot of Cicero's bust,
gleaming in the weak wash of candlelight.

"Could anything have happened to her?" The
countess raised a pleading gaze.

"Good God, Agatha!" burst out Cousin Knox.
"I wish you will not ask that again! He's told you
a brace of times that he has men watching her! They
will see her safe! And if they should fail, the gel's
pluck to the backbone! Aye! A Ransome through
and through! More mettle than sense! I have no
doubt—"

"Take a damper, Arabella!" shouted the earl,
looking as though he would like to gnash his teeth—
with her throat firmly clenched between them.

To Karl's astonishment—and the earl's if his gaping mouth told the tale—Cousin Knox subsided with
a breathy grumble. Karl's gaze, carefully dispas-
sionate, met Darenth's. Both knew Anne could be
protected only so far. Once she was alone with
Shadwell, no one could safeguard her. Damn!
Would she never come?

His raging impatience was concealed by the
indolent drape of his frame and his carefully
schooled features. They would all have the answer
soon. Robert Bragg Ransome, Viscount Langley.
Alive or dead?

Karl envisioned Anne as she had been atop Richmond Hill. The autumn breeze toying with her ebony curls and molding her skirt to her slender hips.

Her lips curving sweetly and her eyes shining brightly, and he, aching with desire and fear.

If anything had happened to Robbie, I would know it, she had said. *Just as I would know if anything happened to you. Some ties of the heart are so strong that—*

Ties of the heart. But there were other ties that bound him: kinship, friendship, and honor. Though he might long to sink his teeth into those bonds and tear them away, he could not. His throat convulsing, Karl yearned for the brandy he could not swallow. Even more, he yearned for the words he had not dared allow Anne to say. The words that would tie him to her, irrevocably.

Suddenly Anne burst into the drawing room, her small feet skimming the carpet as if she might take wing and fly. Her face was pink with exertion and joy. Her eyes sparkled like diamonds over a brilliant smile. "He's alive! Robbie is alive!"

Karl stiffened, straightened, and shot a quick look at Darenth, who had frozen in the act of pulling his watch from his pocket. His shocked gaze followed his daughter to the settee where her mother surged to her feet with a glad cry. They embraced, ebony curls and silvery tears mingling with sobs and laughter.

Anne's vibrant smile tore at Karl's heart. Even now, he could not help but believe she had been duped. The earl, tucking his watch into his pocket and frowning, appeared to think so, too.

"Well, gel!" blared Cousin Knox. "Did he pitch you a bay of moonshine, or do you have proof?"

Anne tossed aside her swansdown muff and yanked at the ribbons of her bonnet. All the while her dancing gaze lingered on her father. "There is no doubt. Only Robbie could have answered my question. Only Robbie knew that I had fallen in the murder hole on—"

"The murder hole!" the countess said weakly.

"Anne, you are sure of this?" asked the earl, his expression that of a man poised on the brink of hope,

but sure that only the chasm of grief awaited his first
tentative step.

She flew to him, her eager hands gripping his
arms, her shining face tilted up. "Yes, Father! Yes!
No one—no one!—but Robbie could have answered
my question."

"Anne," he said, his voice trembling, "you are
sure Friedrich could not have learned this earlier
and—"

"You know what his word of honor means to
Robbie! You know he would never break it! Never!"
she said urgently. "That night we made a pact that
we would never tell what happened. He swore on
his word of honor and I swore on mine—though,
wretch that he is, he considered that to be of little
worth."

The earl drew a long, shuddering breath. Anne
could see her father's belief growing. Acceptance
came at last with a smile and a rush of tears that
clung to the rims of his lashes. Stiffly shrugging from
her light grasp, he turned to the hearth. One shaking hand slipped into his pocket, the other gripped
the mantel, and his proud head bowed.

The countess moved to him slowly, hesitantly. Her
hand trembled against his arm, and he spun around
with a muffled cry, catching her in his arms and
holding her in a crushing grip. "Thank God! Thank
God!" he exulted.

Karl, unable to intrude on that intensely private
moment, looked away and found Anne smiling up
at him.

"He's alive," she said on a pulsating note of happiness.

"I'm glad for you, Anne," he said softly. Though
he was, he couldn't return her smile.

She took a step toward him, then checked, her
eyes widening on a question. He opened his arms,
and she flew into them with a happy laugh. Cradling her close, he drank deep of her joy and of the
fleeting pleasure of having her close.

"I've never been so happy!" Her arms slipped around his waist to hug him close, and her cheek nestled against his broad chest.

She would never be happy again if he took her away, Karl thought heavily. Away from the family she loved, the brother she adored. Her first, most lasting loyalty was to them. She needed them as she would never need him. She was wholly theirs, as she would never be wholly his. And he was a fool to suffer this pain, when she was forever denied him by the circumstances of his birth and the life that had been—and would continue to be—mere existence without her.

His lips pressed gently to her feverish brow. Over her head his eyes met Cousin Knox's steady brown gaze, holding equal measures of pity and dread.

"Am I," she began briskly, hauling herself from the settee, "the only one who has not been driven to distraction by this news? Robbie is alive. Now, what do we do about it?"

Anne tensed in Cantor's arms. Turning slowly, she felt the dragging reluctance of his loosening hold. She had not thought so far ahead. It had been enough to revel in the freedom from grief, in the release from guilt, in the soaring excitement of knowing her brother was alive. It had been easy to silently swear she would do anything to bring him home—when she had forgotten it was not she who would be facing danger and possible death.

"I will leave for Schattenburg as soon as I can to effect his release," Cantor said, his chest vibrating against her tense shoulders.

"No!" The heedless, thoughtless protest rushed from her throat and spilled from her lips.

Cantor froze into a haunting, waiting, breathless stillness. Cousin Knox jerked upright, her brown eyes wide. Her mother wheeled around in the embrace of her father's arms, both wearing expressions of astonishment and disbelief.

Anne's despairing cry lingered on the air. Shame

flooded her with remorse, but the terror would not release her. It screamed that Cantor would enter the frightening realm of von Fersen's utterly ruthless master to rescue her brother. And if he was captured—

"Anne, what are you saying?" her father asked thickly.

His frowning features held disappointment and questions she could not answer. She could not tell him that, no matter how much she wanted Robbie safe, she didn't want Cantor in danger!

"Anne," said Cantor, his melodic voice dipping into its deepest registers, a silver-toned lyric of hope.

But why that hope? she wondered. Surely he knew she would not gladly see him leap into danger. Surely he knew that a choice between him and her brother would tear her apart—as it was doing now.

He touched her arm. She flinched away and heard the swift intake of his breath.

"Anne," her father said, "you cannot mean you do not wish us to rescue Robbie."

No! she wanted to scream. Only . . . only send someone else!

Her sorrowing gaze climbed slowly, pausing at the diamond winking in Cantor's cravat, moving slowly to the hint of a cleft in his chin and up to the rigid line of his mouth. "Won't it be . . . dangerous for . . ."

You. She couldn't say it. She could not betray that her fear was less for her brother than for Cantor, or that, if the choice was hers, she would save him before Robbie.

"For your brother," he finished for her, in a dark and dead tone from which hope had fled. "I give you my word, Anne, I will bring him home to you."

Blindly, her hand groped for his, found it, curled into the broad palm, and felt his impassioned grip return hers. Daring greatly, she raised her gaze to his eyes, dark in the shadows of his tawny lashes. She wanted to plead, to pray, to beg him not to go, but the words—those disloyal words—would not come.

Her father approached with a light, eager step. "Anne, what has Shadwell demanded of you?"

She released Cantor's hand and pulled away, as if distance might still her trembling fear. "M-more of the same," she said hoarsely. "I—I am to go to him on the morrow."

Her father, one arm draped lovingly around her mother, one hand tucking his handkerchief into his pocket, had shed years in minutes. The creases and crevices of grief and anger had smoothed from his face. Though worry carved a frown into his brow, his mouth had softened into a smile.

"Come, dear boy," he said. "We will prepare what Anne will take to Shadwell and make our plans."

Anne's sorrowing gaze followed Cantor to the library.

"He must go," Cousin Knox said gruffly. A sad, weary wisdom darkened her eyes. A wisdom that had plumbed the depths of Anne's shame, understanding and accepting.

"I know," Anne said softly. If only there was a way to save Robbie and protect Cantor.

"Foolish gel," Cousin Knox said in a caressing rumble. "Choices of the heart are never easy."

Even as Karl and the earl hatched their plans, an event was occurring that would change not only those plans but the course of history. The strength of the Allied army, sweeping across the wooded Saxon plains, clashed with Napoleon at Leipzig in a desperate seesaw battle.

While the great armies rested and awaited reinforcements on the following day, Anne hurried to Chumley's to meet Milling-Jemmy Shadwell. Her news was not good for the French, nor would it be of any worth to them by the time they received it. The Bavarians had renunciated their French alliance—the first crack in the Confederation of the Rhine. Wellington, triumphant from Spain, had crossed the Bidassoa into France.

While the sun climbed over the fertile Saxon fields, the reinforced Allies attacked on all points. The French died by the thousands, aged veterans and beardless conscripts. In the afternoon, while Karl met Franz in the fetid depths of Spitalfields to plot Robbie's rescue, Napoleon's strategy was suffering a mortal blow. The Saxon contingent of his German Legion deserted the French and turned their guns on them.

During the long night broken by the screams of the wounded, another man schemed as well. Safely ensconced in a farmhouse guarded by the broken remnant of the Lancers of Schattenburg, Prince Friedrich, his strong white teeth tearing at the flesh of a roast duckling, thought . . . and paused . . . and smiled.

Another sunrise saw the French retreating. The *Völkerschlacht*—the Slaughter of the Nations—was over. Though he survived to fight another day, Napoleon's hegemony in Europe was over.

The French reeled back to the Rhine in headlong flight. The Confederation of the Rhine crumbled. The German princelings scuttled after separate peaces with the Allies—all but the wily Prince Friedrich of Schattenburg, whose strategy was, as ever, tortuous.

Karl's plans were laid. The news was good. A travel-stained messenger panted up to Darenth's doorstep, touting the victory at Leipzig. The earl found the news nearly as welcome as the departure of Cousin Knox for her country seat in Surrey.

For Karl it was the first glimmer of the end of his lifelong wait. Soon he would seek his revenge and his crown. He would go home to Schattenburg, the place he had seldom visited, and then only furtively. He would regain his heritage and his life. He would no longer be a prince without a princedom, a man without a country. His fingers glided over the birthmark on his wrist—the mark of the rightful prince of the House of Schattenburg.

But first he must go in secrecy and danger once more. He must rescue Anne's Robbie. Ah, God! Her shrill *No!* pierced his dreams, wrenching him from sleep into sweating wakefulness. He had thought—he had hoped!—that she feared for *him*. But the fear and the love were all for Robbie. Karl carried that wrenching disappointment like a stone on his chest, until at last the preparations were complete. He and Franz were to sail on the next tide for the mouth of the Rhine . . .

"I fear another spoke has been stuck in the wheel, my lord," said Castlereagh on that chill November day. He sank gracefully into a wing chair, his fair brow puckered. "I have received a billet from Prince Friedrich that offers his personal service to us. A service that can be invaluable in the peace negotiations to come. As you know, he fought in Napoleon's *Grande Armée* and has made extensive contacts among influential Frenchmen. Better still, he has no small amount of influence with the Emperor himself. For the good of the realm, you must delay the rescue of your son."

Karl, standing before the blazing fire, settled a frowning gaze on Castlereagh's austere face.

"Damn!" burst out Darenth. "I cannot leave my son in his hands any longer! I cannot—"

"We have no choice. I must use any avenue of information that I can find. He—"

"And what," Karl interrupted harshly, "does Friedrich expect for his *service*, my lord?"

Castlereagh's gaze dropped. His fair skin flushed. "Nullification of the mediatization of Schattenburg," he said, with a quiver of distaste. "He wants the restitution of his principate as a sovereign nation."

Karl turned back to the fire. Awash in bitterness, he stared into the flames. "Since you have held out the same hope to both Friedrich and me," he asked acidly, "how will you solve this dilemma?"

"Karl, when the Imperial Diet reorganized western Germany in eighteen-hundred and three, it did so partly because it had hundreds of principalities that were too small to defend themselves. By incorporating them into larger states, the country as a whole was made stronger."

"And the mediatized princes became little more than ceremonial figureheads in their own castles," Karl said harshly.

"With certain rights and special status," Castlereagh added.

"And few responsibilities for the people their families had ruled and protected for hundreds of years."

Castlereagh's chair creaked as he rose. His steps whispered over the carpet, and his gentle hand gripped Karl's shoulder. "I'm sorry, but it will be impossible for either of you to hold more than the title and the family wealth and lands. You must understand our position."

"Must I?" Karl rejoined drily.

"I own you have a right to be disappointed, but—"

"Disappointed?" Karl shrugged away Castlereagh's hand and turned to face him. "Your extraordinary sagacity fails you, my lord! Disappointment is the least of the emotions I feel! You and he"—his head jerked at the earl—"have kept me dancing to your tune for twelve years! Why? Because you promised to reinstate my princedom if I would risk my life and that of my man in order to feed your voracious appetite for information. I, my lord, have kept my word. Now will you keep yours?"

Castlereagh's keen gaze met his squarely, revealing a hint of shame amidst a steely determination. "Karl, when the war is won, we will hold a great congress of all of the nations who have fought so bitterly to defeat Napoleon. I will be England's representative, and I have pledged myself to achieving a lasting peace. Through this long struggle, I have learned that nothing is more important than the balance of power in Europe. It cannot again be carved into petty princedoms that are unable to protect themselves."

Karl's chin angled up, his gaze coming around to stab at the earl. "And you, my lord? Have you known this since you came to me twelve years ago? Have you known this all the while you used me to protect *your* country and *your* people? Did you know it even as you pleaded with me to delay my return to Schattenburg, to delay the vengeance Friedrich has earned, to delay freeing my people of his vicious rule?"

The earl stood behind his desk, proudly erect. "No, Karl, I did not know it then, though . . ." He paused, his gaze falling. "I had begun to suspect that restitution of territorial authority to Schattenburg would be impossible."

"And now, my lord? What will you do?"

Darenth's gaze held the flinty light of a battered but rigid rectitude. "Nothing," he said softly. "I will do nothing."

"And your word of honor, my lord?"

"Is less important than a lasting peace for Europe, Karl."

They were right, both Castlereagh and Darenth. The future of a *petty* prince and his *petty* princedom were of less importance than a lasting peace for Europe. Intellectually, Karl accepted it, though everything in him rebelled against it. The House of Schattenburg had ruled from the heights of the Reisenburg for centuries. *Prinz* Karls had looked over the winding, wooded stream of the Neckar and had hunted in the dark silence of the Schattenwald for hundreds of years. Though at first they had been

predatory barons who plundered the river craft, they
had gentled with time. They had been loved by their
people and respected for their firm, but just, benev-
olence. And he, after the horror of Friedrich, had
planned to continue that ancient tradition.

He felt betrayed, and he had been, for the best of
reasons, with the best of intentions. Neither man
allowed him to give full vent to the fury churning
within him. How could he howl "Foul deceivers!"
when they were right? Damn, they were right! Napoleon's lust for conquest had ripped Europe apart.
It could not be allowed to happen again.

He had been raised on the princely virtue of self-
sacrifice for the good of his realm. Whatever his own
disappointment, his people would be stronger and
safer in a stable Europe. He must continue to work
for that end.

But the Countess of Darenth was neither farsighted nor self-sacrificing. She was a mother, her
son was in danger, and her husband could save him,
if only he would. "Why is it *impossible* to rescue Robbie now?" she demanded.

Karl shifted uneasily, fully aware that he was
caught in the midst of a private quarrel with no
graceful way to bow out.

"Agatha," said the earl, "Friedrich has offered his
services to Castlereagh. He has information—"

"What has that to do with Robbie?"

Anne watched her father sink onto the settee and
reach for her mother's hand, which she snatched
from him, as if he were a striking adder. Anne closed
her eyes, unable to watch the pain they inflicted on
each other.

"Aggie, I pray you, try to understand. We must
consider more than our son—"

"As you have always done!" she said bitterly.
"Tell me, John! Tell me it is for the good of England
that my son must suffer longer in Friedrich's hands.

Tell your daughter that you are neither man nor father enough to wrest your son from danger.''

Karl turned toward the curtains, staring through the crack onto the autumn day that held the same cold chill of the room.

''Mother,'' Anne protested softly.

''And you, daughter?'' Her father's ravaged face turned to her. ''Can you understand?''

''I—I know that you have always done, and will always do, what you believe to be right. I can respect that, even if . . .''

''Even if you cannot understand it.'' He stood slowly, his proud shoulders bowed. ''And do you believe that I should risk the safety of England to bring your brother home?''

Anne, like her mother, was not so farsighted. Her loves were more tangible than the love of king and country. Her hurting father; her grieving mother; her endangered brother; and Cantor: for them she would sacrifice anything. But what could she do when safety for one meant danger for another? Her gaze drifted to Cantor, standing with his back to the room. Robbie could be saved only at the risk of Cantor's life. Much as she loved her brother, she was painfully, shamefully glad that the rescue attempt must be delayed.

Her father sighed heavily. ''Agatha, I can do nothing but wait. As soon as Castlereagh gives his permission, I will see your son returned to you.''

''And what, John, will Friedrich have done to him while you await *permission* to save him?''

''Your pardon, my lord.'' Rumford came into the room and presented a letter on a silver salver to Anne.

She read in silent dismay: *My lady, I have the honor to inform you that a cottage bonnet is ready for your pleasure. Your ladyship's obedient servant, Chumley.*

A cottage bonnet. The signal that she was to come without delay. She looked not to her father, but to the silent man who had come to represent all security and hope. ''Cantor, it's from Shadwell. He wants to see me immediately.''

He turned, frowning. ''Does he say what he wants?''

''No, and he's never summoned me like this before,'' she said fearfully. ''What could it mean?''

Karl didn't know, though he didn't like it.

No sooner had Anne departed than another letter arrived, this one for the earl.

He read it rapidly and surged off the settee, his face chalk-white and his eyes dark with a mix of pain and rage. ''He's mad! Utterly mad! Read this! I cannot believe it!''

Karl snatched the stiff parchment from his hand. A bold sprawling signature leaped out at him— Friedrich Auguste, Prinz von Schattenburg.

Chapter 15

The countess wept. The earl paced. Karl stood before the bank of windows, every muscle bulged as if for imminent action. The weak autumn light sparkled over the cold sweat beading on his brow and running in rivulets that dripped from the rigid line of his jaw. Friedrich's letter was crushed in his white-knuckled fist, drawn up before him in a classic pose of threat.

But there was no one upon whom to vent the acid gusts of rage. He should have followed his own inclination twelve years ago. He should have taken Franz and gone to Schattenburg and murdered Friedrich! An eye for an eye! He should have taken his vengeance and won his throne—empty title though it was. He could have saved the earl this heartache, saved Robbie, saved Anne so much grief and fear and pain. He should have seen his duty more clearly. His duty to himself, to the restless dead in their graves, to the people who looked to the House of Schattenburg for succor. By following the earl he had betrayed them all and led them to . . . this. His burning blue stare lowered to his fist, to the creamy vellum crumpled around his clenched fingers.

He heard the distant rasp of the door, the murmur of the porter's voice, and Anne's light footfall. He sensed her presence as he always did, like a candle bringing warmth and light. He turned slowly, his fist dropping to his side, even harder, more strongly clenched than it had been. Did she know? Had Shadwell told her?

She appeared in the broad entry to the drawing room, her gray gaze as cloudy as the sky. He saw a darkness in her carefully schooled features, worry and fear, but nothing that said she knew the news that awaited her.

And when you learn it, Anne, what will you do?

She would keep her fears to herself, Anne determined. Shadwell had informed her that her services were no longer needed. She should have been relieved, but no relief had followed her unheralded release. There was no obvious reason to dismiss her now. The war in Europe was still undecided. The information she gave should still be necessary to Prince Friedrich.

Her cloudy gaze found her mother, sitting on the settee and crying bitter, silent tears. Terror sped through Anne, leaving her icy-cold and swaying. Had they learned what she feared had happened? That Robbie was dead and all was for naught? That Friedrich had taken his revenge on her father when he needed his son no longer?

Her father paced the length of the hearth with long, jerky steps. His jaw jutted, as if he stalked a foe. His hands clasped and unclasped, as if he longed to feel a throat between them. His profile was marked by taut lines of anger.

"Anne!" her mother gasped, bringing her father swinging around.

"Did Shadwell tell you?" he roared on a wrathful note. "Did he tell you what Friedrich has done?"

Anne's hand fluttered to the door frame. Shock leaching her strength away, she struggled to stand upright. A losing struggle until a strong, familiar arm banded her waist, until a deep, mellow voice murmured her name in a tormented, angry caress.

"Cantor," she whispered, turning into his embrace. "What . . . what has happened?"

She felt the rigidity of muscle and bone beneath the fingers gripping his arms. Her gaze rose to his face, finding the pallor beneath the sweat, the rage beneath the love, the measuring look in his stormy eyes.

"What has happened?" she repeated.

His tawny brows swept together in a frown. "What did Shadwell tell you?" he countered.

Her grip tightened on his unyielding arm. "That I am released from spying for him. That I no longer have to—"

"No doubt!" her father barked. "Friedrich will not have you risked now!"

"I—I don't understand." Her gaze raced over her father's face. She saw no sorrow, only a rage akin to Cantor's.

"Show her!" he bit out.

Cantor released her, stepping back and offering his clenched fist. His fingers slowly uncurled, and the crushed vellum crackled and moved like a thing alive.

"Read it," he ordered curtly.

His heat lingered on the creamy white surface with the sprawling signature that leaped out at her like a hand clutching at her throat: *Friedrich Auguste, Prinz von Schattenburg.*

She scanned it rapidly, broken phrases jumping into her mind to writhe in shocked disarray: *marriage to Anne . . . refuse and she will be exposed as a spy . . . your daughter the Prinzessin von Schattenburg, you will see that my principate is returned to me . . . when the question of Napoleon is settled and travel is safe in Europe, you will make the journey to Schattenburg for the marriage . . . refuse me, Darenth, and your son will be killed.*

Your son will be killed! The phrase obliterated Anne's shock and dismay. Robbie was still alive! And hard on its heels, another thought: Cantor would not have to be risked! She could save her brother and protect Cantor.

Karl, standing beside her with every muscle taut and aching, saw the smile that trembled across her lips. A smile! Incredulously, he watched her cradle Friedrich's letter to her breast, as if she cradled the man there instead. Nausea churned inside him, bubbling up to burn the back of his throat.

"Thank God! Thank God!" She sighed, sagging against the door frame.

Karl spun sway, stumbling to the hearth. One fist pressed against the marble mantel, the other dangling uselessly at his side, he stared blindly into the dancing flames.

"Thank God?" thundered the earl. "Have you run mad? That lecher insists on wedding you!"

"I know," said Anne, her voice as unsteady as the jolting beat of her heart. Her loving gaze lingered on Cantor's back. She couldn't say she would do anything to protect him from harm. His pride would not allow that. She could only give half of her reason, and whether it was the most important to her even she was not sure. "I thought I was released because Robbie was dead! But he isn't! He's still alive! There is still hope!"

Karl whipped around, staring at Anne. He should have known! Her brother! Always her brother! For a moment the hatred of Friedrich that boiled in his breast spilled over onto Robbie, the brother whom Anne adored to the exclusion of all else. He himself had been a fool to think he could ever woo her and win her away from her family. A fool—

"Hope?" The earl's voice held the cutting edge of a razor. "Hope, Anne? There is less now than there was! What do you think Friedrich will do when I deny him your hand?"

"But you cannot deny it!" Anne cried.

"Cannot?" came her father's subdued question. "You would not consider wedding that . . . that chartered libertine!"

She could ignore her fear no longer. It devoured her certitude, like a ravenous wolf with a lamb. Could she consider it, marriage to Friedrich? The man who had attempted her mother, dueled with her father, and imprisoned her brother? The man whom even his minion, von Fersen, called "ruthless"? Her wide, frightened gaze moved to Cantor, seeking strength to shore up the rapidly crumbling wall of her will. His hot, intense stare offered her nothing, not love or hope or strength. Yet all of those emotions tugged at her fearful heart. She knew only one thing. A rescue attempt might result in the deaths of both Cantor and her brother. How would she live with herself if she allowed that to happen when she could prevent it by the simple expedient of marrying Prince Friedrich?

Her sorrowing gaze moved over Cantor's face, absorbing its color, its chiseled contours, its captivating vitality, which seemed muted now, like a dying candle gasping in a puddle of wax.

Foolish gel, she remembered Cousin Knox's caressing rumble. *Choices of the heart are never easy.*

"Yes, Father," she said softly. "I would wed the devil himself if it would save Robbie." And Cantor, who turned his back on her to stare into the fire. What was he thinking?

"No, you will not," her father said firmly. "Robbie would not want to be saved at such a price, and I will not expose you to that *lecher!*"

"Nor will I," said her mother, rising slowly. "Anne, you do not know Friedrich as I do. He is vicious and cruel beyond belief."

"Mother, I cannot allow myself to be protected at the price of Robbie's life. You know that you, in my place, would make the choice I have made."

"Perhaps there is another way," interrupted Cantor in a curiously lifeless voice. He did not turn to them, but still stared into the fire, as if it held an undeniable fascination for him. "You could, my lord, agree to Friedrich's terms. We can do nothing until Castlereagh gives us leave to act. When he does, I can leave for Schattenburg and rescue your son. We will, in the meantime, have lost nothing and gained time.''

''Very well,'' agreed her father, his hard gaze shifting from Cantor to Anne. ''But the marriage is out of the question, daughter! We'll speak of it no more.''

''Yes, Father,'' she agreed softly, despite the rebellion in her heart.

''Excellent, Puss.'' His expression softened. ''You are too sensible to believe Friedrich would release Robbie, even with you as hostage to my goodwill in the matter of his principate.''

Her gaze drifted to Cantor, locking with his hooded stare. Even as her heart yearned toward him, a thrill of unease coursed through her. In his cold blue eyes there lingered a suspicion she dreaded and a look of betrayal she knew she had earned.

Betrayal. He shouldn't feel it, but he did. It gnawed at Karl like the hound gnawing on a discarded bone in the cobbled street beneath his bachelor quarters. He had only now come to the full realization that he had been released from those duties and obligations that required a wife of political convenience who could heal and bind the wounds of war. Castlereagh would have his way. The Congress would refuse to nullify the mediatization. Karl would return to Schattenburg not as a head of state but as an honorary prince. He was now free to choose as he pleased. Yet Anne was determined to marry his most bitter enemy in a hapless effort to save her brother. She had done what Karl expected her to do. She had done what she must.

Though the earl had seen only the surface agreement, Karl had heard her thoughts, as if she had spoken them aloud. She had no intention of allowing the rescue attempt. She would, if she must, escape them all and flee to Schattenburg alone. If he let her go, she would run into the arms of danger. If he stopped her, she might hate him. But stop her he would.

Her decision had seemed so easy in the light of day, but in the dark of night it scraped Anne's raw nerves like a stinging nettle. She would wed an old man, the lecherous attacker of her mother and the bitter enemy of her father. She, who was young and innocent, would be bedded by a man who was vicious and cruel and ruthless. She would never know what it was to love and be loved by someone who was young and kind and caring. She would never know what it was to be loved by . . . Cantor.

And she wanted to know what that love would be like. She wanted the whispered confidences in the dark of night, the silent communications of perfect understanding, and the passion that came from shared youth and love and dreams.

She closed her eyes and remembered the moist heat of his mouth cherishing hers. She slept and dreamed a sweet, heated dream that woke her at dawn with a smile. A smile that died under the prodding of an icy finger of fear.

Her father and Cantor could do nothing, but she could. She need not wait for a permission she would not receive. She dared not wait for the war to end, for then it might be too late. Cantor might be on his way. Robbie might have died. She must leave as quickly as she could and by stealth.

Her plan was simple. Perhaps too simple, she fretted. First, she must gain her father's permission to go to their country seat. Then, she would send the carriage on, take a hackney coach to the docks, and arrange transport to the mouth of the Rhine.

For one brief moment she shivered in her bed and wondered if she had the courage to follow her own plan. But the alternative was unthinkable. Lest her weakness betray her, she leaped from bed and summoned Bess.

* * *

Her father was in the midst of a hearty breakfast when Anne hurried into the dining room. The day was cool and gray with fog, but the chandeliers, ablaze with candlelight reflecting from swags of pear-shaped drops, created the aura of sunshine pouring over the sky-blue silk walls.

" 'Morning, Father.'' Did she look as guilty as she felt?

"Anne," he said, laying aside the *Times* and lifting his Sèvres cup.

While he sipped his coffee and regarded her cautiously, Anne moved to the sideboard *en suite*. She fixed a skimpy plate of bacon and toast, poured a cup of tea, and sat at the table, wondering how she would broach her request to leave for their country seat.

"My dear," he began, in a purposeful tone that brought her gaze up to meet his, "I hope you have, after a night's consideration, seen the folly of wedding Friedrich."

She stared at the thick slice of bacon curling over her plate. "Yes, Father."

"Your desire to save your brother is admirable, Anne, but you must see that your mother and I cannot allow you to sacrifice yourself."

"It was foolish, I know," she murmured, her heart thudding painfully. Lying to her father had never been easy for her, but now it was almost impossible. She could barely eke the words through the constriction of her throat.

"You look tired, my dear."

So did he. Anne studied his red-rimmed eyes and the lines of discontent etched around his mouth, the deeper lines of worry carved into his brow. He looked old, she thought with a pang of fear. For the first time he appeared old and worn and weary. She forgot that she had a plan and a purpose and a need to escape. She forgot everything but her father and her agonizing wish that all might be well.

"I wish we might remove to Darenth Hall," she said. "We were all so happy there."

A reminiscent smile softened his mouth. "Do you know what I've been remembering, Anne? The first salmon Robbie caught from the Darent. Gad! It was as big as he was, but he insisted on carrying it to the kitchen himself."

"Robbie was ever his own man, Father," Anne murmured.

"Even as a babe. He has ever been a son to make a man proud."

"It would have meant so much to Robbie to hear you say that, Father."

He looked away. Anne saw the convulsion of his throat and the suspicious brightness of his eyes.

"I wanted to tell him. Many times I came near to doing it, but something always . . ." He stopped and frowned and pressed his fists to his brow. "You never knew my father, Puss. Robbie is his image born again. Not only in looks. They had the same reckless, feckless ways. The same love of life and laughter. The same lust for adventure. They differ only in one way. My father was not an . . ." His fists lowered and his eyes met hers, and Anne saw the dark shadows of shame and pain. "My father was not an honorable man. His only loyalty was to himself."

"And you feared that Robbie would be like him in that, too," said Anne's mother, standing in the doorway.

Their eyes met, her father's a shamed, pained blue and her mother's a sorrowing gray. "Yes," he said raggedly.

"John," she whispered, "what evil did your father do that you now force yourself and your son to pay for his sins?"

He looked sick for a moment, his face stricken and white. Anne saw an expression like panic, a denial of the answer that came to him and a refusal to speak it aloud. The panic died and resignation came, as if he considered it a just punishment.

"After my father died," he began, his voice thin and sharp, "I found in his papers proof that he had sold military secrets to the American colonists during their war for independence."

"John," her mother said softly, "how much that must have hurt you."

And how much it explained, Anne thought. His rigid rectitude, his undying loyalty to king and country, and his stern disapproval of Robbie's childhood pranks.

"Agatha, can you understand why—"

"Yes, my dear, I can," she said, as tormented as he. "But I also understand that my son is in mortal danger, and only you can save him."

"I can save him if I am willing to become a man like my father. Agatha, even for Robbie, I cannot do it!" He tore out of his chair and strode from the room.

Anne now understood what had made her father the man he was. If anything she did stopped Friedrich from giving the English the information they needed, her father would see in her the seeds of his own father's disloyalty. He might despise her as he despised the memory of his father. Yet it seemed even more important that Robbie be rescued, that he and her father be given the chance to know and love each other. If Robbie died, would her father ever forgive himself? Would her mother ever forgive her husband? Anne couldn't weaken now. She must be strong.

"Mother," she said, rising, "I would like to leave for Darenth Hall at noon."

Her mother, knowing how Anne reveled in the peaceful prospects of the Kent countryside, had given her permission easily, which heightened Anne's guilt. A guilt that did not stop her from calling a halt to the traveling chaise and sending it on while she and Bess caught a hackney coach for the London dock. She would have two days before the chaise-and-four returned to St. James's Square. Two days before her parents learned she had not gone to Darenth Hall. What they would think, she wouldn't allow herself to imagine. What they would feel, she dared not consider.

A light fog blanketed the docks where fleets of sailing vessels wallowed and creaked on the heaving, surging Thames. The air was ripe with the scents of tar and hemp and rotting wood. Anne studied the ghostly fretwork of masts and spars and rigging swaying through the cold, wet curtain of the fog. One of those ships would carry her to the mouth of the Rhine—if only she could remove Bess from the safety of the hackney coach.

"Why did I listen to ye, milady!" her abigail wailed, clinging to the door as if a barbarian bent on rapine threatened to drag her away.

"I should have come alone!" said Anne impatiently, her foot rapping an irritated rhythm on the dank, dirty dock.

"No! No, milady!" Bess's bulging eyes blinked rapidly. "Milady, yer on a fool's errand! Ye should have told his lordship! Ye should have told her ladyship! Ye should have—"

"And I'm telling you, I shall leave you here if you do not—"

"No," Bess wailed, releasing the door so precipitately she stumbled over a coil of rope and careened through the fog into a pyramid of wine tuns.

Anne rushed to her side, dusted her off, and adjusted the brim of her poke bonnet. The cluster of cherries atop it trembled like Bess's mouth. "Remember what I told you. Robbie is alive. I must get to Schattenburg, Bess. I must. It is the only way to save him."

"I can scarcely credit it, milady! But his lordship—"

"My father's hands are tied. He can do nothing

at all, and I can do nothing without your help. I pray you, Bess, help me. Help Robbie.''

"Ye should have brought a footman, milady! Traipsing around the London dock without a strong arm, we'll be accosted by"—her frightened gaze followed the drunken sailor lurching past—"all manner of evil men.''

"We'll be perfectly safe, Bess.'' Anne rapped the length of blackthorn against a wine tun. "I've brought my father's sword cane.''

"Oh, milady, milady! Ye . . . ye wouldn't use it,'' she said faintly.

"I assure you, I would not hesitate.''

Bess's eyes rolled up in her head. She oozed a soft whoofing sigh and sank, ungently, to the oaken timbers of the dock. Anne, burning with impatience, scrambled through her well-stuffed reticule for her hartshorn vinaigrette. Kneeling, she cupped Bess's head in her hand and passed the porcelain bottle beneath her nose.

The sounds of the dock mocked her hurry. Water slapped idly against the timbers. Masts creaked lazily. A muffled "Hallo!'' echoed through the fog. Seagulls squabbled nearby.

"Bess! Bess!'' she hissed. "Don't do this to me—''

"Perhaps I can be of service, my lady.''

The deep, melodic voice turned Anne's blood to ice. She swiveled on her knee, staring at Hessian boots whose mirrorlike shine was marred by dewy droplets of water. Her gaze climbed the long length of leather-clad thighs, up to the blue coat decorated with brass buttons, up to a harsh and handsome face.

"C-Cantor,'' she whispered in dismay. The fog shifted around him, masking the expression in his eyes, an expression she feared was as cold as the tone of his voice.

Bess snuffled and coughed and moaned piteously.

"Your woman hasn't the spirit for intrigue, my lady.''

"I-intrigue? I—I'm sure I don't know what you mean. Bess and I were . . . were simply seeing the sights of the London dock."

Bess struggled up, her eyes widening on the welcome sight of a protector. "Mr. Cartwright! Oh, sir! It's all me fault! I would let her embark on this mad escapade!"

"There is no need," Anne warned.

But Bess, once begun, was not to be halted. "Taking ship for Germany, and all to rescue her brother! I pray you, sir, stop her!"

His hard gaze shifted to Anne. "I assure you, Miss Ledbetter, I intend to do just that. And I will begin by taking your weapon, my lady."

Anne's heart trembled in her breast. "Cantor, you can't think that I would use this on you!"

"I think, my lady, that you would do whatever needs to be done."

She could feel rage stirring in him, reaching out to grasp her. "If you really think so ill of me, then let me go! Let me do what I must!"

"Anne," he gritted out, "if you have any care for your own welfare, you will get in that hackney and not speak another word to me."

Karl returned Anne to Darenth House in a thunderous silence, during which even Bess dared not sniffle. He seethed with a rage that threatened to break out into violence every time he dared to glance at Anne. She remained undaunted, uncowed, with her back as straight as a queen's and her expression as proudly haughty. But it was not her expression that curled his hands into fists. It was a fleeting look in her eyes that said *he* had hurt *her!* The temerity of it—by God, the gall!—set his teeth to grinding.

He stared blindly at the passing scenes while the rage gnawed through the best of his intentions. He knew that part of it was given flaming birth by his bitter disappointment. Anne was all too eager to wed Friedrich! Another part came from the fear that she might succeed, and then what would happen to her? What would that vile and vicious man do to his Anne?

Karl's gaze drifted to the dainty profile peeping beyond the brim of her bonnet. A soft sigh parted her lips and set the lower one to trembling. His strong white teeth sank into his own lip, as if he could chew that tremor away.

She had made her choice, he told himself. If he stayed near her, he would be torn apart. Even now desire warred with rage, softening it when he wanted to hold it as close as a lover . . . as close as he wanted to hold Anne. Damn! He'd leave her to her father! He could not, would not, stand watchdog over her any longer!

At Darenth House, he brushed aside the gaping porter and hauled Anne into the library, one hand clamped around her arm. Even that angry touch weakened his resolve and, conversely, hardened it.

"Here, my lord, is your wayward daughter!" He stood her before the desk and backed away, squaring his feet and folding his arms over his chest. "I found her on the London dock preparing to set sail for the mouth of the Rhine."

The earl lurched up from his chair. "The London . . . the mouth . . . Anne! Anne, how could you?"

She stood her ground, her stance proud and her head unbowed. Karl felt a sneaking pride that he quickly squelched.

"You taught me, Father, to do what I believe to be right."

"And you believe this to be right? To sneak away like a thief! To risk your life, Robbie's life, the future of England!"

"Nothing need be risked if I go alone! Friedrich still needs your help in the matter of his principate. He would not dare stop giving the information England needs."

"I have told you, Anne," the earl roared. "I will not allow you to wed Friedrich! And, my headstrong girl, I will see that you do not do this again. You will go to Darenth Hall where a footman will be stationed at your door by night and Cantor at your side to guard you by day.''

That was not part of Karl's plan. He stepped forward. ''My lord, I have no desire to play warden to your daughter, nor can I. Have you forgotten that Shadwell expects reports from me?''

''That, dear boy, can be easily remedied. If Castlereagh releases you from your duties in the Foreign Office, then Shadwell will have no further use for you.''

Chapter 16

⁓⌒◯◯⌒⁓

Darenth Hall gazed down on the winding ribbon of the River Darent from atop a humpbacked hill skirted with winter-bare ash and alder, holly and fir. Save for the red brick that had weathered to a silvery pink, the manor had changed little in its two hundred and twenty-five years. The mullion and transom windows, the bay windows, the balustraded terraces, gardens, and gazebos still spoke of the Elizabethan passion for symmetry and the loyalty of generations of manor lords to their heritage. All was as it had ever been, except for one thing. Robbie wasn't there to fly up the stairs, his cheeks red with cold, his eyes sparkling, his laughter echoing from the wainscoted walls to the geometrically patterned plasterwork ceilings.

Anne climbed to her chamber with a listlessness feigned for the discreetly trailing footman, while Karl abused an expensive brandy in the cozy salon overlooking the moonlit topiary garden.

All had worked as the earl had planned. Karl had been dismissed from the Foreign Office. Shadwell had promptly lost interest in him, something his superior would never have done. Von Fersen enjoyed watching his fish squirm on the hook, while Shadwell knew when to cut bait and run. Karl wished he hadn't. He wished he wasn't here with Anne above and—

The scurry of feet and a wailing, ''Your Grace!

Your Grace!'' heralded the arrival Karl had been awaiting.

"Good God!'' Cousin Knox marched in like a grenadier. "Has my coz run mad? Why have you and the gel been sent here alone?''

"But we aren't alone, your Grace. You have been summoned to give us countenance.''

"Impertinent wretch!'' she trumpeted. "I shan't be fobbed off so easily!''

And she wasn't. She had a ferret's nose for the concealed detail and a magistrate's way with a question. Karl found himself sitting straight as a schoolboy at lessons and sweating like a felon before the bench. She brooked no evasion, saw through every half-truth, and accepted nothing less than a full disclosure. In the end, she had wrung everything from him, just as she had from the earl. Sweating profusely, Karl felt a glimmer of sympathy for Darenth and a malicious desire to see Cousin Knox's bed filled with a knot of toads.

"So!'' She sank back in her chair, thrusting her feet out and wriggling her toes. "You are free to wed her.''

Karl eyed her warily. There were depths to the squat, square Dowager Duchess of Worth he wasn't sure he was man enough to handle. His only comfort was the thought that neither was the Earl of Darenth.

"Well?'' she blustered.

"Well what, your Grace?''

"Well—you impudent bantling!—are you planning to ask her to wed you on the morrow?''

"No, your Grace, I am not.''

"You are not?'' she echoed, sitting forward.

He—the rightful Prince of Schattenburg, a fearless spy who had easily duped men high and low—squirmed in his chair. "The time is not right.''

"The time, my fine Corinthian, has never been more right! You do not deal here with an addlepated moonling, but with a Ransome! She has spirit! Too much spirit to accept a single setback to her plans. The gel is, no doubt, hatching another as we speak. You must see that if you shackle her with a bethrothal, she—"

"Will do precisely what she deems right. When I ask Anne to marry me, it will be for no reason but my desire to have her as my wife."

"If you told her who you are, if you explained—"

"I can't!" Karl shot out of his chair.

"I don't see the problem," she bellowed, then paused. "Surely, you cannot think Anne would betray you to Friedrich!"

Karl raked a savage hand through his hair and clamped his fingers around the nape of his neck to knead the tension away. "I believe, your Grace"— he stared out over the topiary, whose shadows fell in eerie shapes as dark as his thoughts—"that Anne will do whatever is necessary to save her brother."

"Fustian! The gel is mad for you! A choice between you might tear her apart, but she would never betray you!"

"I . . . I would like to believe that, your Grace, but . . ."

A tense silence lingered.

"But you are unwilling to take the chance," she said in a soft, gravelly tone. "Did you ever stop to think that Anne might be as afraid for you as she is for her brother?"

Karl spun around. "What?"

"You wretched boy! I am not yet too old to remember my youth. I had a *parti* who, if he would have had me for more than my dower, I would have waged war on the devil himself to protect. Can you not see that Anne might fear the consequences of a rescue attempt not only for her brother, but for you?"

"She wouldn't—"

"She would."

At that moment, a flustered chambermaid was flitting into Anne's bedchamber carrying an oaken bucket overflowing with a tin of beeswax and clean linen cloths. "Dust, milady?" she said, dipping a curtsy and scanning the chamber. "Where? Where?"

"There is no dust, Hetty. I needed an excuse to summon you here."

"An—an excuse, milady?" Her myopic hazel eyes blinked rapidly.

"I need your help, Hetty."

"Oh, no, milady!" She backed to the door. "I remember the time ye and Lord Robbie caught me up in yer pranks! The bishop, he were ever so angry, milady! Ye'd have thought he'd never seen a grass snake afore!"

"No doubt he hadn't seen one served on his plate." Anne captured the rough work-worn hand that was reaching for the door. "Hetty, this isn't a prank. Robbie's life is in danger—"

"Oh, milady, Lord Robbie's dead! We all know that!"

"No, he's alive and I have to save him. Please, help me."

Hetty Peabody's thin shoulders sank beneath a forlorn, submissive sigh. "Milady, ye and Lord Robbie 'ull be the death o' me yet."

Anne didn't pause for relief, but pulled Hetty across the chamber into the window oriel. "Can you get out of the house tonight and go to Granny Goody's?"

Hetty gave a hesitant nod.

"Tell her I will be bringing a man to her cottage on the morrow. I want her to serve him a sleeping potion in tea."

"Milady! Wh-what are ye doin'?"

"He's guarding me, and I must escape him."

"Guardin' ye, milady!" Hetty's myopic eyes stretched wide. "Well . . . well . . . ye know Granny Goody 'ud do anything for ye, only . . . only me sister Letty's increasin'! Lor', milady, is she increasin'! She'll drop the babe any minute, an' Granny'll be called to midwife."

"Then tell her to leave the potion in a cup on the table if she has to leave." Anne fought back a shudder. Would Cantor ever forgive her for this? "I'll give it to him if need be."

"Then I'll be on me way—"

"No, Hetty, there's something more. I'll need a lady's maid on my journey to the Rhine, and I want you to come with me."

"Lor', milady! Ye got Mistress Ledbetter for that!"

"I can't trust Bess not to betray me. Can you find some reason to leave your duties for a few days?"

"Aye, milady! I've been given leave to help Letty wi' the new babe when it come." Hetty's thin body quivered with a sudden inspiration. "It's a *adventure*, milady, like Lord Robbie was ever speakin' of. Like when he led us all to—"

"Yes, yes, an adventure," Anne said quickly, before Hetty could remember the disastrous ends of most of Robbie's escapades. "You'll have to find a way to Gravesend. I'll meet you at noon by the Church of Saint George."

"If ye'll have yer trunks wi' ye, milady," said Hetty, launching into the spirit of her adventure, "I'll hire—"

"There will be no trunks. I do not—"

"Ye can't travel wi' out yer trunks! Leave 'em to me, milady," said Hetty, blushing to the roots of her hair. "There's one here who'll help me, and none the wiser."

Karl spent a sleepless night cursing her Grace, the Duchess of Worth. As much as he wanted to believe her, he could not. Anne could not labor under the delusion that she could protect him as well as her brother. Yet if she did, he had to tell her who he really was. She must know that he *would* confront Friedrich, either sooner to rescue her brother or later on business of his own.

By morning Karl was in a thoroughly foul mood

that evaporated like sun-kissed mist the moment he saw Anne garbed in dawn's pearlescent light.

She sat in a window seat, sipping tea and staring out over the Elizabethan knot garden below. The day promised to be as foul as Karl's mood had been, but her black velvet riding habit said she planned to risk the uncertain weather.

A growl of thunder rattled the mullioned windows as Karl approached. Would he see it in her eyes, the need to protect not only Robbie but him? She turned to face him. In the starry gray of her gaze he saw caution and fear, grief and guilt.

Grief and guilt. Anne had spent the night in a fruitless battle against them, but neither had abated. Neither had her plans changed. She rose slowly, feeling as weak as cambric tea.

"What is wrong, Anne?" he whispered, his voice low and deep and smooth as the dark velvet of her gown.

"Nothing."

An eddy of pain and doubt darkening his eyes, his head lowered. His lips touched the tremulous curve of her mouth. Gently, so gently, his lips idled over hers, as if their enemy Time had become a friend instead. And indeed it seemed to Anne that Time paused and waited with a smile. Cantor's downy touch tenderly abraded her willing mouth. A touch that tingled in the palms of her hands and in the fulling peaks of her breasts. Her lips flowered beneath his, yielding her all to the sweet wonder of his foraging tongue. She tasted the spice of desire, heady and potent. Moist to moist, hot to hot, velvet to silk, Cantor stroked the recesses of her mouth with the fluttery touches of a bee gathering nectar. A languorous heat melted through her. His lips slid to the corner of her mouth, tarried through infinity, then moved across her cheek to meet the furry barrier of her beaver hat.

"Ah, Anne, Anne," he said softly, her name broken by his rasping breath.

She wanted to respond, but she couldn't summon the strength to speak. Her tongue wafted across her aching lips, seeking the taste of him yet. His thumb caressed the gentle curve of her chin and glided up to the crest of her cheekbone, while the searing heat of his gaze probed hers.

"You are more than a daughter and a sister, Anne. You are a woman, too. A woman capable of great passion and great love. If you think I'll make it easy for you to escape me"—the ruthlessness in his gaze became more pronounced—"I warn you now, I won't. If I can, I will make it impossible."

And he very nearly did. She wanted nothing more than to remain in his arms. She wanted nothing more than a life at his side. But that life could be bought only with her brother's life. She stretched up on tiptoe and pressed her lips to his. The Judas kiss of betrayal.

"Ride with me, Cantor."

The rising wind tumbled fat gray clouds end over end and whipped the lofty crowns of the horse chestnuts guarding the long avenue. Cantor's cupped hands vaulted Anne into the saddle. His stiff collar rode the golden line of his jaw and the blue of his coat matched his eyes, making them seem more brilliant than ever. He had never looked more handsome or more dangerous. Did she imagine the glint of suspicion in his narrowing eyes?

A loop of her knee around the saddle horn, a twitch of her long skirts, and she galloped down the avenue with the wind tearing at her face. She pounded up hill and down, across frost-white fields and around barren cherry orchards. Faster and faster she flew, but she could not outrace her longing, her need, her fear . . . or the hoofbeats of Cantor's dapple gray echoing on the wind.

The charcoal-gray clouds sank lower and lower. The animal roar of thunder reverberated through the chill November day. At last, her dainty white mare flecked with foam and her own breath coming in gasps, Anne slowed to a stop on a chalky eminence overlooking the winding River Darent.

Slipping from the saddle, she moved to the edge and stared down at the whitecaps whipped to a froth. The wind snatched at her hair and snapped the hem of her skirt like the doubts that assailed her. She could delay no longer. She must lead Cantor to Granny Goody Peabody's. Would she be strong enough to watch him drink deep of the tea laced with a sleeping potion?

She would delay only another moment here. If he began to suspect that . . .

. . . something was wrong. Karl smoothed his hand along the restive gray's muscular neck while he studied Anne with suspicion. She could not hope to lose him on the ride today, and she would be watched closely in Darenth Hall. Tonight. That had to be her plan. She would try to slip away tonight—but she would find him sleeping across the threshold of her bedchamber. She would not escape him.

In a smooth, graceful motion, he dismounted and approached Anne. She turned to study him with an apprehension that tore at his heart. He was jealous of her fearful thoughts, as he was jealous of everyone and everything that touched her when he could not. Every smile she bestowed, every word she spoke roused a pang of envy. He even begrudged the errant wind that caressed her cheeks and the smooth fabric that brushed her flesh.

Caw! Caw!

Karl's uneasy gaze shifted to the raven, wheeling in agitated circles against the darkening sky. She was near, as always, watcher and watchman. But what warning did she give now?

Thunder cracked in the distance. He ran his thumb beneath his collar, turning it up against the cold. "Haven't we had enough of this *contredanse*, Anne?" he asked softly. "You are, no doubt, plotting an escape at this very moment. Let us at least have truth between us."

But the truth was as dangerous as Anne's treacherous weakness. And he was a master conspirator, while she was a novice with weak tools to use against him. Her chin angled up, frustration crossing her fragile features. If only she could make him understand a part of why she must escape him.

"Robbie is so much more than a brother," she whispered. "He was my teacher and my friend. Whenever I needed him, he was there. You must understand, Cantor. You told me once that your mother died at your birth—" his every muscle went rigid, and she hesitated, searching his suddenly cold and closed face—"but your father—"

"Was murdered before my birth," he said flatly.

"Then you've never known what it is to have a family."

Karl watched her look away, her eyes filling with tears. Tears that bathed the hard, burning knot of loneliness he carried with him. For her sake, he tried to imagine the ties that bound a family. But he had no one who was bone of his bone, blood of his blood. No one who had shared the laughter and tears, the triumphs and failures, the joys of childhood, the awkwardness of youth, and the insecurities of maturity.

She touched his knotted fist, her palm and fingers cradling it as gently as a mother with a babe. As gently as his mother might have cradled him, had she not been hounded to death by Friedrich. The old rage welled up in him, hot and strong, but mixed with it was a new and painful yearning.

Anne's gaze, misty with sorrow, met his. "The . . . the people who raised you . . ."

The people who raised him. Lady Bragg. Franz. Josef. No one could have taken better care of him. They had protected him, taught him, and . . . loved him. But they had remained ever aware that he was *die königliche Majestät*. To them he was more than a child, more than a man. He was their hope for the future. He was the salvation of Schattenburg and the just sword of vengeance. And in making him more, they had made him less. Try as he might, he could not imagine the loyalty of sister to brother. He knew only the loyalty of prince to subject.

"Cantor"—she moved closer to him, and he longed to have her closer still—"have you never known what it is to be loved?"

Helplessly, he watched tears spill down her cheeks. "Anne, I—"

"You haven't," she said tremulously. "How . . . how sad."

In the glittering depths of her eyes Karl saw an emotion that turned him ice-cold. Fury flushing his face, he caught her caressing hand in a viselike grip. "Don't waste your pity on me, Anne! I neither need it, nor want it!"

But he had it. Pity and love and need as tightly entwined as the ivy scaling the walls of Darenth Hall. Anne's heart ached with it. He had never known what it was to be loved wholly and completely. He had never known a love that was not earned by deed or given by duty. Why did she have to learn that now? Now, when her love could fill his need.

The growling heavens shattered. Sleet and rain poured from the clouds in a drenching deluge.

"We have to find shelter!" he shouted, throwing her into the saddle.

Anne's gaze turned toward Darenth Hall. There lay safety. There lay . . . disloyalty.

"Follow me!" she ordered, urging her mare over the hill to Granny Goody Peabody's tiny thatched cottage.

The spicy scent of potpourri greeted Anne when she flung herself, soaked to the skin and shivering, through the welcoming doorway. Her teeth chattering with cold and fear, she stared around the famil-

iar interior, taking in the fluffy feather bed piled high
with hand-stitched comforters, the chest and rocker
and small trestle table. The familiar, *empty* interior.
No Goody Peabody bustled forward to greet her
with a warm, toothless smile and a promise that all
would be well. The same promise she had given both
Anne and Robbie when they had brought her their
childish hurts.

On the trestle table a chipped china cup sat atop
a square of foolscap. Anne snatched the paper up.
One drachm to cup of tea stared up at her in awkward
block letters. She would have to brew the tea and
give it to Cantor with her own hands. Panic speared
through her. Could she do it? Could she betray him
now, knowing that he needed her as she needed
him?

The foolscap curled and blackened in the low
banked fire, and a shudder shook Anne like the
cherry tree whipping the cottage wall. But there was
no time to indulge in self-pity. She added a log to
the fire and put water on the hob to heat. Her
clammy riding habit dripped a steady, monotonous
rhythm. She had to dry her clothes for the ride over-
land to Gravesend. Her heart throbbing dully against
her ribs, she began shedding her jacket.

Karl tossed the two saddles into a dry corner of
the tiny shed, slapped a hand to the dainty white
mare's rump, and braved the foul weather. The cottage had been dark when they rode over the stub-
bled wheat field into the tiny square of a yard. Now
pale light danced in the windows.

He opened the door, and the wind rushed ahead
of him, snagging the ruffled hem of the wool flannel
nightgown that was settling around Anne's naked
body. The ruffle flapped up, revealing the slight span
of her waist, the creamy swell of her hips, and a
tantalizing triangle of glossy black curls.

Anne's hands dove down, banding the ruffle
around her hips. Her startled gaze collided with

Cantor's, meshing with a swirling blue sea of ardor
and love and longing that kindled kindred emotions
in her. The wanton desire frightened her. The gen-
tler love insisted she admit, if only to herself, that
she wanted him as a woman wants a man, her man.
The man to whom she promises fidelity and yields
up the last secrets of body and soul. She wanted to
freely give him everything that Friedrich would take
from her by force.

The same wild wind that whipped around her
threaded its unseen fingers through Cantor's hair,
lifting his burnished gold curls and flinging them
across his brow. It sucked in his scent, a savory mix
of wool and sandalwood and man, exhaling it beneath her nose. Breathing deep of that essence, she
closed her eyes, the better to resist.

Karl, transfixed in the doorway, was deaf to the
banshee howl of the wind and the cannonade of the
thunder. His enraptured gaze raced over Anne's
face, as if she might disappear at any moment. Her
black curls danced. Her lashes fluttered against her
cheeks, ebony on ivory. Her parted lips invited him
to come close, to drink deep of the nectar that was
his Anne. The gown was molded to her breasts, tantalizing him with the shadows of dusky dark aure-
oles. Her slender legs were smooth, white, and
exquisitely shaped.

His fingers curled into his palms, forming fists that
denied the desire unfurling its forbidden heat in his
loins. If he had any sense at all, he would run. If
there was the least particle of a gentleman in him,
he would wait out the storm in the shed. Instead,
he slammed the door and dropped the bar into place
and turned for the ordeal of watching the hem of
her gown slide, slowly, so slowly that he wanted to
snatch it down and end the torture of watching and
watching, until it fell with a sigh over the tips of her
toes.

He stood in a growing puddle, while the drum
of the sleet on the thatched roof matched the drum of

his pulse. His hot gaze roamed the single room, fleeing the sight of the bed for the safer terrain of the
dark oak beams hung with hams and sausages and
plaited strings of onions.

"There is no one here," he said at random, desperately struggling with the forbidden heat that
snatched at his resolve like the wild, wicked wind
snatching limbs from the trees outside. Why
wouldn't Anne look at him? God help him! He took
a step, and her ebony lashes swept up so suddenly
he froze.

"M-my clothes were wet," she whispered, as if
she needed to explain. "Th-this was all I could
find."

The rosy firelight gleamed through the translucent
fabric of her gown, outlining her hips, her . . .

"Anne," he hastened to say through his closing
throat, unsure whether he was warning himself or
promising her, "I—I give you my word, I will not
take advantage of this . . . this situation."

But she wanted him to. She wanted him to touch
her and hold her and show her, just once, what love
could be like. She wanted him to assuage the growing ache of her breasts and the secret throbbing at
the apex of her thighs. She wanted to reach out and
grab a moment of happiness. And why shouldn't
she? The thought tiptoed through her mind like a
timid child ready to shrink away at the first sign of
disfavor. Why shouldn't she? She had nothing to
look forward to, nothing to hope for, and nothing
to gain by resisting. Why shouldn't she have one
beautiful memory to sustain her through the years
ahead?

Her tongue peeped out, racing across her dry lips.
"And if I want you to . . . to take advantage . . ."

Karl's tawny lashes plunged over his burning
eyes. He grasped for the tattered edges of sanity.
"You don't know what you're saying."

The hem of her gown swayed in an erotic rhythm
around the small pink toes winkling in and out of

sight. Her hands fanned across the soaked fabric of his coat, branding his chest with sensations of heat and cold. She climbed on tiptoe, the gentle bell of her hips sliding into his waiting palms, as if they had been formed for no other purpose.

"I love you," she whispered, her breath fanning across his lips, each word filling an empty space in his heart. "I have loved you since the first time you took my hand and looked into my eyes. I have known since then that I could never truly belong to any other man."

In the silvery depths of her eyes, Karl saw a darkness, a desire, a decision that sent fire raging through him. The ash of a single sane question drifted above that fire: Was this a trick to seduce and lull him? But the eager trembling of her body against his and the petal-soft pressure of her lips on his were not feigned. Banishing sanity to a far corner of his mind, he swept his arms around Anne and yielded to desire. Whether he would find heaven or hell beyond that yielding, he neither knew nor cared. For this moment, she was wholly his.

His mouth opened over hers, that hallowed feast to be savored at his leisure. His supple tongue stroked the seam of her lips, and they melted, submitting to his gentle exploration of the recesses of her mouth.

Anne's every sense quivered with delight. Her fingers threaded his rain-dampened curls, entranced by the silken texture of his hair. Her aching breasts burrowed into the hard plane of his chest. The ache between her thighs sent her surging against him, seeking the hard pressure of his hips. His hands, as supple as his lithely foraging tongue, slid the length of her back, pulling her up to nestle against the hard bulge of his manhood. A cry of pleasure escaped her.

"Anne, Anne." Karl sighed her name in a blissful melody, trembling beneath the tempting, taunting kisses raining along his jaw, beneath his ear. Temptation was not to be resisted. He swept her up and carried her to the soft, downy bed and laid her on that altar, an idol to adore.

His lips lingered over hers, seeking and finding sweet heaven. He had seen passion in all of its guises, save this, the eager giving and taking dared only by the truly innocent. Anne had not learned to guard herself or her heart, to wait and give only as much as was offered to her. It was a burden he had never expected to bear, but one he would wear gladly. He would see that she never had the need to distrust. He would match her, giving for giving and loving for loving. He would be the guard that protected her heart.

A last, lingering kiss, and he pulled away, tearing at his cravat. The diamond stickpin clattered to the flagstone floor and the length of snowy linen went sailing.

Anne, adrift on an enchanted sea of pleasure, curled on her side, tucking her palm beneath her cheek. She watched him with a misty gaze, while his boots thudded to the floor and his wet shirt peeled away from the broad, furred expanse of his chest. The scar flaming red along the bony curve of his ribs and slicing across the ridge of muscle beneath his heart propelled her to her knees.

"Cantor!" Her trembling fingers hovered over the scar while her tear-flooded gaze met his. She had known his work for her father was dangerous, but she had not imagined . . . Her fingers fluttered over the angry red line, and where her fingers went, her lips followed, as if her touch might heal it.

"Anne." His hands cradled her cheeks, tilting her head up. "There is no need—"

"You might have been killed," she said throatily. "I would never have known."

His thumbs caught the tears slipping down her cheeks. "Don't, Anne," he whispered. "Don't cry for me."

But her tears were not only for him. They were

for herself, too. They were for that fearful new awareness that he must have known betrayal many times, beginning with those people who had raised him and loved him not enough. Now she would betray him again. Would he ever understand or believe she did it because she loved him too much? She could not, would not, let him face a danger she could prevent.

She cupped his muscled ribs, as if she held the life-giving chalice of his beating heart in her hands. In her glistening gaze was all she wanted to say: *I love you more than life or hope or breath. Trust me. Love me. Believe me.*

Slowly, she stripped away the gown, that last barrier to him. He came to her, covering her with his strong, hard body, touching her flesh to flesh and heart to heart. And while the sleet rattled against the window panes and the wind screamed around the eaves, he stole from her the last remnants of her heart and the last vestiges of the child she had been. He did it with the lips that adored her and the hands that caressed her. He did it with a tenderness that made her throat ache and with a need that matched her own. A need to give and take and mesh as one.

She was lost to all but the rasp of his breath and the pounding of his pulse and the musky essence of man. She tried to hoard every sensation for the lonely nights to come, but she found at last that she could not think, could only feel—his nuzzling lips and his reverent hands and, at last, the painful glory of their union. That moment when he sheathed himself fully, accepting the innocence she gave him.

He moved, slowly, gently, sliding within her, hot silk to moist satin. She wanted to speak, but her breath caught in her throat. The sensations grew, wild and wondrous warnings of a ravishing paradise to be reached.

Yet she was firmly rooted to the earth by Karl's body, miraculously light as it covered hers. His breath blew in soft flurries beneath her earlobe. His lips grazed the taut line of her jaw. His hands cupped her head, his fingers threaded her hair, and his powerful forearms flanked her shoulders, confining her in the fortress of his love. While his hips rocked against her, his chest teased the tips of her breasts.

And still the sensations grew in fire-storms that raced along her nerves. Her eyes widened. Her fingers dug into his broad back. She arched, waiting in trembling anticipation.

"C-Cantor, I—I—"

"Shh, Anne, let it happen."

He thrust and withdrew, advanced and retreated. The never-ending tension built to the verge of tolerance, and even then it seemed as boundless as the heavens.

She waited, poised on the brink of discovery. One that came in a rush, like sunlight bursting through a cloud and diffusing through her with the golden radiance of Cantor's hair and the loving brilliance of his eyes. It left her shaken and aching and weak from its force, which shuddered through him as it had shuddered through her.

His head bowed to the curve of her neck, and he gasped for breath. While her hands caressed the muscles rippling across his back, Anne's grieving gaze turned to the cracked china cup on the trestle table.

"I love you, Anne," he said softly, nestling his lips against the leaping pulse in the hollow of her throat. The honeyed languor of physical release stole along nerve and vein and sinew, but a stronger release eased his burden of fear. She couldn't leave him now. She couldn't love him like this, offer herself so fully, and then leave him.

He rolled away, pulling her into the curve of his body, glorying in the perfect alignment of back to chest and thigh to thigh. "Trust me, Anne," he whispered against the lustrous curls that stroked his cheek. "Trust me to bring your brother back. I swear I will let no harm come to him."

Did he imagine the sudden stiffening of her body?

"I have trusted you from the first," she said, her voice thick, as though she choked back tears. "Even when you went away without a word, I knew—Cantor, I knew!—there was a reason. And I—I trust you now. I swear I do."

He rolled her onto her back and levered up on an elbow. Tears slid into the springy curls at her temples. The shadow of a frown drifted across his brow. "What's wrong, love?"

"I'm afraid."

"There's nothing to fear," he said softly, wondering that her fear could hurt him so much. Would it always be this way? Would he feel her joy, her sorrow, her pain, as if they were his own? "I will see that no harm comes to you or yours."

No harm would come to her or hers. Anne struggled into her damp clothes, while she steeped the tea with its damning potion. No harm, she thought while Cantor stamped into his boots and she arranged the cups. No harm, she vowed, while he brought the cup to his lips and drank deeply.

"Odd taste," he said, setting it aside.

She looked down into her own steaming cup and willed her voice not to shake. "Granny Goody laces her tea leaves with strengthening herbs."

"Ah," he said, as if that explained it.

A few minutes. She had to hold herself together for a few more minutes. Anne buried her shaking fists in her lap and watched Cantor rise, stretch, smile. That smile. She would never forget it. It held a touch of utterly masculine triumph and a hint of little-boy excitement and more than a suggestion of a lover's satisfaction. If she had done nothing else today, she had pleased him. She would remember that.

"The wind's dying," he said.

Caw! Caw! Caw!

Her heart leaping with fright, Anne swiveled toward the window where a raven battered the glass panes with bedraggled wings.

"What . . ." Cantor strode across the room, faltered, and straightened.

The raven's strong beak pecked at the glass. *Caw! Caw!* it screamed, an almost human sound of rage.

Cantor took a dragging step, another, and paused, raising his hand to his brow.

With the first shattering of the glass, he turned slowly and stared at Anne. In his eyes she saw the death throes of love and trust, the full, painful awareness of what she had done.

"I'm sorry," she whispered. "I'm so sorry."

He stumbled to the bed and tried to hold himself up with an effort that made every muscle tremble. Slowly, he slid to his knees. "Why, Anne?" he asked thickly.

"Because I love you."

"Because you love me," he said, and smiled. An empty smile, as if there were no heart left in him to give it life.

He crumpled to the floor. Anne fell to her knees beside him, cradling his head in her lap while the sound of tinkling glass and the warning *Pruk! Pruk!* of the raven filled the room.

"Forgive me," she wept. "Forgive me."

But he couldn't hear her. Only the raven heard. The raven that came flying through the shattered pane with a deafening beating of wings.

Chapter 17

December 1813
Schattenburg

The ancient castle called Schattenburg, blood-red in the setting sun, loomed above the snow-capped crest of the Reisenberg. A series of curtain walls snaked down the mountainside, each of a brighter red sandstone, each more recently constructed. In a dim and dank cylindrical tower of the lowest wall, Friedrich Auguste, Prince of Schattenburg, stood with his legs spread and his arrogant head thrown back.

He was proud of his great height, proud of his erect body, proud of the silk and satin uniform rippling over the muscular body that might have belonged to a man twenty years younger. There was not a stronger man in Schattenburg, he thought, not a wilier man in all of the German states.

Who but he had the cunning to devise so Machiavellian a plan? One that would regain him the Principate of Schattenburg, stolen in the last convulsion of the Holy Roman Empire, when the tiny secular and religious states were mediatized and grafted to larger ones. Surely they did not think that *he* would gladly retain the empty title of *prince* and accept the loss of his power! But the real joy of his plan was a purely personal one.

His broad, graceful hand crept down to his groin.

Though his eyes blazed with feral hatred, his face twisted with remembered pain. The pain of a sword slash dealt him by the Earl of Darenth. The greater pain later, when he learned that he would never sire an heir of his body, never again lose himself in the lusty fire of passion. Though his mind might burn with desire for a woman's musky flesh, his body would remain cold and untouched. So he filled that empty well with another passion. A passion for revenge that he had nurtured for thirty-five years.

He had exulted when the Earl of Darenth's heir had been born. He had toasted the birth of Darenth's daughter. Through the eyes of his spies he had watched Darenth's children grow, planning, always planning the moment when he would murder them both.

It had been no stroke of luck that the Lancers of Schattenburg had captured an English observer during the bitter Russian winter of Napoleon's first major defeat. Friedrich had known that Robert Ransome, Viscount Langley, was in St. Petersburg acting as an attaché. He had known that adventurous, impetuous youth would not resist the temptation of participating in the war. An act Robbie—how he delighted in that familiarity!—no doubt now bitterly regretted.

Friedrich jerked his head at the two fully uniformed Hessian mercenaries standing at quivering attention by the thick oak door braced with iron. They slipped outside, and Friedrich turned to the rectangular orifice where a single stone yet needed to be mortared into the wall to seal the crypt behind it.

"Robbie!"

A skeletal hand glimmered white against the darkness. A face appeared, its flesh melted away from bones that cut at the skin. Only the eyes were alive, pools of flaming violet staring out of that ravaged face with the savagery of a falcon on the wing. The elegant, laughter-loving Robbie Ransome wasn't a man any longer. He was a dangerous animal who had killed one guard careless enough to get too close to the single opening in his six-by-six-foot hell.

"You won't have to wait much longer," Friedrich said, with a slow, taunting smile. "Anne will be in Schattenburg tomorrow."

"Damn you!" Robbie's deep-throated shout trembled with passionate rage. "Leave her be! You've got me! Isn't that enough?"

"Enough, Robbie?" Friedrich's angry gaze shifted to the adjacent crypt, as yet unwalled and unoccupied. "It will not be enough until your sister has joined you here and your father is chained to watch you both die. And once I have what I want from him, that is exactly what will happen."

"Why?" Robbie screamed at his departing back. "Why?"

Friedrich turned slowly. A ray of sunlight poured across the portal, glittering like gold dust over the regimented waves of his hair. Though his simmering rage threatened to erupt into a full-scale explosion, he ground his teeth, chewing back the need to tell his secret. Everyone else who had learned that his wound had left him impotent was dead. He had seen to that. He flung Robbie a last vicious look and shouldered through the door.

"Damn you, Friedrich!" Robbie's fleshless arm stretched through the opening, the claw of his hand straining after his prey. "Not Anne! She's done nothing to you! Not Anne!"

Anne had arrived at the confluence of the Rhine and the Neckar at midday with a shrinking and tearful Hetty Peabody, whose thirst for adventure had died during the rough crossing of the Channel. Seeking a boatman to take them upriver, Anne met sullen disregard and angry mutters of *die Engländerin*, until she found a gnome of a man with a bent back and a surly look. A game of charades to cross the language barrier proved to be unnecessary.

"Prince Friedrich of Schattenburg" was all she needed to say. The man's surly look was wiped away by one of fear. He nodded briskly, mimed a dawn departure, and shuffled away. She and Hetty slipped and slid across the frozen street to the inn, where the clink of coins caught the sullen innkeeper's avid attention. Not daring to leave her bedchamber and move among the angry Heidelburgians, Anne sat by the window of her chamber staring out over the blackish-brown Neckar to the snow-topped mountains rising beyond it. The setting sun poured liquid gold over the forested heights, a light that was blotted out by the lustrous black raven that flew with a clatter to the windowsill.

Her heart surged into her throat, beating the same wild rhythm as the raven's fluttering wings. She stared at the healing cut buried in a wedge of missing feathers atop its head. It was the same raven that had come whooshing through Granny Goody's shattered windowpane, flapping its wings in her face and shrilling that so-human scream of rage. . . .

Cantor's head had been cradled in her lap, his dusky lashes lying against the pale cheeks and his curls clutching at every tender stroke of her fingers. His broad chest rose and fell in the easy rhythm of deep sleep, a sleep she longed to seek for herself. Perhaps then she might forget the look in his eyes, of a man who had been betrayed by the one he had trusted above all others, of a man who had come to trust neither easily nor casually and now despised both himself and his deceiver. But she couldn't forget, and she was afraid she never would. She was afraid she would forever be haunted by the sight of his dying love for her.

So she cradled him close and stared down at him with hot, dry eyes and listened to the last raindrops thudding on the thatched roof and the fire cackling in the hearth and the raven shattering the window-

pane with a last burst of effort. She didn't care that
she needed to be up and away. She didn't fear the
feathered fury that charged across the tiny cottage,
its eyes a blaze of red, its vicious beak parted on a
shriek, and its wings striking her face. The worst
had already happened to her. She was numb to all
else.

She leaned over Cantor, protecting his face with
her breast, her nose buried in the manly fragrance
of his hair. The beating wings grew silent. The
scream died away to a bad-humored croak.

Anne dared to glance up and found the raven
inches away, hopping on the floor and eyeing her
quizzically. It cocked its head to one side, lifting its
stout beak and flaunting the ruff of fluffy feathers at
its throat. *Why?* it seemed to be asking. *Why did you
do this to him?*

A ridiculous thought, despite the memory of the
Prince and his Lady of the Forest that added the
element of myth to reality, despite the sight of the raven hopping to Cantor's shoulder and stroking the
powerful muscle with a loving beak, despite the
consoling rumble issuing from its deep chest with a
catlike purr. . . .

The same consoling rumble issued from the rav-
en's deep chest now. Anne studied the sheen of its
blue-black wings, her brow puckering in a frown. She
had seen a raven before this one burst through the
cottage window. At Darenth House in London . . .
just before Cantor came to her. At Bragg House in the
Lakelands . . . just after Cantor left her. How strange
that she had only noted that now. They seemed to
travel as a pair.

Her gaze shifted to the door. Would Cantor come
to her now?

She prayed fervently that he would not. Contrar-
ily, she longed as fervently that he would. Nothing
had changed. Everything had changed. She struggled with an overwhelming need to take ship back

to England, back to Cantor. But she was so close now. So close to protecting him and saving Robbie. She couldn't turn back, no matter how desperately she longed to.

She was a stranger moving through a strange land, and that land her own body, heart, and soul. She was as great an oddity to herself as were the sullen Germans with their angry looks and guttural language. Cantor had breathed a new and different life into her. She knew now what it meant to love a man and have a man love her. Though her heart was heavy, her soul sang, soaring easily into the radiant paradise they had discovered together. Even her body seemed different, more acutely attuned to every sense. Her batiste chemise caressed the aching tips of her breasts as gently as Cantor's fingers. Every errant breeze became the moist heat of his breath. Every trailing scent was transmuted into his essence.

She reached out a tentative finger and touched the raven's plumage. Finding that touch welcome, she stroked its long back. ''Where is he?'' she whispered softly.

Rap, rap, rap. The door rattled against its rusted hinges.

The raven squawked and took flight.

Anne bounced from her chair, a hand pressed to her pounding heart. She expected no one! Who could it be?

Hetty, sniffling her forlorn woes on the trundle bed, jerked up, screaming.

A shoulder rammed into the door, setting it to quaking. It flew open with a squeal of rusty hinges and slammed against the wall. Karl von Dannecker charged in, his moth-eaten wig askew, his ribbons flying, and his leg miraculously cured of its limp.

Anne, gaping, was caught in a rough grip that, for all of its brevity, was angry and hurtful. With a sinuous move he snaked a knife from his boot and spun around to face the room, standing guard over her.

Hetty, her mouth yawning wide, shrieked, "Murder! Murder is being done!"

"Anne!" Karl von Dannecker said—but it was her Cantor's voice! Unmistakably her Cantor's voice! "Why is that wretched girl screaming?"

She stared at a pale-gold curl peeping out from under his wig. He had lied to her! He had told her he was Cantor's cousin, when all the while—

"Hetty!" barked the impatient Earl of Darenth. "Calm yourself, or I'll find a muzzle for you!"

Anne darted to the side, peering around the brocade-clad back that blocked her view. Her father stepped through the doorway, scowling at Hetty, whose shrieks choked off on a hapless squeak of "Yer lordship!"

Behind him came Anne's mother, dressed in unrelieved black, and behind her a sea of curious faces filled the doorway. Von Dannecker—now limping, Anne noted—crossed the room, knife in hand, and that sea of faces ebbed away, leaving the door to slam on an empty portal. He deftly slipped the knife into his boot and turned to face the room, obviously on guard.

Anne's curious and horrified gaze raced from the skewed wig to the rose-colored mask with its dark eyeslits and down to the hard, taut mouth beneath it. Cantor's mouth. What a fool she had been to—

"Well, Puss, you've led us a merry chase!" Her father, shifting his scowl from the thoroughly cowed Hetty, clasped his hands behind his back, and rocked on his heels—a sure sign of a commencing lecture. "Cantor did not expect you to take ship from Gravesend, so he wasted his time flying to London. Had we not been favored with fair winds, you would have reached Schattenburg alone. And that, my dear girl, would have been disastrous."

"Father, I won't turn back. I—"

"You"—his threatening finger pointed like the muzzle of a dueling pistol—"will do precisely as I

say! Damn! Was ever a man so cursed in his off-
spring? A scapegrace son and a headstrong daughter! By God, you need a thrashing!''

"John," warned her mother.

"Smooth your feathers, Aggie. I shan't do it, not
but what the chit doesn't need it.''

"Father, I—''

"Not a word from you, Anne! I've suffered *mal de
mer* from the Pool of London to the Heidelburg dock!
I'm in no mood to argue now!'' He strode up to her,
stern and imposing. "Thanks to your cork-brained
flight, I cannot now spare you a meeting with Friedrich. His spies will have told him you are here. If
you do not arrive with von Dannecker and me in
Schattenburg on the morrow, his suspicions will be
aroused.''

"V-von Dannecker!'' she whispered, her gaze
streaking to the silent man standing guard before the
door. Her Cantor. It was all for nothing! Her betrayal
and her flight! He would enter the realm of von Fersen's utterly ruthless master and face danger there.

"What else do you think has gotten us this far?
Herr von Dannecker has and will be our inter-
preter.''

"Of course," she murmured, her gaze drifting
to the window where the distant black speck of the
raven circled through the last bright rays of the
sun.

"Rest well, Anne. We don't know what we will
face on the morrow.''

But she did know what she would have to face
that night. A meeting with Cantor—alone.

The church bell chimed the midnight hour while
Karl, gilded and beribboned in von Dannecker's regalia, limped slowly across the icy street to the quay.
He braced his foot atop a stone block and leaned on
his upraised knee, his forearms crossed over it while
he stared into the viscous Neckar. Schattenburg was
hours away and his revenge was at hand, but he

couldn't think or plan or summon a lifetime's bitter
resolve. He could only look behind the revenge he
would take to the desolate darkness beyond it. He
could only see the empty hours filled with duty.
There would be much work to be done in putting
this war-torn land to rights and bringing prosperity
back to the region—so many widows and orphans
in desperate poverty, so many villages with nothing
but old men to till the land. Though he would no
longer be the official leader of his people, the habit
of responsibility was one he neither could, nor
wanted, to break.

But more than duty was needed to give meaning
to life, and Anne had stolen that from him. He had
wakened to the groggy aftermath of that deep sleep
with Goody Peabody bustling about preparing a
bubbling soup and his ever-present companion, the
raven, perched on his chest. He had wakened to the
delectable memory of Anne in his arms, her eyes
silvery flames of desire and her soft body yielding
to him. But that memory had been seared away in
the brushfire of rage. She had seduced him and betrayed him and left him to despise himself for his
weakness and her for using her body to manipulate
him.

Yet, when he heard Hetty's scream pouring
through the cracks in the door, he knew he would
kill the man who harmed Anne.

He heard the skid of a foot in the street behind
him, and his every sense came alive, alert to danger.
His gaze scouted the dark quay, finding a barrel, a
coil of rope, and an abandoned oar, all waiting to
trap an unwary foot. His fingers inched down his
calf, seeking the cool handle of the knife. He listened to the soft pad of laggard steps, and the night
breeze carried to his nose the sent of damask rose.
Anne.

She must have been watching from her window
and seen him leaving the inn. He waited for her to
approach and waited longer while she stood si-

lently nearby. The seconds ticked away, his hands trembling with the memory of her warm flesh and his heart aching with the knowledge of her betrayal.

"I have heard it said that a woman is the devil in disguise," he said softly, not moving. "What, sweet Anne, are you doing here?" *Sweet Anne*, but there was no loving caress in the heavy sarcasm of his tone.

"I must speak with you, Cantor."

Her voice held a note of strain that tugged at his resisting heart. "Ah, I am unmasked, undone."

"You forgot to limp."

"Yes, the limp. I thought it the perfect touch to the role of von Dannecker." He stared into the swirling water below, wanting to take her captive, whether to vent his anger or assuage his need, he didn't know.

"You played your part to perfection."

"As you played yours," he said bitterly. "I never suspected that you were using your body like a strumpet hawking her wares on the Strand."

It was a cruel thing to say, and Karl regretted it even before he heard the soft hiss of her breath. Yet he could not force himself to offer an apology; the anger was still too strong in him. He heard her light steps, not running away as he wanted but approaching nearer. She was beside him, her small hand touching his arm.

"That was not part of my plan," she whispered. "But . . . I wanted to know what it would be like to be loved by you. I wanted you to be the first, the man I carried in my heart. No matter what you think of me, I cannot regret it."

She turned to go, and Karl caught her wrist. "Anne, I . . ."

She waited, her upturned face bathed in moonlight. Though shame roiled inside him, he could say nothing more.

"I know," she said softly, moving away and

standing at the edge of the quay, staring at the lovers' moon hanging high overhead. "Do you remember the night we first met?"

At the Raeburns' *bal masque*. She had been dressed as an angel with silver gauze wings and a halo that kept slipping. He had been wounded fighting for the Austrians in the Battle of Wagram and was recuperating in England. At his first sight of her, he had blessed the musket ball that almost took his life.

"Brat and Dashwood's older brother were fighting a mock duel for the last place on my dance card, and while they battled you wrote your name in it."

She had watched him do so, her eyes sparkling, her mouth curved in an inviting smile. At that moment he had never wanted anything so much as he had wanted to kiss her.

"When they realized what you had done, I thought you would have to fight a real duel with them both."

The insolent puppies.

"You said, 'Gentlemen, I would not dare cross swords with either of you. Your skill is so execrable you might wound me by accident.' Which quite crushed them both, as they had gone to Italy on their Grand Tour and studied with a master."

The memory of their young, earnest faces falling in dismay brought a reminiscent softening of Karl's mouth.

"And then you smiled at me and I lost my heart," she said.

And she smiled at him, and he lost his.

"I had not believed that love could come so quickly, that one moment I would not know that you existed and the next I could not imagine living without you."

Neither had he. In one moment she had gone from a lovely creature to bear on his arm for a dance to the woman who filled his mind and heart.

"You held out your hand, and I placed mine atop

it.'' She raised her hand, staring into her palm. ''Did you feel it, Cantor? The tie that joined us then?''

Yes, he had felt it. A bond that had been new and wondrous, and frightening because he had been bound by a duty that could not include her. Yet he had returned to her again and again as the Season had progressed. In a few intense weeks she had given him the courage to dream—until duty laid its heavy hand on his shoulder once more in the form of a mission for her father.

Hadn't he betrayed her then? Anne and all that might have been?

''I never thought then that it would come to this,'' she said, turning slowly and walking across the quay to the edge of the street. ''I love you, Cantor.''

The soft words came out of the night, veiled in despair. He wanted to believe her. He wanted to recover the dream that had died when he wakened to the bright light of reality in Goody Peabody's thatched cottage.

''Go back to the inn, Anne,'' he said. ''Rest. Dawn awaits us.''

Dawn arrived with crimson streaks knifing through the sky as Cantor's rejection had knifed through Anne. He would never understand how precious her love for him was. She thought of her parents, so deeply divided it seemed they might never rebuild their shattered love. Had her mother felt like this, as if her heart would literally break?

Teams of straining horses towed the barge upriver. Cantor, in his irritating persona of von Dannecker, limped up and down the long deck, his handkerchief aflutter and his flutelike complaints endless. The wine was too dry and the plum jelly too sweet and the bread too coarse. The trip was too long and the pace was too slow and the deckhands too sullen. He interspersed streams of thickly accented English with harsh German that sounded to Anne's tutored ear like the speech of a native. He never faltered in his role, but still she could not believe that he had fooled her for weeks. The broad span of his shoulders, the muscular strength of his legs, and the firm, bold jaw beneath the lace-trimmed mask should have betrayed him to her then. Why hadn't he told her who he was? Had he mistrusted her, even then? A chill settled around her like a shroud.

Hour after hour they moved against the sluggish current through sinuous walls of red sandstone crowned by a dark and brooding primeval forest. On occasion a hamlet drifted by, the roofs of its half-timbered houses draped in swags of snow. As often the crumbling ruins of a castle clung to the heights like a predatory ghost. Despite the commonplace river scenes—stilt-legged herons standing on gravel shoals and ducks snabbling among the water-weeds—it seemed to Anne the very air breathed of unspoken mysteries.

With dusk encroaching and her destination so near, she was beset by terror. She had not allowed any fear for herself to sway her, but now it came in a rush, like the gray ghost of darkness crawling over the silent forest. What would Friedrich look like? What would he do?

Her hand crept out, touching her father's. His turned and folded tightly around hers. "Puss, Puss," he said softly, "my foolish girl. You must be stronger now than you've ever been."

"Can you forgive me for forcing you to do this, Father? For forcing you to betray England for—"

"Hush, Puss," he said gently. "I could not leave you to fight this battle alone. In truth, I cannot regret, save for your own sake, that you forced my hand."

She looked away, unable to hold his loving

gaze. But relief could not push fear away for very long.

"What is he like, Father?" She had no need to explain who *he* was.

"In his youth he had the charm of a Casanova, the looks of an angel, and the soul of a devil."

The soul of a devil. Anne stared at the raven winging ahead, a black cross etched against the twilight sky.

"Puss," her father began urgently, "you must not by word or deed betray that von Dannecker is other than he appears to be. That disguise will allow . . . Cantor to move freely in search of your brother."

And threaten them both. "Father, if only you will let the wedding take place, then you can have Robbie—"

"That is out of the question! The man is dangerously mad! Why do you think I insisted that your mother await us in Heidelburg?"

Dangerously mad. Anne's hand trembled in his.

The village of Schattenhausen huddled on a crescent of land at the foot of the precipitous slopes of the Reisenberg, a pine-and-beech-clad mountain wreathed in mist. Karl breathed deep of the resinous fragrance of the forest and the fishy odor of the river. He was home, but its smells and sights were strange to him. While all below was cast in the gloom of dusk, the turreted castle called Schattenburg looming on the jagged heights was stained blood-red in the setting sun. As if, he thought, its walls had been bathed in the blood of the victims of his predatory forebears. Those grasping, soulless sires of the House of Schattenburg whose seed had proved true in Friedrich. Crawling down the mountainside were a series of curtain walls with evenly spaced cylindrical towers. At the lowest, unfinished, workmen swarmed like ants, erecting yet another wall to protect Friedrich—from what?

Curling around a loop in the river was a single

row of triple-storied half-timbered houses with scabrous whitewash and pale-ocher beams and stays. There should have been a bustle of activity on the single village street. Old men should have gathered around doorways to discuss the state of crops and fish and game. Old women should have gathered to pluck chickens and cackle like hens themselves. Children should have played, running and laughing. But the only child to be seen had the listless eyes and swollen belly of hunger. The only old man trudged from the river with a bucket of water, taunted by a gaudily uniformed Hessian mercenary.

Overhead the raven flew through the twilight, lighting on the sharp gable of the *Gasthof*, as if she knew she would be as welcome as any traveler to the inn. *Caw! Caw!* she cried.

The old man's head came up. His jaw dropped. The bucket tumbled from his hand, spilling the muddy water of the Neckar across the village street. *"Der Rabe! Der Rabe!"* he screamed, hobbling for the nearest door.

Another raven swooped onto a gabled roof, then another and another, black specters against the dusky sky.

The old man hobbled from door to door, pounding, shouting, drawing the gaping villagers into the street. *"Der Rabe! Der Rabe!"* they murmured with awe, then with growing elation. Soon, the rooftops were lined with ravens and the street was filled with dancing and the Hessians were nervously fingering their weapons.

Karl Auguste Wilhelm II, rightful Prince of Schattenburg, stared through the protection of von Dannecker's mask and smiled on his people.

"Herr von Dannecker," prompted the earl, "the carriage awaits us."

Karl settled against the lush red velvet squabs, noting the fearful looks the coachman flung over his shoulder as he slammed the door shut. Moments later the carriage lurched and rolled up the shallow incline into the hushed natural cathedral of the Schattenwald, heading for the rococo palace of *Chagrin*.

"What was that all about?" asked the earl.

Karl gazed at Anne, sitting tense and silent on the opposite seat. Did she remember the story of the Prince and his Lady of the Forest? "The Legend of Schattenburg says that the ravens will leave if the Master of the Ravens, the rightful prince, is not on the throne. They left thirty years ago"—his gaze shifted to the earl—"on the day Friedrich's brother was murdered. They return today for the first time."

"Superstition," said Darenth, with the hollow tone of uncertainty.

"Perhaps, my lord."

"How strange, Herr von Dannecker, that the ravens should return at the very moment of our arrival." Anne's soft voice came drifting through the dark interior with the pensive note of one awaiting the solution of a puzzle. "Tell me, sir, did Friedrich's brother have a son?"

"When he died, he had no son." It was a truth so precise as to be a lie, but he could not trust Anne with the whole truth. Once, he had doubted that she could betray him. He doubted no longer.

Chagrin rose out of the night in a blaze of light, a white confection of a palace at the foot of a white shell drive nestled among extensive gardens in the French style. Lamps blazed, glittering over marble statuary, shining on Chinese vases set atop scrolled pediments, gleaming like fireflies amidst the shrubbery. Encroaching on the garden's rim was the black and mysterious forest.

The carriage stopped in the elegant oval courtyard at the foot of a flight of broad marble steps where flambeaux danced above the gilded holders march-

ing up the balustrade. At the top of those steps stood
a man, alone.

Anne, alighting from the carriage, paused with her
hand still in Cantor's. Against all hope she had
wished that Robbie might meet her here, but he
was nowhere in sight. There was only the man strutting down the flight of steps. She released Cantor's
hand and moved forward, her sapphire-blue cloak
swirling around her ankles.

"Lady Anne," he said, as if she had no companions, "I am Friedrich Auguste, Prinz von Schattenburg."

She had expected signs of cruelty and dissipa-
tion, but he was physically magnificent. Thickly
muscular, tall and lance-straight, he wore a white
cashmere uniform sashed in sky-blue and dripping with orders and decorations whose jewels reflected the light. He had a wealth of guinea-gold
hair carefully tamed into regimented waves and
an ageless, unlined face. His eyes, wide-spaced,
thickly lashed and the azure of a summer sky,
wore an expression as benign as his smile—until
his gaze shifted to her father. Anne caught a chilling glimpse of the controlled fury and utter ruthlessness that drove him.

"Darenth," he said in nearly accentless English,
"I see you have not brought your lovely countess."

The deliberate provocation pulled a gasp from
Anne.

"My wife, your Highness," said her father, his
voice trembling with suppressed rage, "preferred to
remain behind. May I introduce our companion,
Herr von Dannecker."

"Ah, the musician," Friedrich said in a dismissive
tone.

"Your Highness"—Anne stepped forward—"we
want to see my brother."

His eyes turned to her, narrowing. "You are direct, my dear, like your mother. A flaw in a woman.
You will correct it." He took her chin between his

thumb and forefinger, pinching it much too hard to be comfortable. "I would be a fool to release your brother before the wedding, *Fraulein*. You will have a week to rest from your journey, then we will remove to Schattenburg. There, following ancient family tradition, the ceremony will be performed in the castle chapel."

Chapter 18

O n the marble steps rising to *Chagrin*, Karl saw the ghosts of his father and his mother, of the children they should have had in a long and happy life, and of himself as the child he should have been. It was here that they would have lived and loved, but for Friedrich. Friedrich, who so lusted for the throne that he had murdered his brother for it. Friedrich, who stood before him, unarmed and unsuspecting.

Karl struggled against surging waves of hate and bitterness and rage. They were of a height, he and his uncle. They had the same muscular build. Friedrich's eyes were a lighter blue and his hair a brighter gold. His jaw was a broad square, his chin pointed with a dimple deeply imprinted beneath his supple, well-defined lips. He was a strikingly handsome man, seemingly untouched by his three-score years or by the vicious evil of his life.

That untouched quality inflamed Karl. Had Friedrich never suffered for his cruelty? Had he never known defeat of his overweening ambitions?

Karl struggled for breath. Never had he imagined how hard it would be to wait, to plot, to plan, before he could act. But he must wait. He must, above all, plan very carefully. Anne's life rested in his hands. The thought steadied him, until Friedrich's gaze shifted his way, as if he sensed Karl's inner turmoil.

"Your Highness," Anne was saying, her voice

thin and supplicating, "may I at least see my brother? He—"

"No." Friedrich's gaze, holding a measure of cruel amusement, shifted back to her. "You tremble, *Fraulein*. Come above. The night is too cold for you."

Karl watched him take Anne's hand and saw her flinch. Rage flooding through every muscle, he began to leap after them—and found the earl's iron-hard hand gripping his arm.

"Herr von Dannecker," said the earl in a neutral tone, though his eyes glittered angrily, "beware that patch of ice. You may slip and fall."

His nostrils flaring and his chest heaving, Karl considered wrenching his arm from Darenth's grasp and yielding to the insistent demand that he attack Friedrich now. Undoubtedly, a fool's choice considering the mercenaries standing guard.

He sucked in a breath that whistled through his throat. "Thank you, my lord. I shall take more care."

And he would. He would bury the rage and think of Anne, who must be saved at any cost. Even now, Franz would be waiting in the forest for the pounding night ride back to Schattenburg. Tonight he must make his first plans for finding Robbie. Then, nothing would stop him.

Nothing, Karl vowed hours later. Swathed in a fur-lined black traveling cloak, he stood in the lee of a giant pine tree, blinking the sifting snow from his eyes. On the rising ground a woodcutter's hut snuggled windowsill-deep in virginal white drifts. Through the thick diamond-shaped panes light beckoned with a golden promise of warmth and welcome. Still he hesitated, dreading to destroy the tranquillity that permeated the moonlit clearing.

Rejecting the weakness of hesitation, Karl strode ahead, his heavy Hussar boots gouging scars in the glistening expanse. Before the rough oaken door, he paused to listen to the soft cradle song seeping through the cracks. The melody flowed through his fertile mind, gathering an intricate harmony, while he waited for stolid and faithful Franz to step to the fore.

Franz's beefy fist knocked on the door. Three solid raps echoed away into the moon-glazed woodland, silencing the harsh, hunting *kveck-kveck* of an owl and choking off the soft song within.

The door creaked open a scant crack, and the burly woodcutter peered out, his eyes narrowed with suspicion and his mouth thin beneath a flaxen moustache.

"Willi!" Franz's deep voice drum-rolled as he stepped into the shaft of light.

The crack inched wider. The curling ends of the moustache quivered, and the woodcutter's pale gaze glided to Karl, blending with the shadows in his hooded black cloak. "Come in! Come in!" Willi whispered, as if the winter-blighted forest had ears to hear.

Franz moved into the tiny room, dwarfing it with his bearish size. Karl slipped in with a sleek and predatory step, closing the door behind him. His gaze, sharpened by a lifetime lived in danger's dark shadow, danced from the tiny windows to the wooden door that led through the back. Only then, with escape routes planned, did he allow himself a moment's respite to absorb the heat radiating from the *Kachelofen*, the large stone stove covered with glazed ceramic tiles. Only then did he turn his brilliant gaze on the trio of frowning men and the wrinkled wisp of a woman waiting with a smile of sweet welcome.

Each was tied to him by a past deed done in service to his father. Each had faced the danger of Friedrich's wrath so that Karl, the rightful Prince of Schattenburg, at that time an unborn babe, might live. Franz was convinced that these people remained as true now as then, but Karl was unused to placing his life in the hands of strangers, even those who had once been faithful.

"Why have you demanded we meet you here, Franz? The village has embarked on wild celebration over the return of the ravens. I should not have left them tonight. The Hessians are ever ready with sword and musket." *Der Bürgermeister,* the mayor of Schattenhausen, a shriveled and skeletally thin man, nervously tugged at his pointed chin.

"Yes, Franz, why? You know what danger we face here," echoed *der Hauptmann,* the captain of the castle guards. "Friedrich is ever watching us. He has not forgotten his suspicions that we effected the escape of the Princess Magda."

"And do you, Herr Hauptmann, regret that now?" asked Karl from the shadows of the hood.

The captain's brawny hand slapped against the hilt of his sword, his keen eyes flashing with anger. "Who are you to question my honor or my loyalty? I faithfully served my rightful prince, and I would again was he here."

Karl slid back his hood. "And will you, Herr Hauptmann, serve his son as well?"

Shock rippled visibly through the captain and his companions, freezing them in varied poses of amazement and hope and doubt. A grim set to his mouth, Karl roughly stripped the thick fur glove from his right hand and folded back the cuff of his sleeve, revealing the birthmark on his inner wrist.

Herr Hauptmann's eyes widened. "The Crown of Schattenburg," he breathed, sinking to his knees and tilting up a luminous face. "*Majestät,* we thought never to see you in this lifetime."

"*Majestät,*" said Herr Bürgermeister, bowing low, "we, your people, have long awaited you."

The old woman came to him, reaching up. Karl felt her thin work-roughened hands tremble against his cold cheeks. He knew nothing of her but her name, Trude, and the fact that she had been his father's nurse. She should have been familiar to him.

He should have known the cradle song that she had been singing. He, like his father before him, should have learned her sturdy peasant's wisdom as a babe dandled on her knee. That he had not was another sin to lay at his uncle's feet, as if he had not sins enough. Sins that would soon, very soon, come home to roost with the ravens of Schattenburg.

Trude's eyes, glistening with unshed tears, tenderly searched his. "You have your mother's face," she murmured, her thumb caressing his cheekbone. "But your eyes . . . your eyes are your father's. *Ja*, you are his son."

"I need your help," Karl said.

"We are yours to command, as we were your father's before you," said Willi, the woodcutter, proud tears shining in his eyes.

"*Danke*," said Karl, touched by their expressions of faith. "I swear to you all that my father and my mother will be avenged and you will be released from Friedrich's power. But first, I must have the Englishman whom he has taken captive."

"We know of no Englishman, *Majestät*," said the Bürgermeister, frowning.

"Nor do I," said Herr Hauptmann. "The dungeons are all that remain in the hands of my men, all from Schattenburg. He is not there. All else is guarded by the Hessians. Perhaps he is in one of the castle towers, but . . ."

Karl frowned. He had expected them to at least know the Englishman was captive here. "Herr Hauptmann, if he is in the castle, I must know where."

"*Ja*, I will try, but the Hessians are closemouthed and loyal to Friedrich, as they are loyal to any who pay them."

Karl strode to the window, staring out at the snowdrifts. If Robbie could not be found, then Friedrich must be attacked indirectly, and his reaction would be unpredictable. Karl had hoped he

would not be driven to that last, and most dangerous, resort: the *Bildstock.*

The murder-marker had an old and honored history in the Franconian countryside. A memorial
pillar set up at the scene of a violent death, it often
pointed a finger of accusation at the murderer—and
that was what this one would do. To see the *Bildstock* suddenly appearing on the chapel altar on the
very spot where he had killed his brother would
drive Friedrich mad with rage, and that would make
him both dangerous and careless. Pray it was more
of the latter than the former.

"Willi"—Karl turned to the woodcutter—"you will
carve a *Bildstock* of oak. A simple pillar topped by a
cross with the inscription *An eye for an eye, a tooth for
a tooth.* I will need it in one week's time."

Willi's eyes locked with Trude's. In each face Karl
saw a flowering of worry and fear, not for themselves but for him. This then was what it meant to
take his rightful place. This love and loyalty that
gave unstintingly.

"You must do this thing?" Trude asked, with a
tremor of unease.

"I must," Karl said.

Her eyes searched his once more. "It will be
done."

"You know where—"

"All in Schattenburg know where—and how—our
prince was slain."

Karl's brilliant gaze touched one face, then another, seeking any weakness, any failing. He found
none. "I will meet you all here at midnight tomorrow. We must find the Englishman, and we have
but a week in which to do it."

The week was nearly over. Robbie was nowhere
to be found. Karl had spent his nights sneaking into
the dungeons of Schattenburg, hieing silently
through its secret passages, and exploring its cone-
roofed turrets and dusty cellars in the company of

Herr Hauptmann. He'd spent his days watching Anne's fear grow with every look and word Friedrich turned her way. She had at last, he thought, come to the full realization of her folly. At last, and too late.

As if to mock the morbid depths of Karl's mood, the morning was drenched in golden sunlight. The oval courtyard of *Chagrin* was astir. Horses stamped and blew great streamers of mist. Retainers darted about with cups of hot mulled wine. Anne, having abandoned the black of mourning and dressed in her sapphire-blue riding habit, seemed to spring out of the trampled snow like a summer flower. Her eyes had the wide, vacant look of one who, having been pushed to the limits of her endurance, moves by rote to act as she must.

Karl stared through the slits of von Dannecker's daffodil-yellow mask, cursing the awkward padding and the creaking corset, cursing Friedrich and himself. Between them, they had driven Anne to the edge of desperation. Friedrich with his cold and calculated cruelties. Himself with less calculated, but no less cold cruelty. He had never realized that disillusioned love could have the cutting edge of a knife. Though he wanted to offer Anne assurance through a fleeting touch and a bracing smile, he could not shatter the wall built by her betrayal. Though he understood her reason, he could not forget that she had loved him and left him. He could not forget that she loved him, but not enough.

Anne, mounting with the aid of a groom, sat erect in the saddle, her gloved hands light on the reins. Karl's gaze roamed hungrily over her tiny waist and full breasts. As if she felt that touch, her empty gaze sought him out. He saw no sparkle of laughter, no warmth, no hope, only a dull acceptance. He longed to take her by the shoulders and shake that acceptance away. He longed to plead with her to fight as hard to save their love as she had fought to save her brother's life.

Her gaze lifted to Friedrich on the loggia above them. She trembled visibly, and Karl's hands knotted into fists. Whatever happened, the wedding must not take place. The *Bildstock* had been completed and smuggled into the castle in a tumbril of firewood. Where Friedrich expected to find a bride, he would find instead the accusation of the murdermarker and Herr Hauptmann's men waiting to take him prisoner. Whatever happened, Anne would be safe. If Karl had to sacrifice her brother, her father, himself, she would leave Schattenburg unwed and under safe escort.

His gaze followed Anne's to the loggia and hardened. Friedrich, his hands clasped behind him, stood in the contemptuous stance of a man accustomed to being both feared and obeyed. Did he ever, Karl wondered, remember that his brother had been born to that right? Did he ever see the unhappy ghosts inhabiting every lavish corner of *Chagrin*?

Ghosts. Friedrich frowned on the busy scene below. Magda and his brother, Karl, and his everpresent companion, the raven: they had begun to haunt the exquisite salons, the bedchambers and halls, returning through flashes of memory as real as if they still lived. Memories that had been suppressed for all of these years returned only now with the arrival of the ravens.

The legend said they would return with the rightful prince, but that boy was long dead. Yet now everything seemed to be going wrong at once. Von Fersen had disappeared without a trace, after leaving on a mission so secret he had not told his minions what it was. Napoleon's empire was struggling in its last gasp, and with it would die Friedrich's every hope of expanding his own rule. The ravens had returned and, with them, the memories.

Memories of the twin brother Friedrich had hated because of the few minutes that separated him from the crown. Memories of Magda with her butter-yellow hair and her laugh like the mellow chime of a bell. Memories of Karl and Magda together, dancing, laughing, loving. Reminders of all he had been denied by his wound. And the final blow that decided him on fratricide—they expected a child, while he was half a man whose ambition would end not in a dynasty but in death. Now that ambition rested in Darenth's hands, a man he hated more bitterly than he had his brother.

Yet everything was not going wrong. His gaze fell on the musician with his round corsetted belly, his mask and frills and furbelows. Friedrich's lip curled in disgust. Did Darenth believe him a fool that he would not suspect even so foolish an object as that? He knew every time the "musician" slipped away from *Chagrin* in the dark of night. He knew where he went and whom he saw. Those traitors he would deal with later, a lesson to all who would betray him. Just as he would deal with Darenth and his spy later, when he had what he wanted from his old enemy. They would learn not to underestimate the Prince of Schattenburg.

Friedrich moved beside the balustraded railing and began descending the steps. His gaze followed Darenth, mounted atop a prancing gelding. The strain of the last week was telling on him. He looked as though he had not slept since their arrival, and no wonder. His son was held hostage. His daughter was threatened. He was helpless. Friedrich smiled. It had been many a long year since he had had such pleasure. *Ja*, it was a joy to anticipate his final revenge.

"*Fraulein*"—he approached Anne—"have you ever been on a boar hunt?"

"No, your Highness, the boar has long since died out in England."

"A pity. It is an old custom that a bridegroom of the House of Schattenburg prove his courage by killing a boar and presenting its ears to his bride."

She turned as pale as the lace at her throat, and Friedrich captured her wrist in a deliberately painful grip. "Courage, *Fraulein*." His lips folded back over his teeth in a lupine grimace. "You will have need of it to be a *Prinzessin von Schattenburg*. And I will have no mawkish weakling to wife. Remember your brother, *Fraulein*."

Remember your brother. It was all Anne could do. The reality of Friedrich was far more horrifying than her imaginings had ever been. Lavish in the entertainment of his guests, he had seen to her every comfort—watching her all the while as if she were a calf he was fatting for slaughter. His extravagant compliments meant as little to her as they seemed to mean to him. She knew the look in a man's eyes when he admired and desired a woman, a look that was utterly lacking in Friedrich's passionless gaze. He came alive only when hate blazed across his face, curling his mouth, flaring his nostrils, and turning his eyes the bright hue of a sun-scalded sky.

Her wrist still aching from his deliberately hurtful grip, Anne rode through the silent Schattenwald beneath the canopy of oaks. The voices of the woodsmen, muffled by distance, rippled through the shaded woodland. Friedrich, looking like a pagan warrior of old, rode ahead with a boar spear in one hand and a knife sheathed at his waist. Ahead, the boar-hounds began to bay and the beaters to scream.

"They found him!" Friedrich spurred his black gelding and pounded through the woods, followed closely by a quartet of Hessians ducking low-hanging branches.

"Anne." Cantor, wearing the peacock regalia of von Dannecker, trotted to her side. "You must accept the ears when he presents them. This is no time to whet his anger."

"I—I can't!" She shuddered.

"You can, and you will," he said adamantly.

"Puss, listen to him," added her father. "We dare not test Friedrich's temper. Not now."

Not now. Her gaze danced from her father's

frowning face to the glittering mask that shielded Cantor's from view. "What do you plan?"

"Puss, we cannot tarry!"

"No, I will know what it is!"

"You will know when you need to know, Anne, and no sooner. This is not a game we play," Cantor said harshly, spurring ahead.

He blended with the eerie shadows, vanishing from Anne's sight as he must soon vanish from her life. Though he wore the violet-powdered wig and the garishly colored coat of von Dannecker, it was her Cantor who sat in the saddle as regally as any man born to a crown. She had betrayed him and hurt him, stinging his pride and shattering his trust. She should not be surprised that he held himself aloof, that he spoke little to her and looked upon her seldom. Did he remember those few hours in Granny Goody's tiny cottage? Could he still hear the dull beat of the sleet on the thatched roof and the racing of her heart? Did he remember the fire of every touch, the glory of their union?

She wanted to call him back, to lead him into the deepest woodland glade and stay there forever. Touching. Being touched. Loving. Being loved. Laughing. Would they ever laugh together again? Would she ever again know the sweet heat of his kiss or the comfort of his embrace?

"Come, Puss. We dare not arouse suspicion by lingering."

"Father, I must know! What does he plan?"

"You will learn when the time is right," said her father, his gaze sliding away.

But there could be no right time for plots or plans if Robbie could not be found. And now her father and Cantor were in danger, too. If only they had let her come alone to do what must be done. If only— her gaze sought the beckoning shadows—she could slip away with Cantor and live for love and joy.

The shrill squeal of a boar and the frantic barking of the hounds echoed wildly. Anne's heart leaped into her throat, pounding furiously. "Father, I don't want to see—"

"Nor do I, daughter, but we must."

He urged his restless gelding through the woods. Anne followed to the edge of the clearing where a scene of gory carnage was in progress. The woodsmen, armed with spears and hunting bows, had formed a broad, loose circle. In its center a fallen oak—its rotting limbs thickly covered with woody, winter-browned bramble vines—had formed a lair from which the boar had been flushed. He stood at bay, his back arched, his snout down, and his curving tusks bloodied by the gutted hound that writhed and yelped nearby.

A trio of boar-hounds danced around him, their thick, squarish bodies amazingly agile. The boar's head swung from one to the other, his tusks threatening any that came too close.

"Heigh! Heigh!" Friedrich taunted, shouting over the yelping, yapping hounds. He knelt on the sifting snow atop crackling autumn leaves. The blunt end of his spear gouged the frozen earth and the thick shaft with its sharpened blade pointed at the boar's snout.

The boar's great head swung slowly, his beady eyes glinting red.

"Heigh! Heigh!" Friedrich shouted, his face alight with a savage delight.

The boar's head lowered and one hoof pawed at the earth, sending dirt flying. The other hoof pawed. He grunted, squealed his rage, and charged.

Anne wanted to close her eyes, but they were locked wide open in horror. The smile that sliced across Friedrich's face was no less brutish than the enraged red of the boar's beady eyes. He pounded toward the man, heedless of the deadly spear. Anne felt the vibration of the forest floor as a steady throb in her temples. For one shameful moment she hoped that Friedrich would falter and the boar would end the victor, then she would be free and Robbie would be saved. That hope slammed her eyes shut at the very moment the boar impaled himself on the spear and screamed.

She heard Friedrich's grunting efforts to hold the spear and the boar's crashing, rolling efforts to escape it. Unable to bear the suspense, she opened her eyes. Sprays of blood speckled the earth and spattered Friedrich like a butcher at work in the shambles. The boar's death rattle incited the howling hounds and the cheering men.

Anne turned her head, shivering. Cantor was opposite, his face grim beneath the mask. A heavy tread approached and the great flaps of the boar's ears were thrust into her line of vision. Her stomach churned with revulsion and her mind with rebellion. She wanted to reject both Friedrich and his offering, but she could not look away from his blood-drenched hand.

"*Fraulein,*" Friedrich began on an exultant note, "it is custom now for the bridegroom to ask the bride to wed him. She signifies her yea or nay by accepting the boar's ears or refusing them."

Anne's gaze shrank from his feral stare.

"So, *Fraulein,* will you have me, Friedrich Auguste, Prinz von Schattenburg, to husband?"

Her gaze moved with a will of its own, seeking Cantor. He sat atop his horse, silent and still. Beneath the mask his mouth was a thin, rigid line.

Although everything in her screamed a denial, she extended her gloved hand, slowly, reluctantly. The light weight of the ears fell into her palm. Blood seeped through her glove and turned as cold as her heart.

The small cavalcade, trailed by the woodsmen carrying the boar, entered the long, straight avenue that led to *Chagrin*. The sun glittered over the snowy landscape of carefully planned gardens. Friedrich and her father rode abreast. Anne followed, the boar's ears clasped tightly in her hand, the seeping blood turning sticky in her palm.

"So, Darenth." Friedrich's voice drifted back to Anne. "How will you assure the return of my principate?"

"As you know," her father said, "I have worked closely with our Foreign Minister, Lord Castlereagh—"

"Ah, yes. The Raven's Nest." Friedrich angled around in the saddle, in profile to Anne. "How did you come by such a name?"

It should have been a simple question to answer, but a startled expression brightened her father's darting glance. "You are aware, I am sure, that a raven will pluck out an unprotected lamb's eyes."

Anne stared at the slow beginning of Friedrich's smile—a beautiful, hauntingly familiar smile. Though she tried to remember where she had seen it, she could not.

"You saw the Emperor Napoleon as the lamb and yourself as the raven to pluck his eyes," he said. "I had not thought you so arrogant, Darenth."

"Success warrants arrogance," her father responded, so idly that Anne saw a thrust coming. "You misjudged me once before."

The air was charged with a brutal rage. Though Friedrich uttered no sound, Anne froze, like a deer catching a whiff of the hunter's scent. What was the reason for this rage that had lasted for years after the duel in their youth?

"Which of us, I wonder, will regret that more in the end?" Friedrich said in a deadly tone, and charged ahead down the long avenue to *Chagrin*.

Chapter 19

Friedrich raced between the low evergreen hedges crowned with snow. The geometrically arranged gardens filled with marble statuary flew by, while the taunt echoed on the wind whipping his face: *You misjudged me once before.*

He would have pulled his knife and struck Darenth dead, but he needed the smirking earl yet. The devil take him! He needed him to regain his principate and his full power with it, but when that was done . . .

Caw! Caw!

A thrill of fear coursed through Friedrich. Though the ravens had returned to Schattenburg, this was the first hint that they had arrived at *Chagrin*. He yanked viciously on the reins. The black gelding reared, neighing and pawing the air. Its hooves settling on the white shell avenue, it danced an agitated caracole, while Friedrich's head turned, keeping the raven ever in sight.

She was perched on the marble shoulder of that dreaded god of the ancient Saxons: Wotan, ruler of the kingdom of the dead, god of magic and prophecy. He was symbolized as a warrior with bulging muscles and flowing hair, carrying a spear in his hand. Ranged around his defiantly spread feet were those animals sacred to him: the eagle, the wolf, and the raven.

A superstitious chill scrambled across Friedrich's flesh and writhed like a snake low in his belly.

The raven. He knew her. He would know her anywhere. She had been his brother's faithful companion and protector in many a childhood scuffle. Friedrich bore the marks of her sharp beak on his hands, tiny scars that scissored across his knuckles. He would have worn more scars, but he had locked her out of the chapel on the night he'd killed his brother. Even now he remembered the frantic slamming of her wings against the rose window whose rainbow colors had streaked in columns across the altar where his brother had lain with blood trickling from the sharp blade of the knife embedded in his back. "Why, Friedrich? Why?" Karl had asked, dying without an answer. The raven had grown still then, settling on the delicate tracery and staring down at her master while she sang a mournful *Pruk, pruk*. Then she had flown away, transferring her allegiance to Magda, whose womb protected the future Master of the Ravens.

Magda had escaped Friedrich, but the boy had not. He was dead by von Fersen's hand. Or was he? He had to be! Von Fersen, cunning as he was, would not have dared to lie. The consequences were too great, and that wily henchman was too greedy for his promised honors to chance it.

So why had the raven returned now? Why did Friedrich feel this deep premonition of death and disaster?

He lurched around in his saddle. "Hans! Hans!" he screamed.

The woodsman came at a trot, his bow strung across his back.

Friedrich flung out his arm, pointing at the raven. "Kill her! You are my best bowman! Kill her!"

"*Nein! Nein!*" said Hans, backing away.

In his face Friedrich saw the intolerable echo of his own superstitious fear. "Gottfried! Gottfried!" he bellowed back to the tableau of frozen riders.

The Hessian, a fresh-faced youth of little wit and strong loyalty, galloped forward.

"Kill him!" Friedrich ordered, his long arm pointing not at the raven, but at Hans.

No sooner did the words leave his lips than the Hessian's knife whirred through the air and buried itself in the woodsman's chest. His hands scrabbling feebly at the deer-horn hilt, he fell full-length, twitched, and went still.

From the frozen tableau behind them, Anne's scream rose in full-bodied horror. Friedrich permitted himself a moment to exult. Now she and Darenth would know the danger of thwarting him. But his exultation was short-lived.

Caw! Caw! croaked the raven.

"Take his bow and kill her!" Friedrich ordered, his voice shrill with the fear that melted through bone and sinew to leave him aquiver.

The Hessian leaped from the saddle, yanked the bow from the woodsman's back, notched the arrow in a swift move, and aimed.

Caw! Caw! screamed the raven, as if issuing a challenge.

The arrow whirred over the winter-white garden. The raven soared away. The arrow sped by. Friedrich cursed.

While the raven swooped in a mocking circle overhead, another raven popped up from a Chinese urn, perching on the lip. Another flew from the topmost heights of a cherry tree and settled on the swaying twig of a shrub. Another and another appeared from the concealment of shrubbery and statuary, until the snowy garden was speckled with black. And from every strong beak there came the challenging cry of *Caw! Caw!*

Friedrich, like the dog-baited boar, swung his head from side to side, his ears battered by the cacophony of sound and his fearful heart slinging itself madly against his ribs. Everywhere he saw them. So many they would darken the day if they rose in flight against the sun.

His hands, stained with the dried blood of the boar, trembled around the reins, while his skin turned ashen and his face crumpled, losing its arrogance in ungovernable terror. He wheeled his horse about and fled into the forecourt of *Chagrin*.

Racing incontinently up the flight of stairs, he threw himself through the doors and sank back on them in relief.

His shrinking gaze roamed the colonnaded hall, where the pastoral scenes of the four seasons that flowed across ceiling frescoes were repeated in shallow bas-relief on apple-green chrysoprase cartouches woven round with gilded garlands. In this hall of white marble all was air and light, as delicate as the lovely Magda had been and as flawless as his brother. He hated it as he had hated them, as he hated everything he yearned to call his own. *Chagrin* had never been truly his. Only in Schattenburg, with its thick walls and dark chambers and dank atmosphere, did he feel at home. Only there, with its series of curtain walls stepping down the mountainside, did he feel safe.

He would not wait until the morrow to leave for Schattenburg. He would not wait until the day after to wed Darenth's daughter. He would depart this very day, and on the morrow, he would wed Anne at the altar where his brother had died by his hand.

Shuddering, he closed his eyes and found painted on his mind's eye the sight of the raven perched on Wotan's thick shoulder: Wotan, ruler of the kingdom of the dead, god of magic and prophecy.

Surrounded by a phalanx of hard-faced Hessians armed as if for war, the carriage clattered through the hushed shadows of the Schattenwald, carrying Anne and her betrothed to the ancient seat of his ancestors.

Death seemed to hover around her like a dark,

malevolent presence. She could not forget the
woodsman: his expression of horrified surprise; the
convulsive scrabbling of his hands at the knife; and
the thud of his body slamming into the frozen earth.
She could not forget the death squeal of the boar or
the blood dripping from Friedrich's hands. She
could not forget that Robbie had been his prisoner
for nearly a year. Her assurance that Friedrich would
not have dared harm her brother had been irrepa-
rably shattered. Images of Robbie beaten, brutalized,
and murdered filled her mind.

Friedrich sat opposite her, his shoulders mas-
sively broad against the ruby-red squabs and his face
clouded by a brooding stare. She was eaten by fear
of him; he was eaten by fear of . . . what? The ravens? It did not seem possible. Yet she too, staring
wide-eyed at that sea of croaking black, had felt the
eerie sensation that she was caught in the midst of
an inexplicable and otherworldly threat.

Friedrich's terror would make him more dangerous. He had regained his color, but it was the
flushed pink of remembered shame. Though Anne
hesitated to intrude on his silence, she must plead
with him once more.

"I pray you," she said softly, "let me see my
brother. There will be no tricks or—"

"No tricks, *Fraulein?* Will you promise that for
your father or for his man?" His hard blue gaze
slewed from the window to Anne.

His man. Her thoughts stumbled and reeled. Was
it possible he knew about Cantor? She dared not
look down or away, for fear she would betray her
guilty knowledge. "H-his man?"

His steady stare held a sententious mockery. "The
musician, *Fraulein.* That simpering fool who loses
simper and limp and paunch when he moves in the
dark of night to find your brother."

He knew. He had known all along. Anne sagged
against the squabs, staring blindly at the rosewood
panels carved in a shallow bas-relief of mythical

beasts. She must warn her father and Cantor that their secret was known.

"What will you do?" she asked, every word forced through her aching throat.

"Nothing, *Fraulein*. He will not find your brother. He is, as yet, no threat to me."

As yet. Anne trembled beneath his passionless regard. Strangely familiar, it was the same look her father wore while contemplating a chessboard queen and planning to move her where it suited him.

"And my brother?"

"He is very much alive and eager to see you," he said, his expression sardonic.

Anne's heart misgave her. Did he tell the truth? Or was it a lie? Was she sacrificing so much for nothing? If she was, it was a risk she had to take. "And when will I see him?"

A slow, malicious smile arced across his face. "After the wedding, *Fraulein*. You will be taken to your brother after we are wed on the morrow. Then you will tell your father what you have seen, and I will offer him escort back to England, where he will plead for the return of my principate."

"And if he fails?"

Friedrich's mirthless smile sent a frisson of new fear through Anne.

"He will not dare to fail, *Fraulein*," he said flatly.

The specter of failure haunted Karl. Stiff with tension, he bounced in the rattling carriage that followed Anne's through the pine forest. If he could not effect her escape, she would wed Friedrich on the morrow. On the morrow, when all of his plans had been laid for the day after. Tonight he must slip along the shadowy passages of Schattenburg to seek out Herr Hauptmann and inform him of the change in timing. He, in turn, must inform Franz.

"Dear boy, I should prefer to think the Legend of the Ravens of Schattenburg a superstition. However . . ." The earl paused, his brow wrinkling thoughtfully.

"However, my lord?" Karl prompted.

Darenth shifted restlessly, his expression that of a man confessing something shameful. "I own it gave me pause to ride down the avenue of *Chagrin* through that sea of cawing black."

"You need have no fear, my lord. They will harm neither you nor yours."

"It is quite extraordinary! Do they come at your will?"

"No, my lord. Only one, and she—"

"Leads the rest. Extraordinary!" the earl repeated, his gaze shifting to the window and sharpening. His long body angled forward, a curse hissing beneath his breath. "They followed us!"

"Yes, my lord." Karl's gaze turned to the window, where the ravens soared by, streamers of black flowing over bushes and around branches.

"Is it possible . . ." Darenth's head whipped around. "Is it possible that Friedrich has reason to fear them?"

"Very possible, my lord."

The earl sank back into his seat, his expression hovering between belief and disbelief. "Do you mean to say they would actually attack him?"

"Yes, my lord."

"Good God!" Darenth's wondering gaze returned to the window. "Then why have they waited? We would have been well rid of him."

"They attack only to protect one person, my lord, and that one, me."

The carriage slowed to pass through the first of a series of five gate-towers that permitted access through ring-walls topped with machicolated galleries between evenly spaced towers. In the distance, where the wall curved around the mountainside, workmen swarmed like ants. Stonecutters chiseled great slabs of red sandstone. Men strained against pulley ropes to heft the stones into place. Masons carried hods of mortar.

"If your son is held near the castle, my lord, he will be in one of these towers."

"Then why have they not been searched?"

"They are closely guarded by the Hessians. Our only hope is that Friedrich's feast for the villagers will loosen an unwary tongue, and Franz will learn which tower it is."

Darenth sat forward, his expression intent. "Before the wedding?"

"It is doubtful, my lord," said Karl, flinching from the pain that flashed in the earl's eyes.

Darenth rubbed his brow, as if it ached. "So it has come to this," he said, exhaustion tugging his voice into trembling depths. "I must choose between my daughter and my son."

"No, my lord. That decision is made, and all plans are laid. You cannot escape until the last moment before the wedding, lest Friedrich discover it before I am ready. I will send a guard. Trust him only when he says, 'The Master has come.' Then follow his instructions."

"Are you saying that I am to escape and leave you here?" the earl asked sharply. "I shan't—"

"But you shall! Who else can I trust to see that Anne is traveling down the Neckar while I confront Friedrich? Only you can force her to it."

"And even I may not succeed," Darenth said, scowling.

The carriage strained up the narrow ramp, crossing the wards between the gate-towers, until it exited the last dark cavern into the walled forecourt of Schattenburg. The castle climbed before them, a complex encrustation of circular towers and jutting turrets grafted onto an ancient octagonal keep. Karl descended the carriage under the myriad black eyes of the ravens, solidly lining the height of the forecourt wall, like silent judges at the bench. He limped toward the door, his handkerchief swishing, and was surrounded by a quartet of armed Hessians.

"*Was ist los?* What is going on?" he demanded.

"We are ordered to direct you to your chamber and guard you there until the wedding at dusk tomorrow."

Karl took the incarceration in his chamber lightly. The thick walls of Schattenburg were a honeycomb of secret passages filled with the stale air of centuries. A guard posted outside his door would not prevent him from slipping away to warn Herr Hauptmann and to demand of Anne that she leave with her father. In his chamber, he found the stylized raven carved into the mantel stone and waited for dusk.

The stone moved silently beneath Karl's hand. A section of the wall groaned and creaked open. He stepped into the passage, expecting darkness and finding the light of a flaring torch, expecting emptiness and finding a grinning Hessian pointing a primed pistol. Cold sweat oozed down Karl's spine.

"Return to your chamber, Herr von Dannecker."

The sharp claws of disaster shredding Karl's assurance, he backed into his chamber and watched the creaking door close. His clammy palms scrubbed down his lean hips. Friedrich knew. Not who he was. In that case he would already be dead. But Friedrich knew he had been searching for Robbie, and if he knew that, he also knew about Franz and Herr Hauptmann, Herr Bürgermeister, Willi, and Trude. They had risked their lives so that Anne's brother might be saved. Was Robbie worth the sacrifice?

A thought came. Karl, finding it untenable, thrust it away and turned into his chamber, scowling. But the thought returned, as insistent as a pesky fly. Whatever the political reality of Schattenburg might be, its prince was and would remain its leader. They had not risked their lives for Anne's brother, but for the hope of their future—for him. Was he, a man caught on the triple prongs of duty, desire, and revenge, worthy of their sacrifice, their loyalty?

Karl paced his chamber, wearing the carpet thin while blue-black night crept over the land. Never had he felt so helpless, so full of doubt. Had they been killed? Or had they been sequestered in the dungeon below? That seeping darkness full of skittering rats and skeletons chained to the cold stone walls. And Anne—what had happened to her? If his every hope of help was gone, how would he save her?

He considered entering the passage once more and leaping on the guard. A fool's plan. Dead, he could not save Anne.

At the window slit, he blindly perused the star-spangled sky. Hour after hour crept by, towing the silvery bulk of the moon through the heavens. It vanished above the window, and the hidden door groaned. Karl palmed the knife in his boot, spun around and waited, every muscle tensed to spring.

"*Majestät?*" came Herr Hauptmann's rough whisper.

"Friedrich has found us out," he said urgently. "Has he taken the others?"

"*Nein*," said Herr Hauptmann. "He is like a cat with a mouse. He must play before he springs. We yet have time."

A flood of relief swept through Karl. Whether he was worthy of the loyalty he had been given or not, he could not turn back now. It was more imperative than ever that he seek Friedrich's end. The lives of his people depended on his success. While Anne remained, he would be torn between his duty to his people and his desire to protect her.

"I must see Lady Anne. Are there guards in all of the secret passages?"

"No longer, *Majestät*," said Herr Hauptmann grimly. "My men have seen to that, and they will remain to take care of the others who will come at each change of the watch.''

Buckinghamshire lace foamed around Anne's ankles with her every agitated step. The fire crackling and spitting in the ancient stone hearth failed to take the dank chill from the air. The wan yellow flames of the fat candles burning atop rusty wrought-iron columns failed to pierce the darkness. The ceiling was lost in the cavernous black emptiness that pressed upon the curtained bed. The walls, covered with dusty tapestries depicting the gory carnage of war—haunting reminders of the hunt, of the boar's death rattle, and Friedrich's bloody hands—were lost in the dusky shadows. The musty air seemed to Anne to hold vestiges of ancient evil.

She was alone. Even Hetty had been forbidden to come to her, though Friedrich had promised she would be sent on the morrow to ready Anne for the ceremony. But what of her father? What of Cantor? What had happened to them? If only there was a way to warn them that Friedrich knew what they had been doing.

A rough, ratcheting groan—seeming to come from the stones forming the walls—ached through the air. Icy fear sluiced through Anne. She turned slowly, staring at the tapestry that quivered as if touched by a hand. Beneath it, a crack appeared in the moving wall. It screeched and creaked and sent chills leapfrogging over her flesh. The crack widened. A mirror-shined boot appeared, then another. Fingers curled around the edge of the tapestry and swept it aside.

Cantor, unmasked, glided into her chamber with a sleek and wary step. Anne sagged weakly against the paneled footboard of the burr-oak bed. The hidden door creaking closed behind him, he stood in the dim light. She drank in the sight of him, reacquainting herself with the beloved features that had been barred from her sight since that day in Granny

Goody's tiny thatched cottage. While they were achingly familiar, they were also strange. They wore none of the loving softness she remembered, but instead seemed as hard and unyielding as the marble statuary in *Chagrin*'s sprawling gardens. And in his eyes—those cornflower-blue eyes that had once blazed with passion—there was a cold ruthlessness akin to Friedrich's. A chill prickled her nape.

"Did he hurt you?" he asked roughly.

She had no need to ask who *he* was. "No, he only . . . frightened me." *As you are doing now,* she thought sadly. *What has happened to us, Cantor?*

The tension seeped from him, leaving his flesh supple over the bold bone structure, as if cold marble had been touched with the gift of life. For a moment his gaze met hers. The angry ruthlessness had been swept away by a surging tide of relief.

Anne wanted to fling herself against his broad chest, to slip her arms around his taut waist and hold onto him forever. She wanted to cry, *Save me! Save me from him!*

"You must leave tonight, Cantor," she pleaded, saying *I love you* in the only way she dared. "Friedrich knows you have been spying."

"No, Anne," he said slowly, his expression inexorable. "It is you who must leave on the morrow, with your father. I will send my man for you just before the ceremony—"

"I can't! Friedrich has promised that I will be taken to my brother after we are wed!"

Cantor's body stiffened, alert and waiting. "Did he tell you where?"

"No. He said only that I would be taken to him. Don't you see—"

"I see only that you will sacrifice yourself for nothing!" He crossed to her so swiftly, so angrily, she shrank back against the elaborately carved bedpost. "I will not allow it! You *will* escape with your father."

"And so, I am to flee in craven fear!" Her eyes blazed with an anger equal to his. "I am to leave my brother to the fate chosen by that monstrous man? No! I would rather be dead than to be so cowardly and disloyal!"

"You are not your brother's keeper, Anne!" he said furiously.

"Aren't we all our brothers' keepers? Don't we all have a duty to the people who love us and need us?"

Duty. The hated word glanced off of the armor of Karl's worst expectations. Her brother! Always her brother came first with her! His hands itched to clamp around her arms and shake her into submission. "You will either willingly leave with my man, or you will be trussed up and carried away," he said coldly.

She stepped back, her eyes huge in her ashen face. "You would force me against my will."

"Yes."

"You will leave me no choice?" she asked, her soft voice thin with disbelief.

"Just as you have left me none."

Anne leaned against the carved bedpost, as though her legs threatened to buckle beneath her. She stared after him with tear-flooded eyes, as though he had become a stranger to her.

Frowning, Karl entered the secret passageway and shut the door firmly behind him. He sagged against the wall and breathed deep of the stale air.

"*Majestät*," began the youthful guard, approaching with the torchlight shining over his eager face.

Karl waved him away, wondering if he had ever looked so young and eager, knowing he had never felt either—except once for a few weeks when he first met Anne.

He welcomed the darkness closing in behind the retreating torchlight. Darkness was better for the treacherous thoughts that crowded one after the other. What kind of man lived his life for revenge?

What kind of man would give up the woman he loved for it? It would not bring back his father. It would not give him the life he should have had. He was a man now, coming to Schattenburg as a stranger. He did not know its seasons as he knew those of the Lakeland. He did not know its people as he knew the English. Just as he had not fully belonged in England, he would not fully belong here. His life and his travels had made him a cosmopolitan man, comfortable everywhere, at home nowhere.

He frowned down the passage to the glowing light at the corner turn, where the youth awaited him. That youth knew who he himself was and where he belonged. Karl envied him that. His head sank back against the cool stone wall, his throat working convulsively. At home nowhere.

But was that precisely true? He frowned thoughtfully. Though there was no place and no people who made him feel at home, there was one woman who did. Anne. Only with her did he experience a haven of peace, a sanctuary that would always be his.

Don't we all have a duty to the people who love us and need us? she had said. Was Anne, like he, torn between duty and desire, between loyalty and love? Her capacity for loyalty was what he loved about her, yet he now resisted and resented it. Her loyalty to her brother was no different from his loyalty to the memory of his father and to his people. He was demanding of Anne something he could not give to her. It did not mean he loved her less . . . just as it did not mean that she loved him less?

Karl straightened, his burning gaze turning to the secret door. Wouldn't it be better to have what she could give, knowing that it was his alone?

In the suffocating darkness of her chamber, Anne huddled on the brocade coverlet in the shadows of the lofty canopy. Her cheek rested on her updrawn knees, her gaze following the mesmeric dance of a flame around a candlewick. Cantor would have her trussed up and carried away against her will. He would force her to leave Robbie behind in Friedrich's frightful hands. Though a weak and fearful part of her was giddy with relief that she would not be forced to wed Friedrich, she firmly squelched it. If she yielded to her cowardice and Cantor's demand, she would never forgive herself or him. She had seen an example of Friedrich's rage. She would not allow it to be turned against Robbie.

But what could she do? Her gaze shifted to the massive oak screen folded across a corner of her chamber. Cantor had said he would send his man just before the ceremony. A plan began to form. Yes, it would work. If she hid behind the screen, Hetty, dressed in her hooded cloak, could easily fool Cantor's man.

What would Cantor do when he learned she had deceived him once again? She wouldn't, couldn't, think about that. Thank God, she would not have to see him again until the deed was done. He would have no time to send her away or to weaken her resolve.

She heard a rough, ratcheting groan—coming, she knew, from the stones forming the walls. Cantor was returning. It could be no one else. She slipped from the bed, one hand gripping the corner post and her heart hammering against her ribs. The hidden door screeched and creaked. The tapestry quivered and Cantor appeared.

The candlelight gilded the curls spilled raggedly over his brow by a restless hand. It glowed a matte gold over the planes of his cheeks and lent the radiance of dark stars to his eyes. He stood stiffly, as if unsure whether to approach her or to run.

"What do you want?" she whispered, praying he would say what he had to say and leave her alone.

"You, Anne," he said softly. "I need you."

And she needed him, the strength of his arms and the promise of his love, so desperately she feared she should shun them. But how could she turn him away when the mellow music of his voice wafted through her, a sonorous vibration that harmonized with the delicate song in her heart? That song of love and longing and need that stretched out her hand to him.

He surged across the chamber. The tips of his fingers touched hers, and a thrill ran through her, heedless of all but the delight of his touch. His fingers glided around her hand, clasping it tightly.

"You do understand, Anne. You know why I must send you away."

She gazed up into his unsmiling face, her throat thick with tears she dared not shed. She understood too well. He wanted to protect her, but she could not allow it. Would he understand that? Or would he see only that she had loved him and deceived him once again?

"Yes, I understand," she whispered softly, drawing his hand to the seductive lace at her breast.

The lace caressed Karl's knuckles, intruding on his solemn mood, like the shy knock of a stranger at the door on a wild and stormy night. "Your brother will not be left to his fate, Anne. I will remain here to—"

"Y-you!" Fear smothered the bright light of her gaze. "Why should you remain here? This is none of your trouble. You should never have come at all. You should have remained in England, safe from danger."

The lace trembled against Karl's hand. A stirring of desire stole coherent thought. "I should not have been much of a man to leave you to face Friedrich alone," he said, vaguely aware that another chance was passing to tell her who he was, what he was, what he had to do. But it all seemed so unimportant now. Now, when a night stretched before him. A night alone with his Anne. "Trust me to do what must be done."

His finger idled at the base of Anne's throat. Her pulse leaped at his touch, and a sweet, silken melting stole her fear, leaving desire in its place. His wandering finger found the point of her chin, the corner of her mouth, the tremulous curve of her lower lip.

"Trust me, Anne."

"I would trust you with my life," she murmured thickly. But not with her brother's. Would he understand?

His head lowered, his gaze locked on her lips, which parted for her sigh and yearned for the pressure of his. One hand gently embraced the vulnerable column of her throat; the other spanned low across her back, pulling her against him. Her lashes feathered down, and she waited through a tiny eternity until his mouth claimed hers.

She was no innocent now. She knew what it was to be claimed by him. She knew the velvety heat of his lips, the fragrance of his breath, and the need that sent his mouth slanting hungrily over hers. She knew the desire that came in a scalding flood, the secret yearnings, and the fulfillment that only he could give her. She did not know how much more urgent the drive for fulfillment could be once it had been fully experienced.

Aflame, she surged against him, wrapping her arms around his neck, winnowing eager fingers through his hair, and fitting her trembling frame to his. A low growl sounded deep in his throat and evoked a mewling of need from her.

His hand slid from her throat to the tiny buttons guarding the deep yoke of her gown. One by one, they fell victim to his supple fingers, to the hot, trembling hand that unveiled the tender hollow of her neck and the voluptuous curve of her breast. His seeking lips banished the cool air, while his thumb glided across the sensitive aureola in a gentle friction that left Anne gasping for breath. Where his thumb had been, his lips followed, sucking gently.

Her every nerve seemed to be centered in the peak of her breast, quivering with tormenting ecstasy. "Cantor," she gasped, unsure whether to push him away or pull him closer, and so paralyzed, she suffered and gloried in his touch.

He tugged at the billowing lace of her gown and sent it sliding down her arms, pooling on the carpet like sea waves foaming on a dark shore. His arms swept around her, gathering her close, and she felt the tremors that swept through him as they swept through her, the need that claimed him as it claimed her.

"Anne, Anne." He sighed against her lips. "Sweet Anne."

"I love you."

She slid down his body, feeling the cold brass buttons of his coat, the roughness of wool and the smoothness of satin. Her eager fingers tugged at the knot of his cravat and tore at the fastenings of his shirt, while he shrugged out of his coat and ripped away his waistcoat.

His chest was bared to her. The broad, thickly furred chest that she explored with a wanton delight. Her fingers zealously mapped the interplay of rippling muscles. Her lips lightly danced along his ribs, to the deep pectoral, finding the hard, flat nipple peeping through a forest of gold. Her tongue flicked out. He froze, his breath whistling through his throat.

Her tongue flicked out once more, and she felt the nipple pebble and the shudder that coursed through him. A burgeoning awareness of power came to her. A humbling awareness that her touch could steal his will, as his touch stole hers. Her hands fanned across his chest, moving slowly, so slowly. He swayed beneath her touch, his lashes fanning down over his burning eyes, his tongue slicking across his dry lips.

"Anne," he said roughly, his arms sweeping out. One hand behind her knees, the other behind her back, he held her up and nuzzled her breast. "Two can play at that game, my lady," he said, a smile in his voice.

He tossed her on the bed, laughing at her playfully outraged gasp. He shed his boots and his leather pantaloons, then he lay beside her. One hand worshipped the curve of her hip, and the laughter in his eyes died, replaced by an impatient ardor that found its twin in Anne.

His long, strong body covered hers as lightly as thistledown. She pressed her lips to his throat, while his hips sought the waiting cradle of her thighs. She waited, breath suspended, thought suppressed, sensation supreme. Her lips savored the salty taste of him and gloried in the fierce throb of his pulse. Her breasts ached with every featherlight brush of the golden hair covering his chest. Her palms, exploring the powerful contours of his back, took joy in the tender abrasion of flesh to flesh. But the strongest sensation of all was the secret ache, the hot heaviness that undulated her hips and sent them rising to meet the rigid proof of his desire.

He entered her with an erotic silken slide, sighing when she melted around him, welcoming the swelling fullness, the heat, the pulsation that matched the fierce throb at his throat.

He remained still, as if he had come home after a long dark night and wanted to revel in a moment so sweet he could not bear to let it go.

Then he moved, a zephyrlike stroke. Anne surged to meet it. Another, and she joined him in the escalating cadence of seduction, that realm where temptation is not to be resisted and enchantment is the reward.

In the sweet aftermath, when Cantor held her as

if he were afraid she might wrench herself away and leave him alone, she stroked his cheek and whispered, ''I love you.''

And she wondered whether he would remember or believe her on the morrow when he learned that she had loved him and deceived him once again.

Chapter 20

The narrow, three-storied houses of Schatten-hausen, each floor cantilevered over the one be-low, hunkered down over the narrow village street, protecting it from the brilliant sunlight pouring out of the cold, clear sky. An ox turned on a spit near a sprawling oak. Barrels of beer and a vat of bratwurst welcomed all comers outside the *Gasthof*. The chill air was heady with the aroma of baking bread and the vinegary pungence of sauerkraut.

Prince Friedrich had laid out a feast for the cele-bration of his marriage, but no air of festivity hung over the solemn gathering. The Hessians, every-where in sight, stomped about in their tasseled boots, cashmere trousers, and blue cloaks. Gorging on chunks of bread thickly spread with *Pflaumenmus*, a rustic plum sauce, spindle-limbed children dodged the quick-tempered and quick-fisted soldiers. Gravely silent women, spots of vivid color in the richly embroidered aprons worn over black pleated skirts, shied away from the leering Hessians. The men, both the villagers and the masons that worked on Friedrich's ever-spreading curtain walls, were in-distinguishable in bibbed leather trousers and short coats. They traveled in packs, drinking dark beer, talking quietly among themselves, and secretively eyeing the swaggering mercenaries. Among them, the few young men were missing an arm or a leg or an eye. The others had all been used as fodder by

Friedrich to feed Napoleon's deadly appetite for soldiers.

Franz Grillparzer moved among them, a mug of beer in his hand. The chill wind cut through his fur-lined coat, but he gave little thought to the discomfort of aching fingers and toes. There was a marked difference among the villagers since the return of the ravens. A glint of rebellion could be seen in the men's eyes, spurred by a hope they were only now daring to feel. Friedrich, like his ancient forebears, had stolen from them both their livelihoods and their dignity. There had to be a way to harness their anger and use it.

Franz had spent a week trying to find news of the Earl of Darenth's son. Now time was running out. The fireball of the sun was drifting low in the western sky. The *Bildstock* would soon be in place, awaiting Friedrich's arrival for the wedding at dusk. And what he would do when he saw it, none could say.

Franz leaned against the gnarled trunk of the oak tree, listening first to the low, rough growl of a trio of village men, then to the soft conversation of a group of masons. He heard nothing of significance.

Verdammt! This was a fool's task! Friedrich was their quarry! They should be taking their vengeance, putting Karl on the throne! Then they would have time to find the foolish boy. Whatever they owed the earl, he had received back multifold. Yet, Franz feared, it was not for the earl or the boy, but for the woman, Lady Anne.

Karl had not been the same since he'd met her. His drive for vengeance had been blunted. His sharp edge of suspicion had been dulled. Franz feared that if Karl were put to the choice, he would choose the woman over his own life. And that life was too important.

Chafe as he did against this fool's task, Franz had served the father and now he served the son. As he had loved the father, so he loved the son. Karl had been in his keeping since Princess Magda had laid in Franz's arms a squalling babe still wet from the womb. She had made him swear to protect her son to the death, to lead him as a child and to follow him as a man. And follow him he would, to hell if that was where he led. But he did not like this delay.

His gaze lifted to the ravens, perched in silent rows on the broad ocher roofs. Every moment added to their risk. Now Friedrich knew the musician was a spy for the earl. How long would it be before he learned precisely who that spy was?

Franz frowned. Willi was certain that the mason, Gunter, knew something. In the last year he had changed from a garrulous drinking companion to a morose loner with the look of a man with a guilty secret. Whether that secret was the one they needed, Willi didn't know. But there was no one else. Gunter was their last hope.

Franz headed for the *Gasthof*. The crowded public room had white-washed walls and a parquet floor and polished copper pots lining the deep mantel above the hearth. His dark eyes scanned the room, spying the stonemason, Gunter, in the corner, alone and deep in his cups.

Franz shrugged out of his coat and joined the man, slinging the ladder-backed chair around and straddling it. "Bitter day," he said by way of conversation.

"Bitter day," echoed Gunter, hefting his massive stoneware cup and burying his face to his haggard eyes.

Franz drummed his thick fingers on the scratched tabletop. "You work for Prince Friedrich?"

The cup, on the downward swing to the table, paused in midair. The man's pale, bloodshot eyes darted him a look of suspicion and guilt before dropping cautiously. "*Ja*," he said, with an expression of disgust. "I work for the prince."

If that look of guilt told the tale, he did know something. Franz suppressed a tremor of impatience. If only he could wring the answer from the man and be on his way.

"A *schoppen* of brandy for myself and my friend," he bellowed to the innkeeper.

One *schoppen* followed another and another, while Franz's gaze returned repeatedly to the window, where the sinking sun played a game of catch-me-if-you-can with the diamond-shaped glazing panes. Gunter proved to have an amazing capacity to remain clearheaded. The sun vanished, and at last his stubby, flax-colored lashes sagged over his bloodshot eyes. His thick fingers kneaded his sun-browned temples.

"The Englishman," he muttered around the glass of brandy at his lips.

Franz froze, unsure whether to prompt him with a question or wait for him to say more.

Gunter shuddered. "He is a beast," came his slurred whisper.

"The Englishman?" Franz asked softly.

"*Nein*"—the mason's pale gaze swept the space around them, as if looking to see that none listened—"Prince Friedrich."

"But he always has been. That is nothing new." Franz wanted to grab the man by the throat and choke the answer from him.

"Worse, now," the mason confided, a man with a secret that he both wanted and feared to tell. "Much worse."

"It is said that he murdered his own brother for the throne," Franz whispered. "What could be worse than that?"

The mason's shrinking gaze roamed the public room. He leaned forward, pulling Franz closer. "Just over a year ago, I was called to him. He took me, well-guarded, to the southeast tower of the lowest curtain wall. There, he had me seal an Englishman in a crypt in the tower wall."

A chill pebbled the flesh of Franz's arms. "The Englishman is dead?"

"Nein." The man frowned. "I was told to leave one stone out of the wall so that he might be fed through it. The tower is well-guarded. He must yet live. He must!" the man said desperately. "If he does not, I am guilty of his murder!"

The stonemason was not the only man who thought of murder in the waning light of day. Friedrich strutted around his chamber, his boots mirror-shined and his uniform a pristine white spattered with a rainbow of orders and decorations dangling from ribbons on his chest. He paused before the full-length cheval mirror in a Napoleonic pose. Not a wrinkle betrayed his age. Not a single golden hair strayed from place. Not a doubt assailed him.

He drew strength from the dank air and sturdy walls of Schattenburg. He basked in the remembered glory of its ancient history of rapine and murder, of ancestors who knew what they wanted and took it. Not like those of recent memory who considered themselves enlightened rulers. Enlightened! Another word for weak and spineless!

He curled his hand into a fist. It still had the power to crush a man's throat.

An exultant light gleamed in his eyes. Soon now, it would be done. He would be wed to Darenth's daughter, and then the earl would have no choice but to return his principate to him. And when that was done, he would take his final revenge. At last, he would be at peace.

Nothing would go wrong. The contingent of Hessians should, even now, be knocking at Lady Anne's door to conduct her to the chapel.

Anne longed to latch her fingers onto Hetty Peabody's scrawny shoulders and shake her into submission. Cantor's man was due at any moment, Friedrich's Hessians at any time, and her maid was balking like an obstinate Welsh mule! Hetty's thirst for adventure was now dead ash. Not an ember remained to be fanned back to life. Worse, timidity had been added to obstinacy, driving Anne to the verge of hysteria.

Hetty, her thin arms folded across her narrow chest, firmly shook her head. "His lordship 'ud have me skin, and who's to blame him!"

Anne's appeal "for Robbie's sake" had fallen on deaf ears. Her appeal for her own sake had found Hetty stubbornly silent. She now tried another tack. "Don't you want to get back to Darenth Hall, to Granny Goody and your young man?"

An arrested expression darkened Hetty's myopic gaze. "Oh, milady, if only I could! I'd stay so close to home, I'd not even go to Dartford!"

"Then all you have to do is wear my cloak and remain silent while the guard takes you and my father away. You can be downriver before dusk falls."

"But his lordship—"

The hidden door creaked. Anne caught Hetty's hand and sent her flying behind the screen.

"Milady!" shrieked Hetty, stumbling over a hatbox.

Anne flung up a hand to brace the rocking mahogany panels and heard the guard step through with a click of his heels. She spun to greet him, her cheeks aflame. "My maid," she said breathlessly, "is unusually clumsy today."

"Humph!" came a retort from behind the screen. "And so would ye be if—"

"Hush, Hetty!" Anne threaded her fingers at her waist and clutched at her stomach, which felt as if every butterfly on the Continent had taken up residence in it. "Mein Herr?" she questioned.

The youthful guard's hazel-eyed gaze glided from the screen, where Hetty was bumping and grumbling audibly. He straightened as stiff as the crossed lances in the Great Hall below, fair hair spilling across his brow and a blush of pride staining his cheeks. "The Master has come," he said, as if announcing the Second Coming.

Anne gave scant thought to the oddity of the pass-word. She had more to worry about. Would the stubborn, willful Hetty do as she asked? She nod-ded, spun, and leaped behind the screen.

"Hetty, I pray you, do this for me now!" she hissed. "I'll never ask anything else of you."

"If I had a ha'penny for every time Lord Robbie and ye promised that—"

A rapping at the door set Anne atremble. The Hessians, and she not ready!

"*Fraulein*," commanded a thickly accented voice through the door, "ve haf come to take you to *die Kirche*."

"*Fraulein?*" whispered the youthful guard, his voice climbing and breaking.

"Milady," squealed Hetty.

"A moment, I pray you!" Anne called out shak-ily. "Just a moment! I must dress!"

She made no further plea, simply eyeing her maid with an imploring gaze.

Hetty's pointed chin sank. "His lordship 'ull have me skin!"

"Thank you," Anne whispered fervently, snatch-ing up her cloak and whipping it around her maid's narrow shoulders. Adjusting the hood, she set a hand to Hetty's back and propelled her out into the chamber.

"*Fraulein*," the youthful guard whispered franti-cally, his heels clicking.

Anne waited for the hidden door to groan closed with a last sharp scrape, peeked out, and found her-self alone. But not for long. Friedrich's men waited beyond the door to escort her to *die Kirche*.

Her gaze strayed to the tapestry, still quivering from the rapid passage of Hetty and the guard. It was not yet too late. She had but to turn the stylized raven, and the door would creak open. She could flee down those secret passages and wait safe in En-gland for Cantor to come for her. And he would come. Of that she had no doubt.

She closed her eyes, summoning him in the age-old way of lovers. She felt the moist heat of his lips moving over her mouth, as if he sipped the nectar of life itself. She felt his touch, at once soothing and arousing as his hands slipped over the silken mystery of her flesh. Cantor. Her Cantor. How she needed him.

A bubble of anger rose from the miasma of doubt. If only Robbie had been different. If only he had not always heeded the clarion call of adventure. She might now have Cantor, guiltless and carefree. She might wed him and love him.

A foolish dream. Robbie wasn't different, nor was she.

Where was he? How was he? When she saw him once more, would he, like Brat Raeburn, smile his old devastating smile and look out through eyes that had seen hell?

That thought stilled her trembling and sent her, head high, to the door. She was condemned by her fear for her brother and for Cantor. She could not fail them now. Her hand gripping the blush-pink shawl at her breast, she greeted the quartet of Hessians, come to escort her like a felon to the gallows.

Surrounded by the armed guards, she moved sedately across the common room to the turret stair, where torches gobbled up the darkness. Cantor had had a plan, though what it was he hadn't said. Now that she'd ruined it, was she risking his life?

Close wrapped in the shawl, she moved through the Great Hall overlooked by ancient arms, rusty armor, and battered shields. From the passage there wafted the aromas of a feast in the making. Her stomach threatened to revolt.

The chapel doors loomed at the end of the hall: massive oak timbers, intricately carved and banded in bronze that seemed to bite into the wood as her fear was biting into her heart. She was alone now. Her father would be long gone with Hetty at his side. Though she could give hearty thanks that he was safe away, she wondered at her own foolhardiness. Now that the moment was upon her, she wanted to push through the guards and flee.

She refused to think of what lay ahead; nevertheless, questions crept around the prickly edges of her defenses, of how she would bear Friedrich's kiss, his touch, his intimate knowledge of her body.

Footsteps echoed in the hollow cavern of the Great Hall, bouncing from the soot-blackened beams overhead. She turned slowly, expecting Friedrich. She saw, instead, her father.

Her frantically pounding heart seemed to lodge itself firmly in her throat. He should have been safe away! But here he was, his mane of iron-gray hair framing a dark frown and the frown wrinkling around eyes that seemed to scream across the length of the hall: *Did you think I could be fooled by Hetty wrapped to the eyes in your cloak?*

He came nearer. A muscle in his jaw worked convulsively. His hands clenched spasmodically. "More mettle than sense," he said, without a glimmer of his former pride in that fact.

Would Cantor, too, be so disappointed in her? Would his eyes, like her father's, betray a terrible fear?

The Hessians were crowded around them as thick as her doubts. She stared at the massive chapel doors. Where would Cantor be while she was irrevocably wed to Friedrich?

Inside the chapel, Karl stood near the chancel rail. He was garbed in von Dannecker's stuffing and corset, but not in the musician's garish style. Instead he wore black velvet and white with touches of glittering silver embroidery—the colors of mourning. He stared through the slits of his black velvet mask at the altar where his father had been murdered. It was the completion of a pilgrimage begun at his birth, the fulfillment of his mother's dying wish.

Had she given his father all that Anne had given

him? The treasure of her heart, the gift of her body, the precious burden of her love—and so much more. Had she made his senses sing and his soul float free?

Yet, Karl could not float free of the bonds of hate. He stared at the altar and the *Bildstock*, lovingly crafted by Willi. He read the inscription carved deep into the polished oak column: *An eye for an eye, a tooth for a tooth.* Silently implied was: *A death for a death.*

Another death will not bring my father back. The thought whispered out of nowhere, and he thrust it away as unworthy of him. If ever a man had earned the vengeance of murder, Friedrich was that man! Karl had lived too long with that single purpose to easily turn from it now.

Yet after carefully watching his uncle, he had come to believe that Friedrich's life meant little to him, while the trappings of power meant everything. The greater punishment would be to take his wealth, power, and title, leaving him alive with nothing.

Karl shifted restlessly, a frown clouding his brow. Was that the mercilessness his uncle deserved? Or was Anne's insidious softness weakening his own resolve?

Damn! Friedrich would be shown the mercilessness he had shown! *And you will become another such as he,* the stray thought whispered. Karl clenched his jaw, jutting it fiercely. He would not weaken now!

He stepped onto the altar and moved behind the rood screen, finding Herr Hauptmann hiding behind the organ's shiny silver pipes. "Are your men in place?" Karl asked.

"*Ja,*" said Herr Hauptmann.

"I want him alive," he said firmly. "He will face execution as any murderer would, and I want him to know who is doing it and why."

"*Majestät,*" protested Herr Hauptmann.

"Alive," Karl repeated. "And nothing is to be done until I give the signal, 'The Master has come.' Make sure your men do not move before then."

Herr Hauptmann moved away to warn the men hidden behind columns, lying beneath pews, and secreted in the dark corners untouched by the candlelight. When Friedrich came, he would find armed guards in place of the bride he expected. Karl nodded to the wide-eyed boy waiting to pump the bellows and slipped onto the organ's bench.

The raven flew out of the shadows and landed on the music arch. Agitated, she hopped from foot to foot, refusing to be calmed by Karl's gentle stroking of her back. "Soon," he whispered, "soon, it will be over."

Anne was gone now, safely traveling down the winding Neckar with her father. He was free to take his vengeance.

The swelling tones of Bach's "Kyrie" rose from the organ pipes, an awe-inspiring plea for the Redeemer's mercy from a man who had no mercy in him. The raven deserted Karl, perching on the *Bildstock* to wait. Karl's supple fingers moved through the fluid notes. He would like to lose himself in Bach's majestic vision, but that required peace and he was as taut as the bellows at full prime.

He should be thinking of his father, of the life lost in his youth. He should be thinking of his mother, dying as much from a broken heart as from the complications of childbirth. He should be thinking of his people, soon to be delivered from the yoke of oppression. He should be thinking of what he would do once he assumed his throne and began his duties. But all he could think of was Anne.

He saw her eyes in the silvery moonlight pouring through the great rose window. He felt the downy warmth of her skin with every cool touch of the ivory keys. He tasted the honeyed sweetness of her lips on the musty air of the chapel. He yearned for her with the passion of a man who had learned that his passion could be slaked at the loving, giving breast of only one woman. He gave fervent thanks that she was away and safe, for he knew there was nothing

he would not do to save her. The purpose of the
past had been replaced by the dream of the future.
He now did what he must to ensure the life of that
dream. And when his work here was done, he
would return to England, to Anne. He would woo
her and wed her and bring her home to Schattenburg.

The massive oak doors creaked. His fingers stumbled over the keys, sending a trio of flat notes
whooshing up the organ pipes. He turned slowly on
the bench, preparing to rise and rip away his mask,
revealing himself to Friedrich. Through the delicate
tracery of the rood screen, he saw . . . Anne!

The sick, sinking sensation of imminent disaster
was quickly seared away by the burning heat of a
thunderous rage, savagely spurred by fear. His dis-
believing gaze raced over her white wool gown, her
blush-pink shawl, and the cloud of ebony curls
framing her bloodless face. She had promised him
and deceived him once again. She had stepped
squarely into the deadliest peril. She had ruined his
every plan. If they escaped from this with their lives
it would be a miracle!

Still, there was Franz in the village below. All was
not lost as long as Franz was free.

Karl's mind reeled with the implications. The *Bildstock* was in place and could not be removed with
Anne's Hessian guard in full sight. His men, those
loyal few who followed Herr Hauptmann, were in
place and waiting, but they had not had time to take
all of the Hessians one by one in furtive secretive-
ness. The mercenaries were still too many to be
overcome by brute force, unless Friedrich was taken
first. And Friedrich could only be taken in a melee
that would threaten Anne's life . . . and the earl's.

Damn Darenth! Why hadn't he taken Anne away?
A foolish question. Anne did nothing against her
will.

If Karl could detach them from their guards, then
he could give the order for his men to attack. In the

melee that followed, he could spirit Anne and the earl away to the secret passages and safety.

"Herr Hauptmann!" he called softly to the man hiding behind the soaring wall of the organ pipes. "Await my order, but do nothing without it!"

He moved quickly around the screen, bouquets of black and silver ribbons bouncing at his knees. He approached her, slowing, limping, wafting the lacy handkerchief, posturing for the Hessians' benefit. "*Fraulein*"—he bowed deeply, sending a cloud of white powder sifting from his wig onto the polished oak floor—"you vill, *natürlich*, vish to see de organ vhere I vill play. And you, my lord, vill come vit us."

He took her hand and felt it, icy cold and trembling, in his palm. Her eyes were dark and frightened. His, he knew, must betray his rage and frustration. "Come, *Fraulein*," he commanded.

Behind her, the great oak doors opened with a swoosh. A wedge of full-armed Hessians strode in, making way for Friedrich.

In the village far below, a barge bumped against the stone quay. Heinrich von Fersen leaped nimbly over the waterweeds to land solidly ashore. Though a cap was pulled low over his thinning, mouse-brown hair, he pulled it lower still, shadowing the pale eyes gleaming with a fanatical light. His rough clothes chaffed his skin, another faggot of irritation to lay on the inferno of rage.

Did they really believe he could be held prisoner forever? He had forgotten the bone-rattling terror that had claimed him when he thought Franz Grillparzer would kill him. He remembered nothing but the endless questions and the empty days when he paced the hidden room of a hidden house, seeing none but his jailers. It had taken him weeks to hone the handle of a spoon into a sharp weapon, and more weeks to find the opportunity to use it. As he expected, his jailers grew careless. One was now dead, the other wounded, and he was free.

Free to seek out Prince Friedrich and tell him he had failed. Von Fersen paused for a moment, plunging his shaking hands deep into his pockets. His gaze climbed the forested heights of the Riesenberg to the castle on its crest. Frightened though von Fersen was, Friedrich was his only hope of the life he meant to have.

Scanning the village street, von Fersen saw a man exit the *Gastof* at a run, pale lamplight spilling over his grizzled hair. Von Fersen's eyes narrowed on the man's burly back. Franz Grillparzer! And where Franz was, his master was sure to be! Perhaps Franz was even now heading to him as he strode rapidly into the narrow track that looped like a snake up the mountainside.

Von Fersen watched him blend with the shadows beneath the pines. A man climbing straight up through the trees and brush could cut across the loops and lay in ambush.

He moved quickly, breaking into a run, his teeth chattering with the excitement of new hope. He scrambled up the mountainside, desperately racing against time. At the first loop, he paused to listen to the hurried footsteps slapping against the dusty track ahead of him. He had missed Grillparzer!

Waiting for the footsteps to fade into the distance, he gasped for air, dragging in the resinous scent of the pines. Padding silently across the track, he lunged into the thick undergrowth and began the precipitous climb. Briars snagged at his hands and clutched at his rough wool trousers. An animal scurried away in the dark, leaving behind its musky scent. He stubbed the toe of his heavy boot on a limestone outcropping and cursed beneath his breath. A sliver of moonlight penetrated the night. The loop of the track was ahead. His lungs ached, his bleeding hands stung, but he forced himself to greater effort.

He reached the dusty rim of the track and sank to his knees, gasping for breath. Someday, someday, he vowed, his path would be as smooth as the avenue leading to *Chagrin*. All he had to do was take Grillparzer now.

The slap of footsteps on soggy snow pulled von Fersen up and sent him slinking behind the trunk of a pine tree. His heart pummeled his aching ribs. Every rasping breath seared his lungs. Down the road came the dark figure of a man emerging from the lighter shadows behind him. Von Fersen's hand climbed to the bone-handled knife at his waist, his fingers crawling around the hilt.

Grillparzer came abreast of him, so close he could hear the huff of his breath and smell a whiff of brandy. He waited while his quarry moved one step ahead, two. It would be safer to wrap an arm around Grillparzer's throat and hold the knife at his back, but the man was a burly giant, far too tall for him to reach. Another reason to hate him. Never mind. The knife would cut him down to size!

He leaped out and pressed the point of the blade to Grillparzer's spine. Sensing his shock of fear, von Fersen smiled. "I would not move were I you," he said in a deadly, oily tone.

"Von Fersen!" Franz said, his voice sharp with surprise.

"You did not think I would be gotten rid of so easily, did you?" He dug the point into Grillparzer's back, glorying in the swift, pained hiss of his breath. "Where is he?"

"Who?" The sweat popping on Franz's brow glistened in the moonlight.

"Do not take me for a fool! Where is your master? The one who calls himself Karl Auguste Wilhelm the Second!"

"Far away from here!" said Franz. His hands clenched into meaty fists. The shoulders of his coat climbed beneath his bunching muscles. His breath slowed, stopped.

Von Fersen, sensing that Franz was gathering himself to attack, knew he could not prevail against his greater strength. Grillparzer began to whip around, and von Fersen thrust the knife. The sharp point slipped easily through the coat, penetrated the flesh beneath, and glanced off of a rib before plunging to the hilt. Even that did not stop Franz. He continued unchecked, his brawny fist connecting squarely with von Fersen's jaw.

He felt an explosion of pain and a driving force that sent him flying through the air to land with an angry rustle of branches in the prickly top of a low-growing holly. He rolled off, gasping, staring at Grillparzer who grunted with pain and fell to his knees, plunging full-length across the track.

Chapter 21

The silvery notes of the *Kyrie* were drifting into the Great Hall when Friedrich strode beneath his ancestor's battered accoutrements of war. Never had he felt his power so fully. Where they had needed sword and shield, he needed nothing more than cunning and patience. It had taken him thirty-five years, but at last, he was poised to skewer Darenth on the lance of his vengeance. His mobile lips curled back from his teeth in the semblance of a smile.

Nothing would go wrong now. He had seen to every eventuality, unlike the credulous Earl of Darenth who fully expected him to keep his word.

"Your Highness!" The captain of his Hessian troops came at an uncharacteristic trot. "May I speak with you?"

"This is hardly the time. My bride"—his lip curled from his teeth like a boar-hound anticipating the kill—"awaits me in the chapel."

The captain, a man who sold his skills but never himself, betrayed his distaste with a flare of his patrician nostrils. Friedrich's smile broadened.

"I would not disturb you now, your Highness, but something strange is happening. The men I sent to guard the secret passages have not returned from their watches."

Friedrich stared down his nose at the smaller but no less rigidly erect man. "Must I both pay you and do your thinking for you? Send men after them to see what has happened.''

The captain's chin climbed a notch. ''I have, long since. They have not reported back. I can only assume that they, too, have vanished the way of the others.''

''Is it possible that they desert their posts?''

''*Nein!*'' The captain's firm denial was punctuated by the trio of flatted notes whooshing up the organ pipes.

In the silence that followed, Friedrich's sensation of infinite power faded with the jarringly flat unmusical notes. If he was not safe here in Schattenburg, he would be safe nowhere. Only Darenth would have dared this stealthy attack, but the earl could never rout him here. It was a measure of assurance in a world whose solid earth now quaked beneath his polished boots.

''Summon the troops from the village and send them en masse into the secret passages. Order them to kill every traitor they find!''

Watching the captain march away, aquiver with indignation, Friedrich remembered the raven perched atop Wotan's broad marble shoulder. Wotan, god of magic and . . . prophecy. Though he paid lip service to the church, Friedrich was the incarnation of his ancient Saxon forebears in more than their lust to conquer and rule. He carried the seeds of their archaic superstitions, and those superstitions whispered that the end was near.

His gaze turned to his personal guard of eight, but the comfort he sought was scant. They had been chosen for their reckless courage, skill at arms, blind obedience, and muscular good looks. He could pit them against thrice their number with never a doubt about the outcome, but they were only men. They could not fight the phantom warriors of myth.

He summoned them with a nod, and they marched around him, forming a defensive wedge that moved into the chapel ahead of him. Though his head was high and his shoulders squared, Friedrich's assurance had become simple bravado. Darenth would not see a moment's hesitation in him, not a glimmer of the surely groundless fear that dried his mouth to dust.

The impeccably groomed earl stood behind the last pew, his white-gloved hand gripping the polished oak. Friedrich studied the furrows in Darenth's brow, the lines at the corners of his eyes, and the creping of the skin beneath them. He looked far older than Friedrich, his senior by five years.

That tickling of his vanity brought a lilt to his mouth. His gaze dismissed the earl and shifted to Anne. She stood like a protected child between the lean figure of her father and the taller, broader figure of von Dannecker, who held her hand.

Was it that way between them? Their hands parted reluctantly, Anne's curling beneath the shawl knotted at her breast. Friedrich's smile held a hard edge of frost.

He could feel emanations of anger and resistance, coming, curiously enough, from von Dannecker. No doubt, he suffered his failure to find the earl's son and so deepen the affection of the daughter. And there *was* affection there. It shone in the stricken gray of Anne's eyes, darting to the masked spy, a look of longing and despair.

But she would not escape him now, Friedrich thought. It was too late for whatever they had planned.

"Lady Anne"—his deep voice oozed pride—"you look positively hagged. Did you sleep poorly?"

Her pallid cheeks flamed with color. "I—I slept quite well, your Highness."

She hadn't. That was as obvious as her guilty blush. He studied the lavender smudges beneath her eyes and the tremors racing across her lips. Surely, they were nothing more than signs of her distaste for the coming nuptials.

Pinching her fingers between his, Friedrich

brought her hand to his lips. Her lashes quivered, glossy black as ravens' wings. A chill speared through him.

"Come, *Fraulein*," he said, turning to the altar.

The altar. The *Bildstock*. The raven. The images flashed in his mind with the primeval force of lightning, searing images fraught with superstitious terror. A terror that stormed through him, finding an outlet in the uncontrollable quiver of his taut abdomen.

A tall thick column of polished oak topped by a wooden cross, the *Bildstock* was both a memorial to the slain and an accusation of the slayer. It was set on the exact spot where his brother had died by his hand. Carved deep into the column was the threat *An eye for an eye, a tooth for a tooth.* A human threat, and one Friedrich had no doubt he could thwart. No man alive matched his cunning and will to survive.

But there was another threat, an inhuman one that touched the deep and primitive wellspring of ancient myth. A threat that vowed a return to right an old wrong. The raven, companion and protector of the Master of the Ravens, perched atop the oaken cross, her beady eyes watching him with the wisdom of the ages and the hatred of good for evil.

Caw! Caw! Caw! she cried her accusation.

Terror flayed Friedrich's pride and sent him backing to the door. "Gottfried! Gottfried!" he gasped, summoning the fresh-faced youth. "I want her killed! The raven! Kill! Kill!"

She winged away from the *Bildstock*, soaring high into the vaulted chapel. She circled and screamed, her great black wings flapping and carrying her to an open window. With a last challenging cry, she was gone, meshing with the black of night.

Friedrich sagged against the door, the taste of fear scalding his tongue. It seemed to him another spirit had entered the chapel. Not that of his brother, gentle and forgiving to the end, but that of his brother's wife. Magda, whose gentleness and love for Karl had turned at his death to a mindless and vengeful hate. He had seen her but once before she escaped, and then she had seemed like a Valkyrie imbued with the vision of a seeress. Her finger pointing at him—as it seemed to be pointing now—she had flung a prophecy at him: "On a distant day, Friedrich, the Master of the Ravens will return, and his protector will pluck your eyes. And I will be there, Friedrich, in flesh or in spirit. Listen for me then, and you will hear me laughing."

But the legend said the raven would only return with the Master, and he was dead. Von Fersen had killed him.

So who had dared to accuse him with the *Bildstock?* To bring the ravens back to Schattenburg? Especially that one who had fled with Princess Magda and later convinced von Fersen that Wilhelm von Cramm was her son.

Friedrich's wild gaze fell on Anne, who shrank back in her father's arms, staring at him as if he were mad. Her? Darenth? His spy? If not them, he had to learn who it was—and quickly.

He groped for the brass door handle. "Take them to the dungeon and hold them there!"

He yanked desperately at the door, spun, and fled. Fled across the Great Hall beneath the trappings of war used by his ancestors. Hunted by Magda's vengeful spirit and frightened by the unseen threat of the men who captured his Hessians one by one, he stumbled to a halt, his head swinging, his eyes seeing danger in every corner.

He dared not go to his chamber. It opened onto a secret corridor. Cold sweat oozed from every pore, soaking his tunic and dripping from his brow. His wild gaze found the door of the turret room, and he stumbled toward it, screaming to the guards flanking the entry door. Slamming the door behind him, he listened for the comforting jingle of the men stationing themselves outside with a thump of their musket butts on the cold flagstone floor.

The only sound in the small round room was the harsh rasp of his breath. He was freezing here where no fire warmed the air, but better cold than dead. And it was dark, save for the solid bar of moonlight pointing at him like an accusing finger.

He stepped aside, merging into the shadows, his pristine white uniform a gleam of gray in the dark. He sensed no presence other than his own, and his breath began to slow.

Darenth! Darenth had to be behind it all! Someone had told him about the *Bildstock* and the ravens! Someone had aided him in finding traitors in Schattenburg! Von Fersen, who had vanished without a trace? Impossible! Von Fersen was too greedy for his promised title. Yet who else could it be?

Shame washed over him, hot and strong. Shame for the cowardice that sent him fleeing the chapel. Shame for the fear that, even now, huddled in a quivering lump in his chest.

He closed his burning eyes and watched his scene of vengeance play like a drama on a stage. The last stone mortared over Robbie's crypt. Anne walled up in the adjacent crypt. Darenth chained to the wall to await the slow, smothering death of his children and his own lingering death by starvation.

He had plotted and planned and dreamed of this for thirty-five years, waiting for the earl's love of his children to be firmly fixed, waiting for the perfect opportunity.

But when he killed Darenth's children, he would have to kill him too—and without the use of the earl's influence, all hope of having his principate reinstituted as a sovereign nation would be lost. He would be a prince in name only, stripped of his power. And he needed it! Only power could protect him from the sniggering laughter that would turn on him should any learn he was half a man.

He moved to the window slit, staring out into the night. The rising moon, silvery-bright, was speared through the heart by the sharp peaks of the pines.

Flowing across it, flat black against phosphorescent white, flew a flock of ravens on a silent rustle of wings. They circled down and down, lighting one by one in eerie silence on the machicolated gallery of the curtain wall below.

Friedrich's arid tongue dragging over his dry lips, he fell back. His heart hammered in his chest—like the fist now pounding on the door.

"Go away! I want to see no one!" he cried out, his voice shrill with horror.

"Your Highness! It is I, Heinrich von Fersen!"

Von Fersen! His feet dragging and his head pounding fiercely, Friedrich stumbled to the door and wrenched it open. "Traitor!" he bellowed, fumbling for the ceremonial dagger at his waist.

"*Nein! Nein!*" shrilled von Fersen.

"You vanished for weeks! Without a word! Without a trace!"

"I was prisoner of the English! But I escaped to bring you news—"

"What news could you have that I would need now?"

"Your nephew is alive! The Master of the Ravens is here in Schattenburg! He is a friend of the Earl of Darenth, known in England as Cantor Cartwright."

The blood drained from Friedrich's head in a rush, leaving him reeling like a drunk. He caught the edge of a console table to support himself, desperately swallowing the bitter acid of terror. He wanted to fly at von Fersen and crush his throat in his bare hands, but a pervasive weakness leached his strength away. "Where?" he whispered savagely. "Where is he?"

"Only the earl would know," said von Fersen, falling back a step.

"And I will have an answer from him, if I must tear his son and daughter limb from limb before his eyes!"

The thick slab of the wooden door with its tiny square of rusted window grating slammed behind

Anne. The heavy wooden bar fell into place, thudding like the terrified pulse that surged in her throat.
A scream burbled up against her clenched teeth, and
she fought it back.

The feeble light of an oil lamp turned her father's
flesh a corpse-white. The walls glistened with beads
of dampness that trickled like the sweat sliding between her breasts.

Was Robbie nearby? Behind one of the endless
doors lining the fetid passage? She tried to wash
away the sight of skeletons chained to the walls, but
they clung to her mind's eye like the gelatinous mold
to the stone walls. Her trembling began deep inside,
a subliminal quiver of the soul that moved outward
until her bones seemed to rattle.

Her father's arms wrapped around her, bringing
hazy memories of the comfort offered over childish
woes.

"Wh-what happened, F-Father? I d-don't underst-
stand," she pleaded plaintively.

"Shh, Anne. Someone is coming."

She heard the approach of furtive steps, the whisper of Cantor's full-skirted black coat as he moved
to the door, and the steady thud of her father's
heartbeat. Had he no fear?

The footsteps paused, and Anne's heart seemed
to stop.

"The Master has come," a voice murmured
through the grating. "*Majestät*—"

"*Nein! Verboten!*" said Cantor urgently.

"*Ja, Majes*—" The man hesitated, then launched
into a spate of guttural German.

The man's quiet footsteps fading away, Cantor
turned into the cell, his silver-thread embroidery
shimmering in the dark. He shed the mask and the
wig, tossing them onto the bare wooden bed.

"The Hessians are on guard. We must wait until
they are gone," he whispered, "then someone will
come to take us to the secret passage leading beyond
the curtain walls."

The weak lamplight flickered over his face, leaving his eyes dark wells in his pallid face. "Anne, Anne," he mourned softly, "why didn't you escape while you could?"

There was no answer that did not seem as weak as her knees. She was so glad that his anger had gone. His hand caught hers, and she abandoned her father, flowing into Cantor's arms.

He held her, molding her so tightly to von Dannecker's bulging belly that she could feel the struts of the corset digging into her breast. But it was Cantor's lips that rested warmly in the hollow of her neck and his breath that blew warmly across her flesh. It was his love that bolstered her courage and offered solace for her fear.

"What happened?" she asked. "Prince Friedrich seemed as terrified as a child, but there was nothing there. Nothing . . . but the raven . . ."

She drew back, staring up into his face. "Was that it? Does he really believe the Legend of Schattenburg?"

Cantor paused, and she sensed him gathering himself for a distasteful task. "Yes," he said softly, "he believes it."

"But it is simply a tale! Nothing more!"

"No, Anne, it is much, much—"

"Not now," said her father. "I own it must be told, but not yet."

And so she waited, clasped to Cantor heart to heart, as if the world might crumble around her if she moved away. But tight as he held her, her trembling would not stop.

If Robbie was in this dungeon, how had he stood it for more than a year? Robbie, who loved sunshine and laughter and, as he said, good food, good wine, and bad women. If he survived, would he ever be the same?

Militant footsteps intruded on Anne's thoughts. Rising above the monotonous march was a familiar voice speaking German.

Anne's eyes widened. "Von Fersen!" she whispered. "How did he come—"

"Shh!" Cantor cocked his head, listening. Tension crawled through him, banding his hands at Anne's waist like steel. Despite the chill of the dank air, rivers of sweat ran down his brow. She sensed a sudden deep sorrow, an unbearable grief that flattened her palms against his chest, offering wordless solace.

"My lord," Cantor said, "they plan to take you alone from here. Von Fersen says you know who the Master of the Ravens is. He says," his voice hardened, as if he dared not speak softer, "he has killed Franz."

Lady Bragg's Franz? Anne wondered.

Cantor loosed her and turned away, seeking the darkest shadow. His broad shoulders seemed to carry a weight too heavy to bear.

"I am sorry, my boy," said her father. "He was a good and faithful servant."

"I will tell them who I—"

"No!" Her father caught Cantor's arm, spinning him around. "One of us must remain to get Anne out of here! Don't let your pride be her undoing!"

Cantor flung up his head. "We both know who Friedrich really wants!"

"Nonsense! He wants us all! And he will have us, unless you can belay your pride and—"

The heavy bar scraped up. The door squealed on its hinges.

"Damn!" Cantor cursed beneath his breath as he glided into the thick darkness beyond the blazing torchlight.

"Come out, Darenth," ordered Friedrich. "I will take you to your son."

In the honeycomb of secret passageways was one of recent construction. Every man who had a hand in its making was dead, and though their spirits should have haunted the broad tunnel stretching from the castle's deepest cellar to the lowest curtain wall tower, it was remarkably free of their taint. But not of draping spiderwebs, squealing rats, and seeping damp.

The procession of Darenth, von Fersen, and Friedrich was flanked, fore and aft, by torch-bearing Hessians. Friedrich, his eyes fearfully scanning the black mouth of the tunnel ahead, had lost his arrogance. The Master of the Ravens was alive—and here! He was, no doubt, responsible for the men lost one by one in the secret passages. He had, no doubt, gathered around him a coterie of traitors, men who would be dealt with when the Master was dead—if he must kill every man of Schattenburg to rid it of them!

Friedrich told himself his superstitious fear had been foolish. The Master of the Ravens—known in England, so von Fersen said, as Cantor Cartwright—was no phantom warrior, merely a man.

Friedrich's hard gaze narrowed on von Fersen's delicate back. He had failed, and there was only one reward for failure. Though it would have to wait until he was assured von Fersen would be of no further use to him, Friedrich, gritting teeth that threatened to chatter, contemplated his henchman's execution.

It mattered little to him that von Fersen had brought him a wealth of information: that Darenth worked hand in glove with Castlereagh; that there had never been a chance that Darenth would work for the return of his principate; that Castlereagh would not have agreed if he had. Stiff-necked fools! Like his brother! Honor and loyalty had been his meat and drink, and look where it got him!

Nein! Friedrich had only one loyalty, and that to himself!

The air in the tower was cold but fresh. Friedrich followed his men through the door, the snow crackling underfoot. A murmur began among the leaders, flowing back to him.

"Der Rabe, Der Rabe" was repeated in tones of awe and fear.

Friedrich's gaze climbed to the curtain wall, where the ravens perched atop the gallery. A chill pecked at the base of his spine.

"Hurry! Hurry!" he shouted to his guard, and they set out at a trot, heading for the southeast tower.

Overhead the ravens began grumbling among themselves, a steady buzz that vibrated along Friedrich's nerves. Even as he told himself he had nothing to fear, the superstitious terror was scrabbling around the edges of his mind, seeking the chink in the door that separated sanity from insanity.

Nearing the tower, he ordered his men to guard the door, then pushed Darenth into the circular room. A brawny Hessian wrapped in a cloak, his cheeks red with the cold, huddled before a glowing brazier. Nearby was a hod of damp mortar. His bayonet-fitted musket lay propped against the ladder leading to the guard tower above. The open trapdoor permitted a rush of fresh air that did little to kill the stench of unwashed flesh.

The Hessian leaped to attention, while Darenth looked around in obvious confusion. Friedrich waved the guard to one side, waiting while the earl turned his gaze from the open crypt, to the single opening in the stone wall, to the manacles dangling from chains.

"Darenth, greet your son," he said. "Robbie! Robbie, come forth!"

A skeletal hand glimmered white against the dark orifice where a single stone yet needed to be mortared into place. A face appeared. Only the eyes were alive, pools of savage violet staring out of a wild tangle of blue-black hair and beard. The feral gaze locked on Friedrich, as if no one else existed for him. A growl issued from his throat, rumbling through his bared teeth.

"God! God help us," whispered Darenth weakly, staring at the animal his son had become.

Friedrich gloried in the earl's stricken pallor and the tremors racing through the hand that had once dealt him a deadly blow. Smiling, he watched the earl stumble forward, sink to his knees, and reach for his son's clawlike hand. A hand that jerked away, vanishing into the black maw of the crypt.

"Robbie! Listen! It is I, your father!"

"F-Father?" His face glimmered out of the darkness. His hand reappeared, trembling violently.

"A touching scene," sneered Friedrich.

Darenth spun around, his face contorted with hate. Roaring with outrage and pain, he charged Friedrich with every ounce of his strength. The Hessian leaped up, flinging himself in the earl's path and bellowing for his fellows. They came at a run, falling on the earl with musket butts and bare fists.

"Stop it! Stop it!" Robbie screamed.

Von Fersen melted away, putting the ladder between himself and harm.

Friedrich, his legs spread, his hands locked behind his back, watched the blood spurt from Darenth's mouth and listened to the crack of his ribs.

"Enough," he said firmly. "I don't want him killed. Manacle him and wait outside."

Darenth, subdued and bleeding, hung from the heavy chains that held his wrists at shoulder height. One eye was swollen shut, and the other latched onto Friedrich. "You spawn of hell!" he raged, groaning and breathing in shallow pants. "I should have killed you when I had the chance!"

"Yes, you should have," Friedrich said, his voice low and hard and as vicious as Robbie Ransome's snarl. "I know that the Master of the Ravens is here in Schattenburg. Tell me where I will find him."

"Tell him nothing, Father!"

Friedrich rounded on Robbie. "I suggest you tell him to follow my every order. If he does not, the hod of mortar and the stone awaits. How long do you think you will live without air?''

"You wouldn't!" cried the earl, straining to the full length of the chains.

"You know me better than that," said Friedrich coldly, finding new strength in the terror and rage flaming in the earl's eyes.

"Robbie," the earl choked out, his hand straining against the manacle, reaching for his son. Robbie's skeletal arm, clad in the tattered rags of a once-elegant coat, stretched through the dark opening, striving to reach his father's hand. A span of inches frustrated their efforts.

Friedrich nodded to the Hessian. He scooped up the hod of mortar and rapped Robbie's arm brutally with the scraper. A groan of pain came from his father.

"Where will I find the Master of the Ravens?" Friedrich asked.

"Why are you doing this?" Darenth shouted, watching the guard carefully scrape the mortar into place.

Robbie's hand shot out, grasping the Hessian's wrist, jerking his arm into the black maw, and twisting it brutally. The Hessian screamed. Friedrich shouted for his guards.

They came pouring in, wrenched the Hessian from Robbie's grasp, and aimed a musket at him. "Stand back! Stand back!"

The Hessian cradled his wrenched arm, moaning in a corner, and Friedrich nodded to another to spread the mortar.

"Watch him and think about what will happen when the stone slides into place." Friedrich moved closer, his eyes glittering with a fanatical light. "He will have no air, no light, Darenth. It may drive him mad. Have you ever seen a madman scream himself to death? You will hear it even through the wall—''

"Don't listen to him, Father! Don't listen! Noth-

ing you do will make a difference to him! He plans
to kill us all!''

''And if he does not scream, Darenth,'' Friedrich
said softly, ''he will slowly smother to death. He
will claw at the stone until his fingers bleed. He will
struggle, Darenth, but he will die in the end, his lips
blue and his face contorted. And he will curse you,
Darenth, the father that could have saved him.''

The earl flinched, leaning back against the wall.
''Do you think me a fool? No matter what I tell you,
we are dead.''

The guard hoisted the stone, awaiting Friedrich's
order.

''Slide it in,'' he said in a savage undertone.

The stone scraped into place, the guard grunting
with effort. Darenth sagged against the wall, his
head hanging. He drew a sobbing breath, but said
nothing.

Angry color flooded Friedrich's face. His hands
knotted into frustrated fists. He wanted to beat the
answer from Darenth. He wanted to see him bloodied and cowed into submission, but he knew the earl
too well. He would die with his secret unspoken,
just as he was allowing his son to die now.

But he wasn't done yet, Friedrich thought, trembling with rage. He strode to the door, flinging over
his shoulder, ''What of your daughter, Darenth? Will
you hold your tongue while I have her cut limb from
limb?''

Chapter 22

The tramp of boots shook the earth beneath Franz's cheek. The prick of a holly leaf brought him to agonizing awareness. He had been rolled into the bushes at the side of the track and left for dead, but he was very much alive, in spite of the throbbing pain in his side. He raised his wet hand to his wondering gaze. The black of blood glistened in the moonlight reflecting from the snow.

He peered over a hoary clump of grass. The crackling of the ice-crusted snow roared in his ears, but the mercenaries marching up in triple rows from the village below heard nothing except their own measured tread. His elbow pressing to the knife wound in his side, he watched them disappear from sight.

Why had they been summoned to the castle? Had von Fersen told Friedrich his nephew was alive? Had Friedrich discovered who that nephew was? Was Karl even now prisoner of his uncle, or worse, dead?

Franz closed his eyes and remembered a particular Venetian sunrise long ago: the slap of water against the stone walls; the song of a gondolier; and the babe in his arms, its flesh milky-white and its tiny head crowned in silky gold. "Promise me, Franz!" Princess Magda had said with her last breath. "Promise me you will protect your prince with your life!"

Now, when Karl needed Franz most, he was laid

low by von Fersen. That middling excuse for a man!
A hot flush of shame burned Franz's feverish cheeks.

He shifted. Pain rammed through him like a fist.
He fell back, panting. He must plan first. He dare
not waste energy in pointless movement. Willi and
Trude were in the village. The woodcutter's hut,
though nearer, was empty. The castle was too far;
he'd never make it. He had to return to Schatten-
hausen, and there arouse the rebellion he had seen
stirring in the men's eyes. He must harness their
anger and use it to free his prince and bring about
their salvation.

He tried to stand, but his head swam. He held his
ribs with one hand, pulling himself along with his
elbow and pushing with a knee. He made inching
progress, descending the mountain as von Fersen
had come up, straight as an arrow, but without an
arrow's free flight. Despite the frosty night air, sweat
poured from his brow and soaked through his coat.

"I promise, I promise." He prayed, the vow that
had guided his every waking thought for thirty
years. He wouldn't fail now.

Every clump of grass was a frustration; every
rocky outcropping an obstacle. He skidded the last
few feet into the narrow dirt track, cracking the ice
on a puddle and too exhausted to move. His head
sank to his hand, his breath rasping in his burning
lungs.

The suggestion of a smile softened his hard
mouth. Would he ever remember, when the time
came, to pay his prince the respect he was due? It
was hard to see him as a man, when he remembered
the boy so well. The boy he loved not only as his
prince, but as the son he never had.

Franz struggled up, dragging himself across the
track and into the underbrush. Down and down he
went, toward the flickering lights of Schattenhausen, his promise driving him beyond human
strength.

He reached the village. Overhead, the ravens began to screech, swooping from the ridgelines and diving on the street. The villagers, driven in by the cold, timidly peeped out of doors and windows. The ravens, agleam in the moonlight, streamed in a circle over Franz.

Curiosity tugged the villagers from their snug parlors. Willi and Trude at their head, they crowded around Franz.

"Willi, Willi," he gasped, and the woodcutter knelt beside him. "Von Fersen is here. He has gone above. Prince Karl has need of you all."

"What can we do?"

"What we should have done long ago," he said fiercely. "Gather axes, sickles, and mauls to end Friedrich's life!"

Trude turned to the villagers, her hand flung up. "The Master of the Ravens has returned to us! He is above in the castle now, his life in danger. See! See!"

She pointed to the circling ravens, who soared away, flying up the wooded mountainside above the flocked white treetops.

"But where has he been all of these years?" bellowed a doubter. "How are we to know it is really he?"

"Would the ravens return for another?" scoffed Trude. "And should you doubt, here is Franz Grillparzer, known to you all. Princess Magda herself entrusted him with the care of our Master. Will we now fail him as we failed his father? Will we allow Friedrich to—"

"*Nein! Nein!*" shrieked the innkeeper.

The doubter shouted him down. "What proof have we—"

"My word," said the Bürgermeister, stepping forward. "I have seen the Master. I have seen the Crown of Schattenburg that our rightful prince wears as a birthmark on his wrist."

"But what of the Hessians? Their muskets—"

"We have muskets of our own!" shouted Trude.

"We have axes and sickles and mauls. We have the ravens and the promise of the legend that peace and prosperity will return with our Master. Go! All of you! Gather your weapons!"

A hive of maddened hornets, the villagers buzzed away, returning with torches and weapons. Franz, insisting, was hefted onto a donkey's back for the jolting journey up the twisting track of the mountainside. He lay prone, fading in and out of consciousness, listening with contentment to the crackling anger growing like a well-fed fire.

Near the top, he summoned Willi. "We must cut across the wood and seek the postern gate at the southeast side. Herr Hauptmann has kept a man posted there should we need to send him a message. He will let us through and guide our way."

Pain shot through Franz with the donkey's every stiff-legged lurch, blurring his gaze, weakening him further.

"We'll all be killed!" said the doubter.

Franz struggled up. They had reached the white sward rising from the edge of the trees to the curtain wall guarded by towers.

"The Hessians await us even now. They cannot have missed the torchlight," added the doubter, infecting his fellows with his fear.

"We can do it," Franz croaked.

"*Nein! Nein!* Even now the Hessians gather in the tower! See them with their muskets ready?"

Franz could not wait much longer. Even now he could feel the people's righteous anger dwindling beneath the fear. If he waited longer, they would turn and flee.

He gathered the waning remnants of his strength, kicked the donkey's sides, and went riding, alone, over the barren ground, heading for the postern gate. Behind him, the villagers roared and rushed to follow.

Above, in a window slit, a musket flashed fire.

* * *

Below, in the dungeon, Karl sat on the bare wooden bed, Anne cradled at his side, her cheek pillowed on his shoulder. She was racked by trembling that set his jaw like iron.

While he listened for the furtive step that would herald their release, his hard gaze roamed the cell, from the dark corners to the damp moldy walls to the door. Often he had felt helpless to act, but never so helpless as this.

For so long, only he and Franz had been at risk. Faithful Franz, now dead in service to him. He blinked away tears of grief, seeking anger instead. He must think of the living now.

Where was the guard? With every moment that passed, the danger grew.

Beside him, Anne continued to shudder uncontrollably. He held her closer, one finger gently stroking her cheek and his lips brushing lightly across her brow. "Shh," he murmured softly. "When the guard returns he will see you safe away and I will find your father."

Her eyes glistening in the pale light, she covered his hand and pressed it to her cheek, as if she sought the promise of life to banish the demons of darkness. The warmth of her skin summoned memories of fevered kisses and silken flesh and passion sated in the night. Ah, God! Would they ever have that again? *Where was the guard?*

"What can you do?" she asked softly. "One man, alone."

The quiver of fear in her voice seemed to be evoked by her concern only for him, and he was selfish enough to be glad. It mattered little now that she had loved him and deceived him twice. It mattered only that she had found a place for him in her heart that was his, and only his.

"I am not alone," he whispered. "Herr Hauptmann is the captain of the dungeon guards, all of whom are men of Schattenburg. They will help me, and I swear, we will have your father and brother back safe.''

But her father and brother might now be dead.

A breath whispered through her lips. ''Why is Friedrich doing this?''

Karl closed his eyes. There was so much to explain and not enough time. And when he told her what he was, would she understand? Her father had been right. It was better to wait for those explanations. Later, he would tell her that he had lied to her from the beginning. He would tell her everything and make her understand.

''Anne, I—''

The wary scrape of a boot sent a bolt of hope shooting through Karl. He pressed a finger to Anne's lips, listening.

''*Majestät!*'' whispered the guard through the grill, easing the bar from the door. ''You must hurry!''

''Come, Anne!'' He pulled her up.

''Wait,'' she whispered, holding his arm. ''Cantor, we . . . we don't know what will happen. Whether we will see each other again.''

''Anne, Anne, there's no time!'' Even as he was saying it, he was pulling her into his arms, holding her as if they would never be parted. He was hoarding the memories of her petal-soft lips and her vibrant body clinging desperately to his and her broken pleas of ''Take care, my love, take care.''

And all the while precious time was fleeing and his heart was pounding and his need for her was growing. He wrenched himself away and thrust her at the guard, grabbing his wig and mask from the bare wooden bed and flinging them on. He paused for a moment, tucking a finger in his boot to check the set of the knife.

The guard froze in the door, listening.

The unmistakable tramp of boots echoed dimly through the corridor. ''Damn!'' Karl said fiercely. ''Bar the door! Tell Herr Hauptmann to gather his men and follow where we go.''

The guard melted into the shadows, vanishing into the deepest reaches of the dungeon.

"Courage, Anne! Courage!" Karl whispered. "I will have you out of this yet!"

Whatever happened, he must continue the charade and hope that Herr Hauptmann and his men would come in time.

The fitful glow of torchlight fell across the door. Anne's hand crept into his.

The bar scraped up, the door creaked open, and the hard-faced Hessians marched in, their white cloaks rustling around their boots.

Friedrich appeared, an ominous apparition. An inner light illuminated his grim-visaged face, the diabolical light of a man who nursed malice and madness.

"What have you done to my father?" Anne demanded.

"It is I who will ask the questions here, *Fraulein!*" he shouted, grasping the ornately jeweled hilt of the ceremonial dagger at his waist. "You will give me answers!"

"You will have no answer from me until I know my father is safe!"

Karl squeezed Anne's hand in warning. As proud as he was that she could overcome her fear enough to defy Friedrich, this was no time for that defiance.

Friedrich's eyes narrowed, his vicious gaze dropping to their clasped hands. Unease slithered through Karl, but it was too late to release Anne's hand and move away. The malevolent smile thinning Friedrich's lips said he had seen and understood.

"You think not, *Fraulein,*" he said bitterly, spittle forming at the corners of his mouth, while his arm flung out, pointing at Karl. "Hold him!"

Two guards, fair-haired and empty-eyed, flanked Karl, grasping his arms, brutally wrenching him away from Anne.

"No!" she cried. "Don't hurt him!"

He struggled, watching Friedrich approach Anne and clamp his hand on her shoulder. "Of course, your lover will not be hurt if you tell me what I want to know. Where, *Fraulein*, is the Master of the Ravens?"

Karl grew still, the mercenaries' fingers biting deep into his arms, as deep as the stillness that wrapped around his heart. He saw the confusion in Anne's face, the rising rage in Friedrich's.

An obsessive rage that crushed Anne's will to defy him. It pulsed frenetically in the distended veins in Friedrich's temples. It found an outlet in the massive hand that wrapped around her wrist, squeezing until her bones grated together.

She winced, her breath fluttering in her throat. "I—I don't know what you are talking about," she said breathlessly. "The Master of the Ravens is a legend, nothing more."

"The Master of the Ravens, *Fraulein*"—Friedrich leaned down, his wild, hate-filled face inches from hers—"is a man. A man known as Cantor Cartwright! Tell me where he is!"

Cantor Cartwright! Oh, God! Terror's cold sweat dewed Anne's brow. Her eyes burned with the need to turn from Friedrich to Cantor, to voice the questions she longed to ask. But she dared not betray by word or deed that Cantor was in this very cell, in the hands of Friedrich's guards. Cantor, the Master of the Ravens. Her undeniably English Cantor! Why—

"Where, *Fraulein*?" Friedrich screamed, twisting her wrist, sending her arching back in agony.

Karl felt her pain as if it were being inflicted on himself. He strained against the Hessians, jerking desperately to escape them. "*Schweinehund!* Let her go! I will tell you what you want to know."

The grip on Anne's arm lessened, and she drew a sobbing breath. She couldn't let Cantor betray himself! "England!" she cried, grasping at Friedrich's sleeve. "He is in England!"

Friedrich's fingers wound through her hair, jerking her head back. "You lie! He is here in Schattenburg! And if you will not tell me the truth"—he jerked her around, his forearm across her throat, the point of his dagger beneath her chin—"perhaps your lover will."

A drop of blood oozed down the blade of the knife, glistening in the torchlight. Karl watched it, breath pent behind a grimace of pain and anger. If he kept silent, he had no doubt Friedrich would kill Anne. If he told Friedrich who he was, he might kill them both in rage. A choice that was no choice at all. He straightened, his posture haughtily regal.

"Release me," he commanded, with such authority that the guards were surprised into doing it. He stripped off the mask and wig. "I am here, *mein Onkel*, Karl Auguste Wilhelm the Second, Master of the Ravens, rightful Prince of Schattenburg."

His eyes were fixed not on Friedrich but on Anne. He hadn't wanted her to learn this way. In the awful stillness of the cell, a stunned comprehension darkened her face. He saw her slow, painful acceptance of the fact that he had lied to her from the beginning, that he had never been the man she thought he was. *But he had been*, he wanted to cry out. Only the name was different. He was the man who had loved her then, who loved her now.

Her lashes fell over the tears sparkling in her eyes, as if she could not bear the sight of him. Karl knew he would never again suffer as he suffered in that moment. She did not understand. She might never understand.

He squared his shoulders and shifted his gaze to Friedrich's ashen face with its sagging contours and drooping jaw. Slowly, he lifted his right arm and pulled back the froth of lace, baring the birthmark on his wrist. "I have returned, *mein Onkel*," he said frigidly, "just as my mother promised you I would."

Friedrich, his eyes bulging, stared at Karl, but saw his mother instead. Magda. A Valkyrie imbued with the vision of a seeress. A powerful vessel brimming with the vigor of a hate that reached out from the grave to wrap skeletal fingers around his throat and choke the breath from him.

His parched eyes ached with the need to blink, but he dared not lose sight of Magda's face superimposed over her son's. He could feel her here, a threatening presence that surrounded him, became one with him, and stole his strength.

He gasped for air and struggled to banish his terror. "Hold him," he said, the shriek in his mind coming from his mouth in a whisper. "Hold him!" he shrilled, a high scream of abject fear.

The guards leaped at Karl, grabbing him, and the vision of Magda vanished. Still, Friedrich could not control the panic-stricken tremors that undulated through nerve and sinew. He thrust Anne from him, backing to the door.

"Take them to the tower! Take them away! I'll see them buried alive!"

"No! Let Anne go!" Karl shouted, fighting the unbreakable grip of the guards. "Let them all go! It is me you want!"

"It is all of you! All of you!" Friedrich screamed hysterically. "Take them away! Take them away!"

In the black and seeping tunnel, Anne trudged behind a quartet of Hessians carrying torches. The light spilled over their fair hair and broad shoulders, glistening from the sharpened points of the bayonets attached to their muskets. She pulled her shawl more snugly around her shoulders, knowing as she did that it could not warm her. The chill of the passage was as nothing to the cold block of ice her heart had become.

Cantor—Karl! Karl! She must remember that. Cantor Cartwright, the man to whom she had given herself body and soul, did not exist. The man she would have betrayed her father and brother to save had lied to her all along. He had neither loved nor trusted her enough to tell her who he really was.

He was no longer her exquisite Corinthian, her supremely English Cantor. He was Karl Auguste Wilhelm II, rightful Prince of Schattenburg. Not English, but German. Not Cantor, but Karl. Not the man who loved her, but the man who lied to her.

Now they were going to die with that lie between them. They were going to be . . . buried alive. Fear scurried through her, like the rat scurrying across the damp floor on a collision course with her foot. Sidestepping, she stumbled and began to fall.

Strong arms caught her and set her aright. Cantor's arms, so familiar. Karl's arms, a stranger's. The familiar essence of sandalwood and man awakened memories of his touch, his taste, his smile. Whether Cantor or Karl, those all remained the same. Regret settled like a fog in the aching emptiness of her heart.

For a moment, he held her close to the long, muscular body she knew so well. For a moment, his cornflower-blue gaze searched her face. "Anne," he whispered in the old litany of repentance and regret.

She had forgiven him for so much. For once leaving her without a backward look. For his masquerade as Karl von Dannecker. Karl! she thought with a burst of anger. She could not forgive him for this final betrayal.

Though she longed to yield to the comfort of his touch, she pulled away from him.

Karl, his heart aching, let her go. She could have betrayed Cantor Cartwright to Friedrich. She could have bargained for her life, her father's and her brother's, but she hadn't. Karl suspected she would have died with the secret of Cantor's identity if he hadn't betrayed himself.

He strained for a sound alien to the Hessians' plodding march and Friedrich's uncertain shuffle. Had the guard taken word to Herr Hauptmann? Would he bring his men to the rescue?

A sharp incline of the tunnel opened in a round tower. Outside the tower door, the night was bathed in radiant moonlight, nearly as bright as day. The curtain wall with its machicolated gallery snaked away into the distance, circling around the ward, whose winter-dead grass was crusted with snow. Above, on the gallery, the ravens perched in rows, black specters carved out of the silvery-gray night. They set up a grumbling and mumbling, agitatedly hopping from foot to foot and bobbing up and down. Higher still, silhouetted against the phosphorescent disk of the moon, *she* flew, watcher and watchman.

Always she had been near Karl. His earliest memory was of her perched at the foot of his tiny trundle bed, watching over him. What would she do now?

Pruk, pruk. Pruk-pruk-pruk, pruk, pruk, came the menacing mutters from atop the curtain wall.

At the rear of the procession, Friedrich stumbled from the tower door, his shrinking gaze lifting to the gallery. Superstitious fear crawled over him. He heard in those sinister avian voices the distant echo of laughter. Magda's laughter. Magda's promise that the raven would pluck his eyes.

His shaking hands touched his cheeks and covered his eyes.

From above came the clicking of beaks.

If he left the shelter of the tower, he would have to run that gauntlet. Could the ravens sense murder in his heart like she, the watcher, had sensed it when he was a child? Would they, like she, attack him? Pluck his eyes?

Mind-numbing panic surged over him in cold waves. He forgot the earl and his son, Anne and Karl. He forgot his need for vengeance and power. The only reality was his terror, and his need to escape.

Recoiling, he turned and fled into the dark depths of the tunnel. He ran faster and faster, his breath searing his throat, until he saw the dim glow of torchlight ahead. Behind it came the indistinct figure of Herr Hauptmann followed by his men.

Friedrich stumbled to a halt.

Traitors before him. The ravens behind him.

He spun around, slipping on the slimy floor and falling full-length. His pristine white uniform dripping mold and damp, he pushed himself up and ran up the sharp rise of the tunnel, bursting into the tower and through its door into the clear bright night.

His guards were far ahead, marching Anne and Karl to the southeast tower. The ravens were overhead, harbingers of death and disaster.

For a moment, he saw himself, splattered with slime and maddened by fear. He, Prince Friedrich of Schattenburg! He, with his strength and courage and cunning, was yielding to his fear. The brittle courage of self-conscious pride came creeping back.

He reared his arrogant head and, though his flesh crawled, he forced himself to walk the gauntlet of the restless ravens. A fast walk that gained quickly on the procession ahead.

"Gottfried!" he called out, his voice high and tight. "Order the men on the wall back to the tower door. Traitors come up through the tunnel. I want them all killed!"

Above, in a window slit, a musket flashed fire.

Friedrich flinched, his gaze rising to the guards stationing themselves along the parapet. The animal roar of a mob storming the wall screamed above the musket fire that barked death into the night.

"Your Highness!" shouted a guard from above. "We are being attacked!"

"Who? Who would dare?" shrieked Friedrich.

"The—the villagers," the guard said, as if he could scarcely believe the evidence of his eyes. "I saw the innkeeper and the Bürgermeister!"

"Kill them! Kill them all!" shouted Friedrich. "Hurry! Hurry!" He passed his men at a run, flinging a harried look at Karl.

Karl was at that moment watching a man ease open the postern gate. A bayonet prodded him in the back, and Karl caught Anne, pulling her into the curve of his body and running toward the dark shadow of the tower while the muskets roared overhead and Herr Hauptmann's men poured out of the tower behind them.

"What is happening?" Anne whispered.

"A battle for Schattenburg," he said, cursing the collapse of his plan. If his men could have taken Friedrich in the chapel, so many lives could have been saved.

They reached the massive oak door barred in iron, and a push from behind sent Karl flying into a chilling scene. The Hessians stood, bayonets at the ready, in a semicircle abutting the stone wall. Von Fersen, his blade of a nose buried in his hands, huddled at the edge of the room, near the manacled earl. Friedrich stood beside the ladder leading to the open trapdoor above, his face ashen, his eyes wild.

"I want them walled into the crypt! Walled there, I say!"

"Father!" Anne cried. "Where is Robbie?"

"There!" Friedrich pointed to the solid wall. "Entombed, *Fraulein*, as you will soon be!"

"*No!* Robbie! Robbie!" she screamed, lurching toward the wall.

A Hessian guard captured her flailing wrist and swung her around. She slammed into von Fersen, who careened backward into Darenth. The earl's manacled wrist curled around von Fersen's throat, and Karl saw his chance.

His elbow sank deep into one guard's belly. The Hessian forked over, retching on the floor. Dodging a bayonet, Karl swung his fist. It connected squarely with the man's aquiline nose, smashing it like an overripe peach. His eyes rolled up, and he sagged to the floor.

Karl turned his wary gaze on Friedrich, while he tried to keep the Hessians in view.

''Leave him!'' Friedrich cried, vicious hatred twisting his face. Flexing the fingers of one hand, he feinted with the dagger. ''He is mine! Mine!''

Karl palmed the knife in his boot and cursed von Dannecker's padding and corset. It made him clumsier than he should have been.

The popping of musket fire grew in intensity, but Karl paid scant attention to it. He was, at last, facing his uncle, the man who had murdered his father. He was, at last, free to take his revenge.

Friedrich looked to the left and feinted to the left. He looked to the right and stabbed. Karl danced back, his own blade glittering in the torchlight, while he watched his uncle's eyes.

Eyes that heralded the ultimate cowardice—a moment too late. Friedrich was not a man who would risk himself in single combat once he knew his foe was a match for him. ''Take him! Hold him!'' he bellowed at his guards.

They fell on Karl, pinning him to the wall.

Friedrich advanced, a smile on his face, the dagger in his hand. ''You are as great a fool as your father! He, too, trusted any man at his word!'' he said, swinging the knife in an underhanded arc, burying it to the hilt in Karl's belly.

Caw! Caw! Caw! cried the ravens on a thunder of wings. They poured through the open trapdoor like poppy seeds through a funnel. All was a flash of sleek black feathers, of parted beaks and raking claws and men screaming.

The Hessians released Karl precipitately, charging the door, jostling, shouting, and shoving their way out, while the ravens chivied them on. Friedrich did a macabre dance, beating off the birds that pecked gobbets of flesh from his cheeks, from his neck, from his brow and hands. All the while he screamed shrilly in horror and the ravens flapped around him, their heavy wings thudding against his flesh. He stumbled to the door, falling, scrambling up, plunging through.

"Cantor! Cantor!" Anne screamed, flinging herself against him, her hand pressing against the tear in his black-velvet coat. "You are hurt."

His arm swept around her, and he gazed into her eyes, drinking deep of her sweet concern. "It's little more than a scratch, Anne. The padding. The curst padding!"

"Thank God! Thank God!" she breathed softly, her hand trembling against him.

From the snowy ward there came the clatter of ravens' wings and their shrill caws of victory spinning away on the clear night air. They rose as one from the hulking bulk of a man. Friedrich, caught in the glow of a fallen torch, wavered on his feet, his face a pulpy, bleeding mass with empty eye sockets.

Anne stiffened in Karl's arms, and he caught her face and turned it into his chest, holding her tight. "Don't look, Anne," he whispered, his voice thick.

Friedrich raised his bleeding hands to his tattered ears, as if blocking out an unearthly sound. Screaming, he began running, faster and faster—into the blood-lusting mob of the villagers. They swallowed him up, their axes rising and falling, rising and falling.

Karl sagged against the door, his knees bled of strength. He swallowed and swallowed again, his throat burning with bile. Whatever he had wished on Friedrich, it would have been kinder than the end he had reached.

"Karl!" Darenth shouted. "My son may yet be alive!"

He straightened, frowning. "Where—"

"Here, in the wall." Darenth pointed. "You can see where the mortar is still damp. Take out that stone."

Karl worked feverishly with the scraper, gouging at the setting mortar, working the stone back and forth. Anne knelt beside him, whispering, "Hurry! Please, hurry!"

At last the stone came out, and Anne flung herself before the orifice. ''Robbie! Robbie!''

Silence.

''Bring a torch,'' she cried. ''I can't see him.''

Karl swiveled on his knee, reaching . . .

''Puss, Puss, is that you?'' came Robbie's voice, with the dry rustle of autumn leaves.

Behind them, von Fersen crawled out of the door like a whipped cur.

Chapter 23

Peace descended on Schattenburg with a cleansing fall of snow. Two days had passed since that night of madness and murder. The horror was receding, though Anne feared a part of it would always remain with her.

Robbie slept in the vast bed of state, so thin he barely rippled the covers. His hair and beard as yet untrimmed, he looked like a stranger. He could be fed and fattened to appear more like his old self, but the expression in his eyes could not be changed. That wildness, that marrow-deep rage and desperation. The old laughter-loving Robbie Ransome was dead. What would this new man inhabiting his body be like?

Her father sat in a chair nearby, when he should have been abed himself. The pain on his face had nothing to do with the broken ribs that had been wrapped tightly. He, like Anne, worried about Robbie. He, like she, dared not speak those worries aloud. It would make them too real, too frightening.

Her mother had been summoned from Heidelburg, and she sat now on Robbie's bed, her hand covering his. She touched him, she said, to assure herself that he was real, that this was not a dream.

A fire crackled in the broad, plain hearth with its mantel of heavy stone, while outside the sun sauntered across the powder-blue sky, secure in its domain.

Anne stood at the window, staring down into the ward. From that spot she had seen the Hessians march away in triple files. Her father said they had been paid for the last of their services so they would leave in peace. Apparently they were as eager to be away from here as she was.

A man on horseback trotted out of the shadows of the gate passage into the sunlit ward. The white horse was caparisoned in medieval cloth trappings of silver. The man was enveloped in a flowing black cloak. In his butter-yellow curls there nestled a crown of gold. The man, Prince Karl Auguste Wilhelm II, bore little resemblance to Cantor.

Anne's father had made a point to tell her that Prince Karl went this morning to bury the dead, among them Franz, his oldest and dearest friend. She had suffered a pang of sympathy, quickly squelched, while she ignored her father's unspoken suggestion that she stop hiding in this chamber. But she couldn't leave it. She didn't want to see the Prince in his regalia. She wanted Cantor in his exquisite Corinthian style, but he was gone forever. In his place was a man she didn't know.

She watched that man dismount, flipping the edge of his cloak over his broad shoulders and revealing its silver-fox fur lining. A boy ran for the horse and led it away, while the man tugged off his gloves and frowned at the sky. Slowly his gaze lifted to her window. She wanted to shrink back out of sight, but found herself rooted as firmly as the castle to the mountain crest.

His cornflower-blue eyes—Cantor's eyes—gazed from the lush thicket of dusky lashes. Anne saw his grief and pain and doubt, emotions that found their companions in her. *Come to me, come to me,* she wanted to say. *Be my love, the man you once were.*

An interminable moment trudged by. He looked away, then walked slowly to the entry stair. Anne's pent-up breath eased out on a sigh. What would he have said if he had been at her side?

She heard a flurry of wings and saw the raven wheel out of the sunlight to land on the windowsill. It perched in the snow, watching her through the glass. She shuddered uncontrollably.

Pruk, pruk, the raven murmured, cocking its head and eyeing her curiously.

Anne glimpsed nothing of the murderous rage that had infected the flock that night, but she would never see the raven again without remembering Friedrich . . .

Her thoughts stumbled. Her mind closed.

He would come. The raven always heralded his arrival. Turning to face the chamber, she waited with an eagerness she hated.

Karl shed his cloak and crown, giving them into Hummel's waiting hands.

"*Majestät*," his man said, "Franz would not want you to grieve for him. He fulfilled his promise to Princess Magda and followed you for love. You were as much his prince as you were the son he never had."

"*Danke*, Hummel. I will remember that."

He would remember much else, too. Franz, minion, companion, and mentor, had been faithful to the end. He must have known he would be killed if he led the charge on the walls. It was humbling to know how much Franz and others had been willing to sacrifice for him.

He moved into the Great Hall, standing before the fire and warming his hands. There was so much to do. Friedrich had drained the wealth of his people dry. Now he must rebuild it for them, without Franz at his side. He had not realized how much he had relied on his man's sturdy wisdom. He had not realized how often he had turned to him, that other self who thought as he did.

Now there was no one. Not even Anne. The cavernous emptiness of the Great Hall pressed upon him. His gaze lifted, as if it might pierce the oaken beams to find Anne. He moved slowly, then quickly, eager to be with her in spite of the fear that she would spurn him.

He could not have achieved all he wanted and lost the love that gave it meaning. She must be made to understand why he had kept the secret of his identity from her.

That thought sustained him until he entered Robbie's chamber and saw her standing before the window, a shadowy form haloed in sunlight. He could never hope she would forgive him.

"My lord"—he bowed to the earl—"I thought you would like to know that von Fersen has vanished. My men can find no sign of him."

"Vanished!" Anne moved away from the light, revealing herself as a flesh and blood woman, not the shadow that might vanish before his eyes. "Will he be a danger to you?" She looked away, her face flaming. "To us?" she added weakly.

To you. The words sang with the sweetness of concern. Karl swallowed hard, aching to cross the chamber and sweep her into his arms. "No, he will be no danger to . . . any of us. He will not dare to stay here in Schattenburg, nor can he return to England."

"I—I see."

He yearned to see her smile, to hear her say, *I love you, Karl.* "Anne," he began, his voice low and rough.

"We . . . we would like to thank you for your hospitality, your Highness," she interrupted, dipping into a deep and mocking curtsy. "We will, of course, be leaving as soon as my brother can travel."

He stiffened, every word an arrow piercing his heart. It was too late. It had always been too late for them. He wanted to salve his pride with an abrupt farewell, but found his throat too tight for speech. He bowed, turned, and left.

Anne, her gaze as heavy as her heart, watched him go. He could have said something, she thought bitterly. If he truly cared, he could have asked her to stay.

Her father rose, approaching her. "Willful, wayward chit! Won't you admit that you have a *tendre* for Karl?"

"But I don't, Father." She stared up at him. "I loved Cantor. I don't know who Karl is."

The earl's gaze drifted from Anne to her mother. Though they had reconciled, they had not achieved the loving closeness they once shared. The wounds they had dealt each other were yet raw and unhealed. Anne feared they would never fully mend.

"Karl is not a man to whom trust comes easily, my child," the earl said. "All of his life he has known nothing but danger and death, Anne. His father was murdered by his uncle. His mother fled for her life and died at his birth. He was a child when he survived an assassination attempt by von Fersen. What could he learn of trust from such a life?"

"He has not trusted even you, Father?" Anne asked.

"My child"—he smiled strangely—"Karl has not trusted even himself."

"But isn't that what love is, Father? Belief, faith, trust?"

"Yes, but it is more, too." His wary gaze shifted to her mother. "It is sharing the pain of life, as well as its joys."

Anne's gaze followed his. Her mother's face was vibrant with love in spite of the tears welling in her eyes. Feeling an intruder on the deeply personal moment they shared, Anne glanced at Robbie, who still slept deeply, and excused herself.

Crossing the portal into the hall, she heard the whisper of her mother's skirts and the soft fall of her father's steps.

"Forgive me, my love. Forgive me," he said softly.

"There is nothing to forgive, John. You have loved too much, my dear, not too little."

Anne, her heart both heavier and lighter, glided away silently. Her parents had all they needed in each other. They loved her and Robbie, and they would miss them when they each embarked on their own lives. But Darenth Hall was their world, not hers. She was not a child to cling to them still, as she had clung to them when taking her first unsteady steps. She was a woman with the full knowledge that love was not a warranty against human imperfection or the pain of life. But, if love was strong enough, it could survive imperfection and pain. If it was strong enough, it could teach a man to trust, to share the pain of life as well as its joys.

From the great organ pipes there rose a halting melody that grieved and ached with loneliness and despair, a minor-key lament that foretold only darkness ahead.

Anne paused, listening, her heart weeping. Cantor Cartwright. Karl von Dannecker. Prince Karl Auguste Wilhelm II. Weren't they all one man, and that man her love? Composer, spy, prince, lover: they were all facets of the man who had stolen her heart. Would she punish him and herself for what neither could change?

She moved slowly across the great common room, heading for the turret stair. Faster and faster she flew, spinning down the winding steps. Her skirts lifted, she raced across the Great Hall to the chapel door, down the long center aisle to the altar.

The unfinished melody stopped on a discordant crash of sounds, as if he had drawn up his fists and slammed them into the keyboard. Anne stepped around the rood screen, her heart pounding, her face flushed.

His supple fingers were splayed over the keys, his shoulders drooping wearily and despair tugging at his proud head.

"Karl," she whispered.

His head snapped up. He rose to his feet, his eyes searching hers, not daring to ask, to hope. Her gaze raced over his face, which she knew as well as her own. The face of the man she needed to make her life complete.

"I love you," she said softly.

She expected him to open his arms, to hold her to his heart, to say the words he had never said. Instead he stepped back, his hands clasped behind him and his feet braced apart—as if, Anne thought with shock, she was a troop to be reviewed.

"Perhaps," he began, his voice flat, "you don't understand. My home is Schattenburg now. I will return to England, but my visits there will be few and short. Although my duties as prince will be purely ceremonial, my responsibilities to my people will require much time and hard work. I must help them rebuild the prosperity they lost under Friedrich."

Anne studied the pulse leaping at his throat, the tension thinning his mouth. "Why are you telling me this?"

"Because my wife must be willing to make my home hers, my people hers, my work—"

"You must know that I would."

"But I don't, nor do you," he interrupted quietly. "Anne, your family is everything to you. Think about it! Think about leaving them and living in a country whose people and language are strange to you."

She searched his face. Though he tried to hide it behind a bland expression, she could see his fear—that she, like those others in his life, loved him not enough.

"You are wrong, Karl," she whispered. "I love my family, but you alone are everything to me. When you left me without telling me if you would ever return, I felt so . . . lost. I don't want to feel that way again, and I don't care where we live or how we live so long as we are together."

Still he did not move. "It won't be easy, Anne.

You won't see much of your family. You will have so much to learn, so much to do, so—''

"Do you think this is easy?" A rueful smile sneaked across her lips. "You wretched man, won't you leave me a shred of pride? Must I prostrate myself at your feet and beg you to marry me?"

His face softened, young and yearning. "Are you sure?"

"I've never been more sure of anything."

A smile trembled across his handsome mouth, and his arms reached out to her. She flung herself into his embrace, eagerly, passionately. He held her clasped to him, as if she might try to escape.

"Do you know how much I love you, how much I need you, how little life would be worth without you?" His breath flowed across her cheek. "I've regained my heritage, yet it means nothing to me now. Nothing without you to share it with me."

Anne found his lips waiting for hers, as if he had waited for her, and only her, all his life.

Epilogue

April 1825
Schattenburg

Napoleon was four years dead. Europe was as peaceful as the sprawling gardens of *Chagrin*. Cherry blossoms quivered in the balmy spring breeze. The bed of damask roses, planted and tended by Prince Karl's own hands, breathed their scent on the air that wafted into the state apartments above them. Like a naughty child, the breeze fingered the gold fringe dangling from the apple-green brocade drapes and danced across the ornately appointed chamber to eddy around the bodies lovingly entwined on the tousled bed.

"We need to get up," said Prince Karl, his lips idling over the silken mound of a dainty breast. Duty and desire, the curse of his life. Yet what pleasure it was to have them joined as one in those he loved.

"Yes, we do," whispered Princess Anne, her fingers winnowing through the butter-yellow curls spilling across his brow. Trust. How easily it had come to them both, and how strong it had grown through the years.

"We will, no doubt, be interrupted quite soon," he said, his finger trailing lazily to the fragile hollow of her throat. Her skin was as fine and soft as a girl's, sleep-flushed and warm. As warm as her love. It cradled him now, as it always had, in peace and

contentment. It banished the dark shadows of loneliness so effectively, he could no longer remember
what they had felt like.

"No doubt," said she, cradling his head and pulling it up and melding her mouth to his. Passion
came, as it always did, swiftly, its urgency un-
dimmed by the years. Though she was as familiar
with his body as her own, she must always explore
as if it were new to her. Her lips slipped away from
the mouth she adored to nibble the strong column
of his throat . . .

Rap! Rap! Rap! The door rattled beneath a pounding.

Anne's head rose. Her silvery-gray gaze, sharp
with regret, found the smile sneaking across his lips
and the amusement shining in his eyes. How easily
he laughed now, as if he had been born for it.

"I warned you," he said, his voice a low, musical
rumble, though his pulse had begun to race. Always
her touch inflamed him, as if he were yet a hot-
blooded boy.

"And then you tempted me, you wretch!" She
pouted, eyeing a pillow with mischievous intent.

His hand splayed over it, sun-browned and strong
and liberally sprinkled with gilded hair. "Tch, tch."
His smile spread, and Anne's nerves shimmied with
anticipation.

"Papa! Mama!" piped a voice through the door.

"The invasion," Anne whispered, rolling away to
grab her lacy bed-robe. "Your dressing gown."

"Papa! Mama!"

"One moment," Anne called out, casting a jaundiced gaze at Karl, who casually slipped into his robe
while hers frustrated her every effort to find the
armholes.

"Let me help you with that, my dear." Though
his voice held nothing more than simple concern,
his eyes danced with devilment.

"Oh, no! I haven't forgotten the last time. We'll

not have Tabby blushing to the roots of her hair again."

His low chuckle spilled out, caressing Anne like the hand that slipped around her waist and pulled her to him for a quick kiss. "Odd," he said softly. "As I remember it, sweet Anne, you were the one who blushed."

She gave him a shove. "Into the bed with you."

She hopped in behind him, spreading the covers and leaning back against the pillows piled against the scrolled headboard. Though her cheeks were flushed, she called a sedate "Come in."

The door flew open and banged against the wall. "Mama! Papa!" Two small tornadoes blew in. Ebony-haired and silver-eyed, they scaled the tall bed, flinging a volley of questions that would have done Cousin Knox proud.

"Are we really leaving for England tomorrow?" asked eight-year-old Karl III, hereditary Prince of Schattenburg.

"Will we see Uncle Robbie and Grandpapa and Grandmother?" asked Franz, his brother's junior by three years.

"Will we see Bragg House where Papa was raised?"

"And the Tower and Princess Victoria and the king?"

"Can I catch salmon from the Darent like Uncle Robbie did?"

"And fly his falcons? Can I fly his falcons, Mama?"

"Yes, yes, to everything!" Anne, Franz's sturdy body snuggled against hers, laughed and tweaked his nose.

Karl wriggled on his father's lap, his small face shining. "Will we . . . will we have *adventures*, Papa?" he asked eagerly.

Karl's eyes met Anne's for a brief moment fraught with memories of Robbie and danger and fear and distrust. Once, he had been afraid that marriage to him would kill the best part of her, the innocence he cherished. Though Anne had seen evil and been touched by it, she had not lost her capacity for joy, hope, and faith. Over the years, as their love grew stronger, Karl discovered that Anne was healing the scars of his hard life, just as she was healing the wounds of war for his people. *Die Engländerin*—the Englishwoman—had become not an epithet speaking of hatred and fear but an expression of love and trust. One that was spoken in the humblest cottages in Schattenburg and the palace of their new sovereign, the King of Württemburg. Anne's wisdom and encouragement, her enthusiasm for her new country and its people, had aided Karl's rise in the council of his new king and in his successful efforts to return the region to its former prosperity.

He thought those gifts were all he would ever need, but she had given him more. Two strong sons and a beautiful baby daughter. Children who would never know loneliness or fear, only love and happiness.

"Yes," he said gently, his hand cupping his son's black curls, "we will have adventures."

"I'm afraid we have already had an adventure this morning," came the sweet, peaceful voice of the Quakeress Tabitha Fell, a distant kinswoman of Anne's and governess to the boys. She carried three-month-old Magda to the bed and placed her in her mother's waiting arms.

"Blessings of the day to thee, Friend Anne, Friend Karl," she said gently, her misty gray gaze turning to their eldest son. "Would thee like to tell thy tale?"

"Must I, Tabby?" little Karl implored.

"I think thee must."

He crawled off the bed and stood like a small soldier at attention. "Papa, I took your sword, and I . . . I dueled with the curtains in the parlor."

Anne, chewing her lip, cast Tabby a questioning glance.

"Shredded, Friend Anne," she responded, her gentle gaze dancing.

Karl cleared his throat raucously. Though he could be a stern taskmaster in the duties of his station, he found himself a weak reed indeed in the necessary disciplining of his sons. He suspected he would be hopeless when it came to his daughter. "I see. I will have to consider a just punishment. Come to the library after lunch, and we will discuss it."

"Yes, Papa," said Karl, his small shoulders sinking.

"Perhaps," Karl added, not daring to look at Anne, "it is time we engaged a dueling master. We cannot have you shredding curtains."

"A dueling master! Papa! Papa!" He scrambled on the bed and flung his arms around Karl's neck. "A dueling master, Mama!"

"I heard." Anne smiled, though she wasn't at all sure she welcomed this sign that her son would soon be leaving childhood behind. She gazed down into Magda's tiny face, her finger touching the nubbin nose and trailing gently over the wealth of curls that were the same pale buttery-gold as her father's.

She had so much to be thankful for. Though she had always had a sneaking fear that von Fersen would return to wreck their lives, as the years had passed with no word of him, her fear had faded. Her children were healthy. Karl's love had grown stronger by the day. She had been accepted by his people; he had become a leader who was respected, admired, even adored for the justice that was always tempered by compassion.

The years had not all been happy. There had been the birth of a stillborn child, but they had learned to share that pain as they shared their many joys. As her parents, too, had learned to share the whole of their lives. Her mother's letters were radiant epistles of her father's caring and sharing. Her father's letters, though more restrained, were no less revealing of a man blissfully in love. Only one worry nagged at her—Robbie. She had not seen him since he left Schattenburg after her marriage, for he had, after a short recuperation, left England for a Grand Tour that had lasted for one-and-ten years. His letters had been infrequent and impersonal scribblings about his travels, utterly lacking the devastating verbal caricatures with which he had enlivened their childhood journeys. Robbie had changed, and those changes were, she feared, for the worse. She would know soon, for he was home now.

"Friend Anne," said Tabby, "it is time for the boys' lessons. Should I take the baby with me?"

While Anne transferred her daughter to Tabitha Fell's gentle arms, she studied her face. She saw the deep-rooted serenity, the unbreakable peace, and wished somehow that Robbie could find those qualities for himself.

The boys, tripping after Tabby with a new volley of questions, tumbled through the doorway, slamming the door behind them.

Anne felt the light touch of a finger tracing the shell of her ear and heard the voice she loved above all others whisper, "Now, sweet Anne, we have all morning to put to good use."

She turned slowly, melting into the waiting arms of her lover, her prince, her home.

And on the loggia, heady with ripe spring scents, there landed the raven, cawing.

Avon Romances—
the best in exceptional authors and unforgettable novels!

If you enjoyed this book, take advantage of this special offer. Subscribe now and . . .

GET A *FREE* HISTORICAL ROMANCE

——— NO OBLIGATION (a $3.95 value) ———

Each month the editors of True Value will select the four best historical romance novels from America's leading publishers. Preview them in your home Free for 10 days. And we'll send you a FREE book as our introductory gift. No obligation. If for any reason you decide not to keep them, just return them and owe nothing. But if you like them you'll pay *just* $3.50 each and save at least $.45 each off the cover price. (Your savings are a minimum of $1.80 a month.) There is no shipping and handling or other hidden charges. There are no minimum number of books to buy and you may cancel at any time.

send in the coupon below